The
Lost
Track
of
Time

The
Lost

Track of Time

BY **Paige Britt**

DRAWINGS BY LEE WHITE

SCHOLASTIC INC.

Text copyright © 2015 by Paige Britt
Illustrations © 2015 by Lee White

This book was originally published in hardcover by Scholastic Press in 2015.

ISBN 978-0-545-53813-8

10 9 8 7 6 5 4 3 2 1   16 17 18 19 20

Printed in the U.S.A.   23

First printing 2016

chapter one

Beep. Beep. Beep. Beep.

Penelope dragged one eye open and then the other. She'd been dreaming about a fire-eating lizard that spoke in riddles. The lizard was right in the middle of telling her something important when the alarm went off. She glared at the clock. It glared back: 6:00 a.m.

Here it was, the first day of summer vacation, and even now her mother expected her to get up and get busy. Penelope shut off the beeping and sat up. She dangled her feet over the bed and stared down at her toes. She had to be showered, dressed, and ready for breakfast in 30 minutes, which meant she'd better hurry. She wondered what it would be like to have a day off. Just once.

This won't take long, she told herself. Penelope dropped to the floor and began rummaging underneath her bed for one of the notebooks she kept hidden there.

Penelope's room was extremely neat. Her mother was fond of saying, "A place for everything and everything in its place." That's why Penelope kept everything that had no place in her room underneath the bed. There was the hamster habitat she was building (Penelope didn't own a hamster), the diary she was writing for her twin sister lost at sea (Penelope was an only child), and the invisible ink kit for sending secret messages (just in case she ever got stuck in a Turkish prison). And of course, there were the notebooks. Piles of

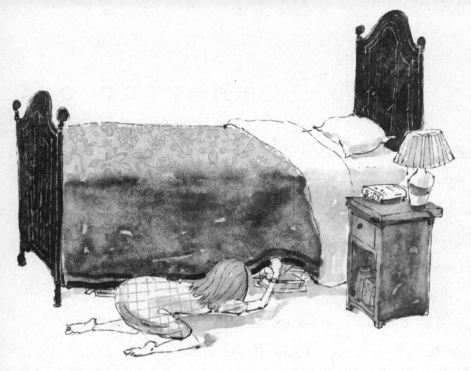

notebooks filled with all the fascinating words she had collected over the years and all the stories she had written with them.

Penelope pushed aside a box of hamster food and pulled out a small red notebook. She flipped it open and used the pencil tucked between its pages to make a quick sketch of the lizard from her dream — big eyes, long body, and a curling tongue, licking up bits of flame. When she finished, she sat back and tried to think of a name for the creature. It wasn't like naming a dog or a cat. It had to be unusual, like Beauregard or Eckbert. No. Too complicated. She needed something simple like . . . Zak. That was it!

Now that she had a name, what next? Zak couldn't just eat fire and speak in riddles. He needed an adventure. Penelope chewed on her pencil to help her think.

The smell of bacon drifted up from the kitchen and her stomach growled. She chewed harder. Maybe Zak belonged to a circus made up entirely of reptiles . . . or maybe he lived in a volcano that was about to blow up the world . . . or . . .

Bacon!

Penelope dropped her pencil. She realized what the smell meant. She was late. Her mother had started making breakfast, and Penelope was expected at the table. She shoved her notebook back under the bed, tore off her pajamas, and threw on some clothes. She raced down the stairs, combing her hair with her fingers. As soon as she stepped into the kitchen, her mother gave her "the look."

"Do you *know* what time it is?"

Penelope slid into her chair. "I know," she mumbled. Penelope couldn't tell the truth — that she'd lost track of time. Her mother wouldn't understand. Not when there was a clock in every room of the house and a watch on her wrist. Just because Penelope wore a watch, though, didn't mean she looked at it. It made her nervous. The second hand never sat still. It swung around and around, sweeping the day away like sand.

Penelope's mother put breakfast on the table and sat down. "Your father will be back from his run any minute now, so we'd better get started." She reached across the table for her leather three-ring binder. "Let's see what's on the schedule for today, shall we?"

Here we go, thought Penelope, slumping over her plate.

"Sit up straight," said her mother without looking up.

Penelope felt a knot form in her stomach as she waited for her mother to begin. The binder held a calendar that served as Penelope's schedule. Each page was a single day and each day was filled with a long list of things she was expected to do. Penelope's mother ripped yesterday's page off the calendar and let out a satisfied sigh. "Looks like you've got a full day ahead of you." She held out the calendar for Penelope to see.

There was the month (May), the date (29), and the quote from Poor Richard (whoever *he* was). After that, lines and lines of her mother's neat handwriting filled the page:

May 29

Be always ashamed to catch thyself idle.

6:30–7:00 Breakfast

7:00–7:30 Daily chores

7:30–8:30 Piano practice

8:30–8:45 Free time

8:45–9:15 Drive to dentist

9:15–10:15 Dentist appt.

10:15–10:45 Drive home from dentist

10:45–11:45 SAT vocabulary drills

11:45–12:15 Wash and polish bike

<u>12:15–12:30 Ride bike</u>

<u>12:30–1:00 Lunch</u>

<u>1:00–2:00 Math tutoring</u>

<u>2:00–3:00 Write b-day thank-you cards NEATLY!</u>

<u>3:00–4:30 Get started on summer reading list</u>

<u>4:30–5:30 Cooking lesson</u>

<u>5:30–6:30 Dinner</u>

<u>6:30–6:45 Free time</u>

<u>6:45–7:00 Call Grandma</u>

<u>7:00–8:00 Tidy room and get ready for bed</u>

Penelope's mother cleared her throat and began to read off all the day's activities. As she did, Penelope wondered for the hundredth time just *who* Poor Richard was. Even though she had never met him, she didn't like him. He was always saying things about "industry" or "sloth." What exactly was *sloth*? It seemed like it had something to do with being lazy. But then again, wasn't a sloth an animal that looked like a sock puppet? Maybe a sloth would make a good sidekick for Zak, the fire-eating lizard . . .

"Penelope!"

Penelope looked up. Her mother was staring at her expectantly. "I *said*, hurry and finish your breakfast. It's almost time for your daily chores."

Just then, the front door swung open and a voice called out, "I'm home!" A minute later her father bounded into the kitchen.

"Hi, pumpkin," he said and rumpled Penelope's hair. "It's another beautiful day out there." He pronounced the word *beautiful* as if it were three words — *beau-ti-ful*.

"How did it go, dear?" asked her mother, flipping to the back of the binder where she kept an account of his daily runs — time, date, distance.

"Great! Five miles, 41:4."

Penelope's mother recorded the information and shut the binder. "Your day is off to a good start," she said, as if the numbers proved it.

"It certainly is!" Her father downed a glass of water and then sat at the table to peel a banana. "I bet you have a lot to look forward to today, huh, kiddo?" he said and reached for the paper.

Penelope crammed a piece of toast in her mouth and mumbled something unintelligible. Her dad wouldn't understand. He looked forward to *every* day. He was an insurance agent, and although he helped people prepare for disasters — death, disease, fire — he was so happy all the time you would have thought he worked at Disneyland.

Penelope finished her toast and got up from the table.

"I guess I'd better get started on my chores."

Her dad glanced up from the sports page. "Go get 'em, tiger," he said, giving her a thumbs-up.

Her mother, who was on the phone, just waved.

Monday was Penelope's day to vacuum the living and dining room floors. As she walked back and forth, vacuuming in neat lines, she thought about the other kids in her class. They probably had summers filled with nothing but hanging out at the pool all day and going to slumber parties at night. Penelope had never been to a slumber party in her life. "Early to bed, early to rise," was another one of Poor Richard's rules.

Penelope changed the vacuum attachment and began sucking up the dirt and crumbs between the couch cushions. She knew it was no use complaining about her schedule. No matter how packed it was, her mother's was even worse. Penelope's mother was an event planner. She planned parties, business meetings, weddings, bar mitzvahs, and anything else that needed to go perfectly. From what Penelope could tell, her mother spent all her time on the phone or the computer organizing other people's lives. Apparently no one minded, because they gave her money to do it.

Penelope knew she should feel lucky to get her mother's help for free, but she didn't. Her mother said that following a daily schedule was the best way to prepare for the future. Penelope didn't know how she could prepare for something that was so impossible to imagine. She could hardly picture herself graduating from middle school, much less going to college. Besides, the only thing she wanted to do was be a writer. Last year her English teacher,

Mr. Gomez, had given her a magazine full of stories written by kids her age. "Keep reading and keep writing," he had told her. "And when you're ready, you should send this magazine one of your stories. I think you have a real chance of getting published." She couldn't get his words out of her mind.

Penelope finished vacuuming the living room and moved on to the dining room. The only other person who encouraged Penelope to write was her neighbor, Miss Maddie. When Penelope was little, before she started school, her mother would drop her off at Miss Maddie's house whenever she had a business meeting to attend or an errand to run. Once in a while, Penelope spent the whole day at Miss Maddie's house. Even though it was just down the street, it felt like a different world. At Miss Maddie's house, Penelope was allowed to do what her mother would call "nothing." It wasn't the nothing where you watched TV for hours, waiting for the day to pass. This nothing was more like a blank page Penelope could fill however she wanted.

Whenever Penelope stayed with Miss Maddie, she would spend all her time reading, writing, or just staring out the window. Miss Maddie didn't mind; in fact, she often joined in. Once they had spent an entire afternoon looking for faces in the wood grain of Miss Maddie's dining room table. After they found a face, they drew it on a piece of paper and gave it a name like "Ichabod" or "Millicent." Next they made up elaborate stories about the characters, which

Penelope wrote down in a notebook. Whenever Penelope asked if they were wasting time, Miss Maddie would just roll her eyes and say, "Don't you worry about the time, it'll keep track of itself."

Penelope wished she believed that.

The grandfather clock chimed 7:30 a.m. and Penelope turned off the vacuum cleaner. "Time for piano practice!" her mother called from the other room.

"I know, I know!" Penelope called back.

She put away the machine as fast as she could and ran down the hall to the living room. She had exactly one hour to complete her sight-reading and theory exercises, practice her scales, and play through all the music assigned by her piano teacher. If she finished by 8:30, she could use her free time to visit with Miss Maddie.

Penelope rushed through her scales and then played all her practice pieces. The piano theory and sight-reading worksheets took longer to complete, and by the time she finished, her hour was almost up. She slammed her workbook closed and headed for the back door. "I'm going to Miss Maddie's," she called over her shoulder.

"Be back in fifteen minutes!" her mother shouted after her. "We leave for the dentist at 8:45 sharp!"

Penelope could almost feel the seconds ticking away as she ran down the street toward Miss Maddie's house. Miss Maddie had lived at the end of Ginger Lane even before there *was* a Ginger Lane or any such thing as the Spicewood Estates housing development. She had once shown Penelope a faded black-and-white picture of her house surrounded by a wide-open field and tall oak trees. Instead of Ginger Lane, a long dirt road ran up to the front gate.

"Once they sold this land and began building Spicewood Estates, houses sprouted up overnight," Miss Maddie had said.

As she ran, Penelope imagined she was racing through a field with houses popping up out of the ground, each with a door, two windows, and a driveway.

Miss Maddie's house wasn't like anyone else's house. It didn't have a mailbox perched on the corner of a neat lawn and a walkway dotted with flowers. Instead, it had an old paint-chipped fence covered with ivy. The front yard had a patch of sunflowers, an overgrown herb garden, and an enormous oak tree. The oak tree spread out across the yard, with branches that almost touched the ground. A pathway ran through the front gate, around the tree, and stopped at a bright purple door.

No one in all of Spicewood Estates had a purple door.

No one except Miss Maddie.

Penelope opened the gate and hurried up the path. She would have preferred to take her time. Sometimes she found stray items along the way — glossy wrappers, colored string, or small toys. Miss Maddie told her that birds would often spot shiny objects on the ground and use them in their nests. Penelope suspected that the little treasures she found were gifts from Miss Maddie meant for the birds.

Today, however, Penelope didn't have time to scavenge for shiny objects. She rushed up to the door and used their secret knock.

Knock-knock-knock. Knock. Knock.

Miss Maddie flung open the door. "What a nice surprise!"

"I've only . . . got . . . a minute," said Penelope, trying to catch her breath.

"Nonsense," said Miss Maddie. "You've got all the time in the world."

Miss Maddie was always saying things like that. Things that made no sense. As far as Penelope was concerned, time was like a bank account, and she was overdrawn.

"I *don't* have all the time in the world," insisted Penelope. "You haven't seen my schedule today."

"Nor do I want to." Miss Maddie stepped back to let Penelope in. "Don't suppose you have time for tea?"

Penelope shook her head.

"All right then, let's just have a sit."

At Miss Maddie's house "a sit" was a very special thing. But then again, it wasn't. It was a little bit like waiting, but at the same time, not like waiting at all. Penelope couldn't quite figure it out. It involved sitting down in a chair and doing nothing. It was wonderful.

Penelope followed Miss Maddie into the living room. A thick rug covered the floor like grass. Miss Maddie had told her it was a Persian rug. *Persian*. It was one of the first words Penelope had ever collected in her notebook. Just the sound of it gave her a shiver of pleasure.

A deep fireplace that burnt real logs took up one end of the room. At the other end, a bay window looked out on Miss Maddie's unruly front yard. There were no curtains on the window. Instead, the sprawling oak tree blocked the view of the street.

As beautiful and exotic as these things were, the best thing about the room was its silence. Not one clock ticked, tocked, chimed, or donged. There wasn't a clock on the mantle or on the wall or on the coffee table. In fact, Penelope had never seen a clock *anywhere* in Miss Maddie's house.

When Penelope had asked her about the missing clocks, Miss Maddie had just shrugged. "I don't need clocks to tell me what time it is. I always do things at the same exact time anyway."

"Really?" Penelope had said. "At the same *exact* time?"

"Yes, ma'am. I do things in my own sweet time. *Every* time."

Penelope couldn't imagine what it must be like not to have a schedule to follow. Having "a sit" with Miss Maddie was the closest she ever got to her "own sweet time." She settled herself in a comfy chair in front of the bay window and curled up her legs. Miss Maddie sat next to her, hands resting loosely on her lap. A hush settled over the room and the sitting began.

Penelope stared at the sunlight playing with the leaves on the oak tree. After a while, a hush crept into her mind and the sunlight stopped being sunlight and the leaves stopped being leaves and for the briefest, smallest moment everything was everything until . . .

Ring!

Penelope sat bolt upright. She glanced over at Miss Maddie. Miss Maddie was still staring out the window, hands in her lap.

Ring!

"The phone is ringing," Penelope blurted out.

"Yup," said Miss Maddie with a slight nod. "That's what they do."

Ring!

It occurred to Penelope that it might be her mother.

"Aren't you going to get it?"

Miss Maddie sighed and got up from her chair.

Penelope wondered how long she had been sitting there. It only felt like a minute, but it could have been longer. There really was only one way to find out. Slowly, slowly Penelope looked down at her wristwatch. For a second, the numbers were nothing but little black marks marching around in a circle. Then they came into focus and Penelope read the time:

8:46.

She was late.

chapter two

At dinner that evening, her mother made an announcement. "Penelope, your father and I have discussed it, and we think it best that you no longer visit Miss Maddie."

Penelope stared at her, fork frozen in midair.

"I know Miss Maddie meant a lot to you when you were little, and heaven knows I appreciated her help looking after you, but now that you're older, I think you need to focus on the future. I've already called and told her not to expect you any longer. So it's settled." She took a large bite of her steak and began to chew.

Penelope looked at her dad. He just shrugged. "Your mother is in charge of your schedule, pal. Besides, she has so many great things planned for you this summer, you're not going to want to miss any of them. Just think, science camp starts in a few days."

Penelope could feel dinner turning to stone in her stomach. She swallowed hard. "But *why?*" she finally blurted out.

"We don't think it's the best use of your time," her mother answered.

"I hardly have any free time as it is," pleaded Penelope.

Penelope's mother placed her fork neatly on her plate and fixed Penelope with a stare. "Time isn't free, Penelope. And neither is college. Do you know how much an Ivy League school costs?"

Penelope shook her head. She didn't even know what an Ivy League school was.

"I can tell you, it costs a lot. How do you expect us to pay for college if you don't get a scholarship? If you weren't so caught up in your fantasies, you would be farther along in your studies. You would be more productive. More *competitive.*"

Penelope sat very still, struggling to focus on what her mother had just said. *If she wasn't so caught up in her fantasies, she would be more competitive?* What was she competing for? Why did her mother treat life like it was a race against time? No matter what Penelope did, she always fell behind.

"Speaking of scholarships," continued her mother, "you'll be taking the pre-pre-SAT this year and you need to be ready. From now on, I want you to focus your writing on the sample essay questions I give you. No more scribbling in your notebook."

Penelope gasped. *Scribbling?* She wasn't scribbling — she was *writing.* There was a difference.

"Hey there, buddy," said her dad. "Your mom is only trying to do what's best for you."

Penelope exhaled slowly. "They're not scribbles," she finally said, trying to keep her voice steady.

"What?" asked her mother, who was busy cutting her steak.

"My notebook. They aren't scribbles. They're stories. Mr. Gomez said I could even be published one day —"

"Stories don't pay the bills, Penelope," said her mother, cutting her off. "In today's economy we can't afford to be impractical."

"Pass the potatoes, will you, sport?" said her father.

Penelope opened her mouth, then closed it. It was no use arguing. Her parents didn't listen anyway. Now there was to be no more writing in her notebook. No more visits to Miss Maddie. No more nothing. "May I be excused?" she asked, pushing back from the table.

"Not yet," said her mother. "I knew you'd be disappointed about not getting to visit Miss Maddie, so I bought you a little something to cheer you up." She put down her fork and napkin and got up from the table. "I'll be right back."

She returned a moment later with a package. Inside the package was a book. The cover featured a man wearing a suit, looking extremely pleased with himself. He was holding up a long to-do list. Next to each entry was a bright red check mark.

"It's your very own copy of *Getting Everything Done*," said her mother excitedly. "I have one, too. I just couldn't *live* without it."

Penelope flipped through the book, trying to think of something nice to say. She stopped when she came to an illustration featuring a series of squares with tiny arrows running back and forth between them. The man stood to the side, pointing at the illustration with a ruler.

"That's a work-flow diagram," explained her mother. "You won't believe how helpful it is. Each square represents a task you need to do and the arrows tell you when to do it. It will make you so much more organized. You're just going to love it!" She beamed down at Penelope. "I'll clear your calendar for the evening. You go ahead and read your book."

Penelope bolted from the table, ran upstairs, and threw the book face-down on her desk. There was the man again! He was posed for a portrait on the back cover, arms crossed, a smug smile on his face. He was wearing a gray suit, gray shirt, and gray tie. Everything about him was the same dull color, except for his teeth, which were unnaturally white. Below the picture was a "personal message." Penelope read:

My work on human productivity resource allocation is the latest and, if I may say so, greatest of the century! If you utilize my proven methods, you'll be a success like me. You'll get everything done! In this book I'll tell you how to follow my time-saving tips and monitor your hourly progress. I'll tell you exactly how to overhaul the logistics of daily life, break down the elements of your must-do tasks, and actualize the hidden potential in the micromoments between project steps.

Ugh. How boring, thought Penelope. She shoved the book in her desk drawer and plopped down on the bed. How on earth could she get through to her parents? Words weren't enough. That was obvious. Her father only listened to her mother and her mother only listened to proof. But how could Penelope *prove* her stories were important? *If I don't do something, my whole life will turn into a work-flow diagram!*

Penelope heard the *thump-thump-thump* of someone running up the stairs. A moment later there was a quick rap on the door and her dad poked his head in. "Hey, pal! Got a minute?"

Penelope shrugged. "I guess so."

"Great!" Her father stepped inside and grabbed the desk chair, flipping it around to face Penelope. He sat down and leaned forward, propping his elbows on his knees. "Time for a pep talk," he announced.

Not again, thought Penelope. Pep talks were her dad's favorite form of communication.

"You know," he said, launching into his speech, "I meant what I said at the dinner table. Your mom really does want what's best for you. All this planning and organizing, it's for your own good."

"I *do* know," said Penelope, who had heard this all before. "But why is it that what I want isn't good enough? She never lets me do my own thing. She only wants me to do *her* thing."

"She doesn't want you to miss out on any opportunities for success. Trust me, she knows what she's doing. I used to sell hot dogs at football games until I met your mother. Now I'm an insurance agent." He sat back in his chair. "Not bad, huh, kid?"

Penelope fought the urge to roll her eyes.

"Just wait and see. Your mom has a plan for your life. It's going to be top-notch."

"But I want to be a writer," Penelope insisted.

"Well, sport, writing is a little iffy." He wobbled his hand back and forth. "I say, life is already full of surprises. Why not go for a sure thing?" He put his fists up like a boxer and began making little jabs at the air. "You've got to be prepared. Ahead of the game. On the ball." He dropped his hands and gave Penelope a meaningful look. "Got it?"

Before Penelope could say a word, he gave her a soft punch on the arm. "'Course you do. That's my girl."

Penelope knew this meant the pep talk was over. He liked to keep them short, which was fine with her.

Sure enough, her father rose to his feet. "I'm glad we had this talk," he said. "See you in the morning?"

"Sure," said Penelope. "See you in the morning."

As soon as the door clicked shut, Penelope fell back on her bed with a groan. Her dad's pep talks always left her exhausted. The person she *really* needed to talk to was Miss Maddie, but she was off-limits. Once Miss Maddie had told her, "When faced with a challenge you have to fight fire with fire!" Penelope wondered what that meant.

Fight fire with fire.

It didn't make any sense. Fighting fire with fire would just make things worse, wouldn't it? Penelope imagined a bonfire growing out of control. You wouldn't fight it by throwing more burning logs on it. That was feeding the fire. You would fight it with water. But that's not what Miss Maddie had said. Penelope knew that fire ate everything in its path. Maybe you *couldn't* stop it. Maybe you just had to let it burn. That didn't seem right either.

Penelope closed her eyes and pretended she was sitting in Miss Maddie's living room. There was the big window and the giant oak tree and the bright blue sky and . . . A thought popped into her head: *If you fight fire with fire, maybe you aren't really trying to put it out.*

Penelope sat up.

She might be onto something. She jumped out of bed, pulled open her desk drawer, and stole another look at the book her mother had given her. There was the man, holding up his to-do list, smiling like he was king of the world.

I could make my own to-do list, she thought.

Her heart skipped a beat.

A list with tasks to accomplish my *goals . . .*

A list of things I *want to do!*

Penelope slammed the drawer shut. Maybe that was it! Maybe that's what fighting fire with fire meant. Maybe you could solve a problem by using the same stuff that made it a problem in the first place.

Penelope grabbed a piece of paper and began to write her very own to-do list. Next to each item, she placed a small box, just waiting for a check mark.

☐ Stay on schedule for one month to keep Mom happy

☐ Steal time to write an AMAZING story

☐ After month is over, submit story to magazine and get published

☐ Prove writing is not a waste of time

☐ Make my own schedule!!

From that moment on, Penelope did everything right on time. She got up at 6:00, dressed, and brushed her teeth. She reached the breakfast table at exactly 6:30 and sat up straight while her mother conducted the daily schedule review. She consulted her wristwatch throughout the day and made sure she was exactly where she needed to be, when she needed to be.

"Seems like that book was a big help," said her dad on the way to science camp a few days later. "Look how smoothly everything is going already!"

Penelope, who was staring out the window, just nodded. She was trying to think up an amazing story idea. Maybe she would write about a super-genius kid who created an endless energy source from bubble gum. Everybody chewed gum all day to power the lights in their houses.

Honk! Honk!

Penelope looked up. Her dad had pulled up to the drop-off zone at the community center where science camp was held. He was waiting for Penelope to get out and so was a line of cars behind them. "Wake up, buddy! It's time to go," he said. Penelope grabbed her backpack and jumped out. Her dad waved apologetically to the car behind him and sped off.

A counselor was waiting at the curb to give Penelope her group assignment. "You're part of the Mad Scientists this week!" she announced cheerfully. "Room 203."

Penelope thought about this for a minute. She wasn't exactly *mad*, she decided, but she wasn't very happy either. She had wanted to go to summer camp, just not for science. Mr. Gomez was teaching a creative writing workshop at the library, but her mother had said no.

"Jobs of the future are in high tech or health care sectors," her mother droned, dropping two brochures on the table. "You can go to computer camp or science camp. Take your pick."

Penelope picked science camp. At least there were experiments.

She glanced at her wristwatch and hurried down the hall to her room. A woman with short brown hair introduced herself as "Ms. Romine." She wore a lab coat and sipped coffee from a beaker.

"Hello, Mad Scientists!" Ms. Romine announced when everyone had taken their seats. "Welcome to the first day of science camp. Today's topic is mushrooms. Does anyone know the difference between a mushroom and a plant?"

Nineteen hands shot up in the air.

Penelope slid down in her chair. Apparently she was the only one at camp who didn't know anything about mushrooms. Well, she knew *one* thing. She didn't like them. They tasted musty. And slimy. And old.

"Mushrooms are a vital part of our ecosystem," continued Ms. Romine. "In fact, fungi are one of the most important organisms on the planet! You might even say they have a role to play in every part of our lives — from food production to waste management."

Penelope found this extremely hard to believe. Everyone else, though, was madly taking notes. Penelope propped her chin on her hand and stared out the window.

Just then Ms. Romine clapped her hands. "All right, everyone, partner up with the person next to you. We're going to work on mushroom identification."

The boy at the desk next to Penelope's was named Ebon. She knew him from Quiz Bowl competition.

"Did you know that some mushrooms have a body that spreads out over several miles?" Ebon asked as soon as they'd pushed their desks together.

Before Penelope could answer, the girl with pigtails seated in front of them swiveled around. "I know. They're called mycorrhizal associations."

Why are you even in science camp if you know everything already? wondered Penelope.

Ms. Romine passed out fungi identification charts, and the rest of the morning was spent drawing and labeling the parts of different mushrooms. That afternoon they took small samples from the mushrooms and looked at them under a microscope. While Ebon recorded the cell diameter of the various samples, Penelope thought about story ideas. Her story needed to be something her parents would like. Maybe a story about a girl who got a perfect score on the SATs and graduated from college at sixteen and became president of the United States. Or maybe a story about a boy who had an internal clock that told him what time it was no matter where in the world he was. He had super-turbo-charged feet and could run faster than the speed of light so he was never late.

Nah. Neither of those seemed right.

When camp was over for the day, Penelope couldn't wait to get home and see if she could come up with something better. She ate dinner as fast as she could. By the time she finished picking up her room and getting ready for bed, she was too tired to concentrate, but she dug her red notebook out from under the bed anyway. A few ideas came to mind.

A girl who starts a business and makes a million dollars . . .

A boy who is smarter than a computer . . .

A really organized kid who can speed-read . . .

Ugh. These were horrible!

"Lights out!" called her mother from downstairs.

Already? Penelope reluctantly turned out the lights and slipped her notebook under the bed. *I'll come up with something better tomorrow,* she told herself.

Penelope rolled over on her back and closed her eyes, letting her mind wander to one of its favorite places . . . After she finished her story, her mother would love it so much that she would clear Penelope's schedule. Every day would be wide open. Filled with nothing. Penelope's stories would be so good her mother would let her display her notebooks on the bookshelf in her bedroom. No more digging them out from underneath the bed. Maybe someday someone would buy what she'd written and there would be a whole shelf in the library filled with her stories. She would be a famous author and travel the world looking for inspiration. She'd travel by hot air balloon, so she could see all the sights. Birds would land on the balloon's basket and she'd tie little notes to their feet, just like messages in a bottle . . .

Penelope drifted off to sleep, where her fantasies took flight and turned into dreams.

chapter three

The next day was very much like the one before except for one thing: homework. Ms. Romine didn't call it that. She called it a "science project," but Penelope knew better.

"This is the perfect thing for a work-flow diagram!" exclaimed her mother when she heard of the assignment. "We'll make one together right after dinner."

Penelope cringed. How was she going to steal time to write if her mother kept crowding her schedule?

As soon as the table was cleared, her mother got busy breaking down the project into tasks and something called "deliverables." Penelope had never heard of a deliverable before, but she had a pretty good idea what it meant. A deliverable must be something you delivered or turned in. Proof that you did something.

Penelope thought about her checklist. *Just wait. In a month, I'm going to turn in my* own *deliverable — the most amazing story ever!*

After identifying the project deliverables, her mother created a timeline. Penelope was shocked to see the entire week mapped out in tiny segments. It looked like her daily schedule, but blown up and stretched out. Was this the future? The future Penelope couldn't imagine? Instead of being wide open and full of possibilities, it was a series of little boxes.

For the rest of the week, each night after dinner was devoted to the science project. All Penelope wanted to do was go to her room and write, but she told herself that keeping her mother happy would pay off in the long run. The only problem was that as soon as she finished one task, another one seemed to pop up. Penelope started carrying her small red notebook in her back pocket and used any spare time during science camp to write down story ideas, but none of them seemed good enough.

It was odd. Ever since she started keeping better track of time, the less of it there seemed to be. The better she got at following her schedule, the busier it became. She was constantly checking the clock to make sure she didn't fall behind, but she fell behind anyway.

On the last night of science camp, Penelope had to work through dinner and late into the night to finish her project. She crawled under the covers, exhausted from the day and ready for sleep, but when she closed her eyes sleep wouldn't come. She tossed this way and that, her head full of worries about getting everything done.

A month has passed, and I still haven't written my story.

Once I finish science camp, Mom expects me to work on those essay questions.

Penelope flipped over onto her side.

If I don't ace those essay questions, I'll never get a scholarship.

Maybe I won't even make it into college.

But if I don't finish this story, I'll never be a writer . . .

She flipped over onto her other side.

Even if I were a writer, who would buy my stories anyway?

I'd probably end up homeless, eating tuna out of a can!

Somehow she managed to fall into a dreamless sleep only to wake the next morning and start all over. It was the last day of camp and Penelope's project won an honorable mention. Her mother was delighted, but Penelope was too tired to care. She moved through the next day and the days that followed on autopilot. By the time another week had passed, she was no closer to coming up with a story idea than before. Science camp was over, but Penelope's schedule was busier than ever. Now she was taking tennis lessons, learning Mandarin, and doing volunteer service hours at the museum in the afternoon.

One morning, Penelope forced herself to wake up before the alarm. She dug out her notebook from under the bed and opened it. She stared at the page, willing herself to write, but for the first time ever nothing came. Not even bad ideas. Her mind was blank. Not blank as in wide open, waiting for something wonderful, but blank like a wall.

That's odd, thought Penelope. She usually had more ideas than she could keep track of. She got out a few old notebooks from under her bed and flipped through them. Detailed notes, elaborate doodles, long lists of words she'd collected, and half-written stories filled the pages. None of them looked familiar. She didn't even remember writing them.

By now she should be writing madly, dreaming up new characters and creating exciting plot twists. But she wasn't. She *couldn't*. Penelope heard her mother's heels clicking down the hall. She threw on her overalls, stuffed a pen and her red notebook in her back pocket, and ran downstairs to breakfast.

"Good morning, sunshine," her mother chirped. "What'll it be?"

"Just some cereal," said Penelope. She wasn't feeling hungry. She wasn't feeling *anything*.

Once breakfast was laid out neatly, her mother sat down. "All right then, let's see what we have to look forward to today." She picked up the calendar and ripped off yesterday's date.

Penelope braced herself for the little sigh her mother always made at this point. But she didn't sigh. Instead, she let out a gasp.

Penelope put down her spoon. "What?"

"Nothing," said her mom and sat back stunned.

"Nothing?"

Penelope's mother nodded slowly.

"Nothing *what*?" Penelope prodded.

"*Nothing*, nothing. That's just it. There's absolutely nothing on the calendar today."

Penelope craned her neck to get a better look. There was the month (July), the date (3), and the quote, but after that the calendar was empty:

July 3

One today is worth two tomorrows.

_____

_____

_____

_____

_____

_____

_____

_____

_____

_____

_____

_____

Penelope's mother frowned at the blank page. "Why is there a hole in your schedule? I'm certain I had you booked until school started." She flipped through the calendar. Sure enough, all the pages were crammed with tiny black notations. When she flipped back to the blank page, she noticed a tiny smudge on the corner. "The pages must have stuck together and now you have nothing to do today," she complained, rubbing at the smudge with her thumb.

This was what Penelope had been dreaming of — an entire day of nothing! Her mind started to race. Maybe her mother would give her the day off. After all, Penelope had been on time all day, every day, for weeks and weeks. A day off wouldn't hurt. She would sit at her desk, stare out the window, and . . .

"All right," said Penelope's mother, "we'd better get busy."

Penelope's mind came to a screeching halt. "Busy? Doing what?"

"What do you mean, 'doing what?' You can't do *nothing* all day."

A familiar knot of dread formed in Penelope's stomach.

"Let's see," said her mother. "We'll start the day with another cooking lesson — you still haven't learned how to make Chicken *Cordon Bleu* — followed by ironing and Mandarin vocabulary drills. This afternoon I'd like you to replant your tomato patch. Your rows are crooked. After dinner, I think you should take up knitting. How does that sound?" She looked at Penelope expectantly, one pencil-thin eyebrow raised as high as it would go.

The knot in Penelope's stomach grew tighter.

"Penelope? I *said*, how does that sound?"

The knot moved from her stomach and into her throat. Penelope took a deep breath. "Can I have a day off instead?" she asked, pushing the words out as best she could.

"Certainly not!" her mother laughed.

"But I've been on time for weeks and weeks . . ."

"Penelope, we've been through this before. There's not the least possibility you can have a day off and get everything done. Now then, help me figure out what to do with the time slot after lunch."

Penelope stared as her mother reached for a pen.

"I know what — you can clean out all the junk under your bed. I've been wanting to do that for weeks."

"What junk?" Penelope's voice was barely a whisper.

Penelope's mother gave her an exasperated look. "You *know* what junk. Those broken toys, that useless hamster cage, not to mention those ratty old notebooks. The new school year begins soon. It's time for a fresh start, don't you think?"

Penelope wanted to yell, "NO!" But the knot in her throat wouldn't let her. Those weren't ratty old notebooks. They were her stories. She'd been a fool to think she could fight fire with fire, and now her plan had gone up in smoke. Penelope watched, unable to move or speak as her mother began to write.

But just at that moment — the *exact* moment when pen touched paper — the doorbell rang.

Ding-dong.

"Oh, dear," said her mother. "Your father must have forgotten his key." She got up from the table and walked briskly toward the front door.

As soon as her mother left the room, Penelope let out the breath she was holding and her head began to clear. There was only one person who could help save her notebooks — help save her dreams! Penelope had just a few seconds to act. It was now or never. She leaned forward, ripped the page out of the calendar, and stuffed it into her pocket. Then she slipped off her wristwatch and shoved it in a drawer before bolting out the back door.

"How'd *you* get here?" said Miss Maddie when she found Penelope at her doorstep.

"There's a hole in my schedule," said Penelope, panting.

"How extraordinary." Miss Maddie motioned Penelope inside, then closed the door. "Does your mother know you're here?"

Penelope shook her head. "No, but I *had* to come. I've run out of ideas and my mother is going to throw away my notebooks and . . . and I'll never be a writer!"

"Ahh . . ." said Miss Maddie. "We'd better have some tea."

When they got to the kitchen, Penelope sat down while Miss Maddie put on the kettle. After the stove was lit and the water was on, Miss Maddie joined her at the table. "So you've run out of ideas?" she asked.

"I thought my parents would give me more time to write if I could prove my stories were important," explained Penelope. "I have to write something good — something *amazing*. But my mind is blank. I can't come up with anything. I've tried for weeks and now it's too late. My mother wants to throw away my notebooks! I've been writing in those notebooks for years. They're my inspiration. Without them, I'll never come up with a story idea. Never!"

Miss Maddie pursed her lips and stared out the window. Penelope stared with her. Usually staring out the window made her feel relaxed, but not this time. The scenery outside looked flat, like the backdrop of a play.

Thwack! Miss Maddie slapped the table with her palm. Penelope sat up.

"Space!" she said.

"*Space?*" asked Penelope.

"Yes, yes. Space. Maybe your ideas are stuck. Maybe they got crowded out and all you need is a little bit of" — she fluttered her fingers around — "you know . . . space."

Space. It *sounded* like a good idea.

"Speaking of space," said Miss Maddie, "just how big is this hole in your schedule?"

Penelope took the calendar page from her pocket and smoothed it out on the table.

Miss Maddie leaned over. "That's pretty big," she said, tapping the calendar page with her finger.

Penelope nodded.

"Watch out," said Miss Maddie, "you could fall into a hole like that."

Penelope glanced up, expecting to see a twinkle in Miss Maddie's eye. But there was no twinkle. Or wink. Or even a smile. Miss Maddie was staring straight at her, a serious expression on her face. Just then the kettle screeched and Miss Maddie got up.

Penelope looked back down at the calendar page with Miss Maddie's words lingering in her mind. *You could fall into a hole like that* . . . Penelope noticed the white of the paper looked brighter than before, and the little black lines seemed faded. The longer she stared, the fainter the black lines grew, until they disappeared altogether. *That's odd*, thought Penelope. She blinked and gave her head a little shake. The lines reappeared.

Penelope looked over at Miss Maddie, who was spooning tea into the pot. "Tea will be ready in no time," Miss Maddie assured her.

Penelope nodded and stole another glance at the page. It happened again! The paper seemed to glow for a moment. Penelope looked closer. The lines were *definitely* growing fainter. *This time I'm not going to blink*, she decided.

Penelope kept her eyes open as wide as they would go. Sure enough, the white grew slowly brighter, and the black lines receded.

Don't blink, don't blink.

Penelope's eyes started to water, but she kept her resolve. The black lines had disappeared altogether and even the white seemed to fade into nothing.

Don't blink, don't blink.

Now the room disappeared. The only thing Penelope could see was the paper, which didn't even seem to be *there* anymore. Instead, a warm, white nothing opened out in front of her. Penelope felt like she was tottering at the edge of a pit. It made her feel queasy. So . . .

She blinked.

And in that brief moment of darkness, the pit rushed up. Or else she fell down. Either way, Penelope heard a whooshing sound and felt a strong wind press against her face. She opened her eyes and flung out her arms to brace herself against the table. But there *was* no table.

A jolt of panic sent Penelope's heart racing. Then the nothing engulfed her, and time slipped away into the rush of air.

chapter four

"Where did *you* come from?" said an unfamiliar voice.

Penelope turned her head in the direction of the sound. All she could see were little black dots dancing against a backdrop of brilliant light.

"Miss Maddie?" she called out.

"Who in the world is Miss Maddie?" the voice demanded.

Penelope squinted and the black dots slowed their dance. A shape wavered in front of her eyes, and she saw the outline of a face. She was lying on her back and a man was standing above her. The man had his hands on his knees and was inspecting her as if she were a beetle. He wore a pair of blue velvet pants and a matching velvet jacket covered in pockets. He seemed unusually tall, with legs as long as fence posts. His brilliant red hair stood straight up and should have made him look silly, except it didn't. Not quite. He looked old and wise and young and foolish all at the same time.

"Wh-where am I?" asked Penelope.

"The Realm of Possibility," the man answered matter-of-factly.

Penelope sat up. Her head was spinning and her back hurt. An uncomfortable lump in her pocket meant she'd landed on her notebook. "The realm of *what?*" she asked.

"The Realm of Possibility," repeated the man. "Used to be anything could happen here, but these days it rarely does. That's why you're so unusual. Bizarre. Highly irregular." He gave her arm a sharp poke, as if checking to see that she was real.

"Ow!" cried Penelope and glared up at him.

"Looks like you're here for good," said the man with a satisfied nod.

"But I can't be here for good," said Penelope, scrambling to her feet. "I have to be somewhere else."

"Impossible."

Penelope gave the man a hard look. "What do you mean, 'impossible'?"

"I mean, you can't be somewhere else if you're already here. It's impossible. Inconceivable. Out of the question."

Penelope felt woozy. Her mother was going to kill her. Not only had she run away to Miss Maddie's, somehow she'd left town altogether! Penelope took a quick look around. She was standing on a small hill. Tall reeds swayed and hummed in the breeze. A well-worn dirt road ran down the hill to meet a field of stubby blue grass. To the right of the field, a forest of pine trees stood like sentries. There was not one house or street sign to be found. The woozy feeling moved from her stomach down to her knees.

Penelope turned back toward the man. "There *must* be a way out of here," she insisted.

But the man wasn't listening. "Do you see that?" he asked suddenly, pointing at the sky above the forest.

Penelope scanned the sky. It was empty except for a dark cloud huddled over the forest's far horizon. "You mean that cloud?" she asked.

When she looked back, the man was running headlong down the hill. "It looks like rain. I must be off!" he called over his shoulder. Once he reached the bottom of the hill, he left the road behind and took a trail through the grass heading straight for the forest.

"Wait!" Penelope shouted after him.

He stopped and turned around.

"I have to get back home! Can you please tell me where this road goes?"

"To the same place every day," he yelled back.

"But where *is* that?"

"If you don't know where you are, you can't possibly care where you're going. Now then, I really must go. Pleased to meet you."

"We *haven't* met!" shouted Penelope. But it was too late. The man had disappeared into the forest.

Penelope took a deep breath and tried to clear her head. *All you have to do is retrace your steps*, she told herself. But that was just it. Penelope didn't remember any steps. She had a vague memory of falling, but from where?

Penelope looked up. The rain cloud she had noticed earlier was moving swiftly across the sky. It didn't drift or roll like a cloud. It spread like a stain, smothering the sun and casting a gray light over the countryside. As the cloud drew closer, the soft breeze died away and the reeds stood still. The birds stopped singing and the bugs stopped twitching and a hush settled over the hill.

Penelope shuddered. Something didn't seem quite right about the cloud. In fact, something felt dreadful, though she couldn't tell what. Penelope's heart started to race and the next thing she knew she was running headlong down the hill in the same direction as the man.

As Penelope ran, she remembered all her mother's warnings about strangers. She considered her situation and decided that while the man certainly *seemed* strange in one way, he wasn't really the kind of stranger she was meant to avoid. Even so, the sooner she introduced herself the better. Then she would ask him for help. What choice did she have? There was no one else around.

Once Penelope reached the bottom of the hill, she veered off the road and onto the trail the man had followed into the forest. She plunged into the woods and the daylight immediately vanished under a thick canopy of shade. Trees crowded around her and tangled branches pressed in on every side. Penelope tried to push her way through the thick undergrowth, but soon lost the trail and with it, her sense of direction.

She heard humming up ahead and followed the sound, scanning the dim woods for a hint of red hair or a flash of blue suit. The humming sounded tantalizingly close, but the man was nowhere to be seen. Soon she was leaping over logs and brushing aside wisps of draping moss. And then, just like that, the humming stopped.

Penelope stood very still as the silence of the forest settled around her. She closed her eyes and held her breath, listening for some clue to the peculiar man's whereabouts. After a moment she heard a soft rustling sound like a mouse making its home. Penelope turned around in a slow circle, scanning the woods. That's when she saw it — a bit of red hair poking out from behind a tree. The man had left the path and was bending over a rotten stump, searching through a pile of decaying leaves.

"Hello?" called Penelope.

The man stood up immediately. "Mushrooms!"

"Wh-what?"

"Mushrooms!" he repeated, making his way toward her. He held out his hand. Two small, unassuming mushrooms sat on his palm. "You do like mushrooms, don't you?"

"They're . . . uh . . . they're very interesting," said Penelope, wishing she could say something intelligent based on what she'd learned at science camp.

The man beamed at her. "I couldn't agree with you more." He slipped the mushrooms into one of his many pockets. "That's settled, then. There's one for me and one for you. Of course, we'll have to wait until dinner."

"B-but I *can't* stay for dinner," stammered Penelope.

"Well, I suppose we could have them for an afternoon snack." He reached back into his pocket.

"You don't understand," she interrupted. "I don't have *time* to eat." Just then Penelope remembered her resolve to introduce herself. "My name is Penelope," she said, sticking out her hand. "And I'm from the Spicewood Estates."

"I'm Dill," he said with a quick shake.

"Like the pickle?" Penelope bit her lip. What a rude thing to say! She knew her mother wouldn't approve, but Dill didn't seem to mind. He smiled as if Penelope had compared him to someone famous.

"Exactly! Like the pickle."

Relieved, Penelope moved on to her request. "I was hoping you could help me. Do you know the way out of this Realm? I know you said it was impossible to leave, but if there's a way in, there must be a way out."

"I never said it was impossible to leave," replied Dill. "I said that if you're here, it's impossible to be anywhere else."

"Oh. So it *is* possible to leave?"

"Of course it's possible," said Dill.

Penelope went slack with relief. "Thank goodness."

"But highly unlikely," he continued.

Penelope suddenly felt very tired. They were going around and around and getting nowhere. She decided to change her approach. "Do you know *anyone* who knows the way out?"

The man frowned. "I suppose Chronos knows."

"*Who?*"

"Chronos." Dill fixed Penelope with a stare. "Ever heard of him?"

Penelope shook her head.

"Lucky you. He's unfriendly. Unpleasant. Actually" — his voice dropped to a whisper — "he's downright wicked."

"Wicked?" said Penelope, taking a step back. "I don't want to meet *him*."

"Indeed, you don't. It's best you stick with me for the time being. Now, I'd better get dinner started," he said, patting the pocket where he'd put the mushrooms. "These won't stay fresh for long."

Dill set off down the trail humming and Penelope hurried after so as not to be left behind. It sounded like she was stuck here, at least until she could figure out how to get home. Except she wasn't much good at figuring things out these days. Not with all her ideas dried up. She thought about poor Miss Maddie, who was probably trying to explain things to her mother at this very moment. Would her mother even *care* that Penelope was gone or would she just be upset that her schedule had been interrupted?

After walking for some time, they came to a clearing in the woods where a tiny sunlit meadow sat. The meadow was ringed by tall trees and topped with a bright blue sky.

"We're almost there!" Dill said and rushed ahead.

Penelope ran after him until — *bam!* — her foot hit something hard and she tumbled to the ground. She got to her feet, expecting Dill to reappear from around a tree or pop up from behind her. But he didn't. She looked left, then right. She looked up, then down. That's when she noticed what had tripped her — a stovepipe sticking up out of the dirt. A stovepipe meant there was a stove and a stove meant there was a kitchen and a kitchen meant . . . *aha!* There it was. A few feet from where she'd fallen was a door level with the ground. The door was open and Penelope peered through it down a deep hole to a pool of light below. Drifting up from the hole was the sound of banging cabinets and slamming drawers.

Penelope followed the noise down a ladder and soon arrived in a large open room fashioned from a cavern. The room had none of the dark dampness associated with caves. It was warm and brightly lit, with a living room on one end and a dining room on the other. The kitchen, where Dill was vigorously stirring something with a wire whisk, sat in the middle.

"Welcome! Greetings! Warmest salutations!" he called out to Penelope and nodded toward the living room. "Make yourself at home."

Penelope picked out a comfy-looking chair facing the kitchen and plopped down. The chair was carved out of a log and had pillows made from grape-colored moss. "Now then," said Dill, once Penelope was settled. "I'm dying to hear about these Spicewood Estates . . ."

"It's just a neighborhood," said Penelope with a shrug. "Lots of people live there."

"And there are spice woods?" he asked eagerly.

Penelope had often wondered about this. "No, there aren't any woods. Maybe there were at one time, but they're gone now. Mostly it's just houses."

"But these houses," pressed Dill, "they're beautiful estates with grounds and gardens?"

"It's not like that," Penelope insisted. "All the houses are the same with small yards."

Dill stopped stirring for a moment. "And you want to go back?"

"I *have* to go back," she explained. "I have a schedule to keep. Things I have to do. The longer I'm away, the farther behind I fall."

"I see." Dill resumed stirring. "I guess they're everywhere," he muttered.

Penelope sat up. "*Who's* everywhere?"

"I'd rather not say. There's no use ruining our appetite." Dill poured whatever he was making into a dish and slipped it into the oven. "I'll be right back. Just have to wash up a bit," he said and disappeared down the hall.

Penelope sat back in her chair and thought about Dill's question. *Did* she want to go back? She had no idea how she had gotten here, so she had no idea how to return. Maybe Dill would let her stay with him until she could come up with a plan. She couldn't help but wonder what she would be going back *to* anyway. By now her mother had probably thrown away all of Penelope's notebooks and was preparing to turn her room into an office.

Penelope got up from her chair to look around. The living room had two chairs and a long couch, each with the same grape-colored moss pillows. The pillows matched the wallpaper, which was every shade of purple imaginable — lavender, mauve, lilac, violet, plum, and wine. The most striking thing about the wallpaper wasn't the color, though. It was the texture. It was *bumpy*.

On closer inspection, Penelope realized the wallpaper wasn't wallpaper at all — it was mushrooms. Huge, spongy, purple mushrooms. Ebon and the other Mad Scientists would flip for these! Penelope reached out to touch one. Her fingertip disappeared in its fleshy exterior and then sprang back.

Bloop.

She couldn't resist doing it again.

Bloop. Bloop.

"Stop that!"

Penelope spun around, hands behind her back. Dill was striding toward her, his wild hair standing up even higher than usual. "Those mushrooms are *very* sensitive! They only grow under the most delicate conditions. You can't go around poking them!"

"I'm sorry," explained Penelope. "I didn't mean to hurt them."

Dill's eyes softened. "All right, then. They *are* hard to resist. They're awfully springy. Bouncy. Downright squishy."

"But what are they for?" asked Penelope.

"Eating, of course! Now then, if you please . . ." Dill escorted Penelope to the dining room and sat her at the head of the table, which was made from an enormous tree stump. He then retrieved a white dish from the kitchen. Spilling over the top of the dish was a gigantic lavender-colored soufflé. *"Bon appétit,"* he said in a hushed tone before placing it gently on the table.

"It looks delicious," said Penelope, who wasn't quite sure it did.

"Shh! You mustn't disturb it."

"Sorry," she whispered.

Dill rolled up his sleeves, took a large flat serving spoon, and approached the soufflé as if it were alive. He adjusted his angle several times before darting forward and swiftly tapping the soufflé along one of the many delicate creases across its top. When he did so, a puff of purple steam rose up and settled several feet above the dinner table.

Dill jumped on his chair and began to shovel bits of steam into his mouth with the serving spoon. "Quick! Grab your spoon!" he urged Penelope.

Penelope picked up her spoon and looked hesitantly at the purple cloud.

"You'll have to stand on your chair," said Dill, puffs of purple air escaping his mouth.

Penelope couldn't resist the idea of eating dinner standing on a chair, so up she went. The steam was thicker than expected and surprisingly easy to scoop up. Inside her mouth it swelled to twice its original size and then burst

into a series of delicate flavors: savory cream sauce, then toasted cheese, and finally vanilla ice cream with a tinge of hazelnut.

Neither of them said a word until the last bit of soufflé was gone. When they were finished, they sat down on their chairs with heavy sighs.

"That was amazing," said Penelope.

Dill let out a lavender-colored burp. "Thank you. I came up with the idea to make a soufflé so light you could only eat the steam, but I had the hardest time figuring out the recipe. The steam kept turning into soup in midair and causing the worst soggy mess. Or the soufflé was too light and only a mist would form. Have you ever tried to eat mist?"

Penelope shook her head.

"Well, I can tell you, it was a disaster. Failure. Total flop."

"What did you do?"

"I just kept moodling. I came up with hundreds of ideas. Most of them were too small, but I kept at it and after a while I moodled up a few big ones. With some tinkering, I turned those big ideas into real possibilities and from there I created my masterpiece — the lightest soufflé in the world!"

A faraway look crossed Dill's face and he stared past Penelope into a memory only he could see. "That was years ago. Years . . . and years . . . long before moodling was declared illegal . . ."

"What exactly *is* moodling?" interrupted Penelope, who was itching to add the word to her collection.

Dill leaned in as if sharing an important secret. "Moodling is daydreaming, letting your mind wander, losing track of time, and, in the most severe cases" — here he mouthed the words — "doing nothing."

Penelope's mouth dropped open. She did these things every chance she could! So did Miss Maddie! "What's so bad about letting your mind wander and . . . and . . . doing nothing?" she asked.

"I say, there's nothing wrong with a bit of moodling — you come up with the most interesting ideas that way. But you can only do it if Chronos isn't around. If he sees you, he'll send the Clockworkers to snatch you up and take you to the tower just like *that*." Dill snapped his fingers.

"Clockworkers!? Tower?" Penelope's voice was a high-pitched squeak.

"I can see it's time to tell you the story of the Great Moodler." Dill looked around the room quickly, as if they might not be alone. Once he seemed satisfied that no one was around, he continued, "Listen closely, but whatever you do, don't repeat a word. Your life just might depend upon it."

chapter five

THE STORY OF THE GREAT MOODLER

Once upon a time, so long ago I don't remember when, the Great Moodler was known far and wide for being exactly that — a *great* moodler. When most people moodle, they come up with a few ideas, but not the Great Moodler. She came up with real possibilities.

First she would moodle on the smallest, faintest notion. Soon it would blossom into an idea. With constant moodling, her ideas took flight, soaring overhead and colliding with one another until sparks flew. From the sparks, her ideas caught fire, streaking into the sky and exploding with possibilities.

In those days, possibilities fell to the ground like rain. Each one was a brilliant bit of light, etched with a message. "It's a possibility," people would say whenever they found one and, if they liked what it said, they'd pop it into their mouths and chew on it. Everyone was full of possibilities in those days — full to the point of bursting.

Most possibilities were quite ordinary, such as, ***Tomorrow it will rain.*** But some were intriguing and delicious, such as, ***There's a man in the moon*** or ***You can fly***. People loved these possibilities the most. Whenever someone discovered one, rather than chew on it, they would sit right down and consider it. When they did, the possibility would grow. Sometimes it grew a little bit and sometimes a lot, but on the average most possibilities were about the size of a watermelon.

One night the Great Moodler had trouble sleeping. She got out of bed and stared up at the stars, moodling on the mysteries of life. When she did, a tiny possibility began to take shape. Even though it was very small, it was brighter and more beautiful than anything ever seen. It was like a sliver of the sun — so dazzling the night around it turned to day.

When the possibility took flight, people woke from their dreams and rushed outside to see what it was. They stared up in awe at the brilliant possibility, waiting for it to fall to the ground so they could consider it. But instead of falling, it streaked across the heavens like a meteor and disappeared from view.

Everyone was crushed. What was this possibility? What did it say? The very next day, explorers set out to find it. Because it was lost in some distant land, they called the treasure they were seeking the Remote Possibility. For years explorers trudged across deserts, slogged through swamps, and hacked their way through jungles, but the Remote Possibility was never found. One by one the explorers gave up their search and the Remote Possibility moved from memory into legend.

One explorer, though, never gave up. He climbed up the highest

mountains and down the deepest valleys in all four directions. When the Remote Possibility remained hidden, he searched harder and farther, traveling into the forgotten corners of the world.

One day while tramping through a rocky wasteland, surrounded by nothing but the dust and debris of a long-dead volcano, the explorer saw a glimmer on the ground up ahead. He was hungry and thirsty and his vision was blurred from exhaustion, but the light refused to fade. Was it a mirage? Or had he finally found what he'd been searching for?

Anything is possible, he told himself and pushed on toward the light. As he drew closer, the faint glimmer became a glow.

Anything is possible, he said again, putting one exhausted foot in front of the other. The light grew brighter still, turning the pebbles in its shadow into diamonds.

Once the treasure was finally within reach, the explorer bent down to pick it up. When he did, he let out a cry. For etched in the light were his very own words!

Anything is possible.

The explorer knew his search was over — the Remote Possibility had been found. He set off for home immediately, carrying his discovery with him. When he reached the border of the wasteland, he met a group of travelers. He shared the Remote Possibility with them, and as he did, the possibility began to grow. This in and of itself wasn't strange — that's what possibilities did. The strange thing was how *much* it grew. And grew. And grew. In just a matter of moments, it was the size of a bush, then a boulder.

"I can't believe it!" said one of the travelers.

"Anything is possible, I suppose," said another. And they all had to agree it was true. The proof was right in front of them.

By now the Remote Possibility was much too big for the explorer to carry, so he sent the travelers for help. But when help arrived, they had never seen a possibility so large and immediately began to consider it themselves. Of course, when they did, it grew even larger. Soon it was the size of a hill.

Word spread rapidly, and more and more people flocked to the wasteland. "Anything *is* possible," they would say when they saw the glittering mound of light. Up, up, up! The Remote Possibility grew bigger still until it was taller than the tallest mountain and wider than the sea.

By now the possibility was so large that people began to wonder what to do with it. Should they climb it? Dance around it? Chip it into pieces? They had no idea, but they knew someone who would — the Great Moodler.

The Great Moodler was a very gifted problem solver. It didn't matter if it was a big problem (like how to build a bridge to a rainbow) or a little problem (like how to catch a cricket), the Great Moodler would come up with a solution. But when she saw the Remote Possibility, even she was overwhelmed.

She moodled all day and all night. Hundreds of tiny notions streamed from her head and ideas bounced back and forth, but no real possibilities formed. So she moodled away the next day and the next night, too. Finally, after a week of almost constant moodling, a big idea began to take shape. Everyone held their breath, watching as she turned the idea this way and that. Suddenly it spun into the air and exploded with possibilities. The crowd cheered and the Great Moodler stood to announce her solution.

"This is what you must do with the Remote Possibility . . ." she shouted. The crowd grew silent, waiting for the answer.

"Live with it!"

Everyone was stunned. This wasn't the answer they were expecting. But the more they considered it, the more it made perfect sense. The Remote Possibility was so wonderful, so beautiful, they should build their lives around it. And that's what they did.

The Great Moodler quickly built a home on top of the gleaming mountain of light. She named the land in all four directions the Realm of Possibility. At the foot of the mountain, the people created a city that was beautiful beyond belief. The buildings were curvaceous and fanciful and went straight up into the clouds. The roads were long and winding and always followed the scenic route. People planted fruit trees along the highways to encourage musing and munching on the way to Wherever.

The city sat on one side of the Remote Possibility and the wasteland where it had been found sat on the other. The wasteland, however, was no longer a wasteland. The rocks and boulders bloomed in the light of the Remote Possibility and became grand mountains in their own right. But these mountains were no ordinary mountains. Instead of being brown or gray, like you might expect, they were blue, orange, green, pink, yellow — every color of the rainbow! People called them the Range of Possibilities and climbed their heights to reach the sun.

The Realm was a peaceful, beautiful place until one day a stranger came walking down the road. He carried nothing with him except a mysterious black book and a gold pocket watch. His name was Chronos and he had come to the Realm to make his mark. Chronos immediately built himself a giant home made of concrete and steel. He called his home, which was really more of a fortress, the Timely Manor. It held twenty-four rooms, one for each hour in the day. The rooms were dark and windowless and filled with ticking clocks. The outside walls were topped with a parapet where grim-faced Clockworkers marched day and night. No one knew exactly where the Clockworkers had come from, but one thing was sure — they lived to serve their master.

The Manor surrounded a central courtyard from which a tremendous clock tower rose. The tower had four clocks — one for each direction of the compass. Chronos was a proud man and he soon became jealous of the Great Moodler's place of importance. He believed the Realm was overrun with useless daydreamers and the Remote Possibility was nothing but a silly notion. He would often stand on the parapet and read aloud from his black book, shouting down to the people in the streets below. The book was filled with time-saving tips and words to live by, but most people ignored them. This made Chronos furious, so he came up with a plan.

In those days, the clock tower was a novelty, and no one paid it much mind. Everyone was too busy moodling to keep track of time. And why should they? There was time enough for everyone. People took as much as they needed and never worried about wasting it. Many had time to spare and would share it with anyone who asked. "There's no present like time," they'd say and give away minutes, hours, even days to those in need.

Chronos changed all that. Every day he ordered his Clockworkers to wind the clocks in the tower and every day, time would run out. People began to watch the clock, first out of curiosity and then in alarm. Time was slipping away. Soon people began to fight among themselves. "Take *your* time. Leave mine alone!" they argued. Neighbors accosted neighbors, demanding borrowed time back. What little time was left at the end of the day was heavily guarded lest it be stolen. It didn't take long before people turned to Chronos for answers. They gathered at the Manor and demanded an explanation. "Where has all the time gone?"

Chronos was prepared. "I'll tell you where it went," he roared, pointing to the Great Moodler's home on top of the Remote Possibility. "It's being wasted by that useless Moodler and by *you*!" This time he pointed an accusing finger at the crowd. "You are killing time with all your moodling. If you want more time, you must do as I say. Immediately!"

This got everyone's attention. "Killing time!" they said to one another. "How horrible. This must stop at once!"

They listened closely as Chronos explained his plan: "The more possibilities you consider, the less likely you are to accomplish anything. And the fewer things you accomplish, the more time you waste. Therefore, the quickest way to make the most of your time is to limit the possibilities." The people looked up at the clock tower in alarm. Sure enough, Chronos was right. Time was running out. There wasn't a minute to waste!

Chronos appointed twelve of his most efficient Clockworkers to a Committee devoted to making every second count. The first thing the Committee did was visit the Great Moodler and demand she stop coming up with new possibilities. "We have quite enough already!" they scolded her.

Next they decided to consider the possibilities they did have and throw out the ones that were a waste of time. After sifting through millions and millions of possibilities, they came up with a master list of 3,763. They passed an amendment to change *Anything is possible* to *3,763 things are possible*.

But they didn't stop there. Even *that* wasn't enough to save time, so they limited the possibilities even further, and as they did, the list became smaller . . .

2,631 . . . and smaller . . .

1,612 . . . and smaller . . .

497 . . . and smaller still . . .

Until it was decided: *217 things are possible*.

Anything struck from the list was deemed "Impossible" and declared illegal. Chronos established a court to prosecute time wasters and turned the

clock tower into a prison. With only 217 things possible, everyone knew *exactly* what they were supposed to be doing and when.

In gratitude for his efforts to save time, the Committee named the great city at the heart of the Realm after their leader. They called it Chronos City. Before long, the City outgrew its borders. As it grew bigger and bigger, it grew uglier and uglier. The Clockworkers shaved the ornamentation off the buildings, cut down the trees, and straightened the roads — all in the interest of efficiency.

The odd thing was, however, that no matter how much time people saved, there never seemed to be enough left over. The more things got done, the faster time ran out. Whether people were winding up or winding down, the clocks in the tower were always ticking. Soon the Realm was full of clocks. People carried them in their pockets, wore them on their wrists, and hung them on every wall. Before long, everyone's internal clock — the clock that told them when to do things in their own time — was completely drowned out.

"There's no such thing as an internal clock," scoffed Chronos. "Has anyone actually ever *seen* one?" People had to admit that no one ever had, whereas the clocks in the tower were undeniably real. Before long, people stopped even trying to check their internal clocks. They doubted they had ever *had* such a thing.

As doubt took hold in their minds, a dark Shadow gathered in the sky. At first it was nothing more than a mist hanging over the City, a slight haziness really. People hardly noticed it was there. But the more the clocks dictated people's every move — when to rise, when to eat, when to sleep — the darker the Shadow grew. The Shadow was darkest right above the tower, forming an impenetrable lid over the City. Before Chronos had arrived, every day had a rhythm, and the sun, moon, and stars kept the beat. Now there was no sun, moon, or stars to be seen. The Shadow had taken the place of the sky.

That's when the Great Moodler disappeared.

"High time!" said some who were glad to see her go.

"Better late than never," said others philosophically.

"It was only a matter of time," advised the Committee smugly.

Everyone had an opinion about where she'd gone. Some said she was banished. Others said she was lost in her own thoughts and couldn't find her way out. No one knew for sure. Either way, she was never seen again.

chapter six

"That's it? *That's* the story of the Great Moodler?" Penelope stared at Dill, willing him to continue.

Dill nodded. "That's it."

"Chronos took over and she disappeared?"

"Poof!" Dill waved his hands in the air. "Just like that."

"What about the Remote Possibility?" cried Penelope.

Dill shook his head sadly. "After the Great Moodler disappeared, the Remote Possibility shrank down to nothing. It hasn't been seen for ages."

Penelope sat in stunned silence. While listening to the story of the Great Moodler, a feeling of excitement had taken hold of her. The Great Moodler was an expert problem solver and a creative genius. If anyone could get her ideas flowing again, it was her! With her ideas back, Penelope could figure out how to make her dreams of being a writer come true. She could even figure out a way to get home, *if* she wanted to. Anything was possible!

But the Great Moodler was gone. And only 217 things were possible.

"I told you leaving was highly unlikely," continued Dill. "Now you know why. If Chronos knew you were here, he'd declare your arrival Impossible and whisk you away to the tower."

"I see what you mean," said Penelope in a daze.

Dill leaned across the table and gave her arm a gentle squeeze. "It's not so bad here. As long as we stay away from the City, we can moodle all we want. Besides, it sounds like your Spicewood Estates are overrun with Clockworkers."

Penelope gave him a weak smile. She couldn't bear to tell him the truth. Staying wasn't the problem. She *liked* it here. There was no daily schedule to follow or work-flow diagram to dictate her days. The problem was moodling. Maybe *Dill* could moodle all he wanted, but she couldn't. Her ideas were stuck. And with the Great Moodler gone, they were likely to stay that way.

"Dill?" said Penelope, her heart caught in her chest. "Have you ever tried to find the Great Moodler?"

Dill's shoulders slumped and his eyes glistened with what looked like tears. "Of course I've tried! I was looking for her when I bumped into you. I've moodled for days, weeks, months. I can't come up with a single idea, much less a real possibility as to where she is. I'm afraid it's hopeless. Useless. Absolutely futile."

Penelope thought about all the bad story ideas she'd come up with in the last few weeks and the blank wall her mind had eventually become. She knew exactly how he felt.

"I don't know what happened," said Dill, wiping his eyes with a handker-chief. "I used to be a great explorer. I could find anything — absolutely *anything*."

He glanced up at Penelope with a wry smile. "I was the one who found the Remote Possibility, you know."

Penelope's mouth dropped open. "You *were?*"

"Oh, yes. Distant memories, buried dreams, lost hopes — I found them all. I was a real hero in those days. You should have heard the people cheering when I came back from an expedition. But that's all over now. Exploring has been declared a waste of time and therefore Impossible by decree of Chronos. I haven't found anything in ages." Dill sighed a deep, unhappy sigh. He stared down at the floor, his shoulders still hunched. A moment later, he popped up and stared at Penelope, as if seeing her for the very first time. "Maybe *you* could give it a try."

Penelope glanced around. "Give *what* a try?"

Dill ignored her question. "Don't go anywhere. I'll be right back . . ." He rushed out of the room and soon returned with a small, shiny object.

"What is it?" asked Penelope.

"It's a moodle hat." Dill gave the hat a quick snap of the wrist and the top popped up. It was shaped like a bowl with a flat rim about three inches wide. He handed the hat gently to Penelope, who examined it. It was made of some sort of silvery mesh material. "How does it work?" she asked.

Dill leaned forward, his eyes practically glowing. "Now *that* is a very good question. On the outside, it looks ordinary. Unremarkable. Extremely plain. But on the inside, it couldn't be more fantastic. The lining is full of very small, very sophisticated traps — sticky snatchers, grabby gadgets, spring-loaded snappers — the works!"

Penelope peered under the hat to see the traps.

"You can't *see* anything," explained Dill. "It's all microscopic. You'll never guess what the traps do. Never, *ever*. So, I'll just have to tell you. They trap ideas, Penelope! All those glorious ideas, streaming and bubbling out of your head, all the ideas you couldn't keep ahold of, until . . . *snap!*" He flung his arms open wide, then slammed his hands together. "The moodle hat traps them for good!

"Imagine!" said Dill, walking wildly about. "The biggest, fattest, grandest ideas are all yours and the skinny, scrawny ones escape into the stratosphere, where they can fatten up a bit before dropping down and lodging in someone else's head." Dill spun around to face her. "Without this hat I never would have found the Remote Possibility. And now you can use it to find the Great Moodler!"

"*Me?*" squeaked Penelope.

"Yes, *you*. Ever since Chronos took over and the Great Moodler disappeared, I've felt lost. And how can I find anyone, if I can't find myself? But *you*," said Dill, giving Penelope's arm a little shake, "you might be able to moodle up an idea of where she went."

Dill looked so hopeful, Penelope couldn't bear to tell him that there was no chance of her coming up with a little idea, much less a big one. "You go first," she said, stalling for time. "To show me how it's done."

"All right." Dill took the hat and put it on. He hurried over to the couch and lay down, propping his head up on the armrest. "Hmmm . . ." he said, tapping his cheek with a long finger, "where is the Great Moodler?"

Penelope sat down on a moss-covered chair to watch. Her feet dangled to the floor and she tapped them nervously. *Tap. Tap. Tap.* There was no way she would be of any help. *Tap. Tap. Tap.* She might come up with a few lame fantasies, but she was all out of good ideas. Dill was sure to be disappointed. *Tap. Tap. Tap.*

Dill glared at her.

"Sorry," she mouthed.

Penelope sat as still as she could, almost not daring to breathe, and waited. After a while, Dill closed his eyes and Penelope thought he had fallen asleep. But every once in a while he'd scrunch his mouth or tweak his nose and the waiting would continue. Watching someone do nothing made Penelope sleepy and soon her head began to dip and sway in a lazy arc. *Snap!* She yanked herself back to attention. But her head dipped again . . . and again. Before long she lost the struggle and fell into a light sleep, her head resting on her chest.

"Drat! Fiddlesticks! Gosh darn it all!"

Penelope jerked awake. "What's wrong?" she asked, trying to sound alert.

"I don't have any ideas," said Dill. "None. Zero. Absolute zilch! It's just like before."

"Try staring out a window," offered Penelope.

"I don't have any windows," grumbled Dill. He took off the hat and held it out to Penelope. "Here, you try. My mind is blank."

Penelope knew the feeling all too well. She took the hat and held it in her lap for a moment. "What am I supposed to do again?" she asked.

"You don't *do* anything," insisted Dill. "If you do something you'll muck it all up. Just let your mind wander and the hat will capture any big ideas. But don't think too hard. And absolutely no analyzing, cogitating, or figuring of any kind."

Penelope slowly raised the hat up to her head. *There's no way this is going to work*, she said to herself. *I'm all out of ideas. I don't know what I'm doing. I hope Dill won't be mad and —*

Penelope's last thought was cut off as she lowered the hat onto her head. She heard, or rather felt, a soft *whir-whir*.

"Now, ask yourself where the Great Moodler is," whispered Dill. "But remember, no thinking! Just let your mind go."

Penelope tried to concentrate on the question while at the same time not thinking. It felt like she was trying to open a door and shut it at the same time. Sometimes a thought floated by — *I wonder what the Great Moodler looks like* or *My foot is falling asleep*. But for the most part, nothing came to mind. Penelope stared at the nothing. It was bright and beautiful. Somehow it made her feel peaceful.

Whir-whir-whir . . . The longer she stared at the nothing, the faster the whirring sound went.

Does the whirring mean it's working? she wondered. *If so, where are all the ideas?*

Penelope let these thoughts slip away and for a minute (or was it an hour?) she slipped away with them. Just then she felt a *snap*. It vibrated through her body and brought her back to reality. She opened her eyes.

Dill was staring at the hat. "That's really something," he said in a hushed voice.

Penelope slowly lowered the hat from her head. It had grown! The silvery mesh material had stretched to the size of a beach ball. Something like a huge bubble struggled to get out. And then — *pop!* — just like that, it disappeared.

Dill turned quickly to Penelope. "So what's the big idea?" he demanded.

Penelope shrugged. "I — I don't know."

"You mean, nothing came to mind?"

"Nothing," said Penelope.

"Nothing? Like nil? *Nada?* Diddly-squat?"

Penelope nodded.

Dill's shoulders sagged. "Oh, well. I suppose the bubble is just an anomaly. We'll try again in the morning."

Penelope wondered what *anomaly* meant. She decided it must be another word for failure.

chapter seven

After the soufflé dish and silverware were washed and put away, Dill escorted Penelope down a long hall, stopping before a door made of dark wood. Inside was a bed made from the roots of a tree growing directly overhead. The roots, which extended down into the room, had been coaxed into the shape of a large, intricately woven basket. The bed, or basket, as it were, was piled ridiculously high with pillows and blankets.

"Sleep well," said Dill.

"Good night," said Penelope and closed the door.

Penelope sat down on the edge of the bed and took out her notebook. She added *moodle* to her list of fascinating words. She also added *anomaly*. Next to *anomaly*, she wrote the word *failure* and a question mark. Afterward, she jotted down the important moments of her day — the hole in her schedule, meeting Dill, the story of the Great Moodler — before slipping off her shoes and crawling under the covers.

The bed rocked back and forth ever so slightly as if the tree above her was swaying in the breeze. The gentle movement should have put Penelope right to sleep, but it didn't. Instead, she lay there thinking about her mother. When her mother had a problem, she got organized. But Penelope wasn't very good at coming up with schedules, action items, and agendas. The only thing she was any good at was moodling, and now she was even a failure at that!

Why can't I come up with any ideas?

Where did they all go?

Penelope rolled over onto her side and squeezed her eyes shut, trying to clear her head.

If I can't come up with any ideas, I'll never find the Great Moodler.

Dill will be so disappointed.

Penelope sat up. She punched her pillow a few times, then lay back down. But as soon as she closed her eyes, the worries started streaming in.

I'll moodle and moodle and nothing will happen . . .

Pop.

Except Chronos will probably catch me . . .

Pop-pop.

And send me to the clock tower!

Penelope was so consumed with the process of worrying that she hardly noticed a very soft popping sound coming from nearby.

I'll starve in the tower or catch pneumonia . . .

Pop-pop.

Or turn into a Clockworker . . .

Pop-pop-pop.

And never be a writer!

Poppity-pop-pop.

Each new worry spawned another worry. And another. Soon they were coming so fast Penelope couldn't keep up. She tossed and turned late into the night. It wasn't until she fell into a fitful sleep that the worries ceased and the popping grew silent.

-- -- --

Penelope woke before dawn to the smell of burnt toast. After stumbling around a bit, she managed to find her notebook and shoes, then made her way to the kitchen.

"Good morning! Ready for . . ." Dill's voice trailed off. He put down the honey jar he was holding and hurried toward Penelope. "Did you sleep all right?"

"Not really," she said, stifling a yawn. "I stayed up half the night worrying about finding the Great Moodler."

"I can see that." Dill took Penelope by the shoulders, turning her this way and that. "It's written *all over* your face."

Penelope put a hand up to her cheek and gasped. She felt bumps. She touched her forehead, nose, and chin. Bumps, bumps, and more bumps. "What happened to me?" she cried.

Dill gripped her shoulder. "I'll tell you on one condition."

"Okay," said Penelope, her heart racing.

"You have to promise me not to worry."

If Penelope hadn't been so dazed, she might have protested. Instead, she limply crossed her heart. "I promise."

Dill dragged Penelope over to the living room and sat her down. He turned to a cabinet nearby and took out a mirror, holding it against his chest. "Remember, you promised not to worry."

Penelope nodded and held out her hand. Dill gave her the mirror.

She immediately forgot her promise. Her face was covered with bumps — wrinkly red bumps. "I have a disease!" she screamed, and right before her eyes — *pop, pop, pop* — three more appeared on her nose.

"*You promised not to worry!*" shrieked Dill and snatched the mirror away.

Penelope snatched it right back. "How can you tell me not to worry? I've got bumps all over my face!"

"Those *aren't* bumps. They're worry warts. If we had a magnifying glass you'd see they're made of teeny-tiny words spelling out your troubles. The more you worry, the worse they get."

Penelope wasn't listening. She was staring at her reflection. *I'm going through the rest of my life covered in ugly red warts*, she thought. *I'll never be able to show my face in public again!* A few more warts squeezed onto her forehead — *Pop! Pop!* Her face was in danger of disappearing altogether.

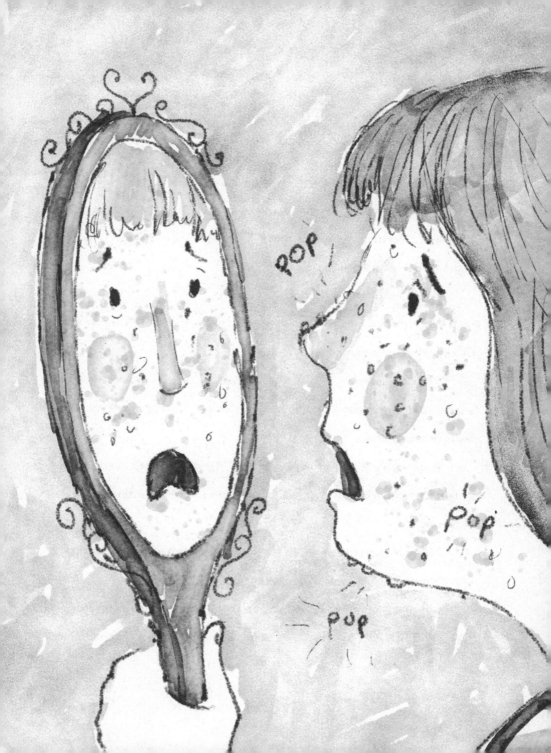

Dill knelt down beside Penelope. "Quick! Tell me what you were worried about."

Penelope dragged her eyes away from the mirror and tried to focus.

"Please," pleaded Dill. "It's important you remember."

Penelope closed her eyes and tried to make a list. "Being captured by Chronos . . . wasting away in the tower . . . catching pneumonia . . . starving to death . . ." She peeked out of one eye.

"Go on, go on," urged Dill.

Penelope took a deep breath and let the words rush out. "Turning into a Clockworker and never moodling again!"

"Horrible, horrible, horrible!" Dill leapt to his feet and began to run around, snatching things from closets and cabinets — bits of rope, flashlights, boots, and hammers.

"Imprisonment! Starvation! Pneumonia!" He dashed off to the next room and came charging back with several boxes of tissues, which he threw onto the growing pile.

"We're almost ready now," he said and disappeared into the hall closet.

"Ready for what?" asked Penelope.

Dill emerged from the closet, holding a stepladder and an inflatable raft. "What do you *mean*, 'for what?' We've got a lot of disastrous matters to take care of."

Penelope scrunched down in her chair. "Not really," she said. "Nothing *actually* happened."

Dill dropped the stepladder. "Nothing?"

Penelope shook her head.

"*Absolutely* nothing?"

Penelope shook her head again.

"You're telling me, you stayed up half the night for no good reason?"

"I had plenty of reasons!" insisted Penelope. "You saw me try the moodle hat. I'm useless. I'll never be able to help you find the Great Moodler or fend off Chronos and his Clockworkers if they find out I'm here."

"Worrying won't change all that. By the way, I think they're spreading," said Dill, pointing at her neck.

Penelope checked. Sure enough, there were more bumps. "What am I going to do?" she cried.

"Stop worrying. They're bound to go away."

"*When?*" Penelope demanded.

Dill's muffled voice came from inside the closet, where he was busily putting away everything he'd just taken out. "It should only take a few hours . . . or a few days."

"A few *days*?" Penelope couldn't believe what she was hearing.

Dill popped out of the closet and tried shoving it closed with his shoulder. "To be honest," he said, huffing and puffing, "I have no idea how long it will take. I've never had worry warts myself, so I'm not sure what the cure is."

"*You don't know what the cure is?*" POP! POP! POP! Penelope's face and neck erupted in a fury of red bumps.

"Nope," said Dill and gave the door a final shove. There was a muffled crash before it clicked obediently closed.

"Can't you think of something?" Penelope pleaded.

"Well," said Dill, drumming his fingers on his chin. "I can certainly give it a try."

Penelope watched him, holding her breath, trying not to worry.

"Pirates!" Dill suddenly shouted.

Penelope looked around quickly. "Where?"

"Not *here*," said Dill. "Last night, in your worries. Did they show up?"

"No . . ."

"How about tigers? Did you worry about them?"

"Of course not. That's ridiculous."

Dill flung open his arms. "There you have it!"

"What do I have?" Penelope said each word very carefully. She was fighting the urge to throw the mirror at him.

"The cure!"

Penelope looked at her reflection. The worry warts hadn't gone anywhere. "*What* are you talking about?" she practically screamed.

"If you got the warts by worrying about all the bad things that *could* have
happened, then the best way to get rid of them is to think about all the bad
things that *couldn't* have happened. It's like worrying, but in reverse."

Penelope stared at Dill, her eyes bulging. *Who ever heard of worrying in
reverse?*

"Here, let me help," he continued. "What's your least favorite thing?"

"Snakes," she answered immediately. That was an easy one.

"Well, then," urged Dill, "tell me something about snakes that couldn't
possibly have happened last night."

Penelope thought about it for a moment. "I didn't get squeezed to death by
a python?" It was really more of a question.

"You're a very lucky girl," said Dill, his voice deep and serious.

Penelope thought she might have felt a slight tingling sensation in her face.
Either the worrying in reverse was working, or she was just embarrassed.

"Go ahead," prompted Dill. "What's another awful thing you didn't have
to worry about?"

"I didn't fall into a pit."

"Or get snapped in two by sharks," Dill added helpfully.

Penelope couldn't help but giggle. "Or swept away by a dust storm . . ."

"Or drowned in a whirlpool. Or run over by an elephant."

"Or frozen inside a glacier!"

By now Penelope's cheeks were burning hot, but she kept going. "I didn't get captured by headhunters . . ."

"Or eaten by cannibals . . ."

"Or thrown into a bed of scorpions!"

"It's working!" shouted Dill, pointing at her face.

Penelope held up the mirror, turning it this way and that. She watched as the last remaining wart faded from bright red to soft pink to the same creamy color as her skin. Then, just like that, it was gone.

"Congratulations!" said Dill, giving Penelope's hand a firm shake. "It's official. You've got nothing to worry about."

chapter eight

Penelope sank back into her chair with relief. The heat from her face melted away, flooding her body with a warm, relaxed feeling. So this was what it felt like to have nothing to worry about.

"Up, up, up!" demanded Dill, clapping his hands.

Penelope, who had just been contemplating going back to bed, didn't budge.

"We've got a sunrise to catch," he insisted. "You don't want to miss it."

Penelope dragged herself to her feet. She followed Dill down the front hall, up the ladder, and out into the cool dark of early morning. But instead of a sun peeking through the trees, they were met by a stark gray sky.

"That's strange," said Dill. "The sun should be here by now."

"Maybe we're up too early." Penelope stifled a yawn. "Maybe it's actually still nighttime."

"If it's nighttime, then where are the stars? No, no, no. Something is definitely wrong. Awry. Out of order."

Penelope looked at the sky. She suddenly felt an odd chill that had nothing to do with the temperature. It seemed to come from her own bones. She remembered the rain cloud Dill had pointed out yesterday and how it had continued to move even after the wind had grown still. How it had blackened the sky and filled her with dread. She felt that same dread now.

Dill must have felt it, too. He turned to Penelope, his face white. "We've got to go. They'll be here soon. Swarms of them."

"Swarms of *what?*" asked Penelope, suddenly awake.

"Clockworkers. That's no cloud," he said, pointing upward. "That's the Shadow."

"The Shadow from Chronos City?" Penelope couldn't believe what she was hearing. "What's it doing *here?*"

"I have no idea, but whatever the reason, it can't be good. We've *got* to get out of here until it passes." Dill hurried back down the ladder and Penelope scrambled after him.

"Where will we go?" she asked as Dill flung odds and ends into a backpack.

"The mountains." Dill's voice was grim, his jaw clenched. "I know a short-cut through the woods to the Range of Possibilities. We'll be halfway there before the Clockworkers reach my meadow. But only if we act fast." He began rifling through drawers and stuffing his many pockets with provisions.

"What about finding the Great Moodler?" Despite all her worries, Penelope wasn't ready to abandon her search.

"The Great Moodler will have to wait." Dill hoisted the pack over his shoulder. "We'll never find her if we're imprisoned in the clock tower. Now *come on.*"

Once outside, Dill and Penelope took off across the meadow. Penelope practically had to run to keep up with Dill's long strides. When they reached the far end of the clearing, a wild, overgrown hedge blocked their way. An ancient wooden sign pointed directly at the impenetrable mass of bushes and brambles. Penelope could just make out the words:

THIS WAY TO THE NAUGHTY WOULDS.

She stifled a laugh. "Shouldn't that say, 'This way to the *Knotty Woods*'?"

Dill looked at the sign and then back at Penelope. "That's *exactly* what it says. 'This way to the Naughty Woulds.'"

"No, it says, 'naughty,' but woods aren't naughty, they're 'knotty.' And what are 'woulds'? I've never heard of such a thing."

"Well, you have now." Dill walked up to the sign and gave it a heave. "Help me out, will you? No use telling the Clockworkers which way we've gone." Together they were able to pull the sign out of the ground. Once they'd hidden it under a bush, Dill found a shrub peppered with little red berries and pulled back one of its branches. "After you," he said with a quick bow.

Penelope leaned forward. A dark tunnel opened out in front of her. Thorny brambles crowded the tunnel as if trying to take it back, and a dank, musty smell filled the air. A path ran forward a few feet and then, with a sharp twist, disappeared.

"Are you *sure* this is the right way?" she asked, looking up at Dill.

"Of course I'm sure! Going around the Woulds takes days and days. If we want to stay ahead of the Clockworkers, there's nothing to do but go through them."

"Maybe you should go first," said Penelope.

"All right, then." Dill stepped inside and Penelope followed. Once they were both inside, he let the branch drop. What little light there was vanished and the air suddenly seemed to thicken. "I recommend you stay on the path," whispered Dill. "You don't want to go wandering around."

"Don't worry," Penelope whispered back. "I won't."

They set off together through the tunnel. Penelope had to hunch down in order to pass, while poor Dill was practically doubled over at the waist. Branches caught their sleeves and hair like long fingers, and they often had to stop and untangle themselves.

Even though the hedge seemed determined to block their path, it eventually opened out into an ancient forest packed with trees. Gnarled branches drooped down across their way and moss hung from every surface. Faint strips of dusty light illuminated the path, which was nearly hidden under a carpet of decaying leaves.

Dill led the way through the woods, humming and pointing out patches of mushrooms growing here and there. Some were light with dark spots, others were dark with light spots, but most were a dull yellow color with strange, fleshy warts. A very few were a translucent white with bright orange underneath. These were Penelope's favorites, but Dill cautioned her against touching them.

"Those will give you an incurable case of the hiccups," he said and then returned to his humming.

Every so often Dill would stop to examine the mushrooms and once or twice he plucked a smaller whitish one, tucking it into one of the pockets covering his jacket. "Just a little something for later," he explained. "Ever tried mushroom-and-halibut goulash?"

"No," said Penelope, hoping she never would.

"How about acorn-and-mushroom pâté?"

"No."

"Mushroom loaf with horseradish sauce?"

"No."

"Pickled mushrooms with prunes?"

"Definitely not!"

Dill shook his head. "You don't know what you're missing."

"How do you know so much about mushrooms?" Penelope asked.

"How come you know so little?"

"I never paid attention to them, even in science camp when I was supposed to. I thought they were gross," admitted Penelope.

"Mushrooms are *not* gross. They're wonderful. Fabulous. Absolutely marvelous. Back when I was searching for the Remote Possibility, I would have starved if it weren't for mushrooms. No matter where I was, I could find a mushroom or two to eat. When I returned from my adventure, I decided to grow them myself. That's why I've come up with so many recipes. I could eat mushrooms for breakfast, lunch, and . . ." Dill suddenly stopped and his voice dropped to a whisper. "Do you see what I see?"

Penelope lowered her voice as well. "What?"

"There! Look at the foot of that tree. The big one, far in the distance."

Penelope could see a cluster of tall, thin trees to her right. Beyond them stood an ancient oak with a trunk as big around as a house. Something glowed faintly among the oak's huge roots. "What are those glowing things?" she asked.

"Mushrooms. Very rare, very delicious mushrooms. Stay right where you are. I'll be back." Dill stepped off the path and darted through the trees.

"Where are you going?" Penelope called out after him.

"To pick them, of course!"

Penelope watched as Dill skipped over the fallen branches and snaking roots that covered the ground. Just before he reached the great tree, he stopped and looked over his shoulder. "I almost forgot," he yelled at Penelope. "Whatever you do, keep up the humming until I get back." Dill stepped behind the tree's giant trunk and was gone.

Penelope pondered his instructions. What was so important about humming? She tried humming a few bars of "Yankee Doodle." When she did, she felt the silence of the forest push against her, and her humming grew softer and softer until it died away altogether. A hush settled around her like a heavy blanket, pressing against her chest. At that moment, Penelope heard, almost imperceptibly, something that sounded like whispering. She strained to listen. There it was — voices in the distant background. Penelope scanned the forest, trying to locate the source of the sound, but all she saw were trees. They loomed over her, backs hunched, leaves limp.

Penelope closed her eyes and listened harder. The voices grew louder. The whispering was more like murmuring now. It seemed to be coming from directly above her. Penelope opened her eyes and thought she saw a slight movement in the branches, but couldn't be sure. She suddenly had the feeling she was being watched.

That's when the voices started in earnest.

The first voice was raspy and high-pitched, like the sound of an old woman. "Wouldn't it be better if she weren't such a scatterbrain?" it cackled.

"Wouldn't it be better if she were smarter?" said a second voice, much like the first.

"Wouldn't it be better if she were more organized?" chimed a third.

"Wouldn't it be better if she were more efficient?" said the fourth.

"It would! It would!" they all exclaimed together.

Penelope stood very still, listening. Were the voices talking about *her*? She looked back up at the trees. There it was again! That little flicker of movement that disappeared when it caught her eye.

"I think we can *all* agree," said the fourth voice, louder than before, "that if she weren't such a scatterbrain, she would be more productive . . ."

"She would be more useful . . ."

"She would be more successful . . ."

"She would be more competitive . . ."

Penelope's mouth dropped open. They *were* talking about her! But who, exactly, were *they*? She felt a sharp branch — or was it a finger? — graze her back. Penelope whirled around. There wasn't anything there — except a tree. Was it closer than before? She heard a snickering sound behind her and spun back to face the way she'd come. The tree in front of her was closer, too! All of the trees looked like they were leaning over her, pushed by a strong wind. Except there *was* no wind. The air was perfectly still.

Just then, the voices started again. This time they were screaming.

"If I were you, I would be ashamed of myself!"

"I would be embarrassed to show my face in public!"

"I would never leave the house!"

Penelope tried to run away, pushing against the branches that now blocked her path. In an instant the earth shifted underneath her and several long, dark roots crept up and around her feet. She kicked at them and they recoiled only to snap back and wrap tightly around her ankles. Once Penelope was anchored to the ground, a thin layer of moss sprouted over her shoes and began to move up her legs.

The voices were laughing now — a horrible screeching sound. Penelope brushed desperately at the moss, trying to knock it away, but it only crept higher. Penelope's knees buckled and she slid to the ground. When she did, the roots leapt up and wrapped around her wrists. Penelope tried to pull her hands free, but the roots were too strong. They held her down as the moss moved around her waist, creeping higher and higher with each second.

Penelope squeezed her eyes closed, fighting back tears. Screams and cheers ricocheted through the forest, until . . .

"Hush!"

Penelope's eyes snapped open. Dill was standing over her, shaking his fists at the trees. "Mind your own business! You're nothing but a bunch of bullies!" he shouted.

To Penelope's complete surprise, the trees fell silent and slowly began to melt back into the forest. Their roots, which had so firmly grasped Penelope, recoiled from her wrists and ankles.

Dill knelt down beside her. "Are you all right?" he asked.

"I — I think so," she stammered.

Dill helped Penelope to her feet and began brushing moss and leaves from her clothes. "The trees are really quite pathetic. If you stand up to them, they'll just go away. If you don't, they'll ensnare you in their chatter. *Wouldn't it be better if she were this, wouldn't it be better if she were that*? Those woulds are troublesome. Nasty. Very naughty."

"So *that's* what you meant by 'Naughty Woulds'!" said Penelope with a shaky laugh. "Now I understand. Why didn't you warn me?"

"I didn't want you to worry," said Dill. "And, really, there's nothing to worry about."

"There's *not*? How do you keep them from trapping you?"

"Humming!" declared Dill, pointing up at the sky as if leading a charge.

"Humming?" Penelope could hardly believe what she was hearing. Humming seemed like such a slight defense against the Naughty Woulds.

"Humming drives away the trees. They can't catch you if you're listening to your own tune," he explained.

Penelope thought about the horrible roots that had gripped her legs and arms. They had almost trapped her! She shook the memory loose and looked at Dill. "And . . . and what if you *don't* listen to your own tune?" she asked softly.

Dill pointed to a large moss-covered rock on the path ahead. "See for yourself."

Penelope approached the rock slowly. On closer inspection, she could see it wasn't a rock at all. She could just make out a hunched figure, anchored to the ground by moss, its features turned to stone.

"That's a person!" cried Penelope.

"Indeed it is," said Dill, joining her alongside the figure.

"But what happened to him?"

"He listened to the trees and believed them."

Penelope took a step back. *So did I,* she thought, her heart thumping.

Dill must have read her mind. He put one long arm around her shoulders and gave her a quick squeeze. "What are friends for, if they can't help keep the Naughty Woulds at bay? After all, who can say how you *would* be if things were one way or another? All we know is how you are, and how you are is exactly how you're meant to be."

Penelope stared up at Dill. He made it sound so simple. The way she was, was exactly how she was meant to be. It was the Naughty Woulds that were twisted and flawed. Her heart slowed its thumping and she smiled. Dill smiled back and then adjusted his coat with a brisk tug. "Ready?" he asked.

"Ready," said Penelope.

Dill set off down the trail humming. This time Penelope joined in.

chapter nine

Once they reached the edge of the Naughty Woulds, Dill and Penelope burst

out of the trees and into the day. They were standing on a high, rocky ridge. A

long valley of waving blue grass opened out below them. Above them, a bright

open sky hung dotted with clouds. They stood for a moment, taking in the view

and letting the memory of the dark woods fade.

Dill pointed to a boulder soaking up the sun. "That's a perfect place for a

picnic." Penelope agreed and together they climbed onto the rock and settled on

the side facing the valley with the Woulds behind them. Dill took out the

glowing mushrooms he'd picked in the forest. He popped the cap off one and

handed it to Penelope. "Eat it quick or the glow will fade," he urged.

Penelope put it in her mouth. When the mushroom touched her tongue it

dissolved, leaving behind a taste that could only be described as *warm*. The

warm slipped down her throat and into her stomach, filling her whole body

with its glow.

Dill and Penelope sat in silence, savoring the heavenly mushrooms. After

a moment, Dill let out a gigantic yawn. "These mushrooms always make me

sleepy. Wake me up in five minutes, would you?" He lay back and closed

his eyes. In a matter of seconds, Dill's breathing dropped to a slow rhythm

and he was asleep. Penelope slipped out her notebook. She might not have any ideas, but at least she would have memories. She wrote about the worry warts and the Shadow and the Naughty Woulds and all the amazing mushrooms she'd seen. She lost track of time, letting it slip away in the stream of words. She didn't stop writing until she was startled by the sound of Dill's snoring. She stuffed her notebook in her pocket and gave him a gentle shove. "Wake up," she urged, hoping five minutes hadn't already passed.

Dill sat up and stretched. "I guess we'd better get going." A sudden frown crossed his face and he pointed back toward the direction they had come. "Will you look at that?" he said, scrambling to his feet. "The Clockworkers have already reached my meadow."

Penelope followed his gaze. From their position high upon the ridge, the Naughty Woulds stretched out behind them. Sure enough, the sky on the far side of the forest looked heavy and dark.

Dill grabbed his pack. "I doubt they'll push on through the Naughty Woulds with evening so close, but still, we'd better get going." He climbed down the boulder and offered Penelope a hand. She took it and jumped down to the ground.

"What do the Clockworkers want with your meadow anyway?" she asked.

Dill shrugged. "It's a mystery. Puzzle. Complete conundrum. They're always on the lookout for time wasters or moodlers, so maybe . . ."

"Maybe they're onto us. . . ." said Penelope, her heart pounding. "Maybe they know I'm here."

Dill looked at Penelope. Penelope looked at Dill. They both nodded. "Let's get going."

Dill turned back toward the valley and pointed to a row of trees on the far side. "Beneath those trees there's a creek we must cross, and beyond that are the foothills of the Range of Possibilities. With luck we'll be in the mountains for dinner."

They scrambled down the ridge and followed a dirt path that zigzagged through the valley. Little white flowers were scattered throughout the deep grass. The blossoms seemed to perk up and salute them as they passed. Dill bobbed his head in greeting to this flower or that. Whenever they reached a clump of bushes or a large rock, he came to a halt and motioned for Penelope to do the same. Then he would peer under the bush or around the rock as if it were hiding something.

"Are you looking for mushrooms?" asked Penelope.

"No," whispered Dill. "Wild Bore."

"Wild boar?" Penelope looked around the sunny, flower-filled pasture. "*Here?*"

Dill waved at her to be quiet. "Keep your voice down. You never know where they might be lurking. It's important to be on guard. They like to sneak up on people."

Penelope imagined a large hairy pig with tusks tiptoeing after them. She fought back the urge to giggle. "How do they sneak up on people?" she whispered, trying to sound serious. "Don't they make a lot of noise grunting and snorting?"

"Oh, no," insisted Dill. "They're very sneaky. And fast. If you get caught by one, don't even bother running. Your only hope is to see it coming."

"What do you do if you see one?"

"Start talking. If you say the first word, they'll leave you alone. If you don't, your only hope is to get a word in edgewise. That usually stops them cold. If you can't do *that* . . ." Dill shook his head. "Let's just say, it's best not to get caught in the first place."

"Got it," said Penelope. But she wasn't sure she did. What good would it do to talk to a pig? Wouldn't it just be better to climb a tree? Penelope decided to drop the subject. Arguing with Dill was like arguing with a cat.

They walked along for some time with Dill stopping every few moments. "You never can be too careful," he'd say and then peer under or around whatever happened to be in their path.

After a while, Penelope decided you *could* be too careful and never make it where you were going. "I think I'll go on ahead a bit," she said, pointing to the trees in the distance. "I'll wait for you there."

Dill stared ahead, his lips pursed. "Well . . ."

"I'll keep an eye out for wild boar, I promise."

"Oh, all right," he agreed.

Penelope ran down the path, relieved to finally be making some progress. She thought about the Shadow moving across the Realm and the Clockworkers swarming underneath it. Dill said they should head for the Range of Possibilities to escape them. But then what? Would that bring them any closer to finding the Great Moodler?

Penelope had hoped she could count on Dill to help her in the search, but now she wasn't so sure. He talked to flowers and thought wild boar were lurking in the bushes. Maybe he hadn't just lost his way — maybe he'd lost his mind as well!

She stopped running. *It's up to me*, Penelope realized. She wasn't used to things being up to her. Her mother usually made the plans and her father rubber-stamped them. That never left Penelope much to do. Until now. She suddenly had the urge to worry again. She couldn't help herself.

How will I ever find the Great Moodler . . .

All on my own . . .

With no help?

Penelope could feel her face growing warmer and warmer, but instead of the *pop-pop-pop* of worry warts, she heard a rustling noise.

Rustle. Rustle.

It was coming from the clump of bushes to her right.

It's probably just a squirrel, she told herself.

Rustle. Rustle. **Snap!**

Penelope froze, her eyes fixed on the spot where the sound had come from. Something was breaking branches. Something large. Penelope was about to run when she heard a series of muffled curses. Just then a man burst out, picking bits of twigs and leaves off his coat sleeves and grumbling loudly.

"Stupid, stupid leaves! What are they doing sticking to *me*? Don't they know who I am?"

Penelope let out a sigh of relief. The man didn't seem very friendly, but at least he wasn't a giant wild pig! He wore gray slacks, a gray shirt, and a gray tie. His skin had a soft gray pallor and his eyes were gray to match. Thin gray hair hung loosely around an angular face, marked by a pinched, unhappy mouth. When he caught sight of Penelope, however, a look of delight crossed his face and then immediately disappeared, as if he were expecting someone else.

"Hello," said Penelope hesitantly.

"Yes, yes, hello, it is." He continued brushing off his jacket, and then asked sharply, "Where are you going all alone, child?"

Penelope objected to being called a child, but was too polite to say so. "Oh, I'm not alone. I . . ."

The man stopped brushing. His eyes locked on Penelope. "Not alone? That's excellent!"

"Well, my friend and I . . ."

"Oh, yes, yes, 'your friend,' and who might that be?" He took an eager step forward.

"Dill and . . ."

"DILL!" shouted the man and rushed past Penelope, almost running over her in an attempt to get by.

Penelope looked back up the trail, and sure enough there was Dill on his hands and knees, looking under some bushes. In a flash the man was upon him. He grabbed Dill's arm and yanked him up. "So pleased to see you, Dill, really, really, it's wonderful. I can't *wait* to tell you what I've been up to."

"Uh . . . ur," stammered Dill. But it was too late. The man had already launched into his speech.

Penelope walked slowly up to the two men. The stranger was talking on and on, while Dill just stood there listening. "I had the most dreadful pain in my tooth," said the stranger. "My tooth hurt so much I woke up at 2:17

this morning. Or was it 2:18? No, it must have been 2:17, because I was in the kitchen for a glass of water by 2:18. Then I put some ice on my tooth, which didn't make a bit of difference. Not a bit, I can tell you."

And he did tell him. The man told Dill in the minutest detail everything about his toothache, rarely pausing for breath. Penelope thought that once he came to the end, he might stop. But he didn't. He just brought up another topic. And another. All the ailments he had ever suffered. All the trips to the post office he had ever taken. All the people who had ever irritated him.

Dill's eyes had a glazed and faraway look, while the strange man positively beamed. Penelope sighed loudly, hoping the man would take the hint. He ignored her. Penelope was used to being ignored, so she did what she always did in this situation. She made herself comfortable and waited. She sat on the ground, crossed her legs, and began to play her waiting games. First she played a game of throwing small rocks at an imaginary target. Then she leaned her head back and watched the clouds for interesting shapes. Next she looked for ants.

All the while, the man kept talking. His brilliant childhood, a book he was writing, tips on what to wear for every occasion. On and on and on. Penelope rested her head in her hands and closed her eyes. The man's voice became a drone in the background. She was just drifting off to sleep when — *plop!* *plop!* — something warm and wet hit the back of her neck.

Penelope jerked her head up. Dill was crying. Not really crying like he had hurt himself — crying like someone had turned on a faucet. His mouth and eyes were frozen in place while huge tears streamed down his cheeks.

Penelope jumped to her feet and gave Dill's arm a shake. It was stiff as a board. "Dill!" she shouted. "What's wrong?" No response. He'd lost the ability to speak, much less move.

The strange man didn't seem to notice. He was talking faster than ever, his mouth moving at an amazing speed. Everything about the man seemed more intense than before. Was his hair black now? And how about his clothes? They seemed more blue than gray.

"Excuse me." Penelope tried to interrupt. The man ignored her. He gripped Dill by the collar, pulled him in close, and began talking about his shopping habits.

"The proper way to shop is to start with the produce section. First you must check the tomatoes. I squeeze each one as hard as I can. I *only* eat firm tomatoes. Then you check the lettuce for bugs . . ."

Dill's tears dried up. The color drained from his face and was now leaving his neck. His bright red hair had faded to light pink. His eyes were like marbles, his body a statue.

Penelope grabbed the man's arm and shook it. "Will you *please* be quiet? Something is terribly wrong with my friend!"

"Hush!" snapped the man. "Don't bore me with your chatter."

"I'm not boring anyone. *You* are!" Before the words were out of her mouth, Penelope knew what was wrong. Dill had tried to warn her, but she hadn't understood. This man was a *Wild Bore*!

Dill wasn't stiff as a board. He was bored stiff! And the tears? Bored to tears. Soon he would be bored to death.

"Stop! Please stop!" Penelope pleaded with the Wild Bore. He never even blinked. His eyes were locked on Dill. Penelope didn't exist.

By now the Bore looked radiant. His once-gray hair was rich as midnight, and his gray eyes flashed every color in the rainbow — red, green, yellow, blue — a new color every few seconds. Dill, on the other hand, was white as chalk. Penelope grabbed his wrist, searching for a pulse. She couldn't feel anything!

Penelope was so desperate she flung herself at the Bore, kicking and screaming. "*Ayyyyyyy!*"

The Bore fought back. "Run along, *child*. The grown-ups are busy!" His chatty, conversational tone was now a vicious snarl. He grabbed Penelope's arm and shoved her to the ground with a thud.

When Penelope fell, she landed on something stiff and lumpy. Her notebook! She sprang to her feet and snatched it from her pocket. Dill had said the only way to stop the Bore was to get a word in edgewise. That was exactly what she would do!

Penelope took out her pen and tore a piece of paper from her notebook. She would fight fire with fire. She would outwit the Wild Bore with words. But not just any words. Interesting words! The Bore might have shut her up, but she knew more than one way to be heard.

Penelope quickly wrote down the most interesting word she had ever seen. This was the bait. Then, on nine separate scraps of paper, she wrote nine more fascinating words. She didn't know what they all meant, but that didn't matter. In fact, that made them all the *more* fascinating. She stood on the tips of her toes and held up the most interesting word in the world for Dill to see:

Taj Mahal

"Stop that this instant!" squealed the Bore, pushing Penelope aside. But it was too late. Penelope had gotten a word in edgewise. Dill turned his head ever so slightly toward Penelope. Quick! She held up the next few words.

First **Ambrosia**, quickly followed by **Nova**.

That did the trick. A blush of color came into Dill's face and slowly he began to move his head away from the Bore and toward Penelope.

Penelope backed away, holding up one word and then the next:

Kumquat . . .

Cowpoke . . .

Conundrum . . .

Dill inched toward Penelope, his eyes locked on the tempting words. The Bore grabbed desperately at Dill, pleading, "Listen to me! Me! *Meeee!*"

Nebula, Doodle, Blurb.

The words were coming faster now and Dill walked with purpose after them. The color was rushing to his face and his red hair was ablaze! The Bore was almost out of earshot when Penelope silenced him with her final, fascinating word:

Skedaddle!

chapter ten

"That was a close call," said Penelope after the Wild Bore was safely behind them.

"Not at all!" countered Dill. He was walking briskly down the trail, swinging his arms and taking deep breaths. "As soon as I realized the Bore was ignoring you, I knew we'd be okay."

"You *did?*"

"Of course! You were a tremendous threat, but the Bore didn't seem to notice."

She was a tremendous threat? Penelope mulled this information over. It hardly seemed possible. She rarely had the upper hand in anything!

"From what I can tell," continued Dill, "the Wild Bore didn't think *you* were the least bit interesting, which means he didn't think you were very dangerous. You and I both know that's bunk. Rubbish. Total nonsense! Young people are the *most* interesting people around. But Wild Bores wouldn't know that. And do you know why?"

"No," said Penelope.

"Because they were never children! Of course, at one time they *looked* like children and could easily be *mistaken* for children, but they were really Little Knowitalls, which is a different thing altogether." Dill glanced over at her. "Certainly you've met a Little Knowitall?"

Penelope thought about the girl with pigtails from science camp. "Oh, yes," she said. "Lots of them."

"Well, then you know exactly what I'm talking about."

By now they had reached the row of trees where they were headed. Just as Dill had said, a creek wound its way through the tree roots. Dill found a shallow area scattered with rocks and leapt lightly from one to the next, chattering all the while. "Almost all Little Knowitalls become Wild Bores. Although now that I think about it, a few *do* manage to avoid that fate by learning to be inquisitive about something besides themselves." Dill reached the other side and turned back to look at Penelope. "Speaking of being inquisitive . . . how do you know all those fascinating words?"

"Oh, well, I don't know them *all*," Penelope explained, balancing her foot on a rock. "But I guess you can say I collect them." She raced across the creek and landed on the other side with a hop. "I never expected them to come in handy."

"Handy?" exclaimed Dill. "They were critical. Vital. Absolutely essential. I wouldn't have survived without them!"

Penelope beamed. She wasn't used to her words being important.

"I suggest you expand your collection immediately!" said Dill.

Penelope's smile faded. She thought about her notebooks filled with drawings and sketches, dreams and ideas. Ideas that would turn into stories if only she could get them flowing again. "I'm not sure there's any use," she mumbled.

Dill's eyes grew large. Huge, actually. For once, he didn't say anything. He just stared at Penelope, waiting for her to continue.

But she didn't *want* to continue. She didn't want to tell Dill the awful truth. It was no use collecting words because she would never use them. She would never be a writer, not if she couldn't moodle. Dill had said it himself — she was an anomaly. A failure.

Penelope stole a glance up at Dill. He was waiting patiently for her to speak. "I want to be a writer," she said, her voice still soft. "And I used to believe that one day I could be, even though my parents didn't think so. I was full of story ideas — so full I couldn't keep track of them all. But out of the blue they . . . they disappeared."

Dill took a step back.

"That's why I wanted to find the Great Moodler," Penelope rushed on. "I thought she could help me find out where all my ideas went, help me become a moodler again. If I can't moodle, I can't write."

"That," said Dill, pointing straight at her, "is a brilliant plan. You find the Great Moodler and get all your ideas back. And then the Great Moodler can find my lost way and I'll be an explorer again!"

This time it was Penelope's turn to take a step back. She hadn't expected Dill to actually *adopt* the plan. "But I've run out of ideas and can't moodle up any new ones. I'm not sure how to find her without . . ."

"You can do it," said Dill, cutting her off. "Look how you handled that Wild Bore!" He turned and began to climb up the creek bank. "You're young and inquisitive, a moodler and a word collector," he called out, listing her qualifications. "What more do you need?"

A lot! thought Penelope. Those traits hadn't led to much success in life so far. Besides, had Dill forgotten about her attempt to use the moodle hat? She had come up with nothing! Penelope was just about to remind Dill of this fact when he let out a sharp cry.

"It's gone!"

Penelope scrambled up the creek bank to join him. Standing atop it, she looked out on a vast plain of rocks and boulders. "What's gone?" she asked.

"The Range of Possibilities," wailed Dill, pointing off into the distance. "It used to be over there, along the horizon, and now it's gone!" He began to pace back and forth, wringing his hands. "You see what I mean? I can't find anything anymore, not even a mountain range. This is bad. Horrible. Completely horrendous!"

Penelope stared at the plain. It was empty of any scenery except for rocks. Miles and miles of rocks. It looked like it would be hard to cross. "What are we going to do now?" she asked.

"We'll just have to follow a hunch," said Dill. He stopped pacing and began to pat his pockets. "Do you have one? I seem to be all out."

"*Me?*" asked Penelope. "Why would I have a hunch? I have no idea where we are, much less where we should go."

"Hunches aren't ideas. They're inklings," explained Dill.

"Don't inklings just pop into your head?"

"Exactly. And they pop out just as quickly. That's why you've got to catch them when you can. Push everything out of your mind and see what pops out when you do. More than likely you'll see a hunch. That's when you snag it!"

"With your hands?"

Dill looked at her as if she'd just said the moon was made of cheese. "Of course not. By listening to it! But be sure not to think while you do it," he instructed. "Thoughts scare them away. Now then, clear your mind and then look around a bit. You look up, and I'll look down."

Penelope couldn't imagine what she was looking for, but she did as she was told. She cleared her mind and then followed Dill's lead. He was walking in circles with his hands clasped behind his back, looking at the ground. Penelope did the same, but looked up at the clouds.

Walking around and around, staring at the sky, made Penelope woozy. Being woozy kept her from thinking too much, which turned out to be a good thing. After walking for a few moments it dawned on her that she might feel less woozy if she stopped walking and focused on one specific spot. With her neck bent back, she locked her eyes on the spot above her nose. When her eyes focused, she saw the most unusual thing. There, on the tip of her nose, sat a small creature, so slight it seemed to be made of air.

Penelope froze, her eyes fixed on the tiny thing. "Dill!" she called in her very quietest whisper. "Dill, come here."

Dill rushed over. "Good job!" he said, slapping Penelope on the back.

Penelope stayed frozen in position. "Now what do I do?" she asked, hardly daring to move her mouth.

"Just relax and concentrate on the question: What do we do now?"

Penelope gently returned her head to an upright position. She crossed her eyes to check on the hunch. It was still there, resting on her nose.

"Hurry up," said Dill. "We don't want to wear the poor thing out."

Penelope looked around, searching for some sign or clue that would tell her what to do next.

"Don't try to figure it out," said Dill. "Just listen to your hunch."

"But I don't hear anything," said Penelope.

"You've got to *really* listen," urged Dill.

Penelope stopped looking around and relaxed. When she did, she heard a small voice coming from what sounded like inside her own head. "Look up," it said. Penelope immediately checked to see if the creature was still on her nose. It had disappeared. *Oh, well*, she thought, *here goes*.

She looked up.

There, along the far horizon, was a black speck moving quickly toward her. It grew larger every second. Dill noticed it, too, and stood still, watching it come closer. The speck was beginning to take shape. It looked like a bird — a *gigantic* bird — a bird the size of a small airplane.

"*RUUUN!*" Dill shouted and, clutching his head, darted this way and that, forward and back, dodging left, then right. Penelope didn't move. Something told her — was it a hunch? — she should stay right where she was. In seconds the bird was upon them. Dill froze in fear and then dove for cover behind a particularly large rock.

The bird circled around them a few times before touching down in a storm of dust. Once the air cleared, Penelope got a better look. It was a bright yellow bird with a long flourish for a tail. Black and gray bands striped its wings and an elaborate looping plume swayed on its forehead. Its beak was brilliant green and would have been beautiful if it didn't look so sharp.

"*Coo-Coo,*" called the bird.

Its voice was loud, but so lyrical that Penelope relaxed. *Something so lovely wouldn't eat a person*, she reassured herself.

The bird made a deep bowing motion, one wing outstretched and the other bent in toward its chest. "*Coo-Coo, Coo-Coo!*" This time it called out with more insistence.

"I think it's trying to tell us something," whispered Dill from behind the rock.

"I think you're right," agreed Penelope. "I'll try to talk back." Mustering her courage, she addressed the gigantic bird. "*Coo-coo, coo-coo,*" said Penelope in her best birdcall.

The bird cocked its head and half sang, half spoke, "How could . . . *you-you* . . . be *Coo-Coo?*"

"Oh, but I'm not," stammered Penelope. "I was just . . . I didn't expect . . . I mean . . ."

"And your friend?" said the bird, jumping onto the rock Dill was hiding behind and peering down at him with interest. "Is he *Coo-Coo . . . too-too?*"

"Certainly not!" said Dill, embarrassed at being caught hiding. He jumped to his feet and made a quick bow. "I'm Dill."

The bird looked him over. Up. Down. Left. Right. When he was done he turned back to Penelope.

"I'm Penelope," she said, introducing herself with a curtsy.

"I'm *Coo-Coo*," said the bird with a deep nod of his head.

"We're looking for the Range of Possibilities," explained Dill. "Do you know where it is?"

"I . . . *do-do*," sang the bird.

"But that's wonderful!" exclaimed Penelope. "Will you take us to it?"

The Coo-Coo made a slight fluttering motion with his wings. "*Coo-coo* . . . if you really want me . . . *to-to*." The giant bird crouched next to a large rock, and Penelope scrambled up and onto his back.

"I hate flying," groaned Dill. "It always upsets my stomach."

"It's the only way," said Penelope, coaxing him up.

When they both were settled, the Coo-Coo leapt into the air. Dill made a sound like a frightened cat and clutched Penelope's waist. Penelope, however, laughed with delight as the bird took off. She was reminded of her fantasy to travel the world by hot air balloon so she could see all the sights. This was much better!

They flew for miles while the rocky wasteland ran beneath them. Here and there boulders rose up, dotting the scenery with their jagged forms. Once, Penelope saw a herd of enormous honey-colored animals picking their way across the landscape. They looked like deer or antelope, but with much longer legs and strangely human faces. Their giant antlers were braided together like elaborate headdresses. When they saw the Coo-Coo, they stopped and bowed their heads in solemn greeting.

The bird called out, "*Coo-coo, coo-coo,*" and dipped his wings in salute.

"What *were* those?" Penelope had never seen such animals.

"Mountain Lopers. It's a . . . *true-true* . . . honor to see them. There are so very . . . *few-few* . . . left."

"Did you see them?" said Penelope with a quick glance back at Dill, but his eyes were clamped shut.

The image of the Mountain Lopers lingered in Penelope's mind — graceful, noble, and, somehow, sad. *Why were there only a few left? Where had they all gone?*

Just then a warm yellow cloud bank rolled across the sky to meet them. It quickly wrapped them in its soft color and the Mountain Lopers disappeared from view. Penelope relaxed her grip on the Coo-Coo's feathered neck and let her fingers trail beside her. She longed to touch the brilliant streaks of yellow and gold that billowed around them. The faster they flew, the richer the yellow grew. Soon the clouds were the color of egg yolk dotted with hints of pink and fuchsia.

When they burst through, a small chain of colorful mountains appeared below them. The range spanned from the deepest, darkest blue to the shiniest, brightest white and everything in between. The foot of each mountain was a single color — midnight blue, mossy green, burnt umber — and this color, whatever it was, was the darkest shade it could be. As the color moved up the mountain, the shade grew lighter and lighter until it reached the peak. The peaks were glorious pastels, shimmering with only the faintest pigment. There were about a dozen mountains surrounded like an island by the desert of rocks and rubble.

"Look!" cried Penelope and nudged Dill with her elbow. "It's the Range of Possibilities!"

Dill peeled one eye open and then, suddenly alert, the other. "But where are all the mountains?" he shouted against the wind.

"What do you mean? They're right *there*!" Penelope pointed at the peaks ahead.

"But how can that be? There used to be hundreds! Where did they all go?"

"*Coo-coo*," called the bird. "I'll show . . . *you-you*."

The little group of mountains huddled below them, but instead of landing, the Coo-Coo caught the wind and let it take them higher. Dill groaned in protest and closed his eyes again. Soon they were soaring over a brilliant blue peak on the northeastern edge of the range, heading straight for a dark cloud swirling above its summit.

As they drew closer, Penelope's heart began to beat faster. This wasn't a cloud. It couldn't be. No cloud was this dark — this thick. It covered the sky like a blanket, casting the translucent peak beneath it into a dull gloom. At that moment, she realized exactly where they were headed. They had come all this way to escape from the Shadow and now the Coo-Coo was taking them directly to it!

Penelope clutched the bird tightly as she felt a cold force emanating from the Shadow. She opened her mouth to warn Dill, and the cold slipped down her throat. "Dill . . ." Penelope gasped, before her voice gave out.

Dill leaned forward, daring a look over Penelope's shoulder, his face turning a slight shade of green. "Turn back!" he shouted at the bird.

But the Coo-Coo only flew faster, heading straight toward the Shadow until it enveloped them. A cold shock hit Penelope like icy water and she felt a painful pressure seize her upper body. The deeper into the Shadow the Coo-Coo flew, the greater the pressure became. It spread up her chest and into her throat, cutting off the air. Even though the great bird flapped his wings harder and faster, Penelope couldn't tell if he was moving or not. Everything inside the Shadow was so still. Penelope gripped the Coo-Coo's neck as a horrible thought crossed her mind.

Is he flying? Or falling?

Just when Penelope felt the blackness creep across her eyes, they burst

back into the day (or what passed for day under the Shadow). Penelope gasped for breath and let her eyes adjust to the dismal light. They had crossed over the peak. On the other side, the earth was barren, marked only by a strange black grid. There were no trees or greenery of any kind. Drifts of smoke climbed into the gray sky, filling the air with a horrible acrid smell. Penelope's eyes stung and her throat felt as if it had been turned inside out.

The Coo-Coo dropped lower. Penelope saw that the grid was a series of freshly tarred roads, crissing and crossing one another for miles. The farther the Coo-Coo flew, the more roads they saw. There were all kinds — highways, byways, toll roads, back roads, front roads — each very long and very straight. Giant trucks crawled like insects across them. Every scrap of earth not already paved was covered in digging, scooping, drilling machines.

Boom. Boom. Boom.

Waves of sound shook the air. The Coo-Coo veered back toward the mountain range in the direction of the sound, flapping his wings with renewed vigor. A massive pillar of smoke hovered at the foot of the mountain they had just flown over. They drew nearer to the smoke until they were almost engulfed in it, and then, as if on cue, the booming began again.

BOOM! BOOM! BOOM!

The Coo-Coo faltered in midflight. Penelope's stomach dropped to her toes, while Dill grasped her waist painfully. The bird regained his balance and flew on. By now they could see the pillar wasn't smoke at all. It was dust.

BOOM! BOOM! BOOM!

The mountain shuddered.

BOOM! BOOM! BOOM!

With a horrible crash, a massive chunk of indigo-colored rock tumbled to the earth. As it fell, the color faded until it hit the ground and broke into a million gray pieces. With each blast of dynamite, more and more of the mountain shattered. Great gashes appeared in its side and the peak wobbled dangerously until a final explosion sent it crashing down. The shimmering blue vanished in a pile of rubble.

When the dust settled, Penelope watched in horror as a swarm of bulldozers scooped up the rocks and dumped them into a great toothy machine.

CRUNCH. CRUNCH. CRUNCH.

The machine ground the rocks to bits and spat them out into a line of waiting dump trucks. Once a truck was full, it drove down a six-lane highway that stretched out of sight.

"I've seen enough!" cried Dill.

The Coo-Coo flapped his gigantic wings and up they went, into the Shadow waiting above.

chapter eleven

Penelope held her breath and closed her eyes, bracing herself for the sickening cold of the Shadow. When it hit, she tried to stay calm by counting down from one hundred.

99, 98, 97 . . .

Her teeth began to chatter . . .

86, 85, 84 . . .

Her hands grew numb . . .

63, 62, 61 . . .

Her head grew lighter and lighter until she forgot what number she was on.

55 . . . or was it 45?

And then, just when Penelope couldn't hold her breath any longer, the Coo-Coo burst out of the Shadow and into the clear evening sky. Penelope took a huge gulp of warm air and willed herself to forget the bitter chill.

The bird headed toward a plum-colored mountain directly below them. Very near its peak a house sat perched on top of two enormous boulders. The house looked like a Swiss chalet covered in elaborately carved figurines. A huge wooden bird sat with outstretched wings on top of a steep roof. Carved oak leaves curled upward on either side of the wooden bird and then cascaded down the house. More oak leaves formed a bed for a gigantic pair of wooden squirrels resting at the base.

Instead of a door, there was an opening with a platform directly under the pitched roof. Below the opening was the most striking feature of all: A clock face took up the entire front of the house.

"It's a cuckoo clock!" gasped Penelope.

Dill didn't even bother to look. "Are we there yet?" he whimpered.

The bird landed expertly on the platform and scurried toward the entrance. Once inside, he knelt so his guests could dismount. "*Coo-coo* . . . kick off your . . . *shoe-shoes*. Make yourself at home," he sang.

Penelope slid to the floor and looked around the room. Her gaze immediately settled on a giant bird's nest in the far corner. Instead of twigs, the Coo-Coo had fashioned his nest from logs. Tucked inside the logs were various odds and ends that spilled out of the nest and onto the floor — an old lawn chair, a bit of fencing, even the chrome handlebars of a bicycle.

The rest of the room was a mess. Every nook, every cranny, every corner was filled with stuff. Not just any stuff, though — *shiny* stuff. Bits of aluminum foil and old street signs papered the walls. A chandelier fashioned from hubcaps and hung with silverware lit the room. Old toys, glass bottles, and knickknacks sat on shelves strewn with silver tinsel.

Penelope found a metal folding chair and sat down, while Dill collapsed gratefully onto a bedraggled sofa. "This is terrible! Horrendous! Unbelievably bad!" He took out a handkerchief and began to wipe his forehead. "Chronos is expanding his reach in every direction. Now I know why the Shadow is over my meadow. Soon the entire Realm will be one big city!"

"But why do they have to tear down the mountains?" asked Penelope. They were so beautiful. So . . . so *extraordinary*. She couldn't believe anyone would want to destroy them.

"To make room for . . . *new-new* . . . buildings and roads," said the bird with a sigh. "These mountains used to be home to an entire flock of . . .

coo-coo . . . birds. But now there are only a . . . *few-few* . . . of us left." The bird shook his head, unable to continue, and his elaborate tail drooped.

Penelope remembered the Mountain Lopers making their way across the wasteland. No wonder they looked so sad. Their homes had been destroyed. She looked around the Coo-Coo's house. Soon it would be a pile of rubble, too.

Dill rested his head in his hands. "Chronos must be stopped," he wailed. "If only we could find the Great Moodler —"

At the sound of the Great Moodler's name, the Coo-Coo snapped to attention. *"COO-COO . . . COO-COO!"* he screeched, erupting into a series of *coo-coos* so loud, so vigorous, he nearly hit his head on the ceiling. Once he'd recovered, he scooped up Dill with his wings. "Only the Great Moodler can . . . *undo-do* . . . this destruction. She can moodle up a whole . . . *slew-slew* . . . of possibilities and restore the Range! I've been hoping someone would find her." The bird dropped his startled guest and stepped back, wings outstretched. "And now here . . . *you-you* . . . are!"

"I'm afraid you are mistaken," objected Dill, straightening his jacket. "I've already tried to find her and failed. Penelope is the one —"

The bird spun around and snatched up Penelope.

"Wait! You don't understand —" insisted Penelope, but her objections were muffled in the bird's feathers. Once the Coo-Coo finally let her go, she tried again to explain. "You don't understand. I can't find her either. I even tried the moodle hat and nothing happened. I have no idea where she is."

"But I . . . *do-do!*" sang out the bird and dashed over to a pile of junk in the corner. He began rummaging through it, tossing things over his shoulder as he did. Penelope ducked just in time to miss a metal trash can followed by its lid. She stood back up, only to drop to the floor again as bits of tin roofing and aluminum foil sailed past.

When the bird spun around, he was holding a shiny, glittering ball for Dill and Penelope to see. "It's a . . . *clue-clue,*" he said with great reverence.

Dill and Penelope leaned in for a better look. The ball was made of pure light. Etched on its surface were a series of words, each one glimmering faintly. The bird turned the ball this way and that so they could read what it said:

Look in the least likely place.

"What is it?" asked Penelope in a hushed voice.

"It's a possibility," answered Dill. He looked up at the bird in awe. "Wherever did you find it?"

The Coo-Coo inhaled a deep, shuddering breath that ruffled his feathers from the top of his head to the tip of his splendid tail. Exhaling, he settled them all back into place and then began his story.

"After the Great Moodler disappeared, I . . . *flew-flew* . . . over the Range of Possibilities every day, looking for a . . . *clue-clue* . . . to where she went.

And every day, my hopes of finding her . . . *grew-grew* . . . smaller and smaller until I gave up altogether. On that day a violent storm . . . *threw-threw* . . . me off course. The wind carried me higher than ever before and I saw, out of the . . . *blue-blue* . . . a shimmering mountain of white light. I was blinded for a moment. When I regained my sight, the mountain was gone from . . . *view-view* . . . and this was falling from the sky." The bird nodded at the possibility.

" 'Look in the least likely place,' " said Dill, almost to himself.

"But where *is* the least likely place?" asked Penelope. She sank down into the couch, but sat right back up again. A thought had occurred to her: The least likely place the Great Moodler would go — and the last place in the world Penelope wanted to visit — was Chronos City!

No sooner had the thought come to mind, than — *woop* — the possibility began to grow.

"*Coo-coo!*" called out the bird in surprise.

Dill turned to look at Penelope. "Are you considering the possibility?" he asked.

Penelope nodded.

"And . . ."

Penelope cringed. "I think it might be Chronos City."

Wooop. The possibility grew even bigger.

Dill put his hand on Penelope's shoulder. "Looks like that's a real possibility," he said.

The bird began hopping from one foot to the other. "Please go look for her. Please, please! Chronos has decreed all . . . *Coo-Coo* . . . birds Impossible. We keep our own time, which is . . . *taboo-boo.* If I went into the City, a . . . *crew-crew* . . . of Clockworkers would snatch me up. But the . . . *two-two* . . . of . . . *you-you* . . . might have a chance." He gave Dill and Penelope a pleading look.

"But isn't it dangerous?" asked Penelope.

"I'm afraid it is," conceded Dill. "Chronos City is unsafe. Risky. Outright hazardous. But we can't stay here and we can't go home. We're surrounded by the Shadow. We have to try."

"*Yahoo-hoo . . . yahoo-hoo!*" hollered the bird. He began dancing around the room, knocking things off shelves and sending the chandelier shaking.

Penelope watched the Coo-Coo dance about. She didn't think there was much to celebrate. She and Dill were heading for the worst place in the world to find the one person who could help them. But Dill was no good at finding things anymore and Penelope was an anomaly, a failure. Still, even though the whole expedition seemed doomed, Dill was right. They had to try. Finding the Great Moodler wasn't just about getting Penelope's ideas flowing again. The homes — maybe even the lives — of Dill and the Coo-Coo and the poor Mountain Lopers depended on it.

At that moment, a chime began to ring. It was seven and the clock was marking the hour. "That's my . . . *cue-cue*," trilled the bird. He tucked the possibility away in a corner and rushed outside. Soon they heard him singing along with the chime. "*Coo-coo, coo-coo. Coo-coo, coo-coo . . .*"

Dill and Penelope walked over to the opening of the great clock and together they watched the bird sing the hour into existence. When he finished, the sun settled lower along the horizon and the noises of the day receded to a hum.

"I'll be back in a . . . *few-few* . . . minutes," called the Coo-Coo and leapt into the early evening sky. The bird dropped down through the high mountain air. Once he reached a lower altitude, he began to dart this way and that, his wide beak snapping.

"What's he doing?" Penelope asked.

"Catching Time Flies, I suppose," answered Dill. "I'm surprised there are any left considering Chronos has decreed fun Impossible." Dill glanced in Penelope's direction. "Time flies only when you're having fun, you know."

Penelope nodded. Oh, yes. She knew.

Dill stretched out his arm and swept it through the air as if to embrace the horizon. "The skies of the Realm used to be filled with Time Flies and Fancies, but now they're almost extinct."

"What are Fancies?" asked Penelope.

"Giant, fantastical creatures that whiz and bounce through the air. Used to be people were always taking off on Flights of Fancy and going on adventures," said Dill. "Chronos insisted Fancies were only figments of the imagination and soon everyone ignored them until they disappeared. Or starved to death. That reminds me . . ." Dill rummaged through his many pockets, pulling out one thing after another — a ball of string, three pairs of glasses, an assortment of screws. Suddenly a smile spread across his face. "Ah, yes! Here they are." He whipped out two small brown-paper packages and held them out to Penelope. "Mushroom butter or mushroom loaf?"

Penelope pointed to the one on the right. "I'll take that one."

"Mushroom butter it is! Wise choice."

Penelope peeled back the wrapping on her sandwich. A nondescript gray substance was spread in a thick layer between two slices of bread. She took a small, uncertain bite and was surprised to find it tasted a little bit like peanut butter and a whole lot like chocolate.

"What did I tell you?" said Dill through a mouthful of sandwich. "Wise choice."

After the first bite, Penelope hardly tasted her sandwich. She was too busy thinking about the journey ahead. "Are you sure we should go to Chronos City?" she prodded Dill.

"I can't think of a more unlikely place to find the Great Moodler," he answered. "Can you?"

"No, but won't there be Clockworkers on the lookout? What if we get caught and taken to the tower?"

Dill stuffed the last bit of sandwich into his mouth and began to lick his fingers clean. "I agree," he said in between licks. "That *is* a possibility."

Penelope put down her sandwich. She wasn't hungry anymore. "And where will we look?"

"No idea," said Dill. "You could try the moodle hat again. I brought it along."

Penelope shook her head. Nothing came to mind before. It was bound to happen again. "I guess we'll just have to hope for some awfully good hunches," she said.

Dill nodded. "A hunch can take you a very long way."

The Coo-Coo returned from his dinner and the rest of the evening was spent planning their search for the Great Moodler.

First thing in the morning, the bird would take Dill and Penelope to the farthest reaches of Chronos City. If he came any closer, he risked being seen and taken away. The Coo-Coo would return to the same spot in three days to see what they had discovered. At that point they would regroup and decide what to do next. Nobody talked about what they would do if Dill and Penelope didn't discover anything, or if they got captured by Clockworkers. It was too terrifying.

Once the plan was settled, they all went to bed. Dill and Penelope slept on the floor on pallets stuffed with the Coo-Coo's giant feathers. The Coo-Coo slept in his nest, head tucked under a wing, his plume bobbing in time to his snores. Every sixty minutes he popped awake and scurried outside to sing the hour. None of this seemed to disturb Dill, but Penelope always woke with a start. At first she used the time to write in her notebook, capturing with words as best she could the events of her day. But soon she grew too tired to hold her pen, so she simply lay awake trying to imagine what her parents were doing. Were they trying to find her? Was her mother organizing a search party? Was her father giving pep talks to worried parents in the neighborhood? Or had they simply gotten on with their lives as if she had never existed? When sleep finally overtook her, Penelope fell into a dream.

She was riding on the Coo-Coo's back, soaring over the Range of Possibilities. Her mother was seated behind her, smiling and laughing, pointing at the beautiful mountains. It was wonderful! Penelope flung open her arms and trailed her fingers in the air. *Splat!* Something soft and sticky stuck to her hands. It smelled like daisies. She licked her fingers. Clouds! She was eating fluffy white clouds and they tasted like cotton candy, just as she always thought they would. Penelope reached out for more, but instead of sticking to her fingers, the clouds shrank back. Penelope looked over her shoulder. The Shadow was rolling across the sky, consuming everything in its path. The clouds were disappearing as if sucked up into a vacuum.

The Coo-Coo sensed the danger and began to struggle, beating his wings harder and faster. "Hold on!" shouted Penelope to her mother. Her mother dug her nails into Penelope's waist, but the pull of the Shadow was too strong. Her grip weakened. "Don't let go!" Penelope pleaded, but it was too late.

Whoosh!

There was a horrible sucking sound and her mother vanished into the darkness.

Penelope longed to cry out, to tell her mother she would save her, but she could hardly breathe, much less speak. She felt like a rock, heavy and dumb. A thousand pounds at least. The Shadow drew closer, stretching out to meet her. Soon it would swallow her.

Penelope felt herself sliding off the bird and everything faded into black.

chapter twelve

"Wake up! Wake up!"

Penelope opened one frazzled eye. Dill was leaning over her, pack in hand.

"Come *on*!" he begged.

She struggled to sit up. "What's wrong?"

The Coo-Coo stood near the doorway, hopping nervously about. "*Coo-coo!* Time we . . . *flew-flew!*"

"Yes, yes, yes! We've got to go!" Dill practically screamed. "No time for explanations."

Penelope stumbled over to the Coo-Coo, slipping on her shoes as she went. Dill cupped his hands together to make a step and Penelope climbed onboard the bird's back. Once she was settled, Dill took a running leap and landed — *umph* — behind her. He was barely able to fling his legs up and over before the agitated bird bolted out the door and into the dawn.

Penelope couldn't understand what was wrong. It was a beautiful morning. The arms of the sun were just beginning to stretch across the sky. Where the sunlight touched, white clouds turned gold. The gold was reflected in the mountaintops and made their pastel peaks shine. Below the peaks, birds were waking the world with the first songs of day.

"Why are we in such a hurry?" she shouted.

Almost as if in answer she heard the boom of dynamite. Penelope looked down. Swarms of trucks were at the foot of the Coo-Coo's mountain.

"A . . . *crew-crew* . . . of workers arrived at my mountain first thing this morning," called the bird.

"They've picked up their pace!" yelled Dill. "We've got to hurry."

The bird veered sharply to the east toward Chronos City — toward the Shadow. Even though morning had arrived over the Coo-Coo's mountain, the air here had a gray pallor, as if the sun were shining through a dirty filter. Penelope stared at the wasteland below them. Now she knew the miles of rocks and boulders were the remains of once-beautiful mountains. The farther they flew, the flatter the terrain below them grew. The rocks and boulders turned to pebbles and dust. The pebbles and dust turned into a dirt road, and the dirt road gave way to asphalt. The City had begun.

The bird started a slow, circling descent before landing near a large rock. Dill and Penelope quickly dismounted. When they were both safely on the ground, Dill turned to the Coo-Coo, hand outstretched. "We'll do our best to find the Great Moodler," he promised. "Thank you for all your help."

"Yes," agreed Penelope, holding her hand out as well. "Thank you."

The Coo-Coo hesitated for a moment before rushing at Dill and Penelope and scooping them up in his wings. Huge tears slid down his face and splashed onto the asphalt. "*Boo-hoo-hoo . . . boo-hoo-hoo,*" he cried. "Please . . . *do-do . . .* be careful."

Dill and Penelope made repeated, although muffled, promises to be as careful as they could and return to this spot in three days with any news of the Great Moodler. The Coo-Coo finally released them and took off into the air. Dill and Penelope watched him until he disappeared, and then they turned to face the road.

"Here goes," said Dill, his voice grim.

Penelope shuddered. "Here goes."

Off they went, heading for the City, their hearts heavy with the memory of the Clockworkers waiting at the foot of the Coo-Coo's mountain.

As they walked, the sun rose higher in the sky and the day grew warm. After a while, the road widened from a single lane to two, then three, before blossoming into an intersection. The intersection was shaped like the spoke of a wheel, with roads stretching in twelve different directions. Off in the distance they could see the outline of the City, running across the entire horizon like a wall.

Dill and Penelope came to a halt. "Which road should we take?" asked Penelope. There were so many to choose from. How would they know which one was right?

Just then Dill's stomach let out a loud growl. "I'd say follow a hunch, but I'm so hungry I doubt I could get very far. Let's eat breakfast." Dill dug around in his pack for a moment before unearthing a small brown envelope. "Hold out your hand," he instructed, and shook a bunch of tiny gray pellets into Penelope's palm. Penelope just assumed they were some sort of mushroom and popped them into her mouth.

"Good gracious," cried Dill. "One at a time!"

Too late. The tiny pellets exploded in Penelope's mouth, filling it with a sticky, puffy substance. The pellets grew to five times their original size. Then ten times. Then twenty.

"You're eating mushmellows," explained Dill. "A cross between mushrooms and marshmallows. I invented them as rations for long trips. But you really *should* eat them one at a time."

Penelope tried to say, "Got it." But it came out more like "*Awt ehh*."

"You could live off these for days and days," Dill rattled on, popping a mushmellow in his own mouth. "They're full of protein and all sorts of nutrients. Not to mention, they're yummy. Delicious. Absolutely scrumptious."

Penelope just nodded. Her cheeks were so full they were beginning to hurt. She tried to move the mushmellows around in her mouth, but there was no room to maneuver.

"Try sucking on it," offered Dill and delicately placed another pellet on his tongue.

Penelope squeezed in her cheeks and tried to draw a breath. *Gurgle.* An odd sound came from the back of her throat as her saliva went to work breaking down the sticky substance. After a few moments the mushmellows began to shrink and slid down her throat.

Gurgle. Gurgle. This time the gurgling sound came from her stomach. Penelope looked down in surprise. The mushmellows had continued to expand. It looked like she was carrying a bowl underneath her overalls.

"Just a minor side effect," said Dill, patting his own protruding belly. "It'll go down in a minute. I might need to fiddle with the recipe a bit." They sat there quietly, digesting their breakfast, until Dill let out a laugh. "Look! I've got a hunch!" He was staring out of the corner of his eye at a tiny, translucent creature on his shoulder. He cocked his head to one side so he could listen to it better. "Someone's coming," he said slowly, as if repeating what he heard.

Penelope didn't like the sound of that. She quickly swallowed the last of her mushmellows. "Someone *who*?" she asked.

Dill listened to his hunch, his thick brows huddled over his eyes. "Someone . . . someone . . . from the City," he said finally.

They heard them before they saw them. Far off in the distance came the sound of sirens. The sound grew louder and louder as it grew closer and closer. Soon they saw the lights — flashing lights that quickly became police cars. The cars approached from every direction, speeding down each of the twelve roads until . . .

Screech. Twelve squad cars came to a stop at the same exact moment.

Click. Twelve car doors opened and twelve uniformed police officers stepped out.

Slam. Twelve car doors closed.

Twelve police officers glared from under twelve hats, their lips flattened in grim frowns. Each officer had a large patch sewn onto his or her left shoulder with black, angular markings on it: I, II, III, IV, V . . . Penelope knew what the markings were — she had seen them before on a grandfather clock. VI, VII, VIII . . . They were Roman numerals and they were used to mark time. IX, X, XI . . . Sure enough, the numbers went all the way to: XII.

Suddenly a voice shouted at them through a bullhorn.

"HALT RIGHT THERE!"

Dill and Penelope stood frozen in the middle of the intersection as a peculiarly short police officer stepped forward. He was shaped like a fire hydrant, with a square lump of a head sitting on a pair of neckless shoulders. "It's 10:00 a.m. and you're under arrest for idling at the crossroads. I am Officer X, man of the hour and keeper of the timepiece." The policeman whipped out a pocket watch and dangled it in front of Penelope and Dill. "As you can see, you've disturbed the piece."

The watch did seem disturbed. The second hand swung wildly around and the minute hand was actually moving backward. Officer X snatched the watch back and snapped the cover closed. "You'll have to come with me," he barked.

Penelope's mouth dropped open. They *couldn't* go with him. This wasn't part of the plan! She whirled around and stared at Dill, willing him to do something.

Dill straightened his jacket and then cleared his throat. "Excuse me, sir, but we —"

"*Now!*" yelled the officer, pointing at the squad car. "We haven't got all day."

Dill and Penelope both cringed and scurried over to the car. Once they reached the door, Officer X leaned forward and snatched Dill's pack from his back. "I'll take that," he said, dumping the contents on the ground. He poked at things with his foot, making sure to stomp on the leftover sandwiches. He stopped when he saw the moodle hat. "What's this?"

Penelope held her breath. What would Dill say? If moodling was illegal, then having a moodle hat was certainly forbidden. Dill just shrugged an innocent shrug. "A toy," he answered.

In its collapsed state, the hat did look like it could be a toy. Officer X must have thought so, too, because he picked it up and threw it as far as it would go. Then he turned back to Dill and Penelope and opened the car door. "Get in."

They did as they were told. Officer X slammed the door and slid behind the wheel. He executed a quick U-turn and sped off in the direction he had come. Eleven police cars followed, sirens screaming.

-- -- --

As they drove, the monstrous skyline of Chronos City came closer and closer. Buildings crowded the sky like giants fighting for air, their heads lost in the Shadow, their feet swarming with cars. The outskirts of the never-ending City were full of bulldozers, concrete mixers, and giant cranes. It seemed like a new building was completed every minute and caravans of moving trucks clogged the highways.

Penelope thought about the Coo-Coo. They were tearing down his mountains for *this*? It was too horrible to think about! And now their plan to help — to find the Great Moodler and stop Chronos — was ruined. Penelope would never moodle again . . . Dill would never find his lost way . . . and the Coo-Coo's home would be destroyed. Penelope felt more like an anomaly than ever!

Just then Dill reached over and gave her hand a squeeze. "Don't worry," he whispered and began poking his face all over as if counting warts.

Penelope smiled weakly. He was right. Now was not the time to worry. It wouldn't help a bit. Instead, she needed to focus and start working on a new plan. She took a deep breath and tapped her forehead. Dill gave her a knowing look and tapped his forehead, too. Good. They were both working on it. Together they would figure out something.

Penelope peered out of the squad car, trying to determine where they were. The city was built around one gigantic structure — the clock tower. It was taller than the tallest skyscraper and visible from every corner of the City. Its sharp spire pointed imperiously at the sky. Beneath the spire were four clock faces, one on each of its four sides. The clock faces shone with a garish green light. They peered down on the City, bathing it in a hateful glow. The sun was nowhere to be seen.

Even from miles away, Penelope could see exactly what time it was on the tower: 10:48 and 32 seconds . . . 33 seconds . . . 34 seconds . . . She was mesmerized by the second hand as it swung around and around. *Where did all the time go?* she wondered.

Dill nudged her sharply. "If you stare at it too long, you'll reset your internal clock."

Penelope looked away from the clock and watched the scenery instead. By now the highway had turned into a twenty-lane expressway. All the cars they passed were either black or white, depending on their size. Officer X merged into a special lane reserved for police, and soon they were moving at high speed, leaving the traffic behind in a blur. Penelope read the billboards whizzing past.

IDLENESS IS THE GREATEST PRODIGALITY.

LOST TIME IS NEVER FOUND AGAIN.

ALL THINGS ARE EASY TO INDUSTRY,
ALL THINGS DIFFICULT TO SLOTH.

Oh, shut up, thought Penelope. There was something irritatingly familiar about these sayings. She glanced back up at the clock tower. *Just to check the time*, she told herself. Penelope could only see one clock face, but it seemed to be staring right at her. The second hand . . .

22 . . . 23 . . . 24 . . .

moved beautifully around . . .

25 . . . 26 . . . 27 . . .

and around.

Penelope scrunched her eyes and gave her head a quick shake. She leaned back in the seat and tried to erase the image of the clock tower from her mind.

Dill had said staring at the tower would reset her internal clock. But what exactly was an internal clock? She remembered a painting she had seen in a book. There was a clock that looked like it was made of Silly Putty. It hung draped over a tree limb, almost ready to slide off onto the ground. *Is that what my internal clock looks like?* she wondered. Penelope didn't think so. Her clock had wings, she decided. Instead of a nasty beeping alarm, it tickled her when it was time to go somewhere.

Just then Dill put his hand on her shoulder. "We're *here*," he whispered. Something about the way he said "here" made Penelope's throat constrict. Before she could take a good look out the window, the car came to an abrupt halt and Officer X hopped out. "Let's go!" he snapped.

Dill and Penelope stepped out of the car and into a dark terminal. The terminal had a low concrete ceiling and concrete walls to match. On each wall a large metal clock chipped away the time, filling the air with its ticking. Everywhere Penelope looked, she saw men and women in identical blue coveralls and hats moving stiffly in and out of dark gray doors.

"Where are we?" she asked.

Officer X turned to look at her, a menacing glare in his eyes. "We're in the clock tower, young lady. It's time for *you* to get busy."

chapter thirteen

Officer X escorted Dill and Penelope to a counter at the far end of the terminal. A few people stopped to stare at them and Dill smiled and nodded politely. "For goodness' sake, stop that!" scolded Officer X. "This isn't a parade." He tried to glare up at Dill, but he was too short. He ended up glaring at Dill's belt buckle, which didn't do much to improve his mood.

At the counter, Officer X was officially assigned to Dill and Penelope's case and given a stack of forms to fill out. After each one was properly signed, stamped, and filed, Officer X turned and pointed to a set of double doors to their right. "March!"

Penelope didn't feel the least bit like marching, but she followed Dill's lead and marched all the same.

Dill's legs were so long he reached the doors first. "Stop!" Officer X screamed at him and ran to catch up. He arrived with a red face and his shirt untucked. "Forget marching." He rearranged his uniform and badge and then pushed past Dill. He brought out a large set of keys, found the right one, and the doors opened with a groan.

Inside was a long, dimly lit hallway filled with doors. Each door was exactly like the others except for the sign posted above it. "Crime Units!" declared Officer X, pointing at the signs. "Dawdling, Dillydallying, Feet Dragging, Frittering, Lollygagging, and Puttering. Never forget," he said, fixing them both with a stare, "the Clockworkers of the Realm are everywhere, protecting the populace against the evils of time wasters."

One of the doors swung open and Penelope caught a glimpse inside. Rows and rows of desks filled a long room. Men and women dressed in identical blue coveralls sat upright at the desks. They looked exactly like the people Penelope had seen in the terminal. They were all typing in unison. *Click-clack. Click-clack. Click-clack.* They struck each key at precisely the same time. *How did they do that?* Penelope wondered, before the door closed and the scene vanished.

At the end of the hall, another set of double doors waited for them. As they approached, the doors slid open with a *hiss* to reveal a cavernous courtroom. Low fixtures dropped yellow pools of light on a massive podium at the far end of the room. Two figures sat expectantly at the podium. Their nameplates read JUDGE JUST RIGHT and JUDGE JUST SO. An enormous 60-second stopwatch hung on the wall behind the judges. Under the stopwatch a sign declared: JUSTICE IN UNDER A MINUTE.

The judges perked up at the sight of the new arrivals. "Don't just stand there, we don't have all day," screeched Judge Just So.

"Time's a-wasting," shrieked Judge Just Right, motioning Dill and Penelope to approach.

Once they were standing in front of the judges, Dill spoke up. "Your Honors . . ."

"Silence," barked Judge Just So and slammed her gavel on the podium. *Bam!*

"Silence," repeated Judge Just Right and slammed *her* gavel. *Bam!*

"*I* said, Silence!" *Bam! Bam!*

"*I* said, SILENCE!" *Bam! Bam! Bam!*

The two judges shouted and banged until both of their faces were red. This might have gone on all day if Officer X hadn't cleared his throat with a cough.

The banging stopped. The gavels hung in the air.

"Well," said Judge Just Right, "speak up."

Officer X stepped forward, his chest outthrust. "These two citizens were caught idling at an intersection on the outskirts of Chronos City."

Judge Just Right fixed Dill with a stare. "And what do you have to say for yourself?"

"Your Honors," Dill said again, this time with a deep bow, "we were simply eating breakfast when —"

"Likely story!" screamed Judge Just Right. *Bam!* went the gavel. "As for *you*, young lady," she said, pointing at Penelope, "what were you doing idling at an intersection?"

Before Penelope could say a word, Judge Just So picked up a large black book from a shelf below her podium. She adjusted her glasses and read solemnly, "Be always ashamed to catch thyself idle."

Judge Just Right snatched her own book out. "Trouble springs from idleness . . ."

"The busy man has few idle visitors," interrupted Judge Just So.

"TO THE BOILING POT THE FLIES COME NOT!"

Penelope groaned. She had the feeling she had heard all this before.

The judges stopped their squalling and looked at her expectantly.

"Go on," demanded Judge Just So. "Tell us what you were doing."

Penelope knew better than to mention their search for the Great Moodler. Before she could think of the right thing to say, she heard herself answer, "Nothing."

"*GUILTY!*" both judges shouted, leaping from their seats and frantically fighting to start the stopwatch.

Judge Just So hit the button first and began the sentencing. "For idling at an intersection . . ."

Tick, tick, tick . . .

"And for doing *ab-so-lutely* nothing," snarled Judge Just Right.

Tick, tick, tick . . .

"You are hereby sentenced to twenty minutes . . ."

Tick, tick, tick . . .

"Around the clock."

Brriiing! The sound of the stopwatch filled the room.

"Take them away!"

— — —

That wasn't so bad, thought Penelope as Officer X ushered them out of the courtroom and into a waiting elevator. They were only sentenced to twenty minutes around the clock. She wasn't sure what that meant, but she knew she could put up with almost anything for twenty minutes.

Once inside the elevator, the doors slid shut and the compartment rushed soundlessly upward. Penelope watched through a small window as the great City flashed by. The higher they went, the smaller the City became, until the buildings looked like toy blocks.

She glanced over at Dill. He raised one eyebrow and tapped his forehead. She tapped back. See? There was nothing to worry about. They were both working on their next move.

The elevator lurched to a stop and the doors opened with a cheerless *ding*. "This way," said Officer X, pointing down an empty hallway toward a thick metal door. The door had a glass-plated window set a few feet from the floor, exactly the right height for Officer X to peer through. He pressed his face against the windowpane and gave a satisfied grunt before unlocking it. He motioned Dill and Penelope inside and flipped a switch. A few lonely lightbulbs sputtered to life, revealing a long corridor flanked by rows and rows of bars.

"Welcome to prison," Officer X said. It was the first time he sounded happy. "This is the north clock tower, where we keep the most serious offenders." He began to stroll down the corridor. "Musty odors, meager lighting, plenty of bedbugs . . . you should be right at home."

Penelope shuddered, which seemed to make him even happier.

He continued his list with gusto. "Tasteless meals, creaky noises, not to mention rock-hard beds."

Dill stopped to peer through the bars of a cell and waved Penelope over. The cell was empty except for a bunch of soft, gray fluff balls. But these weren't ordinary fluff balls. Each one had a pair of small, bare feet and large, black, sleepy eyes. Some of them floated lazily in the air, though most of them were piled in the corner like snowdrifts. A few opened their eyes to look at the new inmates and then closed them again, falling immediately back to sleep.

"Did you say, your most serious offenders are here?" asked Dill. "I can't imagine these dust bunnies are much of a threat."

Officer X wheeled around. "Then stop imagining! It's illegal." He shoved them away from the cell and pointed to a large sign hanging from its door:

DANGER! DO NOT FEED! APPROACH AT YOUR OWN RISK!

"I'd mind that if I were you," he said. "Now keep moving."

As they walked down the corridor, Penelope noticed that every cell was filled with the same creatures and posted with the same warning sign. There was one empty cell at the end of the corridor. Officer X quickly unlocked it. "Home, sweet home," he said and pushed them inside with a nasty snicker before slamming the door shut. "See you soon," he called out and disappeared back down the hall.

"See you in twenty minutes," Penelope called back and then turned to Dill. "All right, what's our plan? What should we do when our time is up and they let us out?"

Dill looked uncertain. "I'm not sure we *will* get out. Those judges are tricky. Cunning. Unmistakably sly. I think it best we start looking for a chance to escape." Dill began to pace the length of the cell, tapping on walls and rattling the bars, checking for possible weaknesses.

"You go right ahead," said Penelope. "I'll join you in a minute." *Actually,* she thought to herself, *I'll join you in twenty minutes.* Surely Dill was overreacting. They would soon be free. After all, they had done absolutely nothing.

Penelope glanced around the cell. A rickety wooden table with four chairs sat in the middle of the room. Two benches that doubled as beds lined the walls on either side. She was just sitting down on one of the benches when she noticed a gigantic mass of cobwebs in a nearby corner. She got up and moved to the chair farthest away.

Dill, on the other hand, went straight up to the cobwebs to get a better look. He was bending over the mass, just about to prod it with an outstretched finger, when a small voice interrupted his examination.

"Excuse me, do you have a hankie?"

Penelope nearly fell out of her chair and Dill took a giant step back. After a moment Dill regained his composure and his manners. "Certainly," he said and produced a neatly folded handkerchief from his front pocket. He held it out toward the cobwebs.

A small hand, matching the small voice, reached out and took the hankie with a polite "Thank you."

Penelope eased over to the corner to get a closer look. Another hand popped out. It was holding a pair of glasses. The first hand began wiping the glasses clean with Dill's handkerchief. After the glasses were spotless, the hand with the hankie began wiping cobwebs off what soon became a face. The face was covered almost entirely in hair — bushy eyebrows, a monstrously large mustache, and an ancient, trailing beard. Once he cleaned his face (more or less), the man offered Dill his hankie back.

Eww, thought Penelope. The hankie was filthy. But Dill didn't skip a beat.

"It's yours to keep," he said with a neat bow.

"Oh, you're so kind," said the man, tucking the hankie back into the mess of cobwebs. "Only the very nicest people come to prison here, if I may say so."

"You may," said Dill.

"Thank you, I believe I will." The strange man cleared his throat and said again with great feeling, "Only the *very* nicest people come to prison here." He smiled at Dill and Penelope as if they were his dearest friends.

Penelope couldn't help but smile back.

The man got to his feet and after several moments of dusting and brushing and straightening his decrepit tie, he took Penelope's hand and gave it a kiss. "Allow me to introduce myself. I am the Timekeeper."

"It's very nice to meet you," said Penelope, who was surprised to discover she meant what she said. Despite his startling appearance, the Timekeeper was delightful.

Dill, however, looked shocked. "Mr. Timekeeper," he said, giving the man's hand a vigorous shake, "I never expected to find *you* here. You have one of the most powerful jobs in all the Realm."

Penelope turned to look at Dill and then back at the little man. *Him? Powerful?* She didn't believe it.

"Well," said the Timekeeper, "you might say I'm taking some time off.

Please," he said, motioning toward the table, "have a seat. I'll tell you all about it." The three inmates took their seats and the Timekeeper let out a satisfied sigh. "It's about time I got up off that floor. I've been sitting there forever, give or take a day."

"Forever," replied Penelope. "That's quite a long while."

"Now that I think about it," continued the Timekeeper, "I might have been there only a few weeks. Actually I have no idea how long I've been sitting on that floor. I've completely lost track of time. Which is *exactly* why I ended up in prison in the first place."

"Sounds serious," said Dill.

"Oh, it is," he said grimly. "Very serious. I used to be the official Timekeeper for the entire Realm. Do you have any idea how many different types of time there are? There's high time, big time, and fun time. Down time, prime time, small time, short time, and dark times. There's time in, time out, time up, time tables, and time frames."

Penelope's head began to swim, but the Timekeeper went on. "There's any time and some time, the right time and the wrong time. Good time, bad time, borrowed time, and due time. I used to keep track of them all! People would bring their spare time to the clock tower for safekeeping and I would file it away. Now I couldn't tell you where the tiniest nanosecond went."

"But what happened?" asked Dill.

"I tripped and fell on hard times. I had a bump on my head for weeks." The Timekeeper absentmindedly rubbed a spot on his head as if remembering the traumatic event.

"That could happen to anyone," offered Penelope.

"True," agreed the Timekeeper. "But unfortunately it happened to me, and I haven't been the same since. From that day on, I wandered around and around in a daze, asking people if they had the time. Of course they didn't! That was *my* job. As you know, time will tell, and it wasn't long before Chronos heard the news. And you can't have a Timekeeper who can't keep track of time. He locked me away as quick as you could say, 'tick-tock.' Now *everyone* is short on time. Chronos is so very stingy. He wouldn't give you the time of day if you asked him." The Timekeeper sat silently for a moment and then shook his head quickly as if to dislodge a memory. He turned to Dill and Penelope and asked brightly, "And how long will you be staying?"

"Well, we were only sentenced to twenty minutes around the clock," answered Penelope. "So we should be out in no time."

"I hate to tell you this," confided the Timekeeper, "but 'no-time' is just a myth. So is a 'jiffy' and the ever-popular 'just-a-moment.' If someone says they'll be back in a jiffy, you know you're in for a wait. Everything takes longer than you think, that much I know. After being here for . . ." The Timekeeper paused with a distressed look on his face. ". . . for . . ."

Dill and Penelope leaned forward expectantly.

". . . for five thousand years," he said triumphantly, "I've figured out a few things. Your prison sentence is connected to how much time you've wasted. Now then, exactly what are you in for?"

"Idling," answered Penelope.

"Well, this is how it works," continued the Timekeeper cheerfully. "You're expected to work around the clock to make up for the time you lost idling. But what they *don't* tell you is that it can't be done. You could work for twenty minutes or twenty years. It won't matter. You can never make up for lost time." The Timekeeper settled back in his chair and smiled pleasantly. "So you see, you'll be here forever. Just like me."

Dill slammed the table with his fist. "I expected something tricky *just* like this!"

"This is a disaster!" cried Penelope.

"It's not *so* bad," offered the Timekeeper, gently patting her arm, "especially if you lose track of time. I'll be happy to show you how." And with that, the Timekeeper buried his face in his beard and promptly fell asleep.

chapter fourteen

"Time to get up!"

A voice from the prison intercom woke Penelope with a start. She lay on her bench, staring at the ceiling as her memory of yesterday came into focus. After the Timekeeper fell asleep, Dill and Penelope had spent the rest of the day and much of the night trying to come up with a plan of escape. Considering what the Timekeeper had told them, they were expected to work around the clock for the rest of their lives! Neither of them knew exactly what their work assignment was, but they assumed they would be building roads, operating machinery, or breaking rocks — the sort of thing convicts usually did. They decided to spend the first work shift on the lookout for escape routes. They would reconvene at the next possible chance, compare notes, and decide how to make their getaway. Once they were free, they would do what they could to find the Great Moodler and then hurry back to meet the Coo-Coo.

Penelope didn't remember falling asleep, but here it was the next morning. She sat up and looked around. Dill was stirring on the bench next to hers, but the Timekeeper, who had not moved from his spot at the table, slept on.

Suddenly there was a loud *click* and the cell was flooded with a garish yellow light. "Time for breakfast!" the intercom blasted again.

Dill and Penelope stumbled out of bed and watched while a mechanical cart rolled down the corridor and stopped in front of a small opening in their cell door. The cart was laden with bowls of lumpy oatmeal, burnt toast, and a pot of tea. They took the items from the cart, one by one, slipping them through the opening.

"Remember," said Dill, busily spreading a glob of oatmeal between two pieces of toast, "today is all about reconnaissance. We keep our heads down, noses clean, and eyes open for a way out of here. Oh, and worse comes to worst, don't forget to hum."

"Got it," said Penelope. She made a mental note to add *reconnaissance* to her notebook. If she ever got the chance, that is. There hadn't been much opportunity for writing since she'd arrived in Chronos City.

Halfway through their breakfast the Timekeeper woke. "What a delightful little nap," he said, stretching and yawning. When he saw the cart he clapped his hands in delight. "Just in time for dinner! Do you mind if I join you?" He immediately began to serve himself.

"But it isn't time for dinner," Penelope tried to explain. "It's time for breakfast."

"All the same to me," said the Timekeeper through a mouthful of toast. Once the Timekeeper had finished his meal, he wiped his mouth with his handkerchief. "Delicious, don't you think?" And then, with a long stretch, he got up from the table, returned to his spot on the floor, and curled up into a ball. "It must be very late. Midnight at least," he said to no one in particular and, after a soft "Good night," he fell back asleep.

Dill and Penelope had just finished loading the cart with their dirty dishes when a loud, unpleasant voice shouted, "Time for work!"

This time the command came from Officer X, who was striding down the corridor as fast as his short legs would go. He stopped at their cell door and, after fumbling around with his keys, yanked it open. "Come along! This isn't a resort, you know." He scowled in the direction of the sleeping Timekeeper.

Officer X led them past the cells full of sleeping fluff balls and out the prison doors into a dark, empty hallway. He took off with purpose. *Click-clack. Click-clack.* His footsteps kept a strict rhythm and, without thinking, Penelope fell into it. *Step-step. Step-step.* Dill, however, kept his own pace and even started humming.

"Stop that this instant!" Officer X swung around, one finger pointed at Dill. "Humming is Impossible, by decree of Chronos. It slows productivity and encourages lollygagging."

"Not another peep." Dill made a motion as if locking his lips with a key.

They walked along in silence, but every so often Penelope saw Dill's head bob back and forth, as if he were listening to some music only he could hear. After a while, the hall took a sharp left, then right, before ending in front of a small alcove.

"Here we are," said Officer X, motioning for them to stop. They were staring at a strange little door. Instead of being rectangular, like most doors, or even square, like some doors, this door was perfectly round, like no other door Penelope had ever seen. It looked like a clock, complete with an hour hand, a minute hand, and twelve numbers.

Officer X took out his pocket watch to check the time — 7:49. Then he rearranged the hands on the door. He moved the hour hand to 7 and the minute hand to 49. Sure enough, there was a sharp *click* and the door slid open.

"After you," said Officer X with a malicious smile.

When Penelope stepped inside, her heart sank. She was standing in a round stone chamber with a staircase hugging its side. Instead of going down, these stairs wound up. They wouldn't be working outside, building roads or breaking rocks. They were going to the top of the tower!

Penelope tried to catch Dill's eye, but he was already moving up the stairs. Officer X pointed for her to follow and she began the slow climb, each step taking her closer to a fate she did not want to discover. A distant roar came from above. It grew louder as they climbed, and as it grew louder, it grew clearer. It moved from an indistinct roar to a booming *tick-tock*.

The stairs ended at another round door. It rattled in its hinges from the force of the sound. Officer X checked the time again and unlocked it.

TICK-TOCK-TICK-TOCK.

They stood looking out on a room at the very top of the tower. Four impossibly E-NOR-MOUS clocks made up its walls. Gigantic hands marched around clock faces that were — eight, nine, ten? — stories high. The vibration of their thunderous ticking shook the air. The clocks glowed a greenish-yellow that robbed everything of its natural color. Blues looked gray. Reds looked brown. And skin tones? They were the worst. Dill and Officer X were both a strange and unhappy olive green.

Through the thick, clear glass of the clocks, Penelope could see the sky, or what she assumed was the sky. The Shadow hung like a blanket over the tower and turned the day a dull gray infused with the tower's unnatural fluorescent light.

An engine made of a million moving parts sat in the middle of the room. Knobs and dials, rods and levers, blinking, beeping consoles — all of them worked to power the great clocks. Whirring, grinding gears churned around and around, endlessly feeding into one another. Gears spun, springs sprang, pistons pumped, and gray-blue smoke rings rose from exhaust pipes.

A swarm of workers dressed in blue coveralls and blue hats tended to all the equipment. They looked exactly like the people Penelope had seen in the terminal and offices outside the courtroom. She realized they must be Clockworkers. They moved with a regimented precision dictated by the beat of the four clocks. *Tick*. A hand went up. *Tock*. A knob was pulled. *Tick*. The knob was released. *Tock.* The hand went down. Several Clockworkers with silver badges on their chests stood on a high platform rhythmically scanning the room.

Just then, the clocks began to chime eight o'clock. *GONG, GONG, GONG . . .* The sound made Penelope's knees shake and her teeth chatter. Dill had the good sense to stick his fingers in his ears, and Penelope quickly followed suit.

When the gonging stopped, Officer X took out his pocket watch. "Right on time," he said smugly. "Which means, you two had better get to work. As you can see, you'll be working around the clock for the duration of your sentence."

Oh, yes, Penelope could see. Now she knew *exactly* what working around the clock meant.

Officer X slapped Dill and Penelope both on the back (a little harder than Penelope thought necessary) and disappeared down the stairs.

One of the Clockworkers approached. She greeted Dill and Penelope with a stiff bow. "You-are-quite-wel-come-to-the-clock-tow-er," she said, each word uttered in time with the ticking clock.

"Oh, hello," said Dill, bowing back.

"Ver-y-well-thank-you." The Clockworker bowed again. There was something off about her response and her excellent manners, as if she were reading them from a script.

The Clockworker turned to Penelope and repeated her greeting, then turned back toward the room. "Right-this-way-please," she said, leading them forward with jerky, halting steps. She walked like she was a piece of machinery.

"This-is-the-time-ma-chine," explained the Clockworker, pausing in front of the engine. Dill and Penelope were careful not to get too close. Even though it was bolted to the floor, it looked like it might run over them. It heaved and moaned, huffed and puffed, churning out billows of smoke. The Clockworker explained how it worked: Every second it spit out a series of silver tokens onto a conveyor belt. Clockworkers were lined up along the belt, sorting the tokens according to size. The tokens were pieces of time — seconds, minutes, and hours. Once they were properly sorted, another set of Clockworkers would feed them — *clink, clink, clink* — into the appropriate time slot.

There were three slots at the end of the conveyor belt — a second slot, a minute slot, and an hour slot. Once a time piece had been spent, it was collected in a large metal box labeled TIME AFTER TIME. These tokens were melted down in a furnace and sent back to the elaborate machine to be used again.

Every so often, a very large time piece would shoot out and land with a thud on the belt. These tokens didn't fit into any of the time slots and were quickly discarded as spare time. Spare time was completely unacceptable and was returned to the machine for reprocessing.

The tokens that *did* fit into a slot rolled down a glass pipe, gathering speed as they went, until — *cling!* — they reached the bottom, where they triggered a long metal rod. The rod was several stories high and had four spokes that spun out at the top. The spokes were attached to the second hand of each clock, propelling them faithfully around and around. There were similar rods for the minute and hour hands. The loud ticking that filled the room actually came from the engine as it made time — second after second, minute after minute, hour after hour.

The Clockworker pointed to the conveyor belt. "If-you-don't-mind," she said, indicating that Dill and Penelope should take their places alongside the other workers.

They did as they were told. Dill sorted time pieces while Penelope put them in the correct slots. Every millisecond the machine flung a token at the conveyor belt. Penelope stared at the time pieces rushing past her. It was like a river and each of the hundreds, thousands, millions of tokens were drops of water rushing toward forever.

Penelope reached for a token. Then another. And another. There were so many of them! How would she ever keep up? She accidentally put a minute token into the hour slot. *Beep! Beep! Beep!* An alarm rang out. A Clockworker pulled a lever, releasing a shriek of steam, and the time machine thundered to a halt just long enough for him to fix the mistake. Then it started up again.

The Clockworkers around Penelope moved with absolute precision. They moved in time with the clock and never misplaced a token or fell behind. Penelope worked so hard to keep up the pace that she didn't have time to even *think* about escape routes. She could feel the seconds as they marched by, turning into minutes that became hours. *Tick-tock-tick-tock* . . . The tide of time went endlessly on. Would it really matter if she went with it?

Tick. A token dropped onto the belt. *Tock.* Penelope's hand reached out. *Tick.* She took the token. *Tock.* She dropped it into the slot.

"Penelope!" hissed Dill.

Penelope snapped out of her reverie.

"Don't move in time with the clock, and remember to hum!" he whispered, before a Clockworker silenced him with a stare.

After that, Penelope tried not to look at the conveyor belt as the time pieces rushed past. She hummed softly under her breath to keep from being sucked into the rhythm. Dill was right. Something about humming helped. It was a reminder that she could sing her own tune in the midst of all the noise. Still, it was a tremendous effort not to give in to the constant ticking. When a chime rang, indicating a change in shift, Penelope was actually relieved to see Officer X. The day was finally over.

-- -- --

Back at their cell, the Timekeeper was awake, munching on a meager dinner. "Welcome!" he said cheerfully, waving a piece of bread in the air before taking a large bite. "Hope you don't mind I started without you. I never know how long I've been waiting so I've stopped waiting altogether." He popped a piece of greenish cheese in his mouth and continued talking. "Have a seat and tell me how you are. You've been gone for ages."

"It *feels* like ages," agreed Penelope, slumping into her chair.

Dill joined them and served himself some dry bread. "Don't suppose you've got any mushrooms growing in this place?" he asked, looking around hopefully.

"Not that I know of," answered the Timekeeper.

Dill stacked a slice of cheese on top of his bread. "Too bad. Mushrooms would come in handy, working around the clock as we are."

"Goodness gracious!" said the Timekeeper. "There's no end to that work. You'll be busy for about, oh, I don't know, eternity. Give or take a millennia."

"So you said," Dill replied and reached for more cheese.

"But we *can't* stay here forever," Penelope blurted out.

"Why not?" asked the Timekeeper and then, before Penelope could answer, he dropped into a snoring heap on the table.

Dill munched away on his dinner, but Penelope had lost her appetite. "What are we going to *do*?" she asked. "I didn't see one possible escape route. What's our plan now? Grow wings and fly away? Another day like today and I'll turn into a Clockworker!"

"Not to worry," said Dill with a tap on his forehead. "I have a plan."

"Let me guess. It involves mushrooms?" Penelope tried to keep the sarcasm out of her voice, but it crept in all the same.

"Of course it does! Lucky for us, I have an emergency supply." Dill reached into his breast pocket and held out something for Penelope to see. It was a dark amber bottle with a black dropper for a lid. A paper label read: MUSHROOM SPORES.

Penelope stared at Dill. They were stuck in prison on the verge of becoming Clockworkers and he wanted to save them with *mushroom spores*? It was all too much!

"I don't want to hear any more about mushrooms!" she shouted. "They won't get us out of here! They won't save your meadow or the Range of Possibilities and they won't help us find the Great Moodler!"

The Timekeeper sat bolt upright in his chair. "Did you say, 'Great Moodler'?"

Before Penelope could answer, a whispering sound like the rustling of trees before a storm filled the air. The sound moved from cell to cell, growing louder as it went.

"What is *that*?" asked Penelope in a low, frightened voice. She wasn't sure she wanted to know the answer, which was just as well, because no one replied. They all sat listening, mouths hanging open, heads cocked to one side.

The whisper grew to a low rumble, and then — *click* — the lights went out. The darkness didn't dampen the sound. In fact, it grew louder. The rumble became a roar like rushing water, and the walls of the prison began to shake. Just when it seemed the walls would break, the sound stopped and a hush, like a layer of fine dust, settled all around them.

As loud and frightening as the noise had been, the silence was even worse.

A mousy squeak burst from Penelope's lips. She clamped her hand over her mouth and peered into the darkness. Thousands upon thousands of shining eyes peered back.

chapter fifteen

"You've woken them," whispered the Timekeeper.

Penelope peeled her hand away from her mouth. "Woken what?" she managed to say.

"The Fancies. This prison is full of them."

"*What?*" asked Dill in surprise. "You mean those dust bunnies sleeping in the cells are Fancies?"

"Indeed," said the Timekeeper. He got up from his chair and shuffled to the cell door, careful not to trip over his trailing beard. The Fancies had somehow managed to escape their cells and were crowding the halls, chattering loudly. The Timekeeper reached through the bars and began to pet the tiny creatures.

"How can these be Fancies?" said Dill, joining the Timekeeper at the door. "The Fancies I remember were glorious. Magnificent. Astonishingly beautiful."

"If they're so wonderful," said Penelope, "why are there warning signs everywhere? Are they dangerous?"

"Some would say they're dangerous," answered the Timekeeper. "They certainly are powerful, but only if they're fed. Which of course they're not. Or at least not anymore. That's why they're so thin and drab."

"What *exactly* do they eat?" asked Penelope. She wanted to know just how dangerous these little creatures were.

"Tickles," said Dill.

"Tickles?" Penelope let out a nervous laugh. When she did, the Fancies began, for just the briefest moment, to glow.

"That's the spirit!" said the Timekeeper.

The Fancies hummed and twittered with pleasure.

"It used to be everyone had their very own Fancy. People tickled them quite regularly and rode them on great adventures. Just like Dill said, they were beautiful — huge and fluffy with wild colors and even wilder antics. But feeding the Fancies was declared Impossible long ago and so they withered away to almost nothing. It wasn't long before they were rounded up and imprisoned as a public nuisance. Now all they do is sleep. I'm sure they haven't been fed for . . ." The Timekeeper searched for the exact time and finally decided on "eons."

Penelope got up and cautiously approached the bars. All the eyes turned in her direction. "How did they get out of their cells?" she asked.

"Oh, my, no cell can keep the Fancies from being free," replied the Timekeeper. "They stay inside the tower because they're simply too weak to go anywhere else. It would take something extraordinary — something truly Impossible — to fatten them up enough to fly away. But that will never happen. Chronos has seen to that."

At the sound of Chronos's name, there was a rushing sound like a thousand birds taking flight, and the Fancies scattered back to their cells. "Ah, well, there they go," said the Timekeeper. He turned toward the table, and Dill helped him to his seat.

"The sound of the Great Moodler's name must have woken them," said the Timekeeper. "I'm sure they miss her terribly. As do I."

"You *do*?" said Dill, nearly dropping the Timekeeper into his chair.

"Of course I do! Oh, I suppose that's Impossible, too," he said with a wave of his hand, "but ever since I lost track of time, I haven't cared a whit for Chronos's decrees. The Great Moodler moodled up the most beautiful possibilities. What's the harm in that?"

Dill and Penelope both sat down and leaned over the table toward the Timekeeper. "Tell me," said Penelope, "do you happen to know where the Great Moodler might be?"

The Timekeeper let out an enormous yawn and then answered, "Certainly!"

"*Where?!*" Dill and Penelope shouted at once.

But the Timekeeper was already asleep, his chin resting on his chest, his head swaying slightly with each breath.

Dill cleared his throat loudly, and the Timekeeper started awake. "Is it time to eat yet?"

"Not yet," said Dill.

The Timekeeper looked longingly at the remnants of dinner on the table. "Pity," he said, picking up an empty plate. "I haven't eaten in three years. Or maybe it's been three hours. Can't really say."

"You were just telling us about the Great Moodler," Dill interrupted him.

"Was I? Wonderful lady. I just saw her . . . um . . . er . . . yesterday."

Neither Dill nor Penelope bothered to contradict him.

"Can you tell us where she is?" Penelope pressed.

"She's outside the Realm of Possibility. Completely outside . . ." His voice trailed off and his eyes began to droop.

"But how do we get outside the Realm of Possibility?" Dill asked.

"Impossible to say. Completely" — *yawn* — "impossible."

"It's *very* important that we find her," insisted Penelope.

The Timekeeper patted her on the arm. "I'm sure you'll find her in no-time." He settled back into his chair and closed his eyes.

"Wait a minute," cried Penelope. "You said yourself, there's no such thing as 'no-time.'"

One eye opened. "Did I?"

"You did."

The second eye opened. "Well, that's not *entirely* true. There *is* no-time like the present. You can bring one about, if you know what you're doing and you're very lucky. But you have to do something very drastic and very dangerous."

"Go on!" urged Penelope. "Whatever it is, we'll do it."

The Timekeeper stroked his considerable beard. "You see, a no-time will only occur if you *stop* time altogether. Once you stop time, you'll be completely outside the Realm of Possibility. That's where you'll find the Great Moodler. It's difficult to do, mind you, but it can be done. Did I mention it was dangerous?"

"You did, you did," Dill and Penelope said, rushing to assure him.

"Well, if you're determined to do it, here's what you'll have to do: First you'll need to climb to the top of the clock tower. Once you're there . . ." The Timekeeper's face suddenly disappeared into the most enormous yawn.

Please don't fall asleep. Please don't fall asleep, prayed Penelope.

When the yawn was over, the Timekeeper propped his head in his hands and continued. "Once you're there, you'll need to find the door leading outside. It's very small. Go through it. You'll be standing directly under the north clock. Now, the next step is *very* important. If you want to create a no-time, you'll have to . . ." Just then the Timekeeper's head slipped out of his hands and dipped down before snapping up again.

Dill and Penelope held their breath.

"You'll have to . . . you'll have to . . ." The Timekeeper's body fell forward and his head hit the table with a soft *thunk*.

"Mr. Timekeeper?" Penelope gave the sleeping man a gentle shake. She was met by the sound of snoring.

"This is bad. Rotten. No good," said Dill, wringing his hands. "We *almost* had him."

Penelope wasn't listening. She took a deep breath and then shouted at the top of her lungs, *"WAKE UP!!"*

The Timekeeper jolted awake.

"Once we're under the clock, what do we do?" Penelope begged, clutching his arm.

For a brief moment he looked at her, eyes wide. "Hold on a second . . ." he mumbled.

So Penelope did. She sat and waited for him, listening for his final words. But they never came. The Timekeeper collapsed onto the table and was immediately engulfed in a tide of sleep, and no amount of shaking would wake him.

-- -- --

Dill and Penelope stayed up late discussing what they'd learned from the Timekeeper. They both agreed they couldn't work around the clock another day. The constant ticking was so overwhelming that if they didn't do something immediately, they would turn into Clockworkers and never find the Great Moodler or see the Coo-Coo ever again! If the Timekeeper didn't wake up and finish giving them instructions by the time Officer X returned, they would have to go on without him. The risk of waiting was too great.

Penelope offered to be the one to find the door. The Timekeeper had said the door was tiny, and that meant Penelope was the one more likely to see it. In the meantime, Dill would create a diversion to keep the Clockworkers from interfering in the search. Once Penelope found the door, they would go through it and position themselves outside the tower under the north clock. There they would figure out how to bring about the no-time. From what the Timekeeper had said, once they caused a no-time they would be outside the Realm of Possibility entirely. That's where they'd find the Great Moodler.

How she fell asleep that night, Penelope never knew. She must have, though, because morning came and a new day began just like the one before.

The intercom announced it was time to get up, breakfast was served, and, as usual, the Timekeeper slept through it all. Both Dill and Penelope tried to rouse him. They waved toast in front of his nose, pulled his beard, and dropped silverware next to his ears. They were both singing as loudly as they could and marching around the table when Officer X came to collect them.

"Hop to it!" Officer X shouted, rattling the cell door and bringing them to attention.

They obediently filed out of the cell and down the corridor. When Officer X wasn't looking, Penelope stole quick peeks at the Fancies. There they were — small, drab, gray creatures, all sound asleep. Did they *really* rush out of their cells last night? It hardly seemed possible.

They exited the prison and once again made their way down the empty hall toward the alcove. Dill took long, quick steps, and Penelope had to practically jog to keep up, but she didn't mind. Watching Officer X scurry after him, red-faced and scowling, was enough to lift her spirits. This little distraction didn't last long, however. Soon they were through the round door, up the stairs, and waiting at the threshold of the clock room.

"In you go," said Officer X, shoving them inside, clearly glad to be rid of them.

The Clockworker who was waiting to receive them bowed with typical exaggerated politeness. Penelope couldn't tell whether it was the same one as the day before. They all looked disturbingly similar. While the Clockworker escorted them to their stations, Penelope tried to look for the tiny door. But the Clockworker kept politely redirecting her steps.

Once they took their places at the conveyor belt, Penelope felt the tug of the familiar rhythm. *Tick-tock-tick-tock.* In a matter of moments, the ticking of the clock felt like the beat of her own heart. She knew it wouldn't be long before it took over completely. They would have to act soon if they were going to act at all.

Penelope looked up from her work to catch Dill's eye. To her surprise, he was standing idly by, fiddling with his ears. The Clockworkers on either side of him were still moving at their steady rhythm, sorting tokens. But without Dill's help, they couldn't keep up. Soon the conveyor belt was strewn with loose time.

Two of the Clockworkers with silver badges climbed down from their platform and walked deliberately toward Dill. "Back-to-work-if-you-please," they repeated over and over as they drew near.

Dill paid them no mind. He picked up a time piece, looked it over, and bit it gently. He made a nasty face and picked up a second token. He held a token in each hand, palms up. He moved his hands up and down, as if comparing their weight.

The Clockworkers were almost upon him, and Penelope knew her time had come. Dill looked right at her and gave her a wink. Then, much to her surprise, he grabbed a whole handful of tokens and stuffed them into his suit pockets.

The two official-looking Clockworkers rushed at Dill. "Stop-right-now! Steal-ing-time-is-for-bid-den." At that moment, a gigantic alarm clock began to ring furiously. It was louder than a freight train and accompanied by all sorts of flashing lights and warning bells.

The Clockworkers didn't seem to know what to do when something out of the ordinary happened. They stood frozen at their stations while the siren wailed.

This was the diversion Penelope was waiting for! She dropped down on all fours and crawled under the conveyor belt. Once she was out of the way of all the commotion, she popped out the other side and ran. She didn't know which was the north clock, so she decided to run around the perimeter of the room until she found the door. Suddenly a Clockworker stepped out from behind a tangle of thick wires connected to the time machine. "If-you-will-excuse-me," he said, moving in front of Penelope and blocking her path. He held a very large wrench in one hand and an oilcan in the other.

Penelope's mind raced. *Use your head!* she told herself. *Fight fire with fire!* What fire did the Clockworkers have besides their stiff, unrelenting politeness?

Well, decided Penelope, *I can be polite, too.* She turned toward the Clockworker and smiled sweetly. "May I please borrow your wrench?" she asked.

"But-of-course." The Clockworker held it out.

"Thank you so much." Once Penelope had the wrench firmly in her grasp she threw it as hard as she could into the heaving mass of gears running the time machine. She heard a loud *clang* followed by a *clunk* and then a horrible *screech*.

"You've been ever so kind," said Penelope with a curtsy and then bolted past the confused Clockworker. She could hear the engine slowing as it tried to spit out the wrench. *Please let that buy me some time. Please, please, please,* she thought and ran toward the nearest clock. Each clock was framed in brick, and Penelope figured that the door, if there really *was* a door, would have to be set inside it.

She had almost run the length of one clock when she heard a *whoosh* and felt a soft gust of air. She looked over her shoulder. A long mechanical arm had emerged from high above the rafters. It swooped down, swinging around the room as if looking for prey. She noticed that the two Clockworkers with badges had dragged Dill up onto their platform and were holding him firmly in place. To her horror, the arm came to a halt directly over him.

Penelope froze as she watched the arm descend with a menacing clicking sound. With one swift movement, it plucked Dill up by the coat collar. The arm swung around the room and stopped over an empty spot on the floor. All the

Clockworkers stepped back, their eyes fixed on Dill. The floorboards lifted. A trapdoor opened to a dark hole.

"Dill!" Penelope shouted.

Dill swung his head around to look at her. "*Ruuuun! Don't stop!*" he shouted back before the arm dropped him into the darkness.

Penelope heard the trapdoor slam shut and stifled a scream. Where were they taking him? She had to get him back! But Dill had told her to run. In a burst of panic and speed, Penelope took off. She turned one corner and started down the length of the next clock. Tears filled her eyes, but she kept on running. She had to find the tiny door. A whirring sound overhead made her look up. The arm had swung back around and was moving swiftly in her direction. Penelope realized why no one had bothered to pursue her. It was useless to run. The arm would catch her.

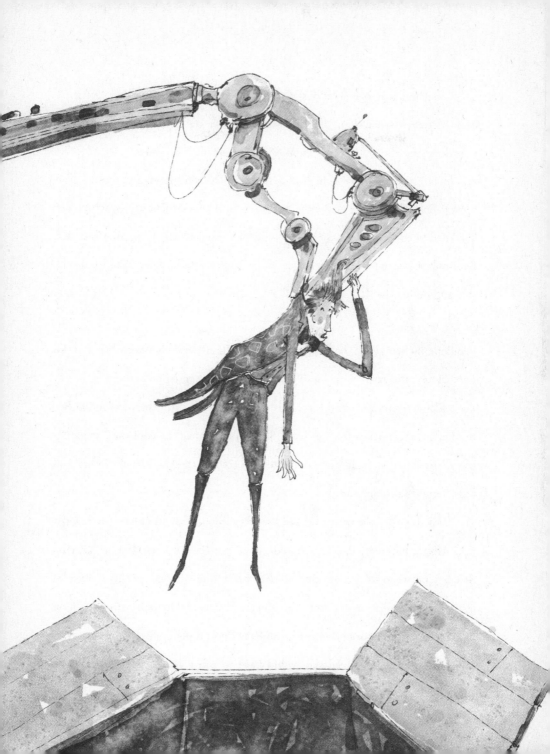

She hunched her shoulders in anticipation. That's when she saw it. A door. A tiny wooden door. It was painted red like the brick, but there was no mistaking the glint of its brass knob. Penelope sprinted forward.

The door was only as high as her waist. She bent down and wrenched it open. *Click!* The fingers of the mechanical arm snapped inches from where her head had been. Penelope saw a narrow ledge poised on the brink of a vast sky. Behind her, the arm's hungry fingers drew back to strike again. She leapt outside and pulled the door shut behind her.

— — —

Penelope inched along the ledge, putting a little distance between her and the door in case the arm opened it. Thankfully the door remained closed.

The ledge ran around the entire tower, and when Penelope stood at her full height, the clock was at her back. She leaned against the cool glass, gripping the VI to steady herself. She could feel the cold of the Shadow above her and kept her eyes straight ahead.

The lights of the tower turned the morning into an unnatural fluorescent day. After a moment, Penelope dared a glance at the City below. The dizzying distance between the ground and her feet was too much. She quickly looked up again just in time to hear a soft *swish* and see the second hand bearing down on her. Her shock evaporated into fear and she ducked just before being knocked off the ledge. She realized she would have to move out of the way or duck every sixty seconds to avoid being hit. Sitting down was not an option. The ledge was so narrow there was barely enough room for her feet, let alone her backside.

Carefully Penelope turned her body around so she could look through the dingy glass of the clock face. She could see the Clockworkers tending the time machine, carrying on as if nothing had happened. Even from this distance, their movements were hypnotic.

Penelope gave her head a shake. *I have to bring about a no-time*, she reminded herself. *There's no looking back now.*

When she heard the *swish* of the approaching second hand, Penelope ducked and let it pass. Something about watching the seconds tick away dislodged a hunch from the edge of her mind. The hunch hovered near her ear, trying to capture her attention. Penelope ignored it. She was too busy trying to figure out what to do. The Timekeeper had told her she would have to do something drastic. Something dangerous. But what?

The hunch started to buzz.

Penelope paid it no mind.

Buzz, buzz, buzz . . .

"Shoo!" said Penelope. She didn't have time for inklings or faint notions. She had to concentrate.

The hunch promptly returned. *Buzz, buzz, buzz . . .*

"Will you hold on a second?" snapped Penelope. "I'm trying to think."

Poof! The hunch disappeared.

That's odd. Doesn't a hunch disappear if you listen to it? thought Penelope. *Had* she listened to it? She recalled what she'd said to the hunch. "Hold on a second. I'm trying to think."

Hold. On. A. Second.

Penelope realized those were the last words the Timekeeper had spoken to her. The words suddenly echoed with a meaning she had never considered. *What if the Timekeeper meant* exactly *what he said?*

There was only one way to find out. Penelope decided to follow her hunch. She looked up at the second hand as it marched toward her. It was quite thick at the base, but it narrowed as it grew longer so that it was only about six inches wide at the tip. Penelope could easily grab ahold of it. But then what?

At that moment, a light rain began to peck at her face. Penelope squinted up at the clock to read the time. It was 8:42 a.m. and 5 seconds. She had exactly 25 seconds before the second hand reached her again. The light drizzle turned to rain accompanied by the not-so-distant sound of thunder. A storm was coming. She would have to act fast.

Penelope watched the second hand grow closer. *Here it comes . . .* she told herself. *Here it comes . . . here it comes . . .* and then it was upon her. Penelope tried to reach up, but fear choked every thought from her mind, and instead of grabbing the second hand and holding it still, she lost her nerve and ducked out of the way.

There was a sudden boom of thunder and rain began to pour down the clock tower. Penelope's time was up. The storm had arrived. She watched the second hand as it crept past the XI mark and up the arch toward the XII. She would have to try and grab it again before she was blown off the ledge completely.

Boom! Another clap of thunder shook the sky and Penelope shook with it. *Hang in there,* she told herself.

Finally the second hand was 10 seconds, 9 seconds, 8 seconds away . . .

Penelope braced herself against the brick wall.

7 . . . 6 . . . 5 . . .

Time had never moved so slowly!

4 . . . 3 . . . 2 . . .

This was it! Penelope reached up and grabbed the second hand, wrapping her arms around it and hugging it with all her might. For a brief moment, the rain disappeared, the clock was silent, and the second hand stood still. *Everything* stood still before . . .

Tick.

The second hand moved, taking Penelope with it. *Tock.* It moved again.

Penelope held on tighter, but every second she held on to disappeared into the next. *Tick-tock-tick-tock.* Up and up Penelope went until her feet dangled uselessly in the air. The second hand was cold and dangerously wet and Penelope could feel her fingers sliding off. The ledge was too narrow to stop her fall. Penelope held on as tightly as she could and reached out with her right foot, desperately straining to lodge it onto the tip of the VII. Thankfully, almost miraculously, her foot caught against the top corner of the sharp metal number.

Before Penelope could feel relief, the second hand moved up another notch and she went with it, leaving the VII below. She craned her neck, looking up. Above her, waiting at the 43 mark, was the minute hand. At that moment, Penelope knew what to do. She would hold on a second *and* on a minute.

Tick-tock-tick-tock. The second hand passed over the minute hand. When the minute hand was at waist level, Penelope raised her legs and wrapped them around its sturdy frame. She locked her ankles and used her position to readjust her grip on the second hand.

Tick. The second hand tried to move forward. Nothing happened. *Tick.* It tried again. Penelope squeezed her eyes shut and, gritting her teeth, pulled down on the second hand as hard as she could. *Tick. Tick. Tick.* She peeled one eyelid open and squinted up. It was working! She was holding on a second. The hand was straining, trying to push its way past 8:43 and 44 seconds.

44 . . . 44 . . . 44 . . .

The second hand struggled to move upward.

44 . . . 44 . . . 44 . . .

Its gears wound tighter and tighter, until . . .

CRACK!

A jagged streak of light danced across the sky and met the spire high above. Blue currents of electricity ran like rivulets down the tower and across the clock face.

The burst of lightning blinded Penelope almost immediately. For a split second, before her eyes were overwhelmed with light, she thought she saw, rising up out of the rain, a glittering white mountain.

Then everything was the flash of lightning and the crack of shattering glass as the great clock exploded and Penelope flew through the air.

-- -- --

If Penelope's world had not turned white, she would have seen the Clockworkers inside the tower stand by helplessly as the clock exploded into the sky. She would have heard a furious ringing fill the air as the mechanical arm swung around and around the vast room, trying to locate the source of all the trouble. Then the great gears that had served the clock so faithfully ground to a halt, sending a chain reaction through the time machine. Springs popped, gears jammed, valves choked, and pistons flew uselessly up and down. Time pieces, unable to fit into overflowing time slots, poured over the conveyor belt and out onto the floor.

A screech, like the sound of a thousand braking cars, pierced the air. For a brief moment, time itself was suspended in the sound. It stretched thinner and thinner and thinner until there was a horrible, earsplitting crack. The time machine shuddered and lay still, steam pouring out of every opening. The three remaining clocks came to a halt, their once unstoppable hands hanging in limp defeat.

Just then the most extraordinary thing happened: A swarm of Fancies spilled into the clock room, dancing and diving like butterflies. The Clockworkers didn't even notice them. They stood motionless, staring out the gaping hole where the north clock had once been. The Fancies surged ahead, streaming out the hole and falling, like the rain, onto the city below.

chapter sixteen

Penelope stared at the emptiness. There was no floor, no wall, no ceiling, no*thing* she could see or touch. Even though there was nothing to see and nothing to touch, the nothing itself was somehow *there*.

She took a tentative step forward and felt herself enveloped in the nothing. It was warm and white and comforting. She took another step, this time with more confidence. To her surprise, she was propelled forward. With each step, she moved with greater and greater ease, until she was gliding gracefully across the space.

Am I walking or flying? Penelope wondered. She was just about to try jumping up into the nothing — just to see if she might float — when a slight vibration ran through the air. She came to a nervous halt. Someone was coming. There was no sound but there was a *feeling* — like standing on a tightwire that had just been plucked.

Penelope listened with her whole body, trying to determine where the movement came from. She turned around in a slow circle, her arms held out from her sides, feeling the air. A sea of horizonless white stretched in every direction. Around she went until she saw, wavering in the distance, a figure moving toward her.

Penelope's heart leapt to her throat. Even though there was, quite literally, nowhere to go, she set off in the opposite direction from the figure.

But the figure picked up its pace, growing larger and closer until Penelope gave up. She stood motionless, waiting.

"Hello! Hello!" An excited voice reached Penelope's ears.

"Hello?" Penelope called back.

Moments later a breathless woman was pumping Penelope's arm up and down in greeting. "So glad you've come! So . . . very . . . very glad," she said between little gasps of air.

Penelope stared down into the face of the little old woman, although *little* and *old* hardly described her at all. She *was* little (shorter than Penelope, in fact). And she *was* old (her wrinkles made that obvious). But her tiny figure filled the air with energy and her eyes sparkled with youth. She wore a black-and-white pin-striped shirt with a black ribbon tied in a loose bow around the collar. A jacket with much broader yellow and blue stripes clashed happily against the shirt. It was an altogether invigorating effect.

"Please *do* sit down." The woman swept her arms open as if indicating an entire auditorium of seats for Penelope to choose from.

"Th-thank — you," stammered Penelope. The absence of anything to sit on didn't seem to bother the old woman. She plopped herself down on nothing and gently swayed back and forth as if seated on a rocker.

Penelope gaped at her. "I — I don't see any chairs."

"Pshaw!" answered the woman. "Don't tell me you only believe in what you see! How do you get through life like that?" The woman stopped rocking and leaned forward expectantly, her elbows sitting on nonexistent armrests.

Before Penelope could figure out what to say, the woman popped up and sat down exactly where she had been before. She patted the air next to her invitingly. "Here, dear," she offered. "We'll sit on the couch together. It might be a little easier for you to imagine."

Penelope walked over and slowly lowered herself down, bracing for a fall. Much to her surprise, something firm materialized beneath her and she relaxed into what seemed to be a very comfy couch. Penelope twisted around to see what she was sitting on, but again, she didn't see a thing. When she turned back around, the woman was holding her hands out toward Penelope. One hand was flat, palm up, while the other grasped the air as though it were the handle of a china cup.

"Tea?"

Penelope nodded and tentatively reached out until her fingers met something firm and smooth.

"Careful now, that's a full cup," the woman cautioned. "Sugar?"

Penelope nodded again and watched, dumbfounded, as the woman dropped nothing into the air where Penelope's teacup should be. *Plop. Plop. Plop.*

"Hope you like it sweet," she said. The woman lifted her palm up to her face, tilted her other hand toward her mouth (pinkie finger outstretched), and took a sip of what appeared to be air.

Penelope followed the woman's example and was stunned by the warm, sugary taste that filled her mouth. "It's delicious," she said.

"Mmm . . ." agreed the woman.

Penelope took another sip and then blurted out, "How is this *possible?*"

"It's not," said the woman, leaning forward and placing a nonexistent napkin on Penelope's knee.

"It's not?"

"Of course not! Nothing we do here is possible."

"Then what *is* it?"

"*Im*possible!" answered the woman, clapping her hands together in delight. She must have noticed Penelope's confused expression because she patted her reassuringly on the arm. "The distance between the impossible and the possible is just a hairsbreadth, but few people make the trip. That's why it's so nice to have company. Which reminds me, I haven't introduced myself. How rude!" The woman stretched out her hand. "I'm the Great Moodler."

"*You're* the Great Moodler?!" Penelope was so surprised she dropped her cup of tea. (Luckily the cup wasn't really there, so there wasn't a mess to clean up.)

"You've heard of me?" The Great Moodler's face turned a light shade of pink.

"Yes, I've heard of you! I — I mean *we* — we've been looking for you. Me and my friend Dill."

"And here I am!" replied the Great Moodler with a tinkling little laugh. "Isn't it lovely how that worked out?"

"Yes — I mean, no!" Penelope shook her head fiercely. "It *isn't* working out at all! I need your help. Desperately. Something horrible has happened to Dill. He's trapped in the tower. If he stays there much longer he'll turn into a . . . a Clockworker." She choked back a sob.

"Oh, my!" said the Great Moodler. She placed her arms around Penelope and gave her a gentle squeeze.

"It's not just Dill," continued Penelope. "The *whole* Realm is in danger. I thought I could help, but all my ideas are dried up. And now our friend the

Coo-Coo has probably lost his home! Chronos is destroying the Range of Possibilities. It's horrible!"

"Well, not quite destroying the Range," the Great Moodler corrected her. "More like disappearing it."

Penelope's jaw dropped. "You *know*?"

"Of course I know! Where do you think it's disappearing *to*?"

"I have no idea . . ."

"Right here," said the Great Moodler with a sweep of her hand. "Whenever Chronos does away with a possibility it has to go *somewhere*. It doesn't just cease to exist. Not any more than you or I cease to exist when someone stops thinking about us. What is *is*, and no decree from Chronos can change that."

"So the possibilities come *here*?" Penelope looked around as if she might see something.

"Exactly," said the Great Moodler, nodding cheerfully.

"But where are we?"

"The Realm of Impossibility." The Great Moodler took a sip of her tea.

"This is a Realm? But how can that be? I don't see anything."

"Nothing," corrected the Great Moodler. "You *see* nothing. If anything is possible, then nothing is impossible." The Great Moodler opened her arms wide. "Here's your nothing."

Penelope looked around. There was something familiar about the bright nothing surrounding her, but she couldn't quite place it. "So this is the Realm of Impossibility," Penelope said, letting the words sink in. "I think I've seen this place before, though I don't know when."

"Understandable," said the Great Moodler. "These days, people don't know anything about nothing. They don't pay the least bit of attention to it. If you can't see it, taste it, hear it, or touch it, it must not be important. Did you know that there's not a thing in the world that didn't start out right here?"

The Great Moodler pointed proudly at what would have been the ground if they had been somewhere. "Back in my day, people popped between the two Realms on a regular basis. Now few people even know the Realm of Impossibility exists. That's why Chronos banished me here. He knew no one would figure out where I was. Which brings up the question: How *ever* did you find me, dear?"

Penelope tried to focus on remembering, but it was all a blur. "I don't really know what I did," she finally said. "All I know is that it had something to do with no-time."

A look of surprise crossed the Great Moodler's face. "*That's* not an easy thing to bring about these days. Especially with the clock tower mucking things up. How did you do it? And start at the beginning, if you don't mind." The

Great Moodler crossed her legs and leaned forward eagerly, eyes fixed on Penelope.

The beginning? It hardly seemed possible to think back that far. "The first thing that happened," said Penelope, trying to collect her thoughts, "was that I landed in the Realm of Possibility."

"Ahhh . . ." said the Great Moodler knowingly.

"I didn't know how I got there or how to get home," continued Penelope. "But then I met Dill, and he told me about you. We went looking for you because he can't find his way and I'm all out of ideas. I want to be a writer, but for some reason I can't moodle anymore. We thought you could help us." By now Penelope's story had started to pick up speed.

"We met the Coo-Coo and he wanted to find you, too. He hoped you could restore the Range of Possibilities. But as soon as we started our search, Chronos's police officers found us idling at an intersection and sent us to prison in the clock tower. That's where we met the Timekeeper. He's the one who told us how to create a no-time. He told me to hang on a second, so I did. I went outside on the ledge of the North Clock and grabbed the second hand. Then there was a storm. A *giant* storm. With lightning . . ."

The Great Moodler nodded her head slowly up and down. "Go on . . ."

Penelope took a jagged breath. "Well, I was hanging on a second when a flash of lightning hit the tower. That's all I remember. Next thing I knew I was here."

The Great Moodler put her cup down on an imaginary table with a firm *chink*. "That's impossible," she said in a hushed and respectful tone.

"It *is?*" asked Penelope, but the Great Moodler didn't seem to be listening.

"*That's* impossible!" she said again, but louder this time. Then she laughed, leaping from the couch and clapping her hands together. She pulled Penelope to her feet and began to dance around, dragging Penelope with her. She

was laughing and shouting at the same time. "That's impossible! That's impossible! Absolutely, fabulously, wonderfully *impossible!*" She stopped to stare intently into Penelope's face. "Do you *know* what you've done?" she asked breathlessly.

"No . . ."

"You broke it."

"The clock?" asked Penelope.

The Great Moodler squeezed Penelope's arms and gave her a tiny shake. "Oh, that was much more than a clock. What you broke, my dear, was a spell. A spell that imprisoned me here and kept the Realm of Possibility under Chronos's control." The Great Moodler flung her hands up in the air. "This is glorious news. Glorious!" She clapped her hands abruptly and began to rub them together. "Come along now! There's not a minute to lose!" The Great Moodler took off running.

"Wait!" Penelope called after her. "What spell did I break?"

"Follow me!" the Great Moodler shouted back.

Penelope ran after her, surprised by how far the little woman had already gone. Once she caught up with her, the Great Moodler began to talk. "When Chronos built the clock tower, he put a spell on it. The clocks of the tower do more than mark time. Much more. They exert a hypnotic power that keeps everyone locked in a horrible malaise."

Penelope wondered what a malaise was. It sounded like a fancy sandwich spread.

"People are so stuck in the spell, they can't think for themselves. After all, the reason only 217 things are possible is because they *believe* only 217 things are possible. The way to snap people out of their malaise is to show them that *anything* is possible. And the best way to show them that anything is possible is to do something absolutely impossible. Which is *exactly* what you did."

"I did?"

The Great Moodler stopped. She turned to Penelope and fixed her with a deep gaze. "Tell me: If only 217 things are possible, as Chronos would have you believe, what does it mean if something *impossible* happens?"

Penelope thought for a minute. "That 218 things are possible?"

"Well, yes," said the Great Moodler, nodding. "But what if that new possibility is so gloriously impossible it makes people stop and think for a *fraction* of a second: If the impossible is possible, then just how many *possibilities* are possible?" The Great Moodler gripped Penelope's arm, her eyes staring at some unseen horizon. "And in that moment, when this thought dawns on them, they might, just might, snap out of their malaise and believe, even for a minute, in the Realm of Impossibility. If —" Her eyes locked on Penelope. "If they can see it. Now then, we really *must* get busy!"

Off she went again, running through the nothing.

"Where are we going?" Penelope called out, chasing after the Great Moodler's quickly disappearing figure. "I have to get back to Chronos City. I have to find Dill!"

"We're going to find the one thing that can free me and your friend — that can free the entire Realm!" called back the Great Moodler. "The Fancies!"

The Fancies? Images of the drab little creatures floating aimlessly in prison came to Penelope's mind. "I hate to tell you this, but the Fancies are in prison!" she shouted after the Great Moodler.

"Don't be ridiculous!" the Great Moodler shouted back and then immediately took a sharp left. Penelope hurried after her. She felt an incline under her feet and noticed that the bright whiteness all around had faded ever so slightly. The small incline turned into a steep rise. Penelope wasn't gliding anymore. She was trudging. The Great Moodler, however, made rapid progress upward. Penelope wondered what would happen if they got separated. How would she find the Great Moodler if there was nowhere to look?

"Just a little farther!" came a shout from above. Penelope looked up to see the Great Moodler waving at her. "One foot after the other!"

Penelope took a few more steps, her breath coming in short gasps. The white of her surroundings was getting thinner and so was the air. When Penelope finally reached the Great Moodler, the little old woman patted her back. "We're almost there," she said.

Where was there? By now the nothing had completely lost any sort of solidity or color. It was more of a fog, with wisps of shimmering dust that clung to Penelope as she walked. Penelope reached out her hand to move the fog away, but it clung to her fingers.

The Great Moodler took Penelope's elbow and whispered in her ear. "A few more steps . . ." Then, just as Penelope decided they were truly going nowhere, the Great Moodler gave Penelope's elbow a sharp squeeze. "Here we are."

She felt a waft of air touch her face and realized that the Great Moodler was blowing the glittering fog away. When the air cleared, Penelope could see she was standing on what must have been a mountain peak. Above her the sky was blue and full of hope. But below her, nestled right up to the mountain of bright nothingness, closer than she had ever imagined it could be, was something. Something massive, cold, and dark. Something that raised the hair on the back of her neck and brought a pang of fear to her throat.

chapter seventeen

The Shadow was so close Penelope could almost touch it. Almost, but not quite. It was as if an invisible wall separating the two Realms held it back. It swirled around and around, breaking apart and reforming, pressing against the bright nothing with an intensity that could only be described as hunger.

Penelope shivered as a thousand icy spiders ran up her neck. "I thought we were going to see the Fancies," she said through chattering teeth.

"And we are!" trilled the Great Moodler, completely unperturbed by the chilling darkness. "The little darlings should be here any minute. I really can't imagine anything tickling the Fancies more than you breaking Chronos's spell."

Penelope watched the Shadow throw itself against the nothing, pummeling it with unsettling power, then retreating only to rush back again. "Is it safe here?" she asked.

The Great Moodler dismissed the writhing darkness with a wave of her hand. "Of course we're safe! Completely beyond the Shadow of Doubt."

"The Shadow of *Doubt*?" cried Penelope. "Is *that* what that is?"

The Great Moodler looked at Penelope in surprise. "What did you think it was?"

Penelope shrugged. "I — I didn't know."

"Used to be the Realm of Impossibility was visible to everyone. All it took was a little moodling and — *ping!* — there it was. But then Chronos appeared and cast doubt in everyone's mind. Now the Shadow hovers over everything in the Realm of Possibility and nobody knows the impossible is within reach, just beyond the Shadow of Doubt. That's why we've got to get those Fancies."

"But what can the Fancies do?" asked Penelope. As far as she was concerned, the Fancies could hardly stay awake, much less fend off the Shadow.

"Oh-ho," said the Great Moodler, wagging her finger at Penelope. "Never underestimate the power of a Fancy. They can do *anything*. To start with, they can lift the Shadow." The Great Moodler cupped one hand around her right eye and stretched out the other hand as if she were holding a spyglass. She moved the hand in front of her eye back and forth, like she was focusing a lens. "I think I see one now!"

"Where?" Penelope scanned the sky.

"Along the far horizon," said the Great Moodler. "Oh, dear, they're shrunken and half-starved. Just as I expected." She put her arms down and looked at Penelope, nodding toward the Shadow. "See for yourself."

Penelope stared at her.

"Go on then." The Great Moodler nudged Penelope with her elbow. "Give it a try."

Penelope lifted her hands as if she, too, were looking through a spyglass.

She closed her left eye and squinted with her right, until . . . "Oh!" There it was. The Shadow seemed so close it was as if Penelope were standing right in it. A soft, silvery haze directly above the Shadow wavered and then moved. "I think I see something . . ." Penelope said.

"That's it! Keep looking!" urged the Great Moodler.

Penelope kept her eye on the movement. It glimmered like dust caught in a shaft of sunshine. Small black dots swam here and there in the dim light. Suddenly a pair of the black dots blinked. They were eyes!

"I see one! I see one!" Penelope cried. Then she saw another. And another. The haze above the Shadow wasn't a haze at all! It was a swarm of Fancies. They moved like a flock of birds skimming over a dark sea. "There must be thousands of them," said Penelope breathlessly. As she watched, the Fancies came to a halt and then, as if they had choreographed the movement, they dove into the Shadow and vanished. Penelope staggered back. "Wh-what happened to them?"

The Great Moodler took a long look through her telescope. "Thank goodness," she muttered. "They're doing *exactly* what I hoped they would."

Penelope couldn't believe what she was hearing. "You *wanted* them to dive into the Shadow? They'll *die*!"

"They aren't going to die," said the Great Moodler in a soothing voice. "Take a look for yourself."

Looking at the Shadow made Penelope feel like it would suck her in, but she did as she was told. She raised her hands to her face and used her spyglass to search for any sign of the Fancies. Nothing disturbed the Shadow's surface until she saw, out of the corner of her eye, a large chunk of darkness float past and fade into the light of the sun. To her surprise a hole in the Shadow appeared, and streaming out of it were the Fancies! They were pushing and tugging at the Shadow as they flew. Some had it by their toes; others were butting it with their heads.

Penelope turned to look at the Great Moodler. "They're lifting the Shadow!" she said in shock.

The Great Moodler smiled an I-told-you-so smile. "Never underestimate the power of a Fancy," she repeated. "There's *nothing* they can't do. Of course, they'll wear themselves out with all that work, the little sweeties, but we'll just have to fatten them up so they can go back out and finish the job. If we both moodle on whatever tickles our Fancy, we'll have a feast for them in no time."

"Moodle?" Penelope squeaked.

"But of course. It's the best way to feed your Fancy."

"I — I can't," Penelope blurted out.

"Nonsense," said the Great Moodler in the most matter-of-fact voice.

"I'm sorry, but it *isn't* nonsense," insisted Penelope. "I used to be able to moodle all the time. But I *told* you, all my ideas disappeared. They dried up or something . . ." Penelope's voice trailed off.

"My dear," countered the Great Moodler, "anyone who can break Chronos's spell isn't just full of ideas, she's full of possibilities."

Penelope's heart skipped a beat.

Her? Full of possibilities? It couldn't be true.

"You don't understand," Penelope said with a shake of her head. "I tried to use the moodle hat to find you. But I couldn't make the hat work. Nothing came to mind. Dill even called it a . . ." Penelope paused. She didn't want to say the word — the word that had been haunting her ever since she'd heard it. But there was the Great Moodler looking at her, eyebrows raised, waiting for her to finish.

Penelope rushed the words out of her mouth. "He called it an anomaly."

"*Exactly!*" said the Great Moodler with one big, exaggerated nod of her head.

Penelope took a step back. "Exactly? Exactly what?"

"Don't you know what an anomaly is?"

"It's a failure, isn't it?"

"My goodness, no! Quite the opposite. An anomaly is an oddity, a quirk, a rarity. You are all those things and I couldn't be more pleased." The Great Moodler beamed up at Penelope as if she'd won a prize. "You see, an ordinary person would have turned into a Clockworker by now. But you figured out exactly where I was right from the start!"

Penelope's heart skipped. "I did?"

"Didn't you say you moodled on my whereabouts and nothing came to mind?" The Great Moodler held out her arms to embrace the nothing all around. "Ta-da!"

Penelope's jaw dropped. The truth of what the Great Moodler said slowly dawned on her. She remembered the gentle whirring of the hat and the bright, beautiful nothing that opened up inside her as she wore it. No wonder this place looked familiar! She *had* seen it all before! "Do you mean I *did* come up with a big idea?" asked Penelope. "I knew where you were all along?"

"Indeed," said the Great Moodler. "You're a first-rate moodler."

Penelope still couldn't quite believe what she was hearing. "My ideas *aren't* stuck? I *can* be a writer?"

"Of course!" said the Great Moodler. "Now then, let's get busy. We've got work to do. The Fancies will be here any minute."

The Great Moodler whirled around and plopped down into a nonexistent chair. She pulled a DO NOT DISTURB sign out of the nothing and hung it above her head. After settling herself in more comfortably, she let out a deep, humming sigh. As she did, small, brightly colored bubbles streamed out of her ears. Penelope watched as the bubbles danced back and forth, growing larger.

I'm free, thought Penelope. *All along I thought I couldn't moodle. But I could. Miss Maddie was right — all I needed was space. This space*. Penelope felt a surge of excitement. She would help fatten up the Fancies, free Dill, and save the Coo-Coo's home — save the entire Realm! All she had to do was moodle.

At that moment, a few Fancies began to trickle into the Realm of Impossibility. They were pale and wan, shriveled by exertion. Penelope watched as they crowded around the bubbles streaming out of the Great Moodler's head, filling the air with their peeps and squeaks. One of the bubbles started to grow bigger and bigger until . . .

POP!

It broke into a million pieces of light. The Fancies sprang into action, swooping through the air and gobbling up the bright shards. The tiny creatures began to glow as the light danced in their stomachs, puffing them up and up until . . . *PFTTTHHH!* They let out a sound like a balloon losing all its air and spun wildly around. Once they came to a halt, they pounced on another morsel. After each bite, the Fancies were bigger and brighter than before. They filled the sky, bobbing about like gigantic balloons. They were every color of the rainbow and then some. They were so fat, so fluffy, that only the tips of their toes could be seen.

Penelope picked a bit of light off her sleeve and examined it closely. There, glimmering in perfect clarity, were the words:

Fudge is a health food.

"It's a possibility!" said Penelope. Just then a particularly energetic Fancy swooped down and snatched it out of her hand. "Hey!" Penelope tried to snatch

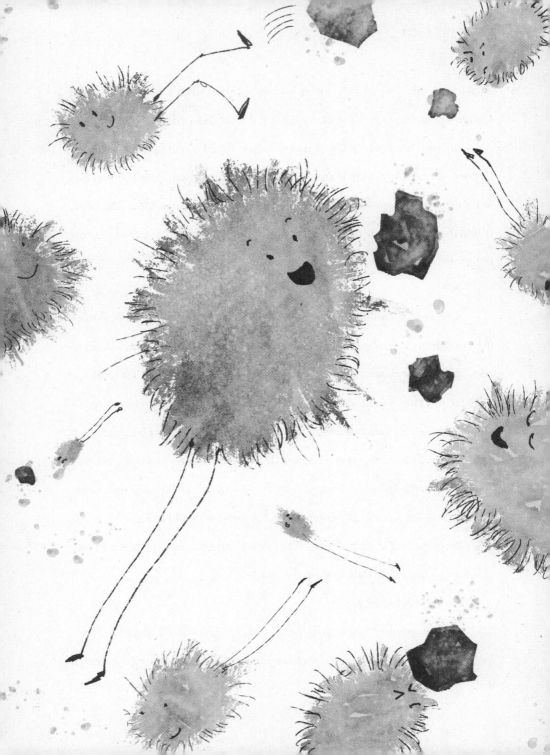

it back, but the Fancy was too fast. It swallowed the possibility and set off to join the others with a loud burp.

Penelope looked at the possibilities falling softly all around her. *I guess there's enough for everybody*, she thought and reached out to catch another one. A flash of light suddenly blinded her and she shielded her eyes before — *plunk* — something soft landed on her chest and tumbled into the front pocket of her overalls. Penelope reached into her pocket and took out a tiny possibility. Squinting, she read the words:

You can do it.

The possibility sent a shock through Penelope and she let out a sharp gasp.

The Great Moodler popped one eye open. "What's all the fuss?"

Penelope cupped her hand around the possibility, hiding it from any hungry Fancies, and walked over to the Great Moodler. "Take a look," she said, opening her hand ever so slightly.

The Great Moodler peered at it and then leaned back with a knowing smile. "You got a good one. That's what I call a Least Possibility. Very tiny, but very powerful. They can grow to be unusually large, if you really consider them. That possibility right there can take you all the way to the moon." She gave Penelope a wink.

Penelope dropped the possibility back into her pocket. By now, more and more Fancies were streaming into the Realm. They

scattered in every direction looking for food. The Great Moodler had returned to her moodling and the air was full of bubbles, some of which had already begun to grow.

Penelope heard a chirping sound and glanced up. An emaciated little Fancy was buzzing around her head. *I'd better get busy*, she thought.

She sat down, crossed her legs, and took out her notebook. She'd been so caught up in trying to escape from the tower, she'd forgotten all about it. Opening it, she stared at a blank page. It was empty, full of nothing, just like the Realm of Impossibility.

She took out her pencil and wrote about all the things that tickled her Fancy. She wrote about drinking tea with the Great Moodler, about following her hunch and discovering the no-time, about the Timekeeper and the Coo-Coo. About everything she'd seen on her journey.

A large group of Fancies crowded around her, vying for spots over her shoulder. They munched hungrily, growing fatter by the moment, feasting on her every word.

On and on she wrote. Here in the Realm of Impossibility, her words took flight above her head, coming to life as the story took shape. And as she wrote, time stood still, waiting

patiently for her to finish.

then Dill ate another mushroom

Clockworkers took...

in the realm

and then we drank tea

chapter eighteen

"That ninny! That — that *twit!*" The Great Moodler was looking through her spyglass, furiously trying to focus the lens.

Penelope looked up from her moodling. "Who's a ninny? Who's a twit?"

"See for yourself," grumbled the Great Moodler, pointing toward the Shadow of Doubt.

Penelope closed her notebook and got to her feet. She brought out her spyglass and quickly scanned the darkness for anything peculiar. Everywhere she looked, she saw Fancies lifting the Shadow. A few were speeding toward the Realm of Impossibility for their next meal. Penelope sent her gaze farther out, this time using the spyglass to follow the line of the horizon. That's when she saw it. Poking above the Shadow was a shiny, pointed spire glinting in a sun it had not seen in ages.

"It's the clock tower," said Penelope glumly.

"That's not all," replied the Great Moodler. "Look again."

Penelope moved her spyglass down the spire to where it met the roof. Clockworkers were swarming all over it. Each Clockworker wore a safety harness secured by ropes to great metal rungs high above them. They were inching along the tower's ledge, carrying ladders, toolboxes, and other gadgets Penelope didn't recognize.

"What are they doing?" Penelope whispered, as if the Clockworkers could hear her.

"They're fixing that awful clock," said the Great Moodler through gritted teeth.

Sure enough, Penelope noticed a new glass plate fitted on the clock face. Some of the Clockworkers had scaled the side of the tower and were welding the plate in place.

Perched on the ledge, polishing the Roman numerals, was a tall, strangely familiar figure. He wore the blue coveralls of the Clockworkers, but his long arms and legs poked out well past the hems. Other than his unusual height, he looked exactly like any other Clockworker. He had the same blank look on his face and he moved with jerky automated movements. Just as with all the other Clockworkers, a blue hat sat on his head, but it couldn't conceal the wild red hair beneath it.

"Dill!" screamed Penelope. Tears sprang to her eyes and the view in front of her vanished. Her calm was shattered and the spyglass along with it. She felt the Great Moodler's hand on her shoulder.

"He's — he's a Clockworker now," Penelope stammered. "We're too late."

"It looks that way," agreed the Great Moodler, "but looks *can* deceive."

The Great Moodler pulled up a chair, and Penelope eased herself into it. Her mind couldn't comprehend the truth, but her stomach did. It began to

churn uncomfortably. Penelope wrapped her arms around her middle and hugged herself to make the pain go away. "How can that be?" she said, more to herself than to the Great Moodler. "Dill *hates* Chronos. He would never serve him in any way. Never! Not in a million years." Penelope looked up into the Great Moodler's sympathetic eyes. "Something horrible must have happened to him," she insisted. "I can't just leave him there!"

"Nobody said anything about leaving him, dear," said the Great Moodler. "But Dill isn't the only captive. The entire Realm of Possibility is held prisoner by Chronos. Once that clock is restored, the spell will be restored, too. Right now, the clock is still broken and we have a chance to help others believe in the impossible. After the clock starts ticking, our chance is ruined. We *must* help the Fancies."

"But there's no time," pleaded Penelope.

"Oh, but there's all the time in the world," the Great Moodler corrected her.

"*Where?*" Penelope practically screamed.

"Right here," said the Great Moodler, opening her arms as wide as they would go, "in the space of this very moment. Chronos would have you believe you need to save time, but for what? The only time you can spend is the time you have right now. And the time you have right now is all the time in the world." The Great Moodler dropped her hands to her sides. "Time isn't precious, Penelope. You are. As long as you remember that, you're sure to use it wisely." The Great Moodler sat down. "Now then, let's start moodling. I have some Fancies to feed and so do you."

Penelope watched as Fancies floated in. They were exhausted from their efforts and in obvious need of nourishment. She sat down and tried to moodle, but images of Dill in those horrible blue coveralls kept coming to mind. *Is his internal clock broken? Does he even remember me anymore? Does he know what happened to him or is he just a machine?*

Penelope gave her head a quick shake. She had to stay calm. She couldn't afford an outbreak of worry warts. She pressed her lips together and tried to focus. Dill needed her help. She was sure of it. But if she returned to the tower, she risked everything. She might be captured and turned into a Clockworker. If it could happen to Dill, it could happen to her! But the Great Moodler said staying here and feeding the Fancies was crucial. Besides, it was safe here. Even if they didn't succeed in lifting the Shadow and the Realm of Possibility was lost in doubt again, Penelope was back to her old moodling self. It felt so amazing she didn't want to stop — if only she had a little more time!

Penelope looked over at the Great Moodler. She was stretched out with her feet up as if she were sitting on a recliner. Her eyes were closed and bubbles streamed out of her head. The Great Moodler had said Penelope would *never* have more time. That people were what really mattered.

Penelope got to her feet. *I can't save time*, she thought. *But I can save Dill.*

She walked right up to the edge of the shimmering mountain and stared out over the Shadow. She remembered Dill telling her that people used to ride the Fancies. All she had to do was capture one and then ride it to the tower. If she moved quickly, maybe she could rescue Dill and be back before the Great Moodler even noticed. That is, if she didn't get caught. Penelope shuddered. She couldn't think about that right now.

A dull blue Fancy about the size of a cantaloupe emerged out of the darkness, and Penelope waved it over. *I'd better fatten you up*, she thought, and took out her notebook. She had already used up all the paper, so she turned to the inside back cover. She only had time for one amazing moodle. Penelope stared at the nothing all around her. For a brief moment she saw it reflected in her own mind. She sat, basking in the nothing until — *pop!* — an idea inspired by Dill came to mind. She started to write:

Mushrooms are a delectable fungus.

Some are small; others humongous.

They grow on the ground.

Can be found all around.

We'll never starve with them among us.

As Penelope wrote, the Fancy gobbled up every word. When she was done, the creature chittered in pleasure and did a series of quick somersaults. After each somersault, it landed in front of Penelope, twice the size it had been before. When it was through bouncing around, it was almost as big as a pony.

Perfect! thought Penelope and glanced quickly over her shoulder at the Great Moodler. The little old lady was still busy moodling. *Well, here goes . . .* Penelope approached the Fancy and, with a little leap, tried to mount it. She grabbed ahold of where she imagined the neck might be, but all she managed to do was knock the Fancy off the mountain ledge. It let out a surprised screech, but then fluttered back to where Penelope stood.

"Sorry," whispered Penelope. She backed away to regroup. *How can I climb on top of a puff of air? It's impossible.* Penelope suppressed a giggle. Of course it was impossible! Everything in this Realm was impossible.

She turned back to the Fancy and imagined a tiny trampoline near her feet. She took two quick steps and a short hop. Sure enough, she landed on a firm but springy surface and shot into the air. She reached for the Fancy and, in her mind, its fluff turned to fur. When she grasped the creature, Penelope felt something soft and thick under her fingers. She held on tight, swinging her legs up and over before landing firmly on the Fancy's back.

To her delight the Fancy lifted into the air and zoomed away, heading

straight for the Realm of Possibility. When they crossed over the Shadow,
Penelope felt a chill grab hold of her toes and move up her legs. She glanced
down and saw the darkness churning like a rough sea below. Doubt gripped her
mind. *I'm riding on nothing but air! I'm going to drop like a rock!*

And so that is *exactly* what she did.

chapter nineteen

The Fancy let out a hideous scream, its little feet paddling helplessly against the rush of air. Penelope tried to scream, too, but her throat clamped shut. Her stomach flattened against her ribs, and she clutched the Fancy, but there was nothing there to hold. The fur just melted in her fingers. She gulped for air, and as her lungs filled, she found her voice again.

"STOP!"

But the Fancy didn't stop. If anything it fell faster, straight through the Shadow. The force of the wind pushed Penelope's cheeks up against her eyes and lifted her mouth into a gruesome grin. Her thoughts ran in every direction, like marbles dumped on the floor. She didn't even try to gather them up as complete panic set in. She began to shiver uncontrollably and her teeth would have chattered if she wasn't clenching them so tightly.

Whoosh! They fell through the Shadow and into the dull sky of the Realm. Penelope looked down and saw the world rushing up to meet her. The Fancy gained speed as it fell, and the wind shifted to a high-pitched whistle. Penelope wanted to cover her ears but was afraid she might fall off. As soon as this thought occurred to her, her knees loosened what little grip they had and she slid forward until . . .

THWACK!

The Fancy fell through a flock of birds, hitting one and sending it spiraling off course. The rest of the birds screeched in dismay and scattered in every direction. One bird flew backward into Penelope's face. Penelope forgot all about falling off the Fancy as she spit out a mouthful of feathers. The feathers reminded her of the Coo-Coo and for a brief moment the delightful memory of flying with the giant bird flashed through her mind. She grabbed the memory and held it tightly, imagining the peaceful exhilaration she felt on the Coo-Coo's back. At that moment, something completely unexpected happened. The Fancy began to slow and the horrible sinking feeling abated. The Fancy was doing exactly what she imagined!

Penelope quickly pictured the Fancy flying along at a gentle pace, with the world passing below like a lazy river. Next she envisioned the force of the wind reduced to a summer breeze. To her great relief, both of these things happened.

Penelope relaxed and dared to take a peek at the ground. It was no longer a blurry mass zooming toward her. Instead, she could clearly make out the contours of the City. The roads were long and narrow, crossing one another at sharp angles, with buildings on either side. Traffic lights dotted the way and cars moved slowly up and back, stopping at regular intervals. One of the roads was three times as wide as the others, heading straight toward the tower.

Even from miles away, the tower's massive bulk dominated the horizon. *It would be so much nicer to be having tea with the Great Moodler right now.* No sooner had this thought crossed Penelope's mind than the Fancy made a sharp turn and headed back in the direction they had come. There was no such thing as wishful thinking when riding a Fancy!

"No!" barked Penelope and emptied her mind of any thoughts except the tower and the task before her. The Fancy whimpered softly and turned back around. "I know," soothed Penelope. "It will be over soon."

As they drew closer to the heart of the City, the sky became a maze of buildings. Penelope flew higher, until the buildings were below her and only the tower loomed ahead, its blank windows and featureless façade blocking their path. Below them, surrounding the tower, was a circular building. A parapet ran along the top and Penelope could see Clockworkers standing guard. She had arrived at the Timely Manor.

Penelope remembered what Dill had told her about the Manor — how it was filled with Clockworkers who followed Chronos's every command. Now Dill was one of those horrible Clockworkers himself.

Penelope pushed aside this thought. She couldn't let it carry her away. She had a job to do. Once she got Dill to the Realm of Impossibility, the Great Moodler would undo whatever awful spell he was under. Penelope took a deep breath and flew up through the Shadow. She clung to the Fancy, focusing on the heat radiating from its back. But its soft warmth was no match for the horrible cold. The chill gripped her body and her mind, robbing her of every sensation but despair.

When they burst through the Shadow, Penelope was startled to find herself face-to-face with the north clock. And it looked brand-new! The glass had been replaced, the Roman numerals restored, and the hands repaired. Fortunately it had not been returned to life. Penelope was relieved to see the hands frozen exactly where she had left them at 8:43:44.

She urged the Fancy forward until it was smack up against the glass face of the clock. When she peered inside, she couldn't believe the scene that lay before her. It was nothing like the well-ordered factory she remembered. The time machine lay still, surrounded by debris and spare parts. Here and there amid the rubble Penelope recognized broken bits of the old north clock, shards of the faceplate, or pieces of metal from its busted springs.

Clockworkers with brooms and dustpans were sweeping up the wreckage while a few sat on the floor sorting through time tokens. A small group of Clockworkers was crowded around the time machine, oiling the gears and replacing damaged parts with new ones. Penelope scanned the Clockworkers for Dill. He was nowhere.

Dang-dung. Dang-dung.

A broken chime rang out meekly. It sounded like someone was trying to strangle the poor thing. As pathetic as the chime sounded, the Clockworkers responded to it immediately. They all dropped what they were doing and lined up at the door leading down the tower stairs. That's when she saw him. Toward the end of the line, standing head and shoulders above the rest, was the unmistakable figure of Dill.

Dang-dung. Dang-dung.

In one single movement, the Clockworkers began to file out of the room.

Penelope pulled the Fancy back from the glass and zoomed over to the little door in the brick wall that led inside the tower. To her great relief it hung open, one of its hinges broken from the force of the explosion.

Penelope carefully dismounted and, bending at the waist, slipped through the door. The Fancy sucked in its breath and tried to squeeze through. "You can't come in here. You might get caught," whispered Penelope. The Fancy made a sad little chirp and tried again, wiggling with all its might, but the door was just too small.

"Wait for me . . . I'll be right back." Penelope crept inside the clock room. By now the line of Clockworkers had almost disappeared, their feet clattering in unison down the stone stairs. Dill, who was near the end of the line, had just reached the door and was about to pass from view.

"*Diiiilllll!*" Penelope didn't care if the other Clockworkers heard her or if she set off the alarm. She just wanted Dill to turn around, snap out of this

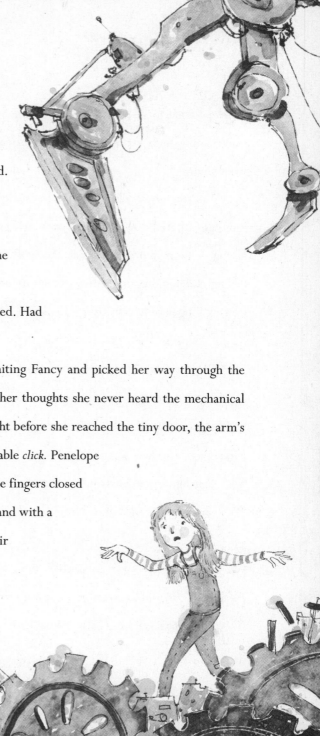

horrible enchantment, and run
to her so they could escape.

But Dill kept walking. He
didn't even look back. No one did.
It was as if their brains had been
switched off. The Clockworkers
continued their stiff march out the
door and Dill went with them.

Penelope stood there stunned. Had
Dill really left her?

She turned back to the waiting Fancy and picked her way through the
debris. She was so caught up in her thoughts she never heard the mechanical
arm snaking through the air. Right before she reached the tiny door, the arm's
fingers opened with an unmistakable *click*. Penelope
looked up, but it was too late. The fingers closed
around the strap of her overalls, and with a
swift tug she was lifted into the air
and dropped into the
waiting trapdoor.

— — —

Penelope tried to sit up but lay back down immediately. Her head felt like it was floating on a string while her stomach danced a jig. *Where am I?* she wondered.

Tall stone walls dripping with moisture surrounded her on every side. A dim light filtered down from an opening high above. She had no memory of falling — no memory other than the swift jerk of the arm and the sickening feeling of being dropped. After that her mind was blank. Penelope closed her eyes, willing her memory back into place.

"Welcome," said a cool, dry voice.

Penelope's eyes popped open. A face was looking down at her from above. It belonged to a man with a sharp nose and an even sharper chin. His mouth was unusually small, with lips so thin they were hardly distinguishable. He reminded Penelope of a snake.

Penelope scrambled to her feet, bracing herself against the cool wall. "Who are you? Let me out of here!"

"I don't think so," said the man with a smug little smile. "Now that I have you, I think I'll keep you. After all, I've had so much fun getting to know your *friend* Dill." He said the word *friend* as if it were a distasteful thing.

Penelope swallowed hard. "What have you done to him?"

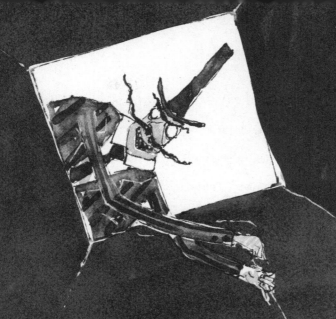

"What have *I* done?" The man leaned over the

pit and pointed a long finger at her. "What have *you* done

is the question. Did you know that you stopped every clock

in the Realm when you destroyed the north clock? Every

single clock came to a complete standstill. Can you imagine

all that wasted time? All those perfectly good seconds, minutes,

and hours gone. Naturally somebody had to make up

for it all, and Dill, well, he practically

volunteered."

Penelope glared up at the man. "Dill

would never volunteer to be a Clockworker. Never!"

The man just smiled. "I want you to know that Dill makes an excellent

Clockworker. As will you . . ." He reached into his pocket and took out a gold watch, which he dangled in the air.

Penelope shrank back against the wall, her heart pounding. She suddenly realized who she was talking to. This man wasn't some Clockworker she could outmaneuver or a Wild Bore she could outwit. This was Chronos himself! If he could cast a spell over the entire Realm and banish the Great Moodler, what would he do to *her*?

Chronos began to lower the watch down into the pit. "Did I say you destroyed *all* the clocks? What I meant to say was all but one. This little watch is actually what keeps the Clockworkers in my power and the Realm running on time. Soon I will use it to reset the north clock and then time will be on *my* side again. But first there's something I need to do."

By now the watch was hanging above Penelope's head, too high to reach, but close enough that she could hear its hands moving rhythmically — *tick-tock-tick-tock* — around its white face.

"Can you tell me what time it is?" asked Chronos.

The words pulled at Penelope with a strange power and she couldn't help but look up. When she did, the watch caught her eye and wouldn't let go. She tried to look away, but her eyes were locked on the endless motion of the second hand. Before she knew it, her arms and legs were frozen as well.

Tick-tock-tick-tock. The incessant ticking grew strangely louder.

Don't listen to it! she told herself. She tried humming a song in her head, reciting important dates, and telling herself familiar stories, but it was impossible to shut out the sound. The ticking seeped in, drowning her in its monotony.

"Penelope . . ." Chronos said in a soft, low voice. "What time is it?"

But Penelope couldn't hear his words — she couldn't even hear her own thoughts. All she could hear was the watch.

TICK-TOCK-TICK-TOCK.

Its sound ricocheted against the walls of the pit until . . .

BBBBBRINGGGG!

A loud alarm shook the air. Chronos let out a shout of delight before quickly retracting the watch. "So sorry, but we'll have to save our fun for later. Time has come and I'm needed elsewhere." He pulled the watch up the rest of the way and snapped it closed.

When he did, Penelope staggered forward, as if released from a spell. She stood there, struggling to make sense of what had just happened.

"I hate to leave a job unfinished," continued Chronos, "but I must go synchronize the clocks in the tower. Until I get back, I suggest you start getting used to the idea of becoming a Clockworker. After all," he added with a nasty little chuckle, "there's not the *least* possibility of escape."

Chronos's words struck Penelope like a blow. A Clockworker? Is that what Chronos used the pocket watch for? To turn people into his slaves?

Penelope looked around wildly. She had to get out of there! She ran her fingers over the wall, searching for a handhold, but the stones were all too smooth and damp. In desperation, she tried digging around the flagstones of the floor, but all she managed to do was bruise her hands.

There has to be a way out of here. Think, Penelope! Think! But no matter how hard she tried, Penelope *couldn't* think. Her head felt clouded and dull. When she searched for the clear, bright nothing — the place inside herself where ideas came from — she found a dense fog hovering in her mind.

Penelope slumped to the ground and rested her head on her knees. *I'll never rescue Dill. Why did I come here? The Great Moodler is probably wondering where I am. Now I'll turn into a Clockworker and be stuck here forever. Chronos is right. There's not the least possibility of escape!*

A cry welled up from deep inside her, bursting from her lips. But instead of a sob ricocheting against the walls, a small speck of darkness flew from her lips and landed at her feet. Penelope jumped up and stared down at the black speck. As she watched, it quickly grew from a speck into a spot and then a puddle. The puddle stretched into a thick ribbon of black. Long wavering appendages sprouted from its sides — four in total. These appendages sprouted appendages of their own. One, two, three, four, five each. They were hands with fingers. And feet with toes. And then, as if on cue, a head grew at the top.

Penelope couldn't look away from the dark shape on the ground. It looked like her shadow, but it was deeper and darker than any shadow she'd ever seen. It moved and swayed of its own accord, free from the mastery of a sun that had not cast it. Its arms drifted open and its fingers waved, beckoning Penelope down.

Penelope backed away into what little corner there was. *This is not happening. This is not happening. This is not happening*, she told herself.

But it was.

The darkness spread soundlessly toward her. Penelope stood shivering, breathing in short, sharp gasps, as the moisture in the air turned to frost. The puddle crept across the stone floor, inching closer and closer until it lapped at Penelope's toes.

Penelope lifted one foot and then the other, but the puddle just grew wider until it seeped under her feet. Her shoes were the first thing to disappear. Her ankles were next. Penelope was frozen, as the darkness gathered around her, sliding up her body, disappearing her bit by bit. There went her knees and thighs, then her torso and arms until, finally, it swallowed her head.

chapter twenty

If Penelope could have fallen she would have, but there was no telling which direction was up and which was down. It was as if she were floating in a dark vacuum. A bitter cold pressed against her like a blanket of ice — dry, heavy ice. She was afraid to breathe. Afraid the cold would grip her lungs and stop her heart.

Penelope held her breath as long as she could, until finally it was too much. She gasped, and when she did, the dark slid down her throat.

That's when the whispering began, speaking with soundless words. *There's not the least possibility of escape. There's not the least possibility of escape.* The words ran over and over through her mind until they found a way out of her mouth.

"There's not the least possibility of escape," she muttered. "There's not the least possibility of escape." Silence quickly swallowed the words, but not before Penelope realized that saying them had given her an odd sort of comfort. Why?

There's not the least possibility of escape. This time she kept the words to herself, looking at them in her mind with a detached curiosity: The darkness had come. It had taken her for its own. There wasn't the least possibility of escape.

And then it struck her. The Least Possibility. Of course! How could she have forgotten? There *was* the Least Possibility. It was in her pocket.

Penelope reached inside her pocket with frozen fingers, fumbling until . . .

there! She felt it. A slight warmth. Penelope carefully brought out the tiny possibility and cradled it in her palm. It was so dull and faded, she could hardly make out the words: *You can do it.*

The darkness immediately began to move. It circled Penelope, slowly at first and then faster and faster until it was a whirling, sucking gloom. Penelope clutched the Least Possibility to her chest. Its warmth spread from her hand and into her heart. She opened her fingers and looked down at the tiny speck. It was glowing again, faint but true.

You can do it.

By now the dark was a feverish tempest, whipping around her with desperate force. Penelope didn't worry that it would knock her to the ground or fling her into the air. There was nowhere to go — the darkness was all there was.

Except . . . except for the light she held in her hand. Did she dare lose it?

Fighting the pressure of the storm, Penelope raised her hand, palm flat, above her head. The Possibility grew heavier and its light shone brighter, but the dark whirled only faster.

You can do it, she told herself.

She braced the Least Possibility with both hands, but even that wasn't enough.

You can do it.

Penelope gritted her teeth as her arms began to shake from the weight.

In a fury of movement, the dark snatched the Least Possibility from her hand and flung it upward and away. But instead of disappearing, it hovered above the dark chaos like a star, piercing it in a hundred places. Penelope looked up and saw something that surprised her — bricks. She had thought the darkness was trying to take her away, but it wasn't. The sucking, pulling, and whirling was just the black disappearing like water down a drain.

More and more of the pit came into view as the dark slipped away. Now Penelope could see her shoulders. Then her waist, her legs, and her feet! Down, down, down went the darkness until it was a puddle on the floor once again. Penelope watched it shrink until it was the teeny tiniest bit of matter and then — *pop!* — it disappeared altogether.

The Least Possibility crashed to the floor, shattering against the stones into a million tiny sparks. The sparks rushed to one another like magnets and soon they formed a small cluster.

Penelope remembered the Great Moodler's words about Least Possibilities. *They can grow to be unusually large, if you really consider them. That possibility right there can take you all the way to the moon.* Penelope didn't need to go all the way to the moon. She just needed to get to the top of the pit.

"I can do it!" Penelope shouted, and the words poured over her like sunshine.

The cluster of light turned into a mound.

"I can do it!"

The mound turned into a hill. Penelope scrambled up it. *I can do it . . . I can do it . . .* The hill was growing so fast that no matter how hard she ran, the top was beyond reach. She could feel the wind in her face as the walls of the pit rushed past. Still the hill grew higher and wider until the pit itself began to crumble. In a matter of seconds, the Least Possibility burst out into the open, sending stones flying. Penelope slid down the side of the hill, landing with a small hop on the ground. And with that, she was free.

— — —

Penelope found herself in a room that was hardly more than a cave. A few lights hung from a low ceiling and a set of worn stairs cut through the rough stone walls. She had no idea when Chronos would return, but she didn't want to be here when he did. Now there was only one thing left to do — find Dill and get back to the Great Moodler!

Penelope sprinted up the stairs for several stories until they stopped at a gray metal door. She caught her breath, then opened it a crack and stuck her head out. She recognized the dark terminal where Officer X had taken her and Dill when they first arrived at the tower. She remembered it as a busy place, filled with Clockworkers and cars. This time, other than a few fluorescent bulbs flickering on and off, it was completely empty.

Penelope saw a driveway off to her left and headed straight for it. She ran up its steep incline, her shoes smacking the concrete floor and her breath coming loud and hard. When she reached the top, the driveway emptied out into the vast courtyard between the tower and the Timely Manor. Above her a blue sky — not gray, but *real* blue — peeked out from behind fading clumps of darkness.

The Fancies are lifting the Shadow! she thought with a thrill of joy. *They're doing it! They're really doing it!*

If the Fancies were still able to lift the Shadow, that meant one thing — Chronos hadn't restored his spell. There was still time to save Dill, *if* she could find him. *You can do it*, she told herself. *You can —*

THWAP!

Penelope staggered backward as a mass of blue fur engulfed her. She laughed and hugged the Fancy. "I'm glad to see you, too," she said and climbed onboard. "Now let's go find Dill and get out of here."

The Fancy took off, heading up the sides of the tower. As they flew, Penelope scanned the ground, but there were no Clockworkers, or cars, or even guards patrolling the parapet around the Manor. "Where is everyone?" she whispered.

In answer, the Fancy sped up. It reached the far corner of the clock tower and rounded it smartly before coming to a halt. Below them, covering every inch of the courtyard's northern quadrant in tight, neat rows, were the Clockworkers.

All of the Clockworkers. Thousands and thousands of them stood facing the Timely Manor, arms at their sides. They looked straight ahead, staring at a set of double doors at the top of a grand staircase. There was a hush in the air, as if they were waiting for something.

Penelope searched the crowd for Dill. He must be there, but which one was he? They were all dressed the same, with blue hats that obscured their faces. Her only hope was to see a hint of his red hair.

At that moment the doors of the Timely Manor opened and Chronos stepped out. Penelope crouched down on the Fancy's back, urging it to fly even higher. The Fancy hugged the side of the tower as it flew, and its blue fur turned gray, blending in with the stone wall and forming a perfect camouflage.

As Penelope watched, Chronos approached a microphone at the top of the ornate staircase and spoke. "You have been off the clock too long. Trouble has sprung from your idleness." He pointed at the sky and the fading Shadow, his thin lips pressed into a frown. "Soon I will restore order to the Realm. The clocks will begin again and so will your work!" He dug into his pocket and brought out his watch. Gripping it in his fist, he held it up in the air. "Never forget," he shouted, "time is on *my* side!"

Penelope stared down at Chronos. The blue sky and sunshine highlighted his pale, pinched face. She remembered looking up at him from the pit. He had looked powerful then, but from here he looked small and . . . and something else. Unhappy? Was that what she saw in his face? *No*, decided Penelope, *he doesn't look unhappy. He looks . . . he looks . . . afraid.*

The thought rang out in Penelope's mind with absolute clarity, and she knew she had hit upon the truth. Chronos was afraid. Afraid the Shadow of Doubt would fade. Afraid the Clockworkers would see beyond it. Afraid the people of the Realm would believe in the impossible and the Great Moodler would return.

Penelope thought about the Realm of Impossibility. Even though she couldn't see it or touch it, it was somehow *there*. And in its there-ness was a great power. According to the Great Moodler, the two Realms — the Realm of Possibility and Impossibility — were intermingled. One couldn't exist without the other. Chronos hid that fact behind the Shadow, but the Shadow was fading and, as it faded, his power went with it.

"Time is on *my* side!" Chronos screamed again. His voice had a whining undertone that Penelope hadn't noticed before. She imagined him stomping his foot like a three-year-old and tried not to laugh.

Chronos opened his fist and the pocket watch swung back and forth on its chain. He held the swaying watch up in front of the microphone and a soft ticking sound filled the air. *Tick-tock-tick-tock-tick-tock.* But just as it had done when Penelope was in the pit, the ticking didn't stay soft for long. It grew louder and more insistent until Chronos didn't need the microphone at all.

The Clockworkers stared straight ahead, eyes trained on the watch. "Tick-tock-tick-tock-tick-tock," they chanted in unison. With each word, a wisp of something like smoke escaped their lips. Soon a dark haze hovered above each Clockworker. Each haze grew thicker as they chanted until it began to take on a shape — a ghostly, human shape.

The shapes sprouted long waving arms and beckoning fingers that sent chills down Penelope's back. She had seen this darkness before — it had plagued her in the pit. Darker than the dark of night, the forms were like small black holes in the sky. Penelope knew they wouldn't stay small for long. Sure enough, as soon as a dark form fully materialized, it lifted up into the air, stretching its long fingers toward the faint Shadow waiting above. With a sickening feeling, Penelope realized what she was seeing. Doubts.

So *that's* what had popped out of her mouth in the pit! She had unleashed her doubts and now the Clockworkers were doing the same.

"Tick-tock-tick-tock-tick-tock," they chanted. There was a horrible sucking sound and a bitter wind raced across the courtyard. The poor Fancy, high up in the air, rocked back and forth from its force.

Penelope's hair whipped across her face, but she kept her eyes locked on the scene below. The wind circled around the Clockworkers, lifting their doubts higher and higher. The wispy remnants of the Shadow now billowed across the sky as the doubts were absorbed into its growing form. The bright blue sky disappeared, and the sunlight vanished.

"Tick-tock-tick-tock-tick-tock." The chanting grew louder and stronger until — *snap!* — Chronos flipped the pocket watch closed. The chanting stopped. A silence hung in the air for a few breathless moments, and then:

GONG.

GONG.

GONG.

The clocks in the tower rang out. Chronos's spell was restored.

chapter twenty-one

The booming shook Penelope's Fancy out of the sky. It plummeted toward the ground, battered by waves of sound. Penelope gathered her wits and focused on the Fancy regaining its balance and flying them to safety. Her imaginings had just taken effect when she heard a sharp cry.

"Stop!" Chronos was standing at the microphone, pointing up at them, his voice pinched with rage. "Stop, right now!"

Penelope urged the Fancy on, ignoring Chronos's command. The Fancy zoomed toward the nearest corner. Once they turned it, they could disappear out of sight. They were close, so close, when Chronos shouted something that stopped Penelope cold and brought the Fancy to a halt.

"Bring *him* to me!"

There was only one person Chronos could be referring to. Penelope slowly turned the Fancy around and saw, far below her, a tall, redheaded figure being led through the crowd by two Clockworkers. Penelope watched, heart in her mouth, as Dill was dragged up the stairs to Chronos.

"Take him to the Passage," snarled Chronos.

The wide doors of the Manor swung open and Dill disappeared behind them. Chronos glanced up at Penelope with a smirk, then turned and swept inside, closing the doors behind him with a bang.

Whatever fear there was left in Penelope melted into rage. "Go!" she shouted to her Fancy. The Fancy flew straight toward the Timely Manor, the wind whistling through its fur. Penelope tried to imagine it flying faster than a rocket — faster than the speed of light. *Whoosh!* She landed at the top of the stairs, jumped off the Fancy, and bolted toward the doors. Above them she saw a stone carving of a clock with rolling ocean waves on either side. The waves crested and then crashed, wrapping long tendrils of foam around an hourglass filled with sand. Below the clock, carved in elaborate scrolling letters, were the words:

TIME AND TIDE WAIT FOR NO ONE.

Penelope wrenched the Manor's doors open and rushed inside. She was met by a long empty corridor lit from the floor. A row of dim lights outlined a path through the gloom and cast a weak glow on the walls, which were lined with grandfather clocks. The clocks were stooped with age, their shoulders hunched as if bearing the weight of time. Each clock had a dull silver pendulum hanging like a beard from its flat gray face. Something about the clocks made them look human.

Penelope ran down the corridor as fast as she could. At first, the corridor followed the curve of the building, but before long it twisted around in a maze of tight spirals. Penelope ran for what seemed like miles, but the corridor never ended. In fact, it never even seemed to change. Every clock she passed looked exactly like the next. Time slipped away (did it even exist?) and still she ran.

Hours must have passed, but not for one moment did Penelope feel tired or winded. Her heart pounded, not from exhaustion but from fear. *I could run forever,* she thought. For the first time in her life, forever seemed like something she could comprehend, like five minutes or an hour. This scared her even more. It scared her so thoroughly that she stopped. And there, standing in the gloom, was Chronos.

"You're late," he snapped.

Penelope took a quick step back. But Chronos shot out his hand with unnatural speed and grabbed her arm. "It's high time I showed you how to behave in a Timely Manor," he said, yanking her toward him.

Penelope struggled against his hold. "Where's Dill?" she demanded. "Where have you taken him?"

"Come with me and you'll see." Chronos dragged Penelope along the corridor. "This is the Passage of Time," he said, pointing to the clocks on either side of them. "I have a new clock made to inaugurate each year of my rule. The clock starts the year standing straight and tall and ends the year like this." He stopped in front of a clock. Its haggard face was blank, its hands unmoving. "Time takes its toll on *them.* Not on me. By the end of the year, they are quite useless. I only keep them around for old time's sake," he said with a nasty laugh.

Chronos pulled Penelope farther along the Passage before stopping in front of another clock. It was brand-new, its wood dark and beautifully oiled, its back straight, standing a few feet higher than Chronos. "Look closely," he whispered in Penelope's ear, pushing her forward until her face was inches away from the glass.

Penelope saw a body pressed underneath the pendulum — torso, arms, and legs. The head disappeared behind the clock face, but she didn't need to see the head to know who the body belonged to.

Penelope yanked her arm free and turned to face Chronos. "Get him out of there!"

"All in good time. All in good time." Chronos took out a key, which he inserted into a small hole in the clock face. He began to wind the key — *screech, screech, screech.* The clock glowed with the same sick green light that permeated the Realm.

"Stop it!" yelled Penelope, reaching up to grab the key.

Chronos swatted her away. "Don't worry. He won't feel a thing — after a while." The clock began to shudder, and the pendulum came to life. But instead of swaying side to side, it moved forward and back, pressing against Dill's body with alarming force. With every thrust of the pendulum, Dill disappeared ever so slightly.

"What are you doing to him?" screamed Penelope.

"Dill is being pressed for time. Every hour, every minute, every second will be drained away. Then *I* will have the time of *his* life."

"*Please* stop it," Penelope begged.

Chronos watched her calmly.

"*Please . . .*"

Chronos's hand hovered over the key. "I suppose I could let him go if you would do *one* thing for me."

"Yes!" cried Penelope, frantic. "Whatever you want."

Chronos removed the key and the clock stood still. He took out his pocket watch. "I don't know how you escaped the pit, but you won't get away from me this time." He raised the watch in the air and let it sway back and forth. "Let's pick up where we left off, shall we? Tell me what time it is, Penelope." His voice was soft and beckoning.

The watch tugged at Penelope, but she looked away.

"*Tell me what time it is,*" repeated Chronos. Now there was an unpleasant edge to the words.

"Just a moment," Penelope pleaded. She knew that if she looked at the watch and listened to its ticking, she would become a Clockworker. If she didn't, Dill would be pressed for time. The situation was impossible!

Nothing is impossible, she told herself. She'd seen that with her own eyes. *If nothing is impossible, then there must be a way out. But what is it?*

"Penelope . . ." Chronos's voice was downright threatening.

"Five minutes," said Penelope. "Just give me five minutes."

Chronos's eyes narrowed and he smiled a tight little smile. "I'll give you thirty seconds." He nodded curtly at the pocket watch. "The clock is ticking."

Penelope sat down on the floor and closed her eyes. She rested her head in her hands and placed her fingers over her ears, blocking out the sound of the watch. *What time is it?*

The watch would tell her a number. But what did that number really mean? To the Timekeeper, time was categorized by type — good time, bad time, borrowed time, and due time. To the Coo-Coo, time was the song of life. To Dill, time was what made mushrooms grow. But what was time to *her*?

Penelope's thoughts drifted this way and that until they ran their course and disappeared. At that moment, a soft sound, like a tiny silver bell, rang inside her head. Penelope forgot everything and listened. The sound danced and leapt, and everywhere it touched thoughts fell away until there was, for the briefest moment, a warm, white nothing.

At that moment, Penelope heard the voice of the Great Moodler: *The only time you can spend is the time you have right now. And the time you have right now is all the time in the world. Time isn't precious, Penelope. You are. As long as you remember that, you're sure to use it wisely.*

"Stop that this instant!" screamed Chronos. "You will *not* moodle under my watch!"

Penelope opened her eyes. She looked up at the watch swaying back and forth and a word popped out of her mouth. She didn't remember thinking the word. It was just there, waiting to be said.

"Now."

A look of horror crossed Chronos's face. "*What* did you say?"

Penelope got to her feet. "I said, the time is Now."

The pocket watch stopped swaying and its hands began to spin at a maddening speed. Chronos snatched the watch back and tapped furiously at its glass face. "What have you done?" he screamed at Penelope. He tried to wind the watch, moving the crown back and forth in a desperate attempt to stop the runaway hands. But they only went faster until there was a loud *crack!* — and the pocket watch shattered. Tiny wheels, screws, and bits of glass spilled everywhere. Chronos fell to his knees. "Nooooo . . ." His hands swept the floor, trying desperately to salvage

the broken bits of

his masterpiece.

At that moment, the air filled with frantic dinging, donging, buzzing, chiming, and ringing as every clock on every wall of the Manor went off at once. The clocks in the tower joined in, their stately peals replaced by a rapid *gongongong*.

The Timely Manor shook as if struck by an earthquake, and the lights along the floor blinked on and off. The grandfather clocks began to sway ominously. Their wooden bones moaned and shuddered before another quake sent them toppling to the floor. Dill's clock, however, remained upright even though a large crack had appeared in a seam along its side. Penelope rushed over, stuck her fingers into the crack, and pulled as hard as she could.

Walls were shaking and clocks were crashing all around her. The ceiling started to collapse and chunks of plaster fell to the floor. Fear coursed through Penelope's body, and she used its energy to yank the crack wide open until there was a space just big enough for Dill to squeeze through.

Penelope reached inside and grabbed Dill's hand. To her relief, his hand grabbed back. Carefully he extracted himself from the horrible contraption. First his legs, then his torso, then finally his head and shoulders until there he was, standing before her, a dazed look on his face.

"Are you all right?" Penelope asked in a rush.

Dill stared at her. "What?"

Penelope gave his arm a desperate shake. "Are you all right? Can you walk?"

But Dill just looked confused, as if Penelope were speaking gibberish. *He isn't all right*, thought Penelope. *I was too late! He'll never be the same again!*

Just then Dill laughed. "I almost forgot." He fiddled with his ears, pulling something out of each one and putting it in his pocket. "Now then, what did you say?"

"Can you walk?" Penelope asked again, articulating each word carefully.

"Of course I can! I'm fit as a fiddle."

Relief flooded through Penelope, clearing her mind and bringing the danger around them back into focus. "Then let's go!"

They ran as best they could, scrambling over fallen clocks and other debris. Penelope knew the Passage stretched on for miles and doubted they would make it out in time. But for some reason, as soon as they turned the first corner, they saw the door a short distance up ahead. It took only a few moments before they burst from the Manor and stepped together out into the sunshine.

chapter twenty-two

Penelope stared up into the biggest, bluest sky she'd ever seen. The Shadow of Doubt was gone and the garish green lights of the tower destroyed. Sunshine poured out over everything, bringing the world alive with color. Even the gray concrete of the Manor was radiant in the light of day.

Penelope felt a slight shudder under her feet and she glanced over at Dill. "Did you feel that?"

He nodded. "Let's get out of here." Before they could move, they heard a loud groan and a fine cloud of dust suddenly filled the air, followed by a rush of falling rocks.

"*Run!*" shouted Dill.

They sprinted across the veranda and took the stairs two at a time (three at a time, in Dill's case), not stopping to look back until they reached the ground. The carved clock above the Manor door was gone. Instead of TIME AND TIDE WAIT FOR NO ONE, the quote now read:

. . . ME AND . . . I . . . WAIT FOR . . . ONE.

"That was close," said Penelope.

"Too close," agreed Dill. "We'd better keep moving."

They set off toward the far side of the courtyard where a set of gates led out into the City. Crossing the courtyard, however, was no easy matter. The earthquake had destroyed much of the Timely Manor and chunks of concrete littered the ground. The wreckage would have been easy to navigate if not for the Clockworkers. They were a mass of confusion. Without the ticking of the clock tower to guide them, their steps had lost all rhythm. They turned this way and that like broken windup toys. They tripped over the rubble and one another, bumping into Dill and Penelope in the process.

"You-must-ex-cuse-me. I-do-beg-your-par-don," they repeated over and over again to no one in particular.

"What's wrong with them?" asked Penelope.

"They're lost," explained Dill. "There aren't any clocks to dictate their movements."

"Well, they certainly haven't lost their manners. Why aren't they trying to stop our escape?"

"Oh, Clockworkers aren't so bad," Dill admitted, neatly sidestepping one who was just about to back into him. "Their worst habit is doing what they're told. Without someone to boss them around, they're harmless."

Penelope looked over at Dill. Although he had lost the hat, he was still wearing the blue coveralls of a Clockworker. "For a while, I thought . . . I thought you were one of them."

"Not for a minute!" said Dill with a shake of his head. "That was just a trick. Ruse. Clever ploy."

"But how did you resist Chronos's spell?"

"Mushrooms, of course!" Dill reached into his pocket and brought out two very small pink fungi. He held them out for Penelope to see. "I grew them in my ears."

Penelope remembered the bottle of mushroom spores Dill had shown her in prison. She knew that spores were something like seeds, but at the time, she couldn't see how they were the least bit important. She had even gotten angry at Dill for thinking they were useful. Now she realized what he had done. "You dropped mushroom spores in your ears when we were working around the clock!"

"Precisely!" Dill beamed. "Ears are a perfect place for mushrooms to grow — so dark and damp. The spores went right to work and I was completely deaf by the time I ended up in the pit underneath the tower. Chronos came along and tried to put me under his spell with the pocket watch, but I couldn't hear the ticking.

"Of course, I could still *see* the pocket watch, but as mesmerizing as that was, it wasn't enough to turn me into a Clockworker. I just pretended the spell had worked so I could bide my time until you returned. And here you are!"

"You *knew* I'd come?" said Penelope. A little bubble of pride formed inside her chest.

Dill stopped in the middle of the courtyard to smile at her. "Never doubted it for a minute."

The bubble grew so big it popped and Penelope began to glow.

Just then a look of panic crossed Dill's face. "What's *that?*"

Penelope spun around in time to see a sudden flash of blue barreling toward her. She braced herself for impact before — *wham!* — a huge furry creature slammed into her, nearly knocking her down.

"Is that what I think it is?" said Dill in wonder. He reached out and softly touched the Fancy's fur. "I'd almost forgotten what a real Fancy looked like. It's been so long since I've seen one."

"I tickled it and it grew!" said Penelope, laughing.

"It certainly did."

"Hop on! They're easy to fly. We'll be out of here in minutes."

Dill's face turned pale. "No. Never. Absolutely not. You know I *hate* flying."

Penelope gave in and they slowly picked their way across the courtyard, with the Fancy bouncing along behind. As they did, Penelope told Dill what had happened to her since they were separated in the tower. When she got to the part about the Great Moodler, he grabbed her arm. "So you found her?"

"You won't believe it, but I had an idea where she was all along!" Penelope told him the whole story of the the no-time and meeting the Great Moodler in the Realm of Impossibility.

Dill hung on every word. When he heard about the Fancies lifting the Shadow of Doubt, he looked back at the Fancy. "That's amazing. Outstanding. Truly impressive." The Fancy turned bright pink and then gold with pride.

"There's nothing a Fancy can't do," said Penelope, quoting the Great Moodler. "All they needed was a little fattening up."

By now they had reached the far side of the tower and the gates to Chronos City loomed in front of them. Pushing against the gates, in a useless attempt to open them, was the Timekeeper. When he saw Dill and Penelope, a huge smile spread across his face. "Hello! Hello!" he cried, waving them over. "You'll never believe what happened. I was having a short nap when the clocks in the tower went crazy. They all went off at once. It was a horrible racket. The earth began to shake and the tower along with it. I thought the tower would collapse, but then the clocks grew silent and I suddenly knew what time it was."

"You *did?*" asked Dill and Penelope at once.

"I did." The Timekeeper grinned. "I knew *exactly* what time it was. It was time to get out of there!"

Everyone laughed at this, including the Fancy, who rolled around on its back chuckling in midair.

"My, my, you've grown," said the Timekeeper, giving the Fancy a gentle poke. He looked at Penelope. "I don't suppose *you* had anything to do with that?"

"Well, I *did* have some help from the Great Moodler."

"Congratulations," said the Timekeeper, clapping in delight. "You found her! No wonder all the clocks are broken." He glanced up at the tower and his smile faded. The tower was leaning across the courtyard at a precarious angle. "Let's get out of here, shall we?"

The three of them pushed against the gate until they had a space wide enough to step through. Outside the Manor, Chronos City was almost unrecognizable. The tall gray buildings were bleached white in the light of a brilliant sun. The air, once thick with doubt, was now filled with glittering possibilities. They drifted down from the clouds and littered the sidewalks. The whizzing cars and bustling crowds were still. People sat on curbs, leaned out windows, or just stood dumbstruck where they were — each holding a possibility they had never considered before.

"Where did they all come from?" asked Dill, his voice soft with awe.

The Timekeeper pointed up. Dill and Penelope slowly raised their eyes to the sky. A giant flock of Fancies was flying overhead. They zoomed in, out, and around the buildings. At the head of the flock was the Great Moodler, flying a Fancy covered in a spiral of colored stripes. Ideas bubbled from her head and burst into flames that immediately turned into beautiful possibilities. After each outburst, a cluster of Fancies broke from formation, carrying the possibilities to the rest of the Realm.

When the Great Moodler caught sight of Penelope, she waved so hard she almost fell off her Fancy. "Penelope, dear!" she called, floating down toward the street. When she was a few feet above the ground, she dismounted, landing with a neat little hop on the sidewalk. "I'm so glad to see you!" she cried and flung open her arms.

Penelope rushed forward. For a split second, she worried that maybe the Great Moodler wouldn't be real — that she might be made of nothing, too. But the arms that wrapped around her were solid and strong and smelled slightly of tea.

"I'm sorry I ran off and left you," Penelope said when the hug was through. "I hope I didn't cause any problems . . . I just had to get to Dill and . . ."

The Great Moodler waved away her apology. "Looks to me like you made good use of your time."

Just then, there was a soft cough and the Timekeeper stepped forward. He carefully smoothed his beard and adjusted his decrepit tie. Then, taking the Great Moodler's hand in his, he gave it a polite kiss. "It's been too long," he said. "I haven't seen you in . . . in . . . at least thirty seconds."

The Great Moodler laughed at this, but when she realized that he really had no idea how long it had been, she immediately offered to moodle on a cure for his condition.

The Timekeeper declined. "Back when I used to keep track of time, there never seemed to be enough," he explained. "I rushed about like a madman. Now I take my time doing whatever I please."

Just then a possibility fluttered down from the sky and landed on the Timekeeper's chest. "What's this?" he said, untangling it from his beard. *"Life is but a dream,"* he read out loud.

"It's a possibility," said the Great Moodler with a sly smile.

"Hmm . . ." said the Timekeeper and wandered over to a bench to consider it. Soon he was snoring.

Next it was Dill's turn to greet the Great Moodler. "Welcome back," he said with a deep bow. Dill was so tall and the Great Moodler so short that he nearly toppled over with the effort. Even so, it was a very solemn moment.

"I do believe we've met before," said the Great Moodler once introductions were made.

Dill blushed with pride. "How kind of you to remember."

"Dill's a great explorer," interrupted Penelope. "He's the one who discovered *Anything is possible* all those years ago."

"Oh, my! I *am* honored." This time it was the Great Moodler who bowed.

Dill's face grew redder than his hair. "What Penelope means," he tried to explain, "is that I *used* to be a great explorer. I've lost my way and now I can't find anything."

At that very moment an idea occurred to Penelope. "You found *me*," she said.

Dill threw her a sideways glance. "What?"

Penelope repeated herself. "You found *me*."

"But I wasn't looking for you," insisted Dill. "I was looking for the Great Moodler."

The Great Moodler took an eager step forward. "But don't you see? Penelope *is* a great moodler. One of the best. Her moodling defeated Chronos, freed you —" She flung her hands up like she was throwing confetti. "Freed the entire Realm!"

Dill's mouth dropped open.

A smile crept across the Great Moodler's face and settled into her eyes. She gave Dill a consoling pat. "You know, dear, sometimes you find what you're looking for, but not what you're expecting."

Dill looked at Penelope. "Y-you mean, *you're* the great moodler I was looking for? I found her after all?"

"I was right under your nose," said Penelope, laughing.

He shook his head in amazement. "Incredible. Extraordinary. Absolutely . . . *Coo-Coo!*"

The Great Moodler looked startled. "Wh-what?"

"The Coo-Coo bird," Dill shouted, pointing at the sky.

Sure enough, there was the Coo-Coo, flying straight toward them. He landed in a rush of air, disrupting a host of Fancies and scattering possibilities everywhere. "*You-you* . . . did it!" the bird called in delight, hugging Dill and then Penelope. "The . . . *two-two* . . . of *you-you* . . . pulled off a . . . *coup-coup!*"

"We had some help," said Penelope, nodding toward the Great Moodler.

The Coo-Coo scurried over to meet her. "*Coo-Coo* . . . at your service," he sang, dipping his head down and nearly knocking her over with his plume.

"Delighted, I'm sure!" laughed the Great Moodler.

"The Coo-Coo helped us find you," explained Penelope. "He lives on the Range of Possibilities . . ." Penelope cringed as the memory of Chronos's bulldozers crossed her mind. "Or at least he used to . . ."

"Were we in time?" asked Dill. "Is your mountain safe?"

The bird shook his head. "The Clockworkers . . . *blew-blew* . . . it up."

Dill and Penelope stood by in shocked silence, unsure of what to say. The Range of Possibilities was gone, the Coo-Coo's home destroyed.

The Great Moodler placed a hand on the bird's wing and gave it a squeeze. "I'm so sorry. We'll all do what we can to help you. It won't be easy, but with two great moodlers on hand" — she motioned toward Penelope — "it shouldn't be a problem. We'll moodle up a Least Possibility. And with thousands of people here in the City to consider it, we'll eventually restore the Range." The Great Moodler turned to Penelope. "Are you willing to give it a try?"

"Oh, yes!"

The Great Moodler turned to Dill. "And you?"

Dill stood up tall. "I'll do what I can even though I don't have my moodle hat."

"*Coo-coo . . . coo-coo*," sang the bird ever so softly. "Would this help . . . *you-you*?" He slipped his head under his wing and pulled it out again. There, between his beak, was a shiny flat object.

"My moodle hat!" Dill rushed forward and the Coo-Coo dropped it into his outstretched hands. "Wherever did you find it?"

"It caught my eye as I . . . *flew-flew* . . . over the wasteland. I thought someone . . . *threw-threw* . . . it away."

"Someone *did*," said Dill. "It was the awful Officer X. I thought I'd never see it again." He clutched the hat to his chest. "Thank you," he said to the bird, his eyes shining.

Just then, they heard a commotion and a figure emerged from the gates of the Timely Manor. His clothes were dusty and torn, and he walked as if in a dream, but Penelope recognized him right away. "It's *Chronos*," she said in alarm.

Everyone watched as Chronos caught sight of a Clockworker. He grabbed

her arm and gesticulated wildly at the tower. The Clockworker didn't seem the

least bit interested and instead held out a possibility for him to consider. Chronos

shoved the possibility aside and ran to the next Clockworker and the next, but no one made a move to help. Possibilities drifted all around them. Chronos swatted at them like flies.

"Poor Richard . . ." said the Great Moodler with a shake of her head. "I'm afraid he'll never recover."

"*That's* Poor Richard?" gasped Penelope.

"Why, yes. He changed his name to Chronos because he thought it sounded more powerful, but Richard is his real name. I just added the 'poor' myself. He seems so pathetic."

Penelope couldn't believe what she was hearing. Chronos was Poor Richard? *The* Poor Richard from her calendar? "Is Chronos always spouting off quotes and sayings?" asked Penelope, just to make sure.

"Oh, yes!" said the Great Moodler. "Endlessly. They're plastered all over the City. I believe he even wrote them all down in a book. It was some sort of almanac or calendar."

"That's the one!" cried Penelope.

Dill turned to Penelope in surprise. "You've heard of it?"

"I definitely have. My mother used to read from it every day."

"Excellent book," said the Great Moodler.

"Wha —?" exclaimed Penelope. "It's not excellent at all! It's horrible and . . . and preachy!"

"Well, that depends on how you look at it," said the Great Moodler. "Poor

Richard had lots of wise things to say, but he was so afraid no one would listen to him that he got carried away. Instead of asking people to consider his words, he demanded they obey them."

Poor Richard, wise? His words, worth considering? The possibility had never occurred to Penelope before. But it did now. It popped out of her head, a single brilliant, blinding seed. She stared at it, caught in the wonder of the words etched in its dazzling brightness. Penelope said them out loud: ***"You might be right."***

Her voice gave this tiny possibility power. It shot up into the air, higher and higher, hovering like a star above the City.

Penelope looked up and held her breath.

Dill held his breath.

The Great Moodler held her breath.

The bird *tried* to hold his breath, but it was no use. He kept interrupting the silence with soft *coo-coos*.

And then the tiny point of light took off like a meteor.

"That's a Least Possibility!" shouted the Great Moodler. "After it!"

"*Coo-coo!*" The bird squawked, running back and forth in excitement. "I can get a . . . *new-new* . . . home!"

"Of course you can," said the Great Moodler. "Once you consider that possibility, who knows how big it will grow." She gave a sharp whistle and an orange-and-blue-plaid Fancy dropped down from the sky. "Get on," she instructed Dill. "We've got to act fast."

Dill took a step backward. "I'm not climbing on that thing." He dodged left, then right, trying to get away. The Fancy, who thought it was a grand game, skittered after him.

"Come on," urged Penelope, jumping aboard her bright blue Fancy. "That Least Possibility could spawn a whole new Range. We've got to find it! Just imagine the easiest, smoothest flight possible, and whatever you do, don't think about falling."

The Fancy butted Dill with its head until his legs (and will) gave way. Next thing he knew, he was perched on top of the creature.

The Great Moodler's whirling spiral Fancy zipped by and she leapt aboard. "After that Possibility!" she shouted and they all took off.

All except Penelope.

When Dill noticed they were leaving without her, he came to a halt. "What's wrong?" he called down.

"I don't know," she called back. "I can't make it go." She imagined rising straight up through the maze of skyscrapers and out into the clear blue sky. But her Fancy didn't budge. Penelope's three friends wheeled around and dropped down to where she floated a few feet above the ground.

"If you can't make it go," said the Great Moodler, "it must be something beyond your wildest imagination."

"What could that be?" asked Dill.

"I think —" answered Penelope, not believing the words herself, "I think I want to go home."

"*Home!*" screeched Dill. "That's absurd. Ridiculous. Out of the question. Your world is full of Clockworkers."

"Is that . . . *true-true?*" sang the bird, his great wings flapping.

"It is," said Penelope. "There are Clockworkers everywhere. But that's just it. I'm a great moodler and . . . and they need me."

Dill released his grip on his Fancy long enough to embrace her. When he leaned back, Penelope could see tears in his eyes to match her own. "I'm sure you're right," he sniffed. "They must be lost without you."

Penelope felt a hand on her arm and turned to look at the Great Moodler. "I suppose your time is up, dear," she said kindly.

Penelope nodded and the tears ran down her face. "I'll never forget what you did for me. Never!" she cried, as her Fancy began to rise.

The Great Moodler waved up at her. "I hope we meet again someday!"

"Thank you! Thank you! Ever more thank you!" Dill shouted.

"*Adieu-dieu . . . adieu-dieu,*" called the Coo-Coo between giant sobs.

Penelope waved and waved until
her friends turned into tiny dots
and then disappeared.

Penelope imagined returning home, and as her thoughts carried her away, the Fancy rose higher and higher. Her time was up and she was going to meet it. As she moodled, her Fancy gained speed, heading straight for a bank of white clouds. It passed through the clouds and popped out the other side, where the sun sat waiting. The Fancy flew straight at the ball of blinding light. Penelope squeezed her eyes shut as she fought back a surge of fear, but the light was just as much inside her head as out. She heard a whooshing sound and felt the Fancy blown out from under her. Her eyes snapped open.

The Fancy was gone.

The sun was gone.

The sky was gone.

Everything was gone.

Even her fear.

All that was left was an unending world of white. Penelope stared at the white. When she did, the glare began to fade and she saw, wavering in the distance, a long, black, horizontal line. As Penelope watched, the line broke apart. Now there were two lines — one above and one below. Then *those* lines broke apart and became four. Then eight.

The lines were stark and black against the white background. They stood very still until the one at the top began to move. It wiggled and stretched, forming what looked like letters. Penelope stared at the letters until she could make out the words:

One today is worth two tomorrows.

chapter twenty-three

"Tea?"

Penelope blinked. Miss Maddie came into sudden focus. She was standing in front of Penelope holding a steaming cup. Penelope nodded dumbly.

Miss Maddie put the cup down on the table. "Careful now, that's full," she cautioned. "Sugar?"

Penelope nodded again and watched as Miss Maddie dropped three sugars into the tea. *Plop. Plop. Plop.* "Hope you like it sweet," said Miss Maddie and winked.

Penelope looked down at her cup. Sitting next to it on the table was a page torn from a calendar — *her* calendar. On it were the words she'd just read. *One today is worth two tomorrows.* Below the words was a series of blank lines.

Miss Maddie sat down at the table next to Penelope and tapped the calendar with her finger. "So then . . . a schedule with a giant hole in it . . . The possibilities are endless."

Penelope took a sip of tea, letting the warm sweetness bring her back to the room. "That's — that's what I thought," she said, "but my mother has other ideas."

Miss Maddie stared at Penelope from over her teacup. "And what do you think about her ideas?"

Penelope put down her cup. "I think they're good."

Miss Maddie put down her cup, too. "I never thought I'd hear you say that."

Penelope shook her head in amazement. "I never did, either. Her ideas aren't the problem. The problem is they're *hers*, not mine."

Penelope stared down at her tea, trying to make sense of her own words.

For a brief moment, the image of a tall, skinny man with red hair stuck inside a clock flashed before her eyes. Time was weighing on him, so heavy. She knew how he felt. She had the feeling her mother did, too.

Penelope looked up. "I think you're right about needing space. I've been so pressed for time, I haven't been able to think for myself. I thought I could prove my writing wasn't a waste of time, but I guess what I really wanted to prove was that *I* wasn't a waste of time."

"The only story that can prove that is your life." Miss Maddie said the words like they were a spell. They dawned on Penelope and a hope she'd never felt before spread its way into her heart. And then she remembered.

Penelope reached around to her back pocket, breath held tight. Would it be there? Was the story real, waiting for her to write?

Her fingers touched her notebook and she slowly drew it out, placing it on the table. She almost didn't dare look. Almost. With one finger, she flipped it open.

There they were. Her notes. The story of her journey. The places she'd seen, the people she'd met, and the things she'd learned. Everything except the end.

Penelope slammed her notebook closed. "I have an idea. An *amazing* idea."

"An idea for a story?"

"Yes," said Penelope and gulped down her tea. "A story that might just get published. It's within the Realm of Possibility. Totally within the Realm!"

"Oh?" said Miss Maddie. "So you've been there?"

But Penelope wasn't listening. "I gotta go!" she said, getting up from the table. "I'm going to talk to my mom and dad. Maybe they'll listen and maybe they won't. If that doesn't work, then I'll find another way to make it happen."

Miss Maddie got up and smoothed down her skirt. "Before you go, there's something I want you to do."

Penelope stopped halfway out the door.

Miss Maddie took a pencil out of her pocket and laid it on the table, next to the calendar. "I want you to make time for yourself. No one else will."

Penelope walked back to the table. She picked up the pencil and looked at it for a moment, toying with it in her hands. She was going back home to do the impossible. She was going to talk to her parents. Usually, at a time like this, she would have been full of doubt. A knot would have formed in her throat and she would have wanted to scream. But Penelope didn't feel like she usually did. Not anymore.

You can do it, said a voice inside her head. *You can do it.*

Penelope took a deep breath and pressed the pencil to the paper, moving it with sure strokes. This is what she wrote:

July 3

One today is worth two tomorrows.

8:00–9:00 Talk to my parents

9:00–?? Anything is possible

To Justin,

for giving me permission to do

ab-so-lutely nothing

--P.B.

acknowledgments

All my thanks to the original Great Moodler — Brenda Ueland — who gave me "the impulse to write one small story." I hope you are pleased.

Profound gratitude to: my editor, Tracy Mack, whose wisdom and kindness brought this book into being; my agent, Marietta Zacker, for making my anything possible — you're a wonder; to Emellia Zamani for recognizing Penelope early on and to Kait Feldmann for her finishing touches; to all the remarkably talented people at Scholastic, especially Marijka Kostiw for her brilliant design and Monique Vescia for her careful copyedits; and to Lee White for bringing it all alive with his illustrations.

I owe a debt to Norton Juster for capturing my imagination so thoroughly with *The Phantom Tollbooth*.

I am grateful to the Writers' Colony at Dairy Hollow for the extraordinary gift of uninterrupted time.

Many thanks to Meredith Davis, Sherrie Peterson, and Cindy Shortt for reading this manuscript when it was lumpy. Your feedback and encouragement helped give it real shape.

To Robyn Cloughley, thank you for holding a supportive space so wide, for so many years.

Deep appreciation to Anne Marie Chenu for teaching me you can't fall off the path; and to Peg Syverson for all her mindful, active care.

Love and endless gratitude to my parents, Darwin and Carolyn Britt, who gave me all the time in the world; and to my family, for always being there.

Special thanks to Jerri Romine, who knew — beyond a shadow of doubt — that this story had to be told. I couldn't have written it without you.

Finally, and forever, thank you to my husband, Justin Pehoski. Your grace and goodness give me courage.

about the author

Paige Britt grew up in a small town, with her nose in a book and her head in the clouds. She studied journalism in college and theology in graduate school but never stopped reading children's books for life's most important lessons. In addition to writing, she loves to sit and moodle. (If you don't know what moodling is, you should probably read this book.) Paige lives in Georgetown, Texas, with her husband. *The Lost Track of Time* is her first novel.

about the illustrator

Lee White is an artist and teacher who loves watercolor, printmaking, and climbing trees. He spends his days splashing paint in his backyard studio, where there are absolutely no clocks allowed! He has illustrated more than fifteen books and shown in galleries across the country, from Los Angeles to New York. He lives in Portland, Oregon, with his wife and their young son.

The
cover art and interior
illustrations for this book were
created in watercolor and digital mixed me-
dia by Lee White. The text of this book was set in
Perpetua, which was designed for Monotype Imaging
by English sculptor and typeface designer Eric Gill. Gill is
known most famously for his self-named face, Gill Sans, a font
that made him a legacy to typography and has stood the test of
time. Gill began work on Perpetua in 1925, but the finished design wasn't released until 1929, when it appeared in a translation
of Walter H. Shewring's *The Passion of Perpetua and Felicity*, from
which the font took its name. Perpetua was selected for this
book both for its classic beauty and its resonance with the
book's theme of time. The display type was set in Love
Letter Typewriter, a modern typeface designed
in 1996 by Dixie's Delights. The book was
designed by Marijka Kostiw.

THE SNOWS OF KILIMANJARO

AND OTHER STORIES

Books by Ernest Hemingway

THE ENDURING HEMINGWAY

THE NICK ADAMS STORIES

ISLANDS IN THE STREAM

THE FIFTH COLUMN AND FOUR STORIES
   OF THE SPANISH CIVIL WAR

BY-LINE: ERNEST HEMINGWAY

A MOVEABLE FEAST

THREE NOVELS

THE SNOWS OF KILIMANJARO AND OTHER STORIES

THE HEMINGWAY READER

THE OLD MAN AND THE SEA

ACROSS THE RIVER AND INTO THE TREES

FOR WHOM THE BELL TOLLS

THE SHORT STORIES OF ERNEST HEMINGWAY

TO HAVE AND HAVE NOT

GREEN HILLS OF AFRICA

WINNER TAKE NOTHING

DEATH IN THE AFTERNOON

IN OUR TIME

A FAREWELL TO ARMS

MEN WITHOUT WOMEN

THE SUN ALSO RISES

THE TORRENTS OF SPRING

THE SNOWS
OF KILIMANJARO

AND OTHER STORIES

by Ernest Hemingway

CHARLES SCRIBNER'S SONS
New York

CONTENTS

THE SNOWS OF KILIMANJARO

AND OTHER STORIES

THE SNOWS OF KILIMANJARO

Kilimanjaro is a snow covered mountain 19,710 feet high, and is said to be the highest mountain in Africa. Its western summit is called the Masai "Ngàje Ngài," the House of God. Close to the western summit there is the dried and frozen carcass of a leopard. No one has explained what the leopard was seeking at that altitude.

"THE MARVELLOUS thing is that it's painless," he said. "That's how you know when it starts."

"Is it really?"

"Absolutely. I'm awfully sorry about the odor though. That must bother you."

"Don't! Please don't."

"Look at them," he said. "Now is it sight or is it scent that brings them like that?"

The cot the man lay on was in the wide shade of a mimosa tree and as he looked out past the shade onto the glare of the plain there were three of the big birds squatted obscenely, while in the sky a dozen more sailed, making quick-moving shadows as they passed.

"They've been there since the day the truck broke down," he said. "Today's the first time any have lit on the ground. I watched the way they sailed very carefully at first in case I ever wanted to use them in a story. That's funny now."

"I wish you wouldn't," she said.

"I'm only talking," he said. "It's much easier if I talk. But I don't want to bother you."

"You know it doesn't bother me," she said. "It's that I've gotten so very nervous not being able to do anything. I think we might make it as easy as we can until the plane comes."

"Or until the plane doesn't come."

"Please tell me what I can do. There must be something I can do."

"You can take the leg off and that might stop it, though I

3

doubt it. Or you can shoot me. You're a good shot now. I taught you to shoot didn't I?"

"Please don't talk that way. Couldn't I read to you?"

"Read what?"

"Anything in the book bag that we haven't read."

"I can't listen to it," he said. "Talking is the easiest. We quarrel and that makes the time pass."

"I don't quarrel. I never want to quarrel. Let's not quarrel any more. No matter how nervous we get. Maybe they will be back with another truck today. Maybe the plane will come."

"I don't want to move," the man said. "There is no sense in moving now except to make it easier for you."

"That's cowardly."

"Can't you let a man die as comfortably as he can without calling him names? What's the use of slanging me?"

"You're not going to die."

"Don't be silly. I'm dying now. Ask those bastards." He looked over to where the huge, filthy birds sat, their naked heads sunk in the hunched feathers. A fourth planed down, to run quick-legged and then waddle slowly toward the others.

"They are around every camp. You never notice them. You can't die if you don't give up."

"Where did you read that? You're such a bloody fool."

"You might think about some one else."

"For Christ's sake," he said, "That's been my trade."

He lay then and was quiet for a while and looked across the heat shimmer of the plain to the edge of the bush. There were a few Tommies that showed minute and white against the yellow and, far off, he saw a herd of zebra, white against the green of the bush. This was a pleasant camp under big trees against a hill, with good water, and close by, a nearly dry water hole where sand grouse flighted in the mornings.

"Wouldn't you like me to read?" she asked. She was sitting on a canvas chair beside his cot. "There's a breeze coming up."

"No thanks."

"Maybe the truck will come."

"I don't give a damn about the truck."

"I do."

"You give a damn about so many things that I don't."

"Not so many, Harry."

"What about a drink?"

"It's supposed to be bad for you. It said in Black's to avoid all alcohol. You shouldn't drink."

"Molo!" he shouted.

"Yes Bwana."

"Bring whiskey-soda."

"Yes Bwana."

"You shouldn't," she said. "That's what I mean by giving up. It says it's bad for you. I know it's bad for you."

"No," he said. "It's good for me."

So now it was all over, he thought. So now he would never have a chance to finish it. So this was the way it ended in a bickering over a drink. Since the gangrene started in his right leg he had no pain and with the pain the horror had gone and all he felt now was a great tiredness and anger that this was the end of it. For this, that now was coming, he had very little curiosity. For years it had obsessed him; but now it meant nothing in itself. It was strange how easy being tired enough made it.

Now he would never write the things that he had saved to write until he knew enough to write them well. Well, he would not have to fail at trying to write them either. Maybe you could never write them, and that was why you put them off and delayed the starting. Well he would never know, now.

"I wish we'd never come," the woman said. She was looking at him holding the glass and biting her lip. "You never would have gotten anything like this in Paris. You always said you loved Paris. We could have stayed in Paris or gone anywhere. I'd have gone anywhere. I said I'd go anywhere you wanted. If you wanted to shoot we could have gone shooting in Hungary and been comfortable."

"Your bloody money," he said.

"That's not fair," she said. "It was always yours as much as mine. I left everything and I went wherever you wanted to go and I've done what you wanted to do. But I wish we'd never come here."

"You said you loved it."

"I did when you were all right. But now I hate it. I don't see why that had to happen to your leg. What have we done to have that happen to us?"

"I suppose what I did was to forget to put iodine on it when I first scratched it. Then I didn't pay any attention to it because I never infect. Then, later, when it got bad, it was probably using that weak carbolic solution when the other antiseptics ran out that paralyzed the minute blood vessels and started the gangrene." He looked at her, "What else?"

"I don't mean that."

"If we would have hired a good mechanic instead of a half baked kikuyu driver, he would have checked the oil and never burned out that bearing in the truck."

"I don't mean that."

"If you hadn't left your own people, your goddamned Old Westbury, Saratoga, Palm Beach people to take me on——"

"Why, I loved you. That's not fair. I love you now. I'll always love you. Don't you love me?"

"No," said the man. "I don't think so. I never have."

"Harry, what are you saying? You're out of your head."

"No. I haven't any head to go out of."

"Don't drink that," she said. "Darling, please don't drink that. We have to do everything we can."

"You do it," he said. "I'm tired."

Now in his mind he saw a railway station at Karagatch and he was standing with his pack and that was the headlight of the Simplon-Orient cutting the dark now and he was leaving Thrace then after the retreat. That was one of the things he had saved to write, with, in the morning at breakfast, looking out the window and seeing snow on the mountains in Bulgaria and Nansen's Secretary asking the old man if it were snow and the old man looking at it and saying, No, that's not snow. It's too early for snow. And the Secretary repeating to the other girls, No, you see. It's not snow and them all saying, It's not snow we were mistaken. But it was the snow all right and he sent them on into it when he evolved exchange of populations. And it was snow they tramped along in until they died that winter.

It was snow too that fell all Christmas week that year up in the Gauertal, that year they lived in the woodcutter's house with the big square porcelain stove that filled half the room, and they slept on mattresses filled with beech leaves, the time the deserter came with his feet bloody in the snow. He said the police were right behind him and they gave him woolen socks and held the gendarmes talking until the tracks had drifted over.

In Schrunz, on Christmas day, the snow was so bright it hurt your eyes when you looked out from the weinstube and saw every one coming home from church. That was where they walked up the sleigh-smoothed urine-yellowed road along the river with the steep pine hills, skis heavy on the shoulder, and where they ran that great run down the glacier above the Madlener-haus, the snow as smooth to see as cake frosting and as light as powder and he remembered the noiseless rush the speed made as you dropped down like a bird.

They were snow-bound a week in the Madlener-haus that time in the blizzard playing cards in the smoke by the lantern light and the stakes were higher all the time as Herr Lent lost more. Finally he lost it all. Everything, the skischule money and all the season's profit and then his capital. He could see him with his long nose, picking up the cards and then opening, "Sans Voir." There was always gambling then. When there was no snow you gambled and when there was too much you gambled. He thought of all the time in his life he had spent gambling.

But he had never written a line of that, nor of that cold, bright Christmas day with the mountains showing across the plain that Barker had flown across the lines to bomb the Austrian officers' leave train, machine-gunning them as they scattered and ran. He remembered Barker afterwards coming into the mess and starting to tell about it. And how quiet it got and then somebody saying, "You bloody murderous bastard."

Those were the same Austrians they killed then that he skied with later. No not the same. Hans, that he skied with all that year, had been in the Kaiser-Jägers and when they went hunting hares together up the little valley above the saw-mill they had talked of the fighting on Pasubio and of the attack on Pertica and Asalone and he had never written a word of that. Nor of Monte Corno, nor the Siete Commum, nor of Arsiedo.

How many winters had he lived in the Voralberg and the Arlberg? It was four and then he remembered the man who had the fox to sell when they had walked into Bludenz, that time to buy presents, and the cherry-pit taste of good kirsch, the fast-slipping rush of running powder-snow on crust, singing "Hi! Ho! said Rolly!" as you ran down the last stretch to the steep drop, taking it straight, then running the orchard in three turns and out across the ditch and onto the icy road behind the inn. Knocking your bindings loose, kicking the skis free and leaning them up against the wooden wall of the inn, the lamplight coming from the window, where inside, in the smoky, new-wine smelling warmth, they were playing the accordion.

"Where did we stay in Paris?" he asked the woman who was sitting by him in a canvas chair, now, in Africa.

"At the Crillon. You know that."

"Why do I know that?"

"That's where we always stayed."

"No. Not always."

"There and at the Pavillion Henri-Quatre in St. Germain. You said you loved it there."

"Love is a dunghill," said Harry. "And I'm the cock that gets on it to crow."

"If you have to go away," she said, "is it absolutely necessary to kill off everything you leave behind? I mean do you have to take away everything? Do you have to kill your horse, and your wife and burn your saddle and your armour?"

"Yes," he said. "Your damned money was my armour. My Swift and my Armour."

"Don't."

"All right. I'll stop that. I don't want to hurt you."

"It's a little bit late now."

"All right then. I'll go on hurting you. It's more amusing. The only thing I ever really liked to do with you I can't do now."

"No, that's not true. You liked to do many things and everything you wanted to do I did."

"Oh, for Christ sake stop bragging, will you?"

He looked at her and saw her crying.

"Listen," he said. "Do you think that it is fun to do this? I don't know why I'm doing it. It's trying to kill to keep yourself alive, I imagine. I was all right when we started talking. I didn't mean to start this, and now I'm crazy as a coot and being as cruel to you as I can be. Don't pay any attention, darling, to what I say. I love you, really. You know I love you. I've never loved any one else the way I love you."

He slipped into the familiar lie he made his bread and butter by.

"You're sweet to me."

"You bitch," he said. "You rich bitch. That's poetry. I'm full of poetry now. Rot and poetry. Rotten poetry."

"Stop it. Harry, why do you have to turn into a devil now?"

"I don't like to leave anything," the man said. "I don't like to leave things behind."

*   *   *

It was evening now and he had been asleep. The sun was gone behind the hill and there was a shadow all across the plain and the small animals were feeding close to camp; quick dropping heads and switching tails, he watched them keeping well out away from the bush now. The birds no longer waited on the ground. They were all perched heavily in a tree. There were many more of them. His personal boy was sitting by the bed.

"Memsahib's gone to shoot," the boy said. "Does Bwana want?"

"Nothing."

She had gone to kill a piece of meat and, knowing how he liked to watch the game, she had gone well away so she would not disturb this little pocket of the plain that he could see. She was always thoughtful, he thought. On anything she knew about, or had read, or that she had ever heard.

It was not her fault that when he went to her he was already over. How could a woman know that you meant nothing that you said; that you spoke only from habit and to be comfortable? After he no longer meant what he said, his lies were more successful with women than when he had told them the truth.

It was not so much that he lied as that there was no truth to tell. He had had his life and it was over and then he went on living it again with different people and more money, with the best of the same places, and some new ones.

You kept from thinking and it was all marvellous. You were equipped with good insides so that you did not go to pieces that way, the way most of them had, and you made an attitude that you cared nothing for the work you used to do, now that you could no longer do it. But, in yourself, you said that you would write about these people; about the very rich; that you were really not of them but a spy in their country; that you would leave it and write of it and for once it would be written by some one who knew what he was writing of. But he would never do it, because each day of not writing, of comfort, of being that which he despised, dulled his ability and softened his will to work so that, finally, he did no work at all. The people he knew now were all much more comfortable when he did not work. Africa was where he had been happiest in the good time of his life, so he had come out here to start again. They had made this safari with the minimum of comfort. There was no hardship; but there was no luxury and he had thought he could get back into training that way. That in some way he could work the fat off his soul the way a fighter went into the mountains to work and train in order to burn it out of his body.

She had liked it. She said she loved it. She loved anything that was exciting, that involved a change of scene, where there were new people and where things were pleasant. And he had felt the illusion of returning strength of will to work. Now if this was how it ended, and he knew it was, he must not turn like some snake biting itself because its back was broken. It wasn't this woman's fault. If it had not been she it would have been another. If he lived by a lie he should try to die by it. He heard a shot beyond the hill.

She shot very well this good, this rich bitch, this kindly care-taker and destroyer of his talent. Nonsense. He had destroyed his talent himself. Why should he blame this woman because she kept him well? He had destroyed his talent by not using it, by betrayals of himself and what he believed in, by drink-ing so much that he blunted the edge of his perceptions, by laziness, by sloth, and by snobbery, by pride and by prejudice, by hook and by crook. What was this? A catalogue of old books? What was his talent anyway? It was a talent all right but instead of using it, he had traded on it. It was never what he had done, but always what he could do. And he had chosen to make his living with something else instead of a pen or a pencil. It was strange, too, wasn't it, that when he fell in love with another woman, that woman should always have more money than the last one? But when he no longer was in love, when he was only lying, as to this woman, now, who had the most money of all, who had all the money there was, who had had a husband and children, who had taken lovers and been dissatisfied with them, and who loved him dearly as a writer, as a man, as a companion and as a proud possession; it was strange that when he did not love her at all and was lying, that he should be able to give her more for her money than when he had really loved.

We must all be cut out for what we do, he thought. However you make your living is where your talent lies. He had sold vitality, in one form or another, all his life and when your affections are not too involved you give much better value for the money. He had found that out but he would never write that, now, either. No, he would not write that, although it was well worth writing.

Now she came in sight, walking across the open toward the camp. She was wearing jodphurs and carrying her rifle. The two boys had a Tommie slung and they were coming along behind her. She was still a good-looking woman, he thought, and she had a pleasant body. She had a great talent and appreciation for the bed, she was not pretty, but he liked her face, she read enormously, liked to ride and shoot and, certainly, she drank too much. Her husband had died when she was still a comparatively young woman and for a while she had devoted herself to her two just-grown children, who did not need her and were embarrassed at having her about, to her stable of horses, to books, and to bottles. She liked to read in the evening before dinner and she drank Scotch and soda while she read. By dinner she was fairly drunk and after a bottle of wine at dinner she was usually drunk enough to sleep.

That was before the lovers. After she had the lovers she did not drink so much because she did not have to be drunk to sleep. But the lovers bored her. She had been married to a man who had never bored her and these people bored her very much.

Then one of her two children was killed in a plane crash and after that was over she did not want the lovers, and drink being no anæsthetic she had to make another life. Suddenly, she had been acutely frightened of being alone. But she wanted some one that she respected with her.

It had begun very simply. She liked what he wrote and she had always envied the life he led. She thought he did exactly what he wanted to. The steps by which she had acquired him and the way in which she had finally fallen in love with him were all part of a regular progression in which she had built

herself a new life and he had traded away what remained of
his old life.

He had traded it for security, for comfort too, there was no
denying that, and for what else? He did not know. She would
have bought him anything he wanted. He knew that. She was
a damned nice woman too. He would as soon be in bed with
her as any one; rather with her, because she was richer, because she was very pleasant and appreciative and because she
never made scenes. And now this life that she had built again
was coming to a term because he had not used iodine two
weeks ago when a thorn had scratched his knee as they moved
forward trying to photograph a herd of waterbuck standing,
their heads up, peering while their nostrils searched the air,
their ears spread wide to hear the first noise that would send
them rushing into the bush. They had bolted, too, before he
got the picture.

Here she came now.

He turned his head on the cot to look toward her. "Hello,"
he said.

"I shot a Tommy ram," she told him. "He'll make you good
broth and I'll have them mash some potatoes with the Klim.
How do you feel?"

"Much better."

"Isn't that lovely? You know I thought perhaps you would.
You were sleeping when I left."

"I had a good sleep. Did you walk far?"

"No. Just around behind the hill. I made quite a good shot
on the Tommy."

"You shoot marvellously, you know."

"I love it. I've loved Africa. Really. If *you're* all right it's the
most fun that I've ever had. You don't know the fun it's
been to shoot with you. I've loved the country."

"I love it too."

"Darling, you don't know how marvellous it is to see you
feeling better. I couldn't stand it when you felt that way. You
won't talk to me like that again, will you? Promise me?"

"No," he said. "I don't remember what I said."

"You don't have to destroy me. Do you? I'm only a middle-aged woman who loves you and wants to do what you want to do. I've been destroyed two or three times already. You wouldn't want to destroy me again, would you?"

"I'd like to destroy you a few times in bed," he said.

"Yes. That's the good destruction. That's the way we're made to be destroyed. The plane will be here tomorrow."

"How do you know?"

"I'm sure. It's bound to come. The boys have the wood all ready and the grass to make the smudge. I went down and looked at it again today. There's plenty of room to land and we have the smudges ready at both ends."

"What makes you think it will come tomorrow?"

"I'm sure it will. It's overdue now. Then, in town, they will fix up your leg and then we will have some good destruction. Not that dreadful talking kind."

"Should we have a drink? The sun is down."

"Do you think you should?"

"I'm having one."

"We'll have one together. *Molo, letti dui whiskey-soda!*" she called.

"You'd better put on your mosquito boots," he told her.

"I'll wait till I bathe . . ."

While it grew dark they drank and just before it was dark and there was no longer enough light to shoot, a hyena crossed the open on his way around the hill.

"That bastard crosses there every night," the man said. "Every night for two weeks."

"He's the one makes the noise at night. I don't mind it. They're a filthy animal though."

Drinking together, with no pain now except the discomfort of lying in the one position, the boys lighting a fire, its shadow jumping on the tents, he could feel the return of acquiescence in this life of pleasant surrender. She *was* very good to him. He had been cruel and unjust in the afternoon. She was a fine woman, marvellous really. And just then it occurred to him that he was going to die.

It came with a rush; not as a rush of water nor of wind; but of a sudden evil-smelling emptiness and the odd thing was that the hyena slipped lightly along the edge of it.

"What is it, Harry?" she asked him.

"Nothing," he said. "You had better move over to the other side. To windward."

"Did Molo change the dressing?"

"Yes. I'm just using the boric now."

"How do you feel?"

"A little wobbly."

"I'm going in to bathe," she said. "I'll be right out. I'll eat with you and then we'll put the cot in."

So, he said to himself, we did well to stop the quarrelling. He had never quarrelled much with this woman, while with the women that he loved he had quarrelled so much they had finally, always, with the corrosion of the quarrelling, killed what they had together. He had loved too much, demanded too much, and he wore it all out.

He thought about alone in Constantinople that time, having quarrelled in Paris before he had gone out. He had whored the whole time and then, when that was over, and he had failed to kill his loneliness, but only made it worse, he had written her, the first one, the one who left him, a letter telling her how he had never been able to kill it. . . . How when he thought he saw her outside the Regence one time it made him go all faint and sick inside, and that he would follow a woman who looked like her in some way, along the Boulevard, afraid to see it was not she, afraid to lose the feeling it gave him. How every one he had slept with had only made him miss her more. How what she had done could never matter since he knew he could not cure himself of loving her. He wrote this letter at the Club, cold sober, and mailed it to New York asking her to write him at the office in Paris. That seemed safe. And that night missing her so much it made him feel hollow sick inside, he wandered up past Taxim's, picked a girl up and took her out to supper. He had gone to a place to dance with her afterward, she danced badly, and left her for a hot Armenian slut, that swung her belly against him so it almost scalded. He took her away from a British gunner subaltern after a row. The gunner asked him outside and they fought in the street on the cobbles in the dark. He'd hit him twice, hard, on the side of the jaw and when he didn't go down he knew he was in for a fight. The gunner hit him in the body, then beside his eye. He swung with his left again and landed and the gunner fell on him and grabbed his coat and tore the sleeve off and he clubbed him twice behind the ear and then smashed him with his right as he pushed him away. When the gunner went down his head hit first and he ran with the girl because they heard the M. P.'s coming. They got into a taxi and drove out to Rimmily Hissa along the Bosphorus, and around, and back in the cool night and went to bed and she felt as over-ripe as she looked but smooth, rose-petal, syrupy, smooth-bellied, big-breasted and needed no pillow under her buttocks, and he left her before she was awake looking blousy enough in the first daylight and turned up at the Pera Palace with a black eye, carrying his coat because one sleeve was missing.

That same night he left for Anatolia and he remembered, later on that trip, riding all day through fields of the poppies that they raised for opium and how strange it made you feel, finally, and all the distances seemed wrong, to where they had made the attack with the newly arrived Constantine officers, that did not know a god-damned thing, and the artillery had fired into the troops and the British observer had cried like a child.

That was the day he'd first seen dead men wearing white ballet skirts and upturned shoes with pompons on them. The Turks had come steadily and lumpily and he had seen the skirted men running and the officers shooting into them and running then themselves and he and the British observer had run too until his lungs ached and his mouth was full of the taste of pennies and they stopped behind some rocks and there were the Turks coming as lumpily as ever. Later he had seen the things that he could never think of and later still he had seen *much worse. So when he got back to Paris that time he could not talk about it or stand to have it mentioned. And there in the café as he passed was that American poet with a pile of saucers in front of him and a stupid look on his potato face talking about the Dada movement with a Roumanian who said his name was Tristan Tzara, who always wore a monocle and had a headache, and, back at the apartment with his wife that now he loved again, the quarrel all over, the madness all over, glad to be home, the office sent his mail up to the flat. So then the letter in answer to the one he'd written came in on a platter one morning and when he saw the handwriting he went cold all over and tried to slip the letter underneath another. But his wife said, "Who is that letter from, dear?" and that was the end of the beginning of that.*

He remembered the good times with them all, and the quarrels. They always picked the finest places to have the quarrels. And why had they always quarrelled when he was feeling best? He had never written any of that because, at first, he never wanted to hurt any one and then it seemed as though there was enough to write without it. But he had always thought that he would write it finally. There was so much to write. He had seen the world change; not just the events; although he had seen many of them and had watched the people, but he had seen the subtler change and he could remember how the people were at different times. He had been in it and he had watched it and it was his duty to write of it; but now he never would.

"How do you feel?" she said. She had come out from the tent now after her bath.

"All right."

"Could you eat now?" He saw Molo behind her with the folding table and the other boy with the dishes.

"I want to write," he said.

"You ought to take some broth to keep your strength up."

"I'm going to die tonight," he said. "I don't need my strength up."

"Don't be melodramatic, Harry, please," she said.

"Why don't you use your nose? I'm rotted half way up my thigh now. What the hell should I fool with broth for? Molo bring whiskey-soda."

"Please take the broth," she said gently.

"All right."

The broth was too hot. He had to hold it in the cup until it cooled enough to take it and then he just got it down without gagging.

"You're a fine woman," he said. "Don't pay any attention to me."

She looked at him with her well-known, well-loved face from *Spur* and *Town and Country,* only a little the worse for drink, only a little the worse for bed, but *Town and Country* never showed those good breasts and those useful thighs and those lightly small-of-back-caressing hands, and as he looked and saw her well known pleasant smile, he felt death come again. This time there was no rush. It was a puff, as of a wind that makes a candle flicker and the flame go tall.

"They can bring my net out later and hang it from the tree and build the fire up. I'm not going in the tent tonight. It's not worth moving. It's a clear night. There won't be any rain."

So this was how you died, in whispers that you did not hear. Well, there would be no more quarrelling. He could promise that. The one experience that he had never had he was not going to spoil now. He probably would. You spoiled everything. But perhaps he wouldn't.

"You can't take dictation, can you?"

"I never learned," she told him.

"That's all right."

There wasn't time, of course, although it seemed as though it telescoped so that you might put it all into one paragraph if you could get it right.

There was a log house, chinked white with mortar, on a hill above the lake. There was a bell on a pole by the door to call the people in to meals. Behind the house were fields and

behind the fields was the timber. A line of lombardy poplars
ran from the house to the dock. Other poplars ran along the
point. A road went up to the hills along the edge of the timber
and along that road he picked blackberries. Then that log
house was burned down and all the guns that had been on deer
foot racks above the open fire place were burned and afterwards their barrels, with the lead melted in the magazines, and
the stocks burned away, lay out on the heap of ashes that were
used to make lye for the big iron soap kettles, and you asked
Grandfather if you could have them to play with, and he said,
no. You see they were his guns still and he never bought any
others. Nor did he hunt any more. The house was rebuilt in
the same place out of lumber now and painted white and
from its porch you saw the poplars and the lake beyond; but
there were never any more guns. The barrels of the guns that
had hung on the deer feet on the wall of the log house lay out
there on the heap of ashes and no one ever touched them.

In the Black Forest, after the war, we rented a trout stream
and there were two ways to walk to it. One was down the valley from Triberg and around the valley road in the shade of
the trees that bordered the white road, and then up a side road
that went up through the hills past many small farms, with
the big Schwarzwald houses, until that road crossed the stream.
That was where our fishing began.

The other way was to climb steeply up to the edge of the
woods and then go across the top of the hills through the pine
woods, and then out to the edge of a meadow and down across
this meadow to the bridge. There were birches along the
stream and it was not big, but narrow, clear and fast, with
pools where it had cut under the roots of the birches. At the
Hotel in Triberg the proprietor had a fine season. It was very
pleasant and we were all great friends. The next year came the
inflation and the money he had made the year before was not
enough to buy supplies to open the hotel and he hanged himself.

You could dictate that, but you could not dictate the Place
Contrescarpe where the flower sellers dyed their flowers in the

street and the dye ran over the paving where the autobus
started and the old men and the women, always drunk on wine
and bad marc; and the children with their noses running in
the cold; the smell of dirty sweat and poverty and drunkenness
at the Café des Amateurs and the whores at the Bal Musette
they lived above. The Concierge who entertained the trooper
of the Garde Republicaine in her loge, his horse-hair-plumed
helmet on a chair. The locataire across the hall whose husband was a bicycle racer and her joy that morning at the
Cremerie when she had opened L'Auto and seen where he
placed third in Paris-Tours, his first big race. She had blushed
and laughed and then gone upstairs crying with the yellow
sporting paper in her hand. The husband of the woman who
ran the Bal Musette drove a taxi and when he, Harry, had to
take an early plane the husband knocked upon the door to
wake him and they each drank a glass of white wine at the
zinc of the bar before they started. He knew his neighbors in
that quarter then because they all were poor.

Around that Place there were two kinds; the drunkards and
the sportifs. The drunkards killed their poverty that way; the
sportifs took it out in exercise. They were the descendants of
the Communards and it was no struggle for them to know
their politics. They knew who had shot their fathers, their
relatives, their brothers, and their friends when the Versailles
troops came in and took the town after the Commune and
executed any one they could catch with calloused hands, or
who wore a cap, or carried any other sign he was a working
man. And in that poverty, and in that quarter across the street
from a Boucherie Chevaline and a wine co-operative he had
written the start of all he was to do. There never was another
part of Paris that he loved like that, the sprawling trees, the
old white plastered houses painted brown below, the long
green of the autobus in that round square, the purple flower
dye upon the paving, the sudden drop down the hill of the rue
Cardinal Lemoine to the River, and the other way the narrow
crowded world of the rue Mouffetard. The street that ran up
toward the Pantheon and the other that he always took with

the bicycle, the only asphalted street in all that quarter, smooth under the tires, with the high narrow houses and the cheap tall hotel where Paul Verlaine had died. There were only two rooms in the apartments where they lived and he had a room on the top floor of that hotel that cost him sixty francs a month where he did his writing, and from it he could see the roofs and chimney pots and all the hills of Paris.

From the apartment you could only see the wood and coal man's place. He sold wine too, bad wine. The golden horse's head outside the Boucherie Chevaline where the carcasses hung yellow gold and red in the open window, and the green painted co-operative where they bought their wine; good wine and cheap. The rest was plaster walls and the windows of the neighbors. The neighbors who, at night, when some one lay drunk in the street, moaning and groaning in that typical French ivresse that you were propaganded to believe did not exist, would open their windows and then the murmur of talk.

"Where is the policeman? When you don't want him the bugger is always there. He's sleeping with come concierge. Get the Agent." Till some one threw a bucket of water from a window and the moaning stopped. "What's that? Water. Ah, that's intelligent." And the windows shutting. Marie, his femme de menage, protesting against the eight-hour day saying, "If a husband works until six he gets only a little drunk on the way home and does not waste too much. If he works only until five he is drunk every night and one has no money. It is the wife of the working man who suffers from this shortening of hours."

"Wouldn't you like some more broth?" the woman asked him now.

"No, thank you very much. It is awfully good."

"Try just a little."

"I would like a whiskey-soda."

"It's not good for you."

"No. It's bad for me. Cole Porter wrote the words and the music. This knowledge that you're going mad for me."

"You know I like you to drink."

"Oh yes. Only it's bad for me."

When she goes, he thought. I'll have all I want. Not all I want but all there is. Ayee he was tired. Too tired. He was going to sleep a little while. He lay still and death was not there. It must have gone around another street. It went in pairs, on bicycles, and moved absolutely silently on the pavements.

No, he had never written about Paris. Not the Paris that he cared about. But what about the rest that he had never written?

What about the ranch and the silvered gray of the sage brush, the quick, clear water in the irrigation ditches, and the heavy green of the alfalfa. The trail went up into the hills and the cattle in the summer were shy as deer. The bawling and the steady noise and slow moving mass raising a dust as you brought them down in the fall. And behind the mountains, the clear sharpness of the peak in the evening light and, riding down along the trail in the moonlight, bright across the valley. Now he remembered coming down through the timber in the dark holding the horse's tail when you could not see and all the stories that he meant to write.

About the half-wit chore boy who was left at the ranch that time and told not to let any one get any hay, and that old bastard from the Forks who had beaten the boy when he had worked for him stopping to get some feed. The boy refusing and the old man saying he would beat him again. The boy got the rifle from the kitchen and shot him when he tried to come into the barn and when they came back to the ranch he'd been dead a week, frozen in the corral, and the dogs had eaten part of him. But what was left you packed on a sled wrapped in a blanket and roped on and you got the boy to help you haul it, and the two of you took it out over the road on skis, and sixty miles down to town to turn the boy over. He having no idea that he would be arrested. Thinking he had done his duty and that you were his friend and he would be rewarded. He'd

helped to haul the old man in so everybody could know how
bad the old man had been and how he'd tried to steal some feed
that didn't belong to him, and when the sheriff put the hand-
cuffs on the boy he couldn't believe it. Then he'd started to
cry. That was one story he had saved to write. He knew at least
twenty good stories from out there and he had never written
one. Why?

"You tell them why," he said.

"Why what, dear?"

"Why nothing."

She didn't drink so much, now, since she had him. But if he
lived he would never write about her, he knew that now. Nor
about any of them. The rich were dull and they drank too
much, or they played too much backgammon. They were dull
and they were repetitious. He remembered poor Julian and his
romantic awe of them and how he had started a story once that
began, "The very rich are different from you and me." And
how some one had said to Julian, Yes, they have more money.
But that was not humorous to Julian. He thought they were
a special glamourous race and when he found they weren't
it wrecked him just as much as any other thing that wrecked
him.

He had been contemptuous of those who wrecked. You did
not have to like it because you understood it. He could beat
anything, he thought, because no thing could hurt him if he
did not care.

All right. Now he would not care for death. One thing he
had always dreaded was the pain. He could stand pain as well
as any man, until it went on too long, and wore him out, but
here he had something that had hurt frightfully and just when
he had felt it breaking him, the pain had stopped.

He remembered long ago when Williamson, the bombing
officer, had been hit by a stick bomb some one in a German
patrol had thrown as he was coming in through the wire that
night and, screaming, had begged every one to kill him. He

was a fat man, very brave, and a good officer, although addicted to fantastic shows. But that night he was caught in the wire, with a flare lighting him up and his bowels spilled out into the wire, so when they brought him in, alive, they had to cut him loose. Shoot me, Harry. For Christ sake shoot me. They had had an argument one time about our Lord never sending you anything you could not bear and some one's theory had been that meant that at a certain time the pain passed you out automatically. But he had always remembered Williamson, that night. Nothing passed out Williamson until he gave him all his morphine tablets that he had always saved to use himself and then they did not work right away.

Still this now, that he had, was very easy; and if it was no worse as it went on there was nothing to worry about. Except that he would rather be in better company.

He thought a little about the company that he would like to have.

No, he thought, when everything you do, you do too long, and do too late, you can't expect to find the people still there. The people all are gone. The party's over and you are with your hostess now.

I'm getting as bored with dying as with everything else, he thought.

"It's a bore," he said out loud.

"What is, my dear?"

"Anything you do too bloody long."

He looked at her face between him and the fire. She was leaning back in the chair and the firelight shone on her pleasantly lined face and he could see that she was sleepy. He heard the hyena make a noise just outside the range of the fire.

"I've been writing," he said. "But I got tired."

"Do you think you will be able to sleep?"

"Pretty sure. Why don't you turn in?"

"I like to sit here with you."

"Do you feel anything strange?" he asked her.

"No. Just a little sleepy."

"I do," he said.

He had just felt death come by again.

"You know the only thing I've never lost is curiosity," he said to her.

"You've never lost anything. You're the most complete man I've ever known."

"Christ," he said. "How little a woman knows. What is that? Your intuition?"

Because, just then, death had come and rested its head on the foot of the cot and he could smell its breath.

"Never believe any of that about a scythe and a skull," he told her. "It can be two bicycle policemen as easily, or be a bird. Or it can have a wide snout like a hyena."

It had moved up on him now, but it had no shape any more. It simply occupied space.

"Tell it to go away."

It did not go away but moved a little closer.

"You've got a hell of a breath," he told it. "You stinking bastard."

It moved up closer to him still and now he could not speak to it, and when it saw he could not speak it came a little closer, and now he tried to send it away without speaking, but it moved in on him so its weight was all upon his chest, and while it crouched there and he could not move, or speak, he heard the woman say, "Bwana is asleep now. Take the cot up very gently and carry it into the tent."

He could not speak to tell her to make it go away and it crouched now, heavier, so he could not breathe. And then, while they lifted the cot, suddenly it was all right and the weight went from his chest.

It was morning and had been morning for some time and he heard the plane. It showed very tiny and then made a wide circle and the boys ran out and lit the fires, using kerosene, and piled on grass so there were two big smudges at each end of the level place and the morning breeze blew them toward the camp and the plane circled twice more, low this time, and then glided down and levelled off and landed smoothly and, coming walking toward him, was old Compton in slacks, a tweed jacket and a brown felt hat.

"What's the matter, old cock?" Compton said.

"Bad leg," he told him. "Will you have some breakfast?"

"Thanks. I'll just have some tea. It's the Puss Moth you know. I won't be able to take the Memsahib. There's only room for one. Your lorry is on the way."

Helen had taken Compton aside and was speaking to him. Compton came back more cheery than ever.

"We'll get you right in," he said. "I'll be back for the Mem. Now I'm afraid I'll have to stop at Arusha to refuel. We'd better get going."

"What about the tea?"

"I don't really care about it you know."

The boys had picked up the cot and carried it around the green tents and down along the rock and out onto the plain and along past the smudges that were burning brightly now, the grass all consumed, and the wind fanning the fire, to the little plane. It was difficult getting him in, but once in he lay back in the leather seat, and the leg was stuck straight out to one side of the seat where Compton sat. Compton started the motor and got in. He waved to Helen and to the boys and, as the clatter moved into the old familiar roar, they swung around with Compie watching for wart-hog holes and roared, bumping, along the stretch between the fires and with the last bump rose and he saw them all standing below, waving, and the camp beside the hill, flattening now, and the plain spreading, clumps of trees, and the bush flattening, while the game trails ran now smoothly to the dry waterholes, and there was a new water that he had never known of. The zebra, small rounded backs now, and the wildebeeste, big-headed dots seeming to climb as they moved in long fingers across the plain, now scattering as the shadow came toward them, they were tiny now, and the movement had no gallop, and the plain as far as you could see, gray-yellow now and ahead old Compie's tweed back and the brown felt hat. Then they were over the first hills and the wildebeeste were trailing up them, and then they were over mountains with sudden depths of green-rising forest and the solid bamboo slopes, and then the heavy forest again, sculptured into peaks and hollows until they crossed, and hills sloped down and then another plain, hot now, and purple brown, bumpy with heat and Compie looking back to see how he was riding. Then there were other mountains dark ahead.

And then instead of going on to Arusha they turned left, he evidently figured that they had the gas, and looking down he saw a pink sifting cloud, moving over the ground, and in the air, like the first snow in a blizzard, that comes from nowhere, and he knew the locusts were coming up from the South. Then they began to climb and they were going to the East it seemed, and then it darkened and they were in a storm, the rain so thick it seemed like flying through a waterfall, and then they were out and Compie turned his head and grinned and pointed and there, ahead, all he could see, as wide as all the world, great, high, and unbelievably white in the sun, was the square top of Kilimanjaro. And then he knew that there was where he was going.

Just then the hyena stopped whimpering in the night and started to make a strange, human, almost crying sound. The woman heard it and stirred uneasily. She did not wake. In her dream she was at the house on Long Island and it was the night before her daughter's début. Somehow her father was there and he had been very rude. Then the noise the hyena made was so loud she woke and for a moment she did not know where she was and she was very afraid. Then she took the flashlight and shone it on the other cot that they had carried in after Harry had gone to sleep. She could see his bulk under the mosquito bar but somehow he had gotten his leg out and it hung down alongside the cot. The dressings had all come down and she could not look at it.

"Molo," she called, "Molo! Molo!"

Then she said, "Harry, Harry!" Then her voice rising, "Harry! Please, Oh Harry!"

There was no answer and she could not hear him breathing.

Outside the tent the hyena made the same strange noise that had awakened her. But she did not hear him for the beating of her heart.

A CLEAN, WELL–LIGHTED PLACE

It was late and every one had left the café except an old man who sat in the shadow the leaves of the tree made against the electric light. In the day time the street was dusty, but at night the dew settled the dust and the old man liked to sit late because he was deaf and now at night it was quiet and he felt the difference. The two waiters inside the café knew that the old man was a little drunk, and while he was a good client they knew that if he became too drunk he would leave without paying, so they kept watch on him.

"Last week he tried to commit suicide," one waiter said.

"Why?"

"He was in despair."

"What about?"

"Nothing."

"How do you know it was nothing?"

"He has plenty of money."

They sat together at a table that was close against the wall near the door of the café and looked at the terrace where the tables were all empty except where the old man sat in the shadow of the leaves of the tree that moved slightly in the wind. A girl and a soldier went by in the street. The street light shone on the brass number on his collar. The girl wore no head covering and hurried beside him.

"The guard will pick him up," one waiter said.

"What does it matter if he gets what he's after?"

"He had better get off the street now. The guard will get him. They went by five minutes ago."

The old man sitting in the shadow rapped on his saucer with his glass. The younger waiter went over to him.

"What do you want?"

The old man looked at him. "Another brandy," he said.

"You'll be drunk," the waiter said. The old man looked at him. The waiter went away.

29

"He'll stay all night," he said to his colleague. "I'm sleepy now. I never get into bed before three o'clock. He should have killed himself last week."

The waiter took the brandy bottle and another saucer from the counter inside the café and marched out to the old man's table. He put down the saucer and poured the glass full of brandy.

"You should have killed yourself last week," he said to the deaf man. The old man motioned with his finger. "A little more," he said. The waiter poured on into the glass so that the brandy slopped over and ran down the stem into the top saucer of the pile. "Thank you," the old man said. The waiter took the bottle back inside the café. He sat down at the table with his colleague again.

"He's drunk now," he said.

"He's drunk every night."

"What did he want to kill himself for?"

"How should I know."

"How did he do it?"

"He hung himself with a rope."

"Who cut him down?"

"His niece."

"Why did they do it?"

"Fear for his soul."

"How much money has he got?"

"He's got plenty."

"He must be eighty years old."

"Anyway I should say he was eighty."

"I wish he would go home. I never get to bed before three o'clock. What kind of hour is that to go to bed?"

"He stays up because he likes it."

"He's lonely. I'm not lonely. I have a wife waiting in bed for me."

"He had a wife once too."

"A wife would be no good to him now."

"You can't tell. He might be better with a wife."

"His niece looks after him. You said she cut him down."

"I know."

"I wouldn't want to be that old. An old man is a nasty thing."

"Not always. This old man is clean. He drinks without spilling. Even now, drunk. Look at him."

"I don't want to look at him. I wish he would go home. He has no regard for those who must work."

The old man looked from his glass across the square, then over at the waiters.

"Another brandy," he said, pointing to his glass. The waiter who was in a hurry came over.

"Finished," he said, speaking with that omission of syntax stupid people employ when talking to drunken people or foreigners. "No more tonight. Close now."

"Another," said the old man.

"No. Finished." The waiter wiped the edge of the table with a towel and shook his head.

The old man stood up, slowly counted the saucers, took a leather coin purse from his pocket and paid for the drinks, leaving half a peseta tip.

The waiter watched him go down the street, a very old man walking unsteadily but with dignity.

"Why didn't you let him stay and drink?" the unhurried waiter asked. They were putting up the shutters. "It is not half-past two."

"I want to go home to bed."

"What is an hour?"

"More to me than to him."

"An hour is the same."

"You talk like an old man yourself. He can buy a bottle and drink at home."

"It's not the same."

"No, it is not," agreed the waiter with a wife. He did not wish to be unjust. He was only in a hurry.

"And you? You have no fear of going home before your usual hour?"

"Are you trying to insult me?"

"No, hombre, only to make a joke."

"No," the waiter who was in a hurry said, rising from pulling down the metal shutters. "I have confidence. I am all confidence."

"You have youth, confidence, and a job," the older waiter said. "You have everything."

"And what do you lack?"

"Everything but work."

"You have everything I have."

"No. I have never had confidence and I am not young."

"Come on. Stop talking nonsense and lock up."

"I am of those who like to stay late at the café," the older waiter said. "With all those who do not want to go to bed. With all those who need a light for the night."

"I want to go home and into bed."

"We are of two different kinds," the older waiter said. He was now dressed to go home. "It is not only a question of youth and confidence although those things are very beautiful. Each night I am reluctant to close up because there may be some one who needs the café."

"Hombre, there are bodegas open all night long."

"You do not understand. This is a clean and pleasant café. It is well lighted. The light is very good and also, now, there are shadows of the leaves."

"Good night," said the younger waiter.

"Good night," the other said. Turning off the electric light he continued the conversation with himself. It is the light of course but it is necessary that the place be clean and pleasant. You do not want music. Certainly you do not want music. Nor can you stand before a bar with dignity although that is all that is provided for these hours. What did he fear? It was not fear or dread. It was a nothing that he knew too well. It was all a nothing and a man was nothing too. It was only that and light was all it needed and a certain cleanness and order. Some lived in it and never felt it but he knew it all was nada y pues nada y nada y pues nada. Our nada who art in nada, nada be thy name thy kingdom nada thy will be nada in nada as it is in nada. Give us this nada our daily nada and nada us our nada as we nada our nadas and nada us not into nada but deliver us from nada;

pues nada. Hail nothing full of nothing, nothing is with thee. He smiled and stood before a bar with a shining steam pressure coffee machine.

"What's yours?" asked the barman.

"Nada."

"Otro loco mas," said the barman and turned away.

"A little cup," said the waiter.

The barman poured it for him.

"The light is very bright and pleasant but the bar is unpolished," the waiter said.

The barman looked at him but did not answer. It was too late at night for conversation.

"You want another copita?" the barman asked.

"No, thank you," said the waiter and went out. He disliked bars and bodegas. A clean, well-lighted café was a very different thing. Now, without thinking further, he would go home to his room. He would lie in the bed and finally, with daylight, he would go to sleep. After all, he said to himself, it is probably only insomnia. Many must have it.

HE CAME into the room to shut the windows while we were still in bed and I saw he looked ill. He was shivering, his face was white, and he walked slowly as though it ached to move.

"What's the matter, Schatz?"

"I've got a headache."

"You better go back to bed."

"No. I'm all right."

"You go to bed. I'll see you when I'm dressed."

But when I came downstairs he was dressed, sitting by the fire, looking a very sick and miserable boy of nine years. When I put my hand on his forehead I knew he had a fever.

"You go up to bed," I said, "you're sick."

"I'm all right," he said.

When the doctor came he took the boy's temperature.

"What is it?" I asked him.

"One hundred and two."

Downstairs, the doctor left three different medicines in different colored capsules with instructions for giving them. One was to bring down the fever, another a purgative, the third to overcome an acid condition. The germs of influenza can only exist in an acid condition, he explained. He seemed to know all about influenza and said there was nothing to worry about if the fever did not go above one hundred and four degrees. This was a light epidemic of flu and there was no danger if you avoided pneumonia.

Back in the room I wrote the boy's temperature down and made a note of the time to give the various capsules.

"Do you want me to read to you?"

"All right. If you want to," said the boy. His face was very white and there were dark areas under his eyes. He lay still in the bed and seemed very detached from what was going on.

I read aloud from Howard Pyle's *Book of Pirates;* but I could see he was not following what I was reading.

"How do you feel, Schatz?" I asked him.

"Just the same, so far," he said.

I sat at the foot of the bed and read to myself while I waited for it to be time to give another capsule. It would have been natural for him to go to sleep, but when I looked up he was looking at the foot of the bed, looking very strangely.

"Why don't you try to go to sleep? I'll wake you up for the medicine."

"I'd rather stay awake."

After a while he said to me, "You don't have to stay in here with me, Papa, if it bothers you."

"It doesn't bother me."

"No, I mean you don't have to stay if it's going to bother you."

I thought perhaps he was a little lightheaded and after giving him the prescribed capsules at eleven o'clock I went out for a while.

It was a bright, cold day, the ground covered with a sleet that had frozen so that it seemed as if all the bare trees, the bushes, the cut brush and all the grass and the bare ground had been varnished with ice. I took the young Irish setter for a little walk up the road and along a frozen creek, but it was difficult to stand or walk on the glassy surface and the red dog slipped and slithered and I fell twice, hard, once dropping my gun and having it slide away over the ice.

We flushed a covey of quail under a high clay bank with overhanging brush and I killed two as they went out of sight over the top of the bank. Some of the covey lit in trees, but most of them scattered into brush piles and it was necessary to jump on the ice-coated mounds of brush several times before they would flush. Coming out while you were poised unsteadily on the icy, springy brush they made difficult shooting and I killed two, missed five, and started back pleased to have found a covey close to the house and happy there were so many left to find on another day.

At the house they said the boy had refused to let any one come into the room.

"You can't come in," he said. "You mustn't get what I have."

I went up to him and found him in exactly the position I had left him, white-faced, but with the tops of his cheeks flushed by the fever, staring still, as he had stared, at the foot of the bed.

I took his temperature.

"What is it?"

"Something like a hundred," I said. It was one hundred and two and four tenths.

"It was a hundred and two," he said.

"Who said so?"

"The doctor."

"Your temperature is all right," I said. "It's nothing to worry about."

"I don't worry," he said, "but I can't keep from thinking."

"Don't think," I said. "Just take it easy."

"I'm taking it easy," he said and looked straight ahead. He was evidently holding tight onto himself about something.

"Take this with water."

"Do you think it will do any good?"

"Of course it will."

I sat down and opened the *Pirate* book and commenced to read, but I could see he was not following, so I stopped.

"About what time do you think I'm going to die?" he asked.

"What?"

"About how long will it be before I die?"

"You aren't going to die. What's the matter with you?"

"Oh, yes, I am. I heard him say a hundred and two."

"People don't die with a fever of one hundred and two. That's a silly way to talk."

"I know they do. At school in France the boys told me you can't live with forty-four degrees. I've got a hundred and two."

He had been waiting to die all day, ever since nine o'clock in the morning.

"You poor Schatz," I said. "Poor old Schatz. It's like miles and kilometers. You aren't going to die. That's a different thermometer. On that thermometer thirty-seven is normal. On this kind it's ninety-eight."

"Are you sure?"

"Absolutely," I said. "It's like miles and kilometers. You know, like how many kilometers we make when we do seventy miles in the car?"

"Oh," he said.

But his gaze at the foot of the bed relaxed slowly. The hold over himself relaxed too, finally, and the next day it was very slack and he cried very easily at little things that were of no importance.

THE GAMBLER, THE NUN, AND THE RADIO

THEY BROUGHT them in around midnight and then, all night long, every one along the corridor heard the Russian.

"Where is he shot?" Mr. Frazer asked the night nurse.

"In the thigh, I think."

"What about the other one?"

"Oh, he's going to die, I'm afraid."

"Where is he shot?"

"Twice in the abdomen. They only found one of the bullets."

They were both beet workers, a Mexican and a Russian, and they were sitting drinking coffee in an all-night restaurant when some one came in the door and started shooting at the Mexican. The Russian crawled under a table and was hit, finally, by a stray shot fired at the Mexican as he lay on the floor with two bullets in his abdomen. That was what the paper said.

The Mexican told the police he had no idea who shot him. He believed it to be an accident.

"An accident that he fired eight shots at you and hit you twice, there?"

"Si, señor," said the Mexican, who was named Cayetano Ruiz.

"An accident that he hit me at all, the cabron," he said to the interpreter.

"What does he say?" asked the detective sergeant, looking across the bed at the interpreter.

"He says it was an accident."

"Tell him to tell the truth, that he is going to die," the detective said.

"Na," said Cayetano. "But tell him that I feel very sick and would prefer not to talk so much."

"He says that he is telling the truth," the interpreter said. Then, speaking confidently, to the detective, "He don't know who shot him. They shot him in the back."

"Yes," said the detective. "I understand that, but why did the bullets all go in the front?"

"Maybe he is spinning around," said the interpreter.

"Listen," said the detective, shaking his finger almost at Caye-tano's nose, which projected, waxen yellow, from his dead-man's face in which his eyes were alive as a hawk's. "I don't give a damn who shot you, but I've got to clear this thing up. Don't you want the man who shot you to be punished? Tell him that," he said to the interpreter.

"He says to tell who shot you."

"Mandarlo al carajo," said Cayetano, who was very tired.

"He says he never saw the fellow at all," the interpreter said. "I tell you straight they shot him in the back."

"Ask him who shot the Russian."

"Poor Russian," said Cayetano. "He was on the floor with his head enveloped in his arms. He started to give cries when they shoot him and he is giving cries ever since. Poor Russian."

"He says some fellow that he doesn't know. Maybe the same fellow that shot him."

"Listen," the detective said. "This isn't Chicago. You're not a gangster. You don't have to act like a moving picture. It's all right to tell who shot you. Anybody would tell who shot them. That's all right to do. Suppose you don't tell who he is and he shoots somebody else. Suppose he shoots a woman or a child. You can't let him get away with that. You tell him," he said to Mr. Frazer. "I don't trust that damn interpreter."

"I am very reliable," the interpreter said. Cayetano looked at Mr. Frazer.

"Listen, amigo," said Mr. Frazer. "The policeman says that we are not in Chicago but in Hailey, Montana. You are not a bandit and this has nothing to do with the cinema."

"I believe him," said Cayetano softly. "Ya lo creo."

"One can, with honor, denounce one's assailant. Every one does it here, he says. He says what happens if after shooting you, this man shoots a woman or a child?"

"I am not married," Cayetano said.

"He says any woman, any child."

"The man is not crazy," Cayetano said.

"He says you should denounce him," Mr. Frazer finished.

"Thank you," Cayetano said. "You are of the great translators. I speak English, but badly. I understand it all right. How did you break your leg?"

"A fall off a horse."

"What bad luck. I am very sorry. Does it hurt much?"

"Not now. At first, yes."

"Listen, amigo," Cayetano began, "I am very weak. You will pardon me. Also I have much pain; enough pain. It is very possible that I die. Please get this policeman out of here because I am very tired." He made as though to roll to one side; then held himself still.

"I told him everything exactly as you said and he said to tell you, truly, that he doesn't know who shot him and that he is very weak and wishes you would question him later on," Mr. Frazer said.

"He'll probably be dead later on."

"That's quite possible."

"That's why I want to question him now."

"Somebody shot him in the back, I tell you," the interpreter said.

"Oh, for Chrisake," the detective sergeant said, and put his notebook in his pocket.

Outside in the corridor the detective sergeant stood with the interpreter beside Mr. Frazer's wheeled chair.

"I suppose you think somebody shot him in the back too?"

"Yes," Frazer said. "Somebody shot him in the back. What's it to you?"

"Don't get sore," the sergeant said. "I wish I could talk spick."

"Why don't you learn?"

"You don't have to get sore. I don't get any fun out of asking that spick questions. If I could talk spick it would be different."

"You don't need to talk Spanish," the interpreter said. "I am a very reliable interpreter."

"Oh, for Chrisake," the sergeant said. "Well, so long. I'll come up and see you."

"Thanks. I'm always in."

"I guess you are all right. That was bad luck all right. Plenty bad luck."

"It's coming along good now since he spliced the bone."

"Yes, but it's a long time. A long, long time."

"Don't let anybody shoot you in the back."

"That's right," he said. "That's right. Well, I'm glad you're not sore."

"So long," said Mr. Frazer.

Mr. Frazer did not see Cayetano again for a long time, but each morning Sister Cecilia brought news of him. He was so uncomplaining she said and he was very bad now. He had peritonitis and they thought he could not live. Poor Cayetano, she said. He had such beautiful hands and such a fine face and he never complains. The odor, now, was really terrific. He would point toward his nose with one finger and smile and shake his head, she said. He felt badly about the odor. It embarrassed him, Sister Cecilia said. Oh, he was such a fine patient. He always smiled. He wouldn't go to confession to Father but he promised to say his prayers, and not a Mexican had been to see him since he had been brought in. The Russian was going out at the end of the week. I could never feel anything about the Russian, Sister Cecilia said. Poor fellow, he suffered too. It was a greased bullet and dirty and the wound infected, but he made so much noise and then I always like the bad ones. That Cayetano, he's a bad one. Oh, he must really be a bad one, a thoroughly bad one, he's so fine and delicately made and he's never done any work with his hands. He's not a beet worker. I know he's not a beet worker. His hands are as smooth and not a callous on them. I know he's a bad one of some sort. I'm going down and pray for him now. Poor Cayetano, he's having a dreadful time and he doesn't make a sound. What did they have to shoot him for? Oh, that poor Cayetano! I'm going right down and pray for him.

She went right down and prayed for him.

In that hospital a radio did not work very well until it was dusk. They said it was because there was so much ore in the ground or something about the mountains, but anyway it did not work well at all until it began to get dark outside; but all night it worked beautifully and when one station stopped you could go farther west and pick up another. The last one that you could get was Seattle, Washington, and due to the difference in time, when they signed off at four o'clock in the morning it was five o'clock in the morning in the hospital; and at six o'clock you could get the morning revellers in Minneapolis. That was on account of the difference in time, too, and Mr. Frazer used to like to think of the morning revellers arriving at the studio and picture how they would look getting off a street car before daylight in the morning carrying their instruments. Maybe that was wrong and they kept their instruments at the place they revelled, but he always pictured them with their instruments. He had never been in Minneapolis and believed he probably would never go there, but he knew what it looked like that early in the morning.

Out of the window of the hospital you could see a field with tumbleweed coming out of the snow, and a bare clay butte. One morning the doctor wanted to show Mr. Frazer two pheasants that were out there in the snow, and pulling the bed toward the window, the reading light fell off the iron bedstead and hit Mr. Frazer on the head. This does not sound so funny now but it was very funny then. Every one was looking out the window, and the doctor, who was a most excellent doctor, was pointing at the pheasants and pulling the bed toward the window, and then just as in a comic section, Mr. Frazer was knocked out by the leaded base of the lamp hitting the top of his head. It seemed the antithesis of healing or whatever people were in the hospital for, and every one thought it was very funny, as a joke on Mr. Frazer and on the doctor. Everything is much simpler in a hospital, including the jokes.

From the other window, if the bed was turned, you could see the town, with a little smoke above it, and the Dawson mountains looking like real mountains with the winter snow on them. Those were the two views since the wheeled chair had proved to be premature. It is really best to be in bed if you are in a hospital; since two views, with time to observe them, from a room the temperature of which you control, are much better than any number of views seen for a few minutes from hot, empty rooms that are waiting for some one else, or just abandoned, which you are wheeled in and out of. If you stay long enough in a room the view, whatever it is, acquires a great value and becomes very important and you would not change it, not even by a different angle. Just as, with the radio, there are certain things that you become fond of, and you welcome them and resent the new things. The best tunes they had that winter were "Sing Something Simple," "Singsong Girl," and "Little White Lies." No other tunes were as satisfactory, Mr. Frazer felt. "Betty Co-ed" was a good tune too, but the parody of the words which came unavoidably into Mr. Frazer's mind, grew so steadily and increasingly obscene that there being no one to appreciate it, he finally abandoned it and let the song go back to football.

About nine o'clock in the morning they would start using the X-ray machine, and then the radio, which, by then, was only getting Hailey, became useless. Many people in Hailey who owned radios protested about the hospital's X-ray machine which ruined their morning reception, but there was never any action taken, although many felt it was a shame the hospital could not use their machine at a time when people were not using their radios.

About the time when it became necessary to turn off the radio Sister Cecilia came in.

"How's Cayetano, Sister Cecilia?" Mr. Frazer asked.

"Oh, he's very bad."

"Is he out of his head?"

"No, but I'm afraid he's going to die."

"How are you?"

"I'm very worried about him, and do you know that absolutely no one has come to see him? He could die just like a dog for all those Mexicans care. They're really dreadful."

"Do you want to come up and hear the game this afternoon?"

"Oh, no," she said. "I'd be too excited. I'll be in the chapel praying."

"We ought to be able to hear it pretty well," Mr. Frazer said. "They're playing out on the coast and the difference in time will bring it late enough so we can get it all right."

"How many tubes has the radio?" asked the one who did not drink.

"Seven."

"Very beautiful," he said. "What does it cost?"

"I don't know," Mr. Frazer said. "It is rented."

"You gentlemen are friends of Cayetano?"

"No," said the big one. "We are friends of he who wounded him."

"We were sent here by the police," the smallest one said.

"We have a little place," the big one said. "He and I," indicating the one who did not drink. "He has a little place too," indicating the small, dark one. "The police tell us we have to come—so we come."

"I am very happy you have come."

"Equally," said the big one.

"Will you have another little cup?"

"Why not?" said the big one.

"With your permission," said the smallest one.

"Not me," said the thin one. "It mounts to my head."

"It is very good," said the smallest one.

"Why not try some," Mr. Frazer asked the thin one. "Let a little mount to your head."

"Afterwards comes the headache," said the thin one.

"Could you not send friends of Cayetano to see him?" Frazer asked.

"He has no friends."

"Every man has friends."

"This one, no."

"What does he do?"

"He is a card-player."

"Is he good?"

"I believe it."

"From me," said the smallest one, "he won one hundred and eighty dollars. Now there is no longer one hundred and eighty dollars in the world."

"From me," said the thin one, "he won two hundred and eleven dollars. Fix yourself on that figure."

"I never played with him," said the fat one.

"He must be very rich," Mr. Frazer suggested.

"He is poorer than we," said the little Mexican. "He has no more than the shirt on his back."

"And that shirt is of little value now," Mr. Frazer said. "Perforated as it is."

"Clearly."

"The one who wounded him was a card-player?"

"No, a beet worker. He has had to leave town."

"Fix yourself on this," said the smallest one. "He was the best guitar player ever in this town. The finest."

"What a shame."

"I believe it," said the biggest one. "How he could touch the guitar."

"There are no good guitar players left?"

"Not the shadow of a guitar player."

"There is an accordion player who is worth something," the thin man said.

"There are a few who touch various instruments," the big one said. "You like music?"

"How would I not?"

"We will come one night with music? You think the sister would allow it? She seems very amiable."

"I am sure she would permit it when Cayetano is able to hear it."

"Is she a little crazy?" asked the thin one.

"Who?"

"That sister."

"No," Mr. Frazer said. "She is a fine woman of great intelligence and sympathy."

"I distrust all priests, monks, and sisters," said the thin one.

"He had bad experiences when a boy," the smallest one said.

"I was acolyte," the thin one said proudly. "Now I believe in nothing. Neither do I go to mass."

"Why? Does it mount to your head?"

"No," said the thin one. "It is alcohol that mounts to my head. Religion is the opium of the poor."

"I thought marijuana was the opium of the poor," Frazer said.

"Did you ever smoke opium?" the big one asked.

"No."

"Nor I," he said. "It seems it is very bad. One commences and cannot stop. It is a vice."

"Like religion," said the thin one.

"This one," said the smallest Mexican, "is very strong against religion."

"It is necessary to be very strong against something," Mr. Frazer said politely.

"I respect those who have faith even though they are ignorant," the thin one said.

"Good," said Mr. Frazer.

"What can we bring you?" asked the big Mexican. "Do you lack for anything?"

"I would be glad to buy some beer if there is good beer."

"We will bring beer."

"Another copita before you go?"

"It is very good."

"We are robbing you."

"I can't take it. It goes to my head. Then I have a bad headache and sick at the stomach."

"Good-by, gentlemen."

"Good-by and thanks."

They went out and there was supper and then the radio, turned to be as quiet as possible and still be heard, and the stations finally signing off in this order: Denver, Salt Lake City, Los Angeles, and Seattle. Mr. Frazer received no picture of Denver from the radio. He could see Denver from the *Denver Post*, and correct the picture from *The Rocky Mountain News*. Nor did he ever have any feel of Salt Lake City or Los Angeles from what he heard from those places. All he felt about Salt Lake City was that it was clean, but dull, and there were too many ballrooms mentioned in too many big hotels for him to see Los Angeles. He could not feel it for the ballrooms. But Seattle he came to know very well, the taxicab company with the big white cabs (each cab equipped with radio itself) he rode in every night out to the roadhouse on the Canadian side where he followed the course of parties by the musical selections they phoned for.

He lived in Seattle from two o'clock on, each night, hearing the pieces that all the different people asked for, and it was as real as Minneapolis, where the revellers left their beds each morning to make that trip down to the studio. Mr. Frazer grew very fond of Seattle, Washington.

The Mexicans came and brought beer but it was not good beer. Mr. Frazer saw them but he did not feel like talking, and when they went he knew they would not come again. His nerves had become tricky and he disliked seeing people while he was in this condition. His nerves went bad at the end of five weeks, and while he was pleased they lasted that long yet he resented being forced to make the same experiment when he already knew the answer. Mr. Frazer had been through this all before. The only thing which was new to him was the radio. He played it all night long, turned so low he could barely hear it, and he was learning to listen to it without thinking.

Sister Cecilia came into the room about ten o'clock in the morning on that day and brought the mail. She was very handsome, and Mr. Frazer liked to see her and to hear her talk, but the mail, supposedly coming from a different world, was more important. However, there was nothing in the mail of any interest.

"You look *so* much better," she said. "You'll be leaving us soon."

"Yes," Mr. Frazer said. "You look very happy this morning."

"Oh, I am. This morning I feel as though I might be a saint."

Mr. Frazer was a little taken aback at this.

"Yes," Sister Cecilia went on. "That's what I want to be. A saint. Ever since I was a little girl I've wanted to be a saint. When I was a girl I thought if I renounced the world and went into the convent I would be a saint. That was what I wanted to be and that was what I thought I had to do to be one. I expected I would be a saint. I was absolutely sure I would be one. For just a moment I thought I was one. I was so happy and it seemed so simple and easy. When I awoke in the morning I expected I would be a saint, but I wasn't. I've never become one. I want so to be one. All I want is to be a saint. That is all I've ever wanted. And this morning I feel as though I might be one. Oh, I hope I will get to be one."

"You'll be one. Everybody gets what they want. That's what they always tell me."

"I don't know now. When I was a girl it seemed so simple. I knew I would be a saint. Only I believed it took time when I found it did not happen suddenly. Now it seems almost impossible."

"I'd say you had a good chance."

"Do you really think so? No, I don't want just to be encouraged. Don't just encourage me. I want to be a saint. I want so to be a saint."

"Of course you'll be a saint," Mr. Frazer said.

"No, probably I won't be. But, oh, if I could only be a saint! I'd be perfectly happy."

"You're three to one to be a saint."

"No, don't encourage me. But, oh, if I could only be a saint! If I could only be a saint!"

"How's your friend Cayetano?"

"He's going to get well but he's paralyzed. One of the bullets hit the big nerve that goes down through his thigh and that leg is paralyzed. They only found it out when he got well enough so that he could move."

"Maybe the nerve will regenerate."

"I'm praying that it will," Sister Cecilia said. "You ought to see him."

"I don't feel like seeing anybody."

"You know you'd like to see him. They could wheel him in here."

"All right."

They wheeled him in, thin, his skin transparent, his hair black and needing to be cut, his eyes very laughing, his teeth bad when he smiled.

"Hola, amigo! Que tal?"

"As you see," said Mr. Frazer. "And thou?"

"Alive and with the leg paralyzed."

"Bad," Mr. Frazer said. "But the nerve can regenerate and be as good as new."

"So they tell me."

"What about the pain?"

"Not now. For a while I was crazy with it in the belly. I thought the pain alone would kill me."

Sister Cecilia was observing them happily.

"She tells me you never made a sound," Mr. Frazer said.

"So many people in the ward," the Mexican said deprecatingly. "What class of pain do you have?"

"Big enough. Clearly not as bad as yours. When the nurse goes out I cry an hour, two hours. It rests me. My nerves are bad now."

"You have the radio. If I had a private room and a radio I would be crying and yelling all night long."

"I doubt it."

"Hombre, si. It's very healthy. But you cannot do it with so many people."

"At least," Mr. Frazer said, "the hands are still good. They tell me you make your living with the hands."

"And the head," he said, tapping his forehead. "But the head isn't worth as much."

"Three of your countrymen were here."

"Sent by the police to see me."

"They brought some beer."

"It probably was bad."

"It was bad."

"Tonight, sent by the police, they come to serenade me." He laughed, then tapped his stomach. "I cannot laugh yet. As musicians they are fatal."

"And the one who shot you?"

"Another fool. I won thirty-eight dollars from him at cards. That is not to kill about."

"The three told me you win much money."

"And am poorer than the birds."

"How?"

"I am a poor idealist. I am the victim of illusions." He laughed, then grinned and tapped his stomach. "I am a professional gambler but I like to gamble. To really gamble. Little gambling is all crooked. For real gambling you need luck. I have no luck."

"Never?"

"Never. I am completely without luck. Look, this cabron who shoots me just now. Can he shoot? No. The first shot he fires into nothing. The second is intercepted by a poor Russian. That would seem to be luck. What happens? He shoots me twice in the belly. He is a lucky man. I have no luck. He could not hit a horse if he were holding the stirrup. All luck."

"I thought he shot you first and the Russian after."

"No, the Russian first, me after. The paper was mistaken."

"Why didn't you shoot him?"

"I never carry a gun. With my luck, if I carried a gun I would be hanged ten times a year. I am a cheap card player, only that." He stopped, then continued. "When I make a sum of money I gamble and when I gamble I lose. I have passed at dice for three thousand dollars and crapped out for the six. With good dice. More than once."

"Why continue?"

"If I live long enough the luck will change. I have bad luck now for fifteen years. If I ever get any good luck I will be rich." He grinned. "I am a good gambler, really I would enjoy being rich."

"Do you have bad luck with all games?"

"With everything and with women." He smiled again, showing his bad teeth.

"Truly?"

"Truly."

"And what is there to do?"

"Continue, slowly, and wait for luck to change."

"But with women?"

"No gambler has luck with women. He is too concentrated. He works nights. When he should be with the woman. No man who works nights can hold a woman if the woman is worth anything."

"You are a philosopher."

"No, hombre. A gambler of the small towns. One small town,

then another, another, then a big town, then start over again."

"Then shot in the belly."

"The first time," he said. "That has only happened once."

"I tire you talking?" Mr. Frazer suggested.

"No," he said. "I must tire you."

"And the leg?"

"I have no great use for the leg. I am all right with the leg or not. I will be able to circulate."

"I wish you luck, truly, and with all my heart," Mr. Frazer said.

"Equally," he said. "And that the pain stops."

"It will not last, certainly. It is passing. It is of no importance."

"That it passes quickly."

"Equally."

That night the Mexicans played the accordion and other instruments in the ward and it was cheerful and the noise of the inhalations and exhalations of the accordion, and of the bells, the traps, and the drum came down the corridor. In that ward there was a rodeo rider who had come out of the chutes on Midnight on a hot dusty afternoon with the big crowd watching, and now, with a broken back, was going to learn to work in leather and to cane chairs when he got well enough to leave the hospital. There was a carpenter who had fallen with a scaffolding and broken both ankles and both wrists. He had lit like a cat but without a cat's resiliency. They could fix him up so that he could work again but it would take a long time. There was a boy from a farm, about sixteen years old, with a broken leg that had been badly set and was to be rebroken. There was Cayetano Ruiz, a small-town gambler with a paralyzed leg. Down the corridor Mr. Frazer could hear them all laughing and merry with the music made by the Mexicans who had been sent by the police. The Mexicans were having a good time. They came in, very excited, to see Mr. Frazer and wanted to know if there was anything he wanted them to play, and they came twice more to play at night of their own accord.

The last time they played Mr. Frazer lay in his room with the door open and listened to the noisy, bad music and could not keep from thinking. When they wanted to know what he wished played, he asked for the Cucaracha, which has the sinister lightness and deftness of so many of the tunes men have gone to die to. They played noisily and with emotion. The tune was better than most of such tunes, to Mr. Frazer's mind, but the effect was all the same.

In spite of this introduction of emotion, Mr. Frazer went on thinking. Usually he avoided thinking all he could, except when he was writing, but now he was thinking about those who were playing and what the little one had said.

Religion is the opium of the people. He believed that, that dyspeptic little joint-keeper. Yes, and music is the opium of the people. Old mount-to-the-head hadn't thought of that. And now economics is the opium of the people; along with patriotism the opium of the people in Italy and Germany. What about sexual intercourse; was that an opium of the people? Of some of the people. Of some of the best of the people. But drink was a sovereign opium of the people, oh, an excellent opium. Although some prefer the radio, another opium of the people, a cheap one he had just been using. Along with these went gambling, an opium of the people if there ever was one, one of the oldest. Ambition was another, an opium of the people, along with a belief in any new form of government. What you wanted was the minimum of government, always less government. Liberty, what we believed in, now the name of a Mac-Fadden publication. We believed in that although they had not found a new name for it yet. But what was the real one? What was the real, the actual, opium of the people? He knew it very well. It was gone just a little way around the corner in that well-lighted part of his mind that was there after two or more drinks in the evening; that he knew was there (it was not really there of course). What was it? He knew very well. What was it? Of course; bread was the opium of the people. Would he remember that and would it make sense in the daylight? Bread is the opium of the people.

"Listen," Mr. Frazer said to the nurse when she came. "Get that little thin Mexican in here, will you, please?"

"How do you like it?" the Mexican said at the door.

"Very much."

"It is a historic tune," the Mexican said. "It is the tune of the real revolution."

"Listen," said Mr. Frazer. "Why should the people be operated on without an anæsthetic?"

"I do not understand."

"Why are not all the opiums of the people good? What do you want to do with the people?"

"They should be rescued from ignorance."

"Don't talk nonsense. Education is an opium of the people. You ought to know that. You've had a little."

"You do not believe in education?"

"No," said Mr. Frazer. "In knowledge, yes."

"I do not follow you."

"Many times I do not follow myself with pleasure."

"You want to hear the Cucaracha another time?" asked the Mexican worriedly.

"Yes," said Mr. Frazer. "Play the Cucaracha another time. It's better than the radio."

Revolution, Mr. Frazer thought, is no opium. Revolution is a catharsis; an ecstasy which can only be prolonged by tyranny. The opiums are for before and for after. He was thinking well, a little too well.

They would go now in a little while, he thought, and they would take the Cucaracha with them. Then he would have a little spot of the giant killer and play the radio, you could play the radio so that you could hardly hear it.

THERE had been a sign to detour in the center of the main street of this town, but cars had obviously gone through, so, believing it was some repair which had been completed, Nicholas Adams drove on through the town along the empty, brick-paved street, stopped by traffic lights that flashed on and off on this traffic-less Sunday, and would be gone next year when the payments on the system were not met; on under the heavy trees of the small town that are a part of your heart if it is your town and you have walked under them, but that are only too heavy, that shut out the sun and that dampen the houses for a stranger; out past the last house and onto the highway that rose and fell straight away ahead with banks of red dirt sliced cleanly away and the second-growth timber on both sides. It was not his country but it was the middle of fall and all of this country was good to drive through and to see. The cotton was picked and in the clearings there were patches of corn, some cut with streaks of red sorghum, and, driving easily, his son asleep on the seat by his side, the day's run made, knowing the town he would reach for the night, Nick noticed which corn fields had soy beans or peas in them, how the thickets and the cut-over land lay, where the cabins and houses were in relation to the fields and the thickets; hunting the country in his mind as he went by; sizing up each clearing as to feed and cover and figuring where you would find a covey and which way they would fly.

In shooting quail you must not get between them and their habitual cover, once the dogs have found them, or when they flush they will come pouring at you, some rising steep, some skimming by your ears, whirring into a size you have never seen them in the air as they pass, the only way being to turn and take them over your shoulder as they go, before they set their wings and angle down into the thicket. Hunting this country for quail as his father had taught him, Nicholas Adams started thinking about his father. When he first thought about him it was always the eyes. The big frame, the quick movements, the wide shoulders, the hooked, hawk nose, the beard that covered the weak chin, you never thought about—it was always the eyes. They were protected in his head by the formation of the brows; set deep as though a special protection had been devised for some very valuable instrument. They saw much farther and much quicker than the human eye sees and they were the great gift his father had. His father saw as a big-horn ram or as an eagle sees, literally.

He would be standing with his father on one shore of the lake, his own eyes were very good then, and his father would say, "They've run up the flag." Nick could not see the flag or the flag pole. "There," his father would say, "it's your sister Doro-thy. She's got the flag up and she's walking out onto the dock."

Nick would look across the lake and he could see the long wooded shore-line, the higher timber behind, the point that guarded the bay, the clear hills of the farm and the white of their cottage in the trees but he could not see any flag pole, or any dock, only the white of the beach and the curve of the shore.

"Can you see the sheep on the hillside toward the point?"

"Yes."

They were a whitish patch on the gray-green of the hill.

"I can count them," his father said.

Like all men with a faculty that surpasses human require-ments, his father was very nervous. Then, too, he was sentimen-tal, and, like most sentimental people, he was both cruel and abused. Also, he had much bad luck, and it was not all of it his own. He had died in a trap that he had helped only a little to set, and they had all betrayed him in their various ways before he died. All sentimental people are betrayed so many times. Nick could not write about him yet, although he would, later, but the quail country made him remember him as he was when Nick was a boy and he was very grateful to him for two things; fishing and shooting. His father was as sound on those two things as he was unsound on sex, for instance, and Nick was glad that it had been that way; for some one has to give you your first gun or the opportunity to get it and use it, and you have to live where there is game or fish if you are to learn about them, and now, at thirty-eight, he loved to fish and to shoot exactly as much as when he first had gone with his father. It was a passion that had never slackened and he was very grateful to his father for bring-ing him to know it.

While for the other, that his father was not sound about, all the equipment you will ever have is provided and each man

learns all there is for him to know about it without advice; and
it makes no difference where you live. He remembered very
clearly the only two pieces of information his father had given
him about that. Once when they were out shooting together
Nick shot a red squirrel out of a hemlock tree. The squirrel fell,
wounded, and when Nick picked him up bit the boy clean
through the ball of the thumb.

"The dirty little bugger," Nick said and smacked the squirrel's head against the tree. "Look how he bit me."

His father looked and said, "Suck it out clean and put some
iodine on when you get home."

"The little bugger," Nick said.

"Do you know what a bugger is?" his father asked him.

"We call anything a bugger," Nick said.

"A bugger is a man who has intercourse with animals."

"Why?" Nick said.

"I don't know," his father said. "But it is a heinous crime."

Nick's imagination was both stirred and horrified by this and
he thought of various animals but none seemed attractive or
practical and that was the sum total of direct sexual knowledge
bequeathed him by his father except on one other subject. One
morning he read in the paper that Enrico Caruso had been arrested for mashing.

"What is mashing?"

"It is one of the most heinous of crimes," his father answered.
Nick's imagination pictured the great tenor doing something
strange, bizarre, and heinous with a potato masher to a beautiful lady who looked like the pictures of Anna Held on the inside
of cigar boxes. He resolved, with considerable horror, that when
he was old enough he would try mashing at least once.

His father had summed up the whole matter by stating that
masturbation produced blindness, insanity, and death, while a
man who went with prostitutes would contract hideous venereal
diseases and that the thing to do was to keep your hands off of
people. On the other hand his father had the finest pair of eyes
he had ever seen and Nick had loved him very much and for a
long time. Now, knowing how it had all been, even remembering the earliest times before things had gone badly was not good
remembering. If he wrote it he could get rid of it. He had gotten
rid of many things by writing them. But it was still too early for

that. There were still too many people. So he decided to think of something else. There was nothing to do about his father and he had thought it all through many times. The handsome job the undertaker had done on his father's face had not blurred in his mind and all the rest of it was quite clear, including the responsibilities. He had complimented the undertaker. The undertaker had been both proud and smugly pleased. But it was not the undertaker that had given him that last face. The undertaker had only made certain dashingly executed repairs of doubtful artistic merit. The face had been making itself and being made for a long time. It had modelled fast in the last three years. It was a good story but there were still too many people alive for him to write it.

Nick's own education in those earlier matters had been acquired in the hemlock woods behind the Indian camp. This was reached by a trail which ran from the cottage through the woods to the farm and then by a road which wound through the slashings to the camp. Now if he could still feel all of that trail with bare feet. First there was the pine-needle loam through the hemlock woods behind the cottage where the fallen logs crumbled into wood dust and long splintered pieces of wood hung like javelins in the tree that had been struck by lightning. You crossed the creek on a log and if you stepped off there was the black muck of the swamp. You climbed a fence out of the woods and the trail was hard in the sun across the field with cropped grass and sheep sorrel and mullen growing and to the left the quaky bog of the creek bottom where the killdeer plover fed. The spring house was in that creek. Below the barn there was fresh warm manure and the other older manure that was caked dry on top. Then there was another fence and the hard, hot trail from the barn to the house and the hot sandy road that ran down to the woods, crossing the creek, on a bridge this time, where the cat-tails grew that you soaked in kerosense to make jack-lights with for spearing fish at night.

Then the main road went off to the left, skirting the woods and climbing the hill, while you went into the woods on the wide clay and shale road, cool under the trees, and broadened for them to skid out the hemlock bark the Indians cut. The hemlock bark was piled in long rows of stacks, roofed over with more bark, like houses, and the peeled logs lay huge and yellow

where the trees had been felled. They left the logs in the woods
to rot, they did not even clear away or burn the tops. It was only
the bark they wanted for the tannery at Boyne City; hauling it
across the lake on the ice in winter, and each year there was
less forest and more open, hot, shadeless, weed-grown slashing.

But there was still much forest then, virgin forest where the
trees grew high before there were any branches and you walked
on the brown, clean, springy-needled ground with no undergrowth and it was cool on the hottest days and they three lay
against the trunk of a hemlock wider than two beds are long,
with the breeze high in the tops and the cool light that came
in patches, and Billy said:

"You want Trudy again?"

"You want to?"

"Uh Huh."

"Come on."

"No, here."

"But Billy——"

"I no mind Billy. He my brother."

Then afterwards they sat, the three of them, listening for a
black squirrel that was in the top branches where they could
not see him. They were waiting for him to bark again because
when he barked he would jerk his tail and Nick would shoot
where he saw any movement. His father gave him only three
cartridges a day to hunt with and he had a single-barrel twenty-
guage shotgun with a very long barrel.

"Son of a bitch never move," Billy said.

"You shoot, Nickie. Scare him. We see him jump. Shoot him
again," Trudy said. It was a long speech for her.

"I've only got two shells," Nick said.

"Son of a bitch," said Billy.

They sat against the tree and were quiet. Nick was feeling hollow and happy.

"Eddie says he going to come some night sleep in bed with
you sister Dorothy."

"What?"

"He said."

Trudy nodded.

"That's all he want do," she said. Eddie was their older half-brother. He was seventeen.

"If Eddie Gilby ever comes at night and even speaks to Dorothy you know what I'd do to him? I'd kill him like this." Nick cocked the gun and hardly taking aim pulled the trigger, blowing a hole as big as your hand in the head or belly of that half-breed bastard Eddie Gilby. "Like that. I'd kill him like that."

"He better not come then," Trudy said. She put her hand in Nick's pocket.

"He better watch out plenty," said Billy.

"He's big bluff," Trudy was exploring with her hand in Nick's pocket. "But don't you kill him. You get plenty trouble."

"I'd kill him like that," Nick said. Eddie Gilby lay on the ground with all his chest shot away. Nick put his foot on him proudly.

"I'd scalp him," he said happily.

"No," said Trudy. "That's dirty."

"I'd scalp him and send it to his mother."

"His mother dead," Trudy said. "Don't you kill him, Nickie. Don't you kill him for me."

"After I scalped him I'd throw him to the dogs."

Billy was very depressed. "He better watch out," he said gloomily.

"They'd tear him to pieces," Nick said, pleased with the picture. Then, having scalped that half-breed renegade and standing, watching the dogs tear him, his face unchanging, he fell backward against the tree, held tight around the neck, Trudy holding, choking him, and crying, "No kill him! No kill him! No kill him! No. No. No. Nickie. Nickie. Nickie!"

"What's the matter with you?"

"No kill him."

"I got to kill him."

"He just a big bluff."

"All right," Nickie said. "I won't kill him unless he comes around the house. Let go of me."

"That's good," Trudy said. "You want to do anything now? I feel good now."

"If Billy goes away." Nick had killed Eddie Gilby, then pardoned him his life, and he was a man now.

"You go, Billy. You hang around all the time. Go on."

"Son a bitch," Billy said. "I get tired this. What we come? Hunt or what?"

"You can take the gun. There's one shell."

"All right. I get a big black one all right."

"I'll holler," Nick said.

Then, later, it was a long time after and Billy was still away.

"You think we make a baby?" Trudy folded her brown legs together happily and rubbed against him. Something inside Nick had gone a long way away.

"I don't think so," he said.

"Make plenty baby what the hell."

They heard Billy shoot.

"I wonder if he got one."

"Don't care," said Trudy.

Billy came through the trees. He had the gun over his shoulder and he held a black squirrel by the front paws.

"Look," he said. "Bigger than a cat. You all through?"

"Where'd you get him?"

"Over there. Saw him jump first."

"Got to go home," Nick said.

"No," said Trudy.

"I got to get there for supper."

"All right."

"Want to hunt tomorrow?"

"All right."

"You can have the squirrel."

"All right."

"Come out after supper?"

"No."

"How you feel?"

"Good."

"All right."

"Give me kiss on the face," said Trudy.

Now, as he rode along the highway in the car and it was getting dark, Nick was all through thinking about his father. The end of the day never made him think of him. The end of the day had always belonged to Nick alone and he never felt right unless he was alone at it. His father came back to him in the fall of the year, or in the early spring when there had been jack-snipe on the prairie, or when he saw shocks of corn, or when he saw a lake, or if he ever saw a horse and buggy, or when he saw, or heard, wild geese, or in a duck blind; remembering the time an eagle dropped through the whirling snow to strike a canvas-covered decoy, rising his wings beating, the talons caught in the canvas. His father was with him, suddenly, in deserted orchards and in new-plowed fields, in thickets, on small hills, or when going through dead grass, whenever splitting wood or hauling water, by grist mills, cider mills and dams and always with open fires. The towns he lived in were not towns his father knew. After he was fifteen he had shared nothing with him.

His father had frost in his beard in cold weather and in hot weather he sweated very much. He liked to work in the sun on the farm because he did not have to and he loved manual work, which Nick did not. Nick loved his father but hated the smell of him and once when he had to wear a suit of his father's under-wear that had gotten too small for his father it made him feel sick and he took it off and put it under two stones in the creek and said that he had lost it. He had told his father how it was when his father had made him put it on but his father had said it was freshly washed. It had been, too. When Nick had asked him to smell of it his father sniffed at it indignantly and said that it was clean and fresh. When Nick came home from fishing without it and said he lost it he was whipped for lying.

Afterwards he had sat inside the woodshed with the door open, his shotgun loaded and cocked, looking across at his father sitting on the screen porch reading the paper, and thought, "I can blow him to hell. I can kill him." Finally he felt his anger go out of him and he felt a little sick about it being the gun that his father had given him. Then he had gone to the Indian camp, walking there in the dark, to get rid of the smell. There was only one person in his family that he liked the smell of; one sister. All the others he avoided all contact with. That sense blunted when he started to smoke. It was a good thing. It was good for a bird dog but it did not help a man.

"What was it like, Papa, when you were a little boy and used to hunt with the Indians?"

"I don't know," Nick was startled. He had not even noticed

the boy was awake. He looked at him sitting beside him on the seat. He had felt quite alone but this boy had been with him. He wondered for how long. "We used to go all day to hunt black squirrels," he said. "My father only gave me three shells a day because he said that would teach me to hunt and it wasn't good for a boy to go banging around. I went with a boy named Billy Gilby and his sister Trudy. We used to go out nearly every day all one summer."

"Those are funny names for Indians."

"Yes, aren't they," Nick said.

"But tell me what they were like."

"They were Ojibways," Nick said. "And they were very nice."

"But what were they like to be with?"

"It's hard to say," Nick Adams said. Could you say she did first what no one has ever done better and mention plump brown legs, flat belly, hard little breasts, well holding arms, quick searching tongue, the flat eyes, the good taste of mouth, then uncomfortably, tightly, sweetly, moistly, lovely, tightly, achingly, fully, finally, unendingly, never-endingly, never-to-endingly, suddenly ended, the great bird flown like an owl in the twilight, only it daylight in the woods and hemlock needles stuck against your belly. So that when you go in a place where Indians have lived you smell them gone and all the empty pain killer bottles and the flies that buzz do not kill the sweetgrass smell, the smoke smell and that other like a fresh cased marten skin. Nor any jokes about them nor old squaws take that away. Nor the sick sweet smell they get to have. Nor what they did finally. It wasn't how they ended. They all ended the same. Long time ago good. Now no good.

And about the other. When you have shot one bird flying you have shot all birds flying. They are all different and they fly in different ways but the sensation is the same and the last one is as good as the first. He could thank his father for that.

"You might not like them," Nick said to the boy. "But I think you would."

"And my grandfather lived with them too when he was a boy, didn't he?"

"Yes. When I asked him what they were like he said that he had many friends among them."

"Will I ever live with them?"

"I don't know," Nick said. "That's up to you."

"How old will I be when I get a shotgun and can hunt by myself?"

"Twelve years old if I see you are careful."

"I wish I was twelve now."

"You will be, soon enough."

"What was my grandfather like? I can't remember him except that he gave me an air rifle and an American flag when I came over from France that time. What was he like?"

"He's hard to describe. He was a great hunter and fisherman and he had wonderful eyes."

"Was he greater than you?"

"He was a much better shot and his father was a great wing shot too."

"I'll bet he wasn't better than you."

"Oh, yes he was. He shot very quickly and beautifully. I'd rather see him shoot than any man I ever knew. He was always very disappointed in the way I shot."

"Why do we never go to pray at the tomb of my grandfather?"

"We live in a different part of the country. It's a long way from here."

"In France that wouldn't make any difference. In France we'd go. I think I ought to go to pray at the tomb of my grandfather."

"Sometime we'll go."

"I hope we won't live somewhere so that I can never go to pray at your tomb when you are dead."

"We'll have to arrange it."

"Don't you think we might all be buried at a convenient place? We could all be buried in France. That would be fine."

"I don't want to be buried in France," Nick said.

"Well, then, we'll have to get some convenient place in America. Couldn't we all be buried out at the ranch?"

"That's an idea."

"Then I could stop and pray at the tomb of my grandfather on the way to the ranch."

"You're awfully practical."

"Well, I don't feel good never to have even visited the tomb of my grandfather."

"We'll have to go," Nick said. "I can see we'll have to go."

IN ANOTHER COUNTRY

In the fall the war was always there, but we did not go to it any more. It was cold in the fall in Milan and the dark came very early. Then the electric lights came on, and it was pleasant along the streets looking in the windows. There was much game hanging outside the shops, and the snow powdered in the fur of the foxes and the wind blew their tails. The deer hung stiff and heavy and empty, and small birds blew in the wind and the wind turned their feathers. It was a cold fall and the wind came down from the mountains.

We were all at the hospital every afternoon, and there were different ways of walking across the town through the dusk to the hospital. Two of the ways were alongside canals, but they were long. Always, though, you crossed a bridge across a canal to enter the hospital. There was a choice of three bridges. On one of them a woman sold roasted chestnuts. It was warm, standing in front of her charcoal fire, and the chestnuts were warm afterward in your pocket. The hospital was very old and very beautiful, and you entered through a gate and walked across a courtyard and out a gate on the other side. There were usually funerals starting from the courtyard. Beyond the old hospital were the new brick pavilions, and there we met every afternoon and were all very polite and interested in what was the matter, and sat in the machines that were to make so much difference.

The doctor came up to the machine where I was sitting and said: "What did you like best to do before the war? Did you practise a sport?"

I said: "Yes, football."

"Good," he said. "You will be able to play football again better than ever."

My knee did not bend and the leg dropped straight from the knee to the ankle without a calf, and the machine was to bend the knee and make it move as in riding a tricycle. But it did not bend yet, and instead the machine lurched when it came to the bending part. The doctor said: "That will all pass. You are a fortunate young man. You will play football again like a champion."

In the next machine was a major who had a little hand like a baby's. He winked at me when the doctor examined his hand, which was between two leather straps that bounced up and down and flapped the stiff fingers, and said: "And will I too play football, captain-doctor?" He had been a very great fencer, and before the war the greatest fencer in Italy.

The doctor went to his office in a back room and brought a photograph which showed a hand that had been withered almost as small as the major's, before it had taken a machine course, and after was a little larger. The major held the photograph with his good hand and looked at it very carefully. "A wound?" he asked.

"An industrial accident," the doctor said.

"Very interesting, very interesting," the major said, and handed it back to the doctor.

"You have confidence?"

"No," said the major.

There were three boys who came each day who were about the same age I was. They were all three from Milan, and one of them was to be a lawyer, and one was to be a painter, and one had intended to be a soldier, and after we were finished with the machines, sometimes we walked back together to the Café Cova, which was next door to the Scala. We walked the short way through the communist quarter because we were four together. The people hated us because we were officers, and from a wine-shop some one would call out, "A basso gli ufficiali!" as we passed. Another boy who walked with us sometimes and made us five wore a black silk handkerchief across his face because he had no nose then and his face was to be rebuilt. He had gone out to the front from the military academy and been wounded within an hour after he had gone into the front line for the first time. They rebuilt his face, but he came from a very old family and they could never get the nose exactly right. He went to South America and worked in a bank. But this was a long time ago, and then we did not any of us know how it was going to be afterward. We only knew then that there was always the war, but that we were not going to it any more.

We all had the same medals, except the boy with the black silk bandage across his face, and he had not been at the front long enough to get any medals. The tall boy with a very pale face who was to be a lawyer had been a lieutenant of Arditi and had three medals of the sort we each had only one of. He had lived a very long time with death and was a little detached. We were all a little detached, and there was nothing that held us together except that we met every afternoon at the hospital. Although, as we walked to the Cova through the tough part of town, walking in the dark, with light and singing coming out of the wine-shops, and sometimes having to walk into the street when the men and women would crowd together on the sidewalk so that we would have had to jostle them to get by, we felt held together by there being something that had happened that they, the people who disliked us, did not understand.

We ourselves all understood the Cova, where it was rich and warm and not too brightly lighted, and noisy and smoky at certain hours, and there were always girls at the tables and the illustrated papers on a rack on the wall. The girls at the Cova were very patriotic, and I found that the most patriotic people in Italy were the café girls—and I believe they are still patriotic.

The boys at first were very polite about my medals and asked me what I had done to get them. I showed them the papers, which were written in very beautiful language and full of *fratellanza* and *abnegazione,* but which really said, with the adjectives removed, that I had been given the medals because I was an American. After that their manner changed a little toward me, although I was their friend against outsiders. I was a friend, but I was never really one of them after they had read the citations, because it had been different with them and they had done very different things to get their medals. I had been wounded, it was true; but we all knew that being wounded, after all, was really an accident. I was never ashamed of the ribbons, though, and sometimes, after the cocktail hour, I would imagine myself having done all the things they had done to get their medals; but walking home at night through the empty streets with the cold wind and all the shops closed, trying to keep near the street lights, I knew that I would never have done such things, and I was very much afraid to die, and often lay in bed at night by myself, afraid to die and wondering how I would be when I went back to the front again.

The three with the medals were like hunting-hawks; and I was not a hawk, although I might seem a hawk to those who had never hunted; they, the three, knew better and so we drifted apart. But I stayed good friends with the boy who had been wounded his first day at the front, because he would never know now how he would have turned out; so he could never be accepted either, and I liked him because I thought perhaps he would not have turned out to be a hawk either.

The major, who had been the great fencer, did not believe in bravery, and spent much time while we sat in the machines correcting my grammar. He had complimented me on how I spoke Italian, and we talked together very easily. One day I had said that Italian seemed such an easy language to me that I could not take a great interest in it; everything was so easy to say. "Ah, yes," the major said. "Why, then, do you not take up the use of grammar?" So we took up the use of grammar, and soon Italian was such a difficult language that I was afraid to talk to him until I had the grammar straight in my mind.

The major came very regularly to the hospital. I do not think he ever missed a day, although I am sure he did not believe in the machines. There was a time when none of us believed in the machines, and one day the major said it was all nonsense. The machines were new then and it was we who were to prove

them. It was an idiotic idea, he said, "a theory, like another."
I had not learned my grammar, and he said I was a stupid impossible disgrace, and he was a fool to have bothered with me.
He was a small man and he sat straight up in his chair with
his right hand thrust into the machine and looked straight
ahead at the wall while the straps thumped up and down with
his fingers in them.

"What will you do when the war is over if it is over?" he
asked me. "Speak grammatically!"

"I will go to the States."

"Are you married?"

"No, but I hope to be."

"The more of a fool you are," he said. He seemed very angry.
"A man must not marry."

"Why, Signor Maggiore?"

"Don't call me 'Signor Maggiore.'"

"Why must not a man marry?"

"He cannot marry. He cannot marry," he said angrily. "If he
is to lose everything, he should not place himself in a position
to lose that. He should not place himself in a position to lose.
He should find things he cannot lose."

He spoke very angrily and bitterly, and looked straight
ahead while he talked.

"But why should he necessarily lose it?"

"He'll lose it," the major said. He was looking at the wall.
Then he looked down at the machine and jerked his little
hand out from between the straps and slapped it hard against
his thigh. "He'll lose it," he almost shouted. "Don't argue with
me!" Then he called to the attendant who ran the machines.
"Come and turn this damned thing off."

He went back into the other room for the light treatment
and the massage. Then I heard him ask the doctor if he might
use his telephone and he shut the door. When he came back
into the room, I was sitting in another machine. He was wearing his cape and had his cap on, and he came directly toward
my machine and put his arm on my shoulder.

"I am so sorry," he said, and patted me on the shoulder with his good hand. "I would not be rude. My wife has just died. You must forgive me."

"Oh—" I said, feeling sick for him. "I am *so* sorry."

He stood there biting his lower lip. "It is very difficult," he said. "I cannot resign myself."

He looked straight past me and out through the window. Then he began to cry. "I am utterly unable to resign myself," he said and choked. And then crying, his head up looking at nothing, carrying himself straight and soldierly, with tears on both his cheeks and biting his lips, he walked past the machines and out the door.

The doctor told me that the major's wife, who was very young and whom he had not married until he was definitely invalided out of the war, had died of pneumonia. She had been sick only a few days. No one expected her to die. The major did not come to the hospital for three days. Then he came at the usual hour, wearing a black band on the sleeve of his uniform. When he came back, there were large framed photographs around the wall, of all sorts of wounds before and after they had been cured by the machines. In front of the machine the major used were three photographs of hands like his that were completely restored. I do not know where the doctor got them. I always understood we were the first to use the machines. The photographs did not make much difference to the major because he only looked out of the window.

THE KILLERS

THE DOOR of Henry's lunch-room opened and two men came in. They sat down at the counter.

"What's yours?" George asked them.

"I don't know," one of the men said. "What do you want to eat, Al?"

"I don't know," said Al. "I don't know what I want to eat."

Outside it was getting dark. The street-light came on outside the window. The two men at the counter read the menu. From the other end of the counter Nick Adams watched them. He had been talking to George when they came in.

"I'll have a roast pork tenderloin with apple sauce and mashed potatoes," the first man said.

"It isn't ready yet."

"What the hell do you put it on the card for?"

"That's the dinner," George explained. "You can get that at six o'clock."

George looked at the clock on the wall behind the counter. "It's five o'clock."

"The clock says twenty minutes past five," the second man said.

"It's twenty minutes fast."

"Oh, to hell with the clock," the first man said. "What have you got to eat?"

"I can give you any kind of sandwiches," George said. "You can have ham and eggs, bacon and eggs, liver and bacon, or a steak."

"Give me chicken croquettes with green peas and cream sauce and mashed potatoes."

"That's the dinner."

"Everything we want's the dinner, eh? That's the way you work it."

"I can give you ham and eggs, bacon and eggs, liver——"

"I'll take ham and eggs," the man called Al said. He wore a derby hat and a black overcoat buttoned across the chest. His face was small and white and he had tight lips. He wore a silk muffler and gloves.

"Give me bacon and eggs," said the other man. He was about the same size as Al. Their faces were different, but they were dressed like twins. Both wore overcoats too tight for them. They sat leaning forward, their elbows on the counter.

"Got anything to drink?" Al asked.

"Silver beer, bevo, ginger-ale," George said.

"I mean you got anything to *drink?*"

"Just those I said."

"This is a hot town," said the other. "What do they call it?"

"Summit."

"Ever hear of it?" Al asked his friend.

"No," said the friend.

"What do you do here nights?" Al asked.

"They eat the dinner," his friend said. "They all come here and eat the big dinner."

"That's right," George said.

"So you think that's right?" Al asked George.

"Sure."

"You're a pretty bright boy, aren't you?"

"Sure," said George.

"Well, you're not," said the other little man. "Is he, Al?"

"He's dumb," said Al. He turned to Nick. "What's your name?"

"Adams."

"Another bright boy," Al said. "Ain't he a bright boy, Max?"

"The town's full of bright boys," Max said.

George put the two platters, one of ham and eggs, the other of bacon and eggs, on the counter. He set down two side-dishes of fried potatoes and closed the wicket into the kitchen.

"Which is yours?" he asked Al.

"Don't you remember?"

"Ham and eggs."

"Just a bright boy," Max said. He leaned forward and took the ham and eggs. Both men ate with their gloves on. George watched them eat.

"What are *you* looking at?" Max looked at George.

"Nothing."

"The hell you were. You were looking at me."

"Maybe the boy meant it for a joke, Max," Al said.

George laughed.

"*You* don't have to laugh," Max said to him. "*You* don't have to laugh at all, see?"

"All right," said George.

"So he thinks it's all right." Max turned to Al. "He thinks it's all right. That's a good one."

"Oh, he's a thinker," Al said. They went on eating.

"What's the bright boy's name down the counter?" Al asked Max.

"Hey, bright boy," Max said to Nick. "You go around on the other side of the counter with your boy friend."

"What's the idea?" Nick asked.

"There isn't any idea."

"You better go around, bright boy," Al said. Nick went around behind the counter.

"What's the idea?" George asked.

"None of your damn business," Al said. "Who's out in the kitchen?"

"The nigger."

"What do you mean the nigger?"

"The nigger that cooks."

"Tell him to come in."

"What's the idea?"

"Tell him to come in."

"Where do you think you are?"

"We know damn well where we are," the man called Max said. "Do we look silly?"

"You talk silly," Al said to him. "What the hell do you argue with this kid for? Listen," he said to George, "tell the nigger to come out here."

"What are you going to do to him?"

"Nothing. Use your head, bright boy. What would we do to a nigger?"

George opened the slit that opened back into the kitchen. "Sam," he called. "Come in here a minute."

The door to the kitchen opened and the nigger came in. "What was it?" he asked. The two men at the counter took a look at him.

"All right, nigger. You stand right there," Al said.

Sam, the nigger, standing in his apron, looked at the two men sitting at the counter. "Yes, sir," he said. Al got down from his stool.

"I'm going back to the kitchen with the nigger and bright boy," he said. "Go on back to the kitchen, nigger. You go with him, bright boy." The little man walked after Nick and Sam, the cook, back into the kitchen. The door shut after them. The man called Max sat at the counter opposite George. He didn't look at George but looked in the mirror that ran along back of the counter. Henry's had been made over from a saloon into a lunch-counter.

"Well, bright boy," Max said, looking into the mirror, "why don't you say something?"

"What's it all about?"

"Hey, Al," Max called, "bright boy wants to know what it's all about."

"Why don't you tell him?" Al's voice came from the kitchen.

"What do you think it's all about?"

"I don't know."

"What do you think?"

Max looked into the mirror all the time he was talking.

"I wouldn't say."

"Hey, Al, bright boy says he wouldn't say what he thinks it's all about."

"I can hear you, all right," Al said from the kitchen. He had propped open the slit that dishes passed through into the kitchen with a catsup bottle. "Listen, bright boy," he said from the kitchen to George. "Stand a little further along the bar. You move a little to the left, Max." He was like a photographer arranging for a group picture.

"Talk to me, bright boy," Max said. "What do you think's going to happen?"

George did not say anything.

"I'll tell you," Max said. "We're going to kill a Swede. Do you know a big Swede named Ole Andreson?"

"Yes."

"He comes here to eat every night, don't he?"

"Sometimes he comes here."

"He comes here at six o'clock, don't he?"

"If he comes."

"We know all that, bright boy," Max said. "Talk about something else. Ever go to the movies?"

"Once in a while."

"You ought to go to the movies more. The movies are fine for a bright boy like you."

"What are you going to kill Ole Andreson for? What did he ever do to you?"

"He never had a chance to do anything to us. He never even seen us."

"And he's only going to see us once," Al said from the kitchen.

"What are you going to kill him for, then?" George asked.

"We're killing him for a friend. Just to oblige a friend, bright boy."

"Shut up," said Al from the kitchen. "You talk too goddam much."

"Well, I got to keep bright boy amused. Don't I, bright boy?"

"You talk too damn much," Al said. "The nigger and my bright boy are amused by themselves. I got them tied up like a couple of girl friends in the convent."

"I suppose you were in a convent?"

"You never know."

"You were in a kosher convent. That's where you were."

George looked up at the clock.

"If anybody comes in you tell them the cook is off, and if they keep after it, you tell them you'll go back and cook yourself. Do you get that, bright boy?"

"All right," George said. "What you going to do with us afterward?"

"That'll depend," Max said. "That's one of those things you never know at the time."

George looked up at the clock. It was a quarter past six. The door from the street opened. A street-car motorman came in.

"Hello, George," he said. "Can I get supper?"

"Sam's gone out," George said. "He'll be back in about half an hour."

"I'd better go up the street," the motorman said. George looked at the clock. It was twenty minutes past six.

"That was nice, bright boy," Max said. "You're a regular little gentleman."

"He knew I'd blow his head off," Al said from the kitchen.

"No," said Max. "It ain't that. Bright boy is nice. He's a nice boy. I like him."

At six-fifty-five George said: "He's not coming."

Two other people had been in the lunch-room. Once George had gone out to the kitchen and made a ham-and-egg sandwich "to go" that a man wanted to take with him. Inside the kitchen he saw Al, his derby hat tipped back, sitting on a stool beside the wicket with the muzzle of a sawed-off shotgun resting on the ledge. Nick and the cook were back to back in the corner, a towel tied in each of their mouths. George had cooked the sandwich, wrapped it up in oiled paper, put it in a bag, brought it in, and the man had paid for it and gone out.

"Bright boy can do everything," Max said. "He can cook and everything. You'd make some girl a nice wife, bright boy."

"Yes?" George said. "Your friend, Ole Andreson, isn't going to come."

"We'll give him ten minutes," Max said.

Max watched the mirror and the clock. The hands of the clock marked seven o'clock, and then five minutes past seven.

"Come on, Al," said Max. "We better go. He's not coming."

"Better give him five minutes," Al said from the kitchen.

In the five minutes a man came in, and George explained that the cook was sick.

"Why the hell don't you get another cook?" the man asked. "Aren't you running a lunch-counter?" He went out.

"Come on, Al," Max said.

"What about the two bright boys and the nigger?"

"They're all right."

"You think so?"

"Sure. We're through with it."

"I don't like it," said Al. "It's sloppy. You talk too much."

"Oh, what the hell," said Max. "We got to keep amused, haven't we?"

"You talk too much, all the same," Al said. He came out from the kitchen. The cut-off barrels of the shotgun made a slight bulge under the waist of his too tight-fitting overcoat. He straightened his coat with his gloved hands.

"So long, bright boy," he said to George. "You got a lot of luck."

"That's the truth," Max said. "You ought to play the races, bright boy."

The two of them went out the door. George watched them, through the window, pass under the arc-light and cross the street. In their tight overcoats and derby hats they looked like a vaudeville team. George went back through the swinging-door into the kitchen and untied Nick and the cook.

"I don't want any more of that," said Sam, the cook. "I don't want any more of that."

Nick stood up. He had never had a towel in his mouth before.

"Say," he said. "What the hell?" He was trying to swagger it off.

"They were going to kill Ole Andreson," George said. "They were going to shoot him when he came in to eat."

"Ole Andreson?"

"Sure."

The cook felt the corners of his mouth with his thumbs. "They all gone?" he asked.

"Yeah," said George. "They're gone now."

"I don't like it," said the cook. "I don't like any of it at all."

"Listen," George said to Nick. "You better go see Ole Andreson."

"All right."

"You better not have anything to do with it at all," Sam, the cook, said. "You better stay way out of it."

"Don't go if you don't want to," George said.

"Mixing up in this ain't going to get you anywhere," the cook said. "You stay out of it."

"I'll go see him," Nick said to George. "Where does he live?"

The cook turned away.

"Little boys always know what they want to do," he said.

"He lives up at Hirsch's rooming-house," George said to Nick.

"I'll go up there."

Outside the arc-light shone through the bare branches of a tree. Nick walked up the street beside the car-tracks and turned at the next arc-light down a side-street. Three houses up the street was Hirsch's rooming-house. Nick walked up the two steps and pushed the bell. A woman came to the door.

"Is Ole Andreson here?"

"Do you want to see him?"

"Yes, if he's in."

Nick followed the woman up a flight of stairs and back to the end of a corridor. She knocked on the door.

"Who is it?"

"It's somebody to see you, Mr. Andreson," the woman said.

"It's Nick Adams."

"Come in."

Nick opened the door and went into the room. Ole Andreson was lying on the bed with all his clothes on. He had been a heavyweight prizefighter and he was too long for the bed. He lay with his head on two pillows. He did not look at Nick.

"What was it?" he asked.

"I was up at Henry's," Nick said, "and two fellows came in and tied up me and the cook, and they said they were going to kill you."

It sounded silly when he said it. Ole Andreson said nothing.

"They put us out in the kitchen," Nick went on. "They were going to shoot you when you came in to supper."

Ole Andreson looked at the wall and did not say anything.

"George thought I better come and tell you about it."

"There isn't anything I can do about it," Ole Andreson said.

"I'll tell you what they were like."

"I don't want to know what they were like," Ole Andreson said. He looked at the wall. "Thanks for coming to tell me about it."

"That's all right."

Nick looked at the big man lying on the bed.

"Don't you want me to go and see the police?"

"No," Ole Andreson said. "That wouldn't do any good."

"Isn't there something I could do?"

"No. There ain't anything to do."

"Maybe it was just a bluff."

"No. It ain't just a bluff."

Ole Andreson rolled over toward the wall.

"The only thing is," he said, talking toward the wall, "I just can't make up my mind to go out. I been in here all day."

"Couldn't you get out of town?"

"No," Ole Andreson said. "I'm through with all that running around."

He looked at the wall.

"There ain't anything to do now."

"Couldn't you fix it up some way?"

"No. I got in wrong." He talked in the same flat voice. "There ain't anything to do. After a while I'll make up my mind to go out."

"I better go back and see George," Nick said.

"So long," said Ole Andreson. He did not look toward Nick. "Thanks for coming around."

Nick went out. As he shut the door he saw Ole Andreson

with all his clothes on, lying on the bed looking at the wall.

"He's been in his room all day," the landlady said downstairs. "I guess he don't feel well. I said to him: 'Mr. Andreson, you ought to go out and take a walk on a nice fall day like this,' but he didn't feel like it ."

"He doesn't want to go out."

"I'm sorry he don't feel well," the woman said. "He's an awfully nice man. He was in the ring, you know."

"I know it."

"You'd never know it except from the way his face is," the woman said. They stood talking just inside the street door. "He's just as gentle."

"Well, good-night, Mrs. Hirsch," Nick said.

"I'm not Mrs. Hirsch," the woman said. "She owns the place. I just look after it for her. I'm Mrs. Bell."

"Well, good-night, Mrs. Bell," Nick said.

"Good-night," the woman said.

Nick walked up the dark street to the corner under the arclight, and then along the car-tracks to Henry's eating-house. George was inside, back of the counter.

"Did you see Ole?"

"Yes," said Nick. "He's in his room and he won't go out."

The cook opened the door from the kitchen when he heard Nick's voice.

"I don't even listen to it," he said and shut the door.

"Did you tell him about it?" George asked.

"Sure. I told him but he knows what it's all about."

"What's he going to do?"

"Nothing."

"They'll kill him."

"I guess they will."

"He must have got mixed up in something in Chicago."

"I guess so," said Nick.

"It's a hell of a thing."

"It's an awful thing," Nick said.

They did not say anything. George reached down for a towel and wiped the counter.

"I wonder what he did?" Nick said.

"Double-crossed somebody. That's what they kill them for."

"I'm going to get out of this town," Nick said.

"Yes," said George. "That's a good thing to do."

"I can't stand to think about him waiting in the room and knowing he's going to get it. It's too damned awful."

"Well," said George, "you better not think about it."

A WAY YOU'LL NEVER BE

THE ATTACK had gone across the field, been held up by machine-gun fire from the sunken road and from the group of farm houses, encountered no resistance in the town, and reached the bank of the river. Coming along the road on a bicycle, getting off to push the machine when the surface of the road became too broken, Nicholas Adams saw what had happened by the position of the dead.

They lay alone or in clumps in the high grass of the field and along the road, their pockets out, and over them were flies and around each body or group of bodies were the scattered papers.

In the grass and the grain, beside the road, and in some places scattered over the road, there was much material: a field kitchen, it must have come over when things were going well; many of the calf-skin-covered haversacks, stick bombs, helmets, rifles, sometimes one butt-up, the bayonet stuck in the dirt, they had dug quite a little at the last; stick bombs, helmets, rifles, intrenching tools, ammunition boxes, star-shell pistols, their shells scattered about, medical kits, gas masks, empty gas-mask cans, a squat, tripodded machine gun in a nest of empty shells, full belts protruding from the boxes, the water-cooling can empty and on its side, the breech block gone, the crew in odd positions, and around them, in the grass, more of the typical papers.

There were mass prayer books, group postcards showing the machine-gun unit standing in ranked and ruddy cheerfulness as in a football picture for a college annual; now they were humped and swollen in the grass; propaganda postcards showing a soldier in Austrian uniform bending a woman backward over a bed; the figures were impressionistically

82

drawn; very attractively depicted and had nothing in common with actual rape in which the woman's skirts are pulled over her head to smother her, one comrade sometimes sitting upon the head. There were many of these inciting cards which had evidently been issued just before the offensive. Now they were scattered with the smutty postcards, photographic; the small photographs of village girls by village photographers, the occasional pictures of children, and the letters, letters, letters. There was always much paper about the dead and the débris of this attack was no exception.

These were new dead and no one had bothered with anything but their pockets. Our own dead, or what he thought of, still, as our own dead, were surprisingly few, Nick noticed. Their coats had been opened too and their pockets were out, and they showed, by their positions, the manner and the skill of the attack. The hot weather had swollen them all alike regardless of nationality.

The town had evidently been defended, at the last, from the line of the sunken road and there had been few or no Austrians to fall back into it. There were only three bodies in the street and they looked to have been killed running. The houses of the town were broken by the shelling and the street had much rubble of plaster and mortar and there were broken beams, broken tiles, and many holes, some of them yellow-edged from the mustard gas. There were many pieces of shell, and shrapnel balls were scattered in the rubble. There was no one in the town at all.

Nick Adams had seen no one since he had left Fornaci, although, riding along the road through the over-foliaged country, he had seen guns hidden under screens of mulberry leaves to the left of the road, noticing them by the heat-waves in the air above the leaves where the sun hit the metal. Now he went on through the town, surprised to find it deserted, and came out on the low road beneath the bank of the river. Leaving the town there was a bare open space where the road slanted down and he could see the placid reach of the river and the low curve of the opposite bank and the whitened, sun-baked mud where the Austrians had dug. It was all very lush and over-green since he had seen it last and becoming historical had made no change in this, the lower river.

The battalion was along the bank to the left. There was a series of holes in the top of the bank with a few men in them. Nick noticed where the machine guns were posted and the signal rockets in their racks. The men in the holes in the side of the bank were sleeping. No one challenged. He went on and as he came around a turn in the mud bank a young second lieutenant with a stubble of beard and red-rimmed, very bloodshot eyes pointed a pistol at him.

"Who are you?"

Nick told him.

"How do I know this?"

Nick showed him the tessera with photograph and identification and the seal of the third army. He took hold of it.

"I will keep this."

"You will not," Nick said. "Give me back the card and put your gun away. There. In the holster."

"How am I to know who you are?"

"The tessera tells you."

"And if the tessera is false? Give me that card."

"Don't be a fool," Nick said cheerfully. "Take me to your company commander."

"I should send you to battalion headquarters."

"All right," said Nick. "Listen, do you know the Captain Paravicini? The tall one with the small mustache who was an architect and speaks English?"

"You know him?"

"A little."

"What company does he command?"

"The second."

"He is commanding the battalion."

"Good," said Nick. He was relieved to know that Para was all right. "Let us go to the battalion."

As Nick had left the edge of the town three shrapnel had burst high and to the right over one of the wrecked houses and

since then there had been no shelling. But the face of this officer looked like the face of a man during a bombardment.
There was the same tightness and the voice did not sound natural. His pistol made Nick nervous.

"Put it away," he said. "There's the whole river between
them and you."

"If I thought you were a spy I would shoot you now," the
second lieutenant said.

"Come on," said Nick. "Let us go to the battalion." This
officer made him very nervous.

The Captain Paravicini, acting major, thinner and more
English-looking than ever, rose when Nick saluted from behind the table in the dugout that was battalion headquarters.

"Hello," he said. "I didn't know you. What are you doing in
that uniform?"

"They've put me in it."

"I am very glad to see you, Nicolo."

"Right. You look well. How was the show?"

"We made a very fine attack. Truly. A very fine attack. I
will show you. Look."

He showed on the map how the attack had gone.

"I came from Fornaci," Nick said. "I could see how it had
been. It was very good."

"It was extraordinary. Altogether extraordinary. Are you
attached to the regiment?"

"No. I am supposed to move around and let them see the
uniform."

"How odd."

"If they see one American uniform that is supposed to make
them believe others are coming."

"But how will they know it is an American uniform?"

"You will tell them."

"Oh. Yes, I see. I will send a corporal with you to show you
about and you will make a tour of the lines."

"Like a bloody politician," Nick said.

"You would be much more distinguished in civilian clothes.
They are what is really distinguished."

"With a homburg hat," said Nick.

"Or with a very furry fedora."

"I'm supposed to have my pockets full of cigarettes and postal cards and such things," Nick said. "I should have a musette full of chocolate. These I should distribute with a kind word and a pat on the back. But there weren't any cigarettes and postcards and no chocolate. So they said to circulate around anyway."

"I'm sure your appearance will be very heartening to the troops."

"I wish you wouldn't," Nick said. "I feel badly enough about it as it is. In principle, I would have brought you a bottle of brandy."

"In principle," Para said and smiled, for the first time, showing yellowed teeth. "Such a beautiful expression. Would you like some Grappa?"

"No, thank you," Nick said.

"It hasn't any ether in it."

"I can taste that still," Nick remembered suddenly and completely.

"You know I never knew you were drunk until you started talking coming back in the camions."

"I was stinking in every attack," Nick said.

"I can't do it," Para said. "I took it in the first show, the very first show, and it only made me very upset and then frightfully thirsty."

"You don't need it."

"You're much braver in an attack than I am."

"No," Nick said. "I know how I am and I prefer to get stinking. I'm not ashamed of it."

"I've never seen you drunk."

"No?" said Nick. "Never? Not when we rode from Mestre to Portogrande that night and I wanted to go to sleep and used the bicycle for a blanket and pulled it up under my chin?"

"That wasn't in the lines."

"Let's not talk about how I am," Nick said. "It's a subject

I know too much about to want to think about it any more."

"You might as well stay here a while," Paravicini said. "You can take a nap if you like. They didn't do much to this in the bombardment. It's too hot to go out yet."

"I suppose there is no hurry."

"How are you really?"

"I'm fine. I'm perfectly all right."

"No. I mean really."

"I'm all right. I can't sleep without a light of some sort. That's all I have now."

"I said it should have been trepanned. I'm no doctor but I know that."

"Well, they thought it was better to have it absorb, and that's what I got. What's the matter? I don't seem crazy to you, do I?"

"You seem in top-hole shape."

"It's a hell of a nuisance once they've had you certified as nutty," Nick said. "No one ever has any confidence in you again."

"I would take a nap, Nicolo," Paravicini said. "This isn't battalion headquarters as we used to know it. We're just waiting to be pulled out. You oughtn't to go out in the heat now—it's silly. Use that bunk."

"I might just lie down," Nick said.

Nick lay on the bunk. He was very disappointed that he felt this way and more disappointed, even, that it was so obvious to Captain Paravicini. This was not as large a dugout as the one where that platoon of the class of 1899, just out at the front, got hysterics during the bombardment before the attack, and Para had had him walk them two at a time outside to show them nothing would happen, he wearing his own chin strap tight across his mouth to keep his lips quiet. Knowing they could not hold it when they took it. Knowing it was all a bloody balls—If he can't stop crying, break his nose to give him something else to think about. I'd shoot one but it's too late now. They'd all be worse. Break his nose. They've put it back to five-twenty. We've only got four minutes more. Break that other silly bugger's nose and kick his silly ass out of here. Do you think they'll go over? If they don't, shoot two and try to scoop the others out some way. Keep behind them, sergeant. It's no use to walk ahead and find there's nothing coming behind you. Bail them out as you go. What a bloody balls. All right. That's right. Then, looking at the watch, in that quiet tone, that valuable quiet tone, "Savoia." Making it cold, no time to get it, he couldn't find his own after the cave-in, one whole end had caved in; it was that started them; making it cold up that slope the only time he hadn't done it stinking. And after they came back the teleferica house burned, it seemed, and some of the wounded got down four days later and some did not get down, but we went up and we went back and we came down—we always came down. And there was Gaby Delys, oddly enough, with feathers on; you called me baby doll a year ago tadada you said that I was rather nice to know tadada with feathers on, with feathers off, the great Gaby, and my name's Harry Pilcer, too, we used to step out of the far side of the taxis when it got steep going up the hill and he could see that hill every night when he dreamed with Sacré Cœur, blown white, like a soap bubble. Sometimes his girl was there and sometimes she was with some one else and he could not understand that, but those were the nights the river ran so much wider and stiller than it should and outside of Fossalta there was a low house painted yellow with willows all around it and a low stable and there was a canal, and he had been there a thousand times and never seen it, but there it was every night as plain as the hill, only it frightened him. That house meant more than anything and every night he had it. That was what he needed but it frightened him especially when the boat lay there quietly in the willows on the canal, but the banks weren't like this river. It was all lower, as it was at Portogrande, where they had seen them come wallowing across the flooded ground holding the rifles high until they fell with them in the water. Who ordered that one? If it didn't get so damned mixed up he could follow it all right. That was why he noticed everything in such detail to keep it all straight so he would know just where he was, but suddenly it confused without reason as now, he lying in a bunk at battalion headquarters, with Para commanding a battalion and he in a bloody American uniform. He sat up and looked around; they all watching him. Para was gone out. He lay down again.

The Paris part came earlier and he was not frightened of it except when she had gone off with some one else and the fear that they might take the same driver twice. That was what frightened about that. Never about the front. He never dreamed about the front now any more but what frightened him so that he could not get rid of it was that long yellow house and the different width of the river. Now he was back here at the river, he had gone through that same town, and there was no house. Nor was the river that way. Then where did he go each night and what was the peril, and why would he wake, soaking wet, more frightened than he had ever been in a bombardment, because of a house and a long stable and a canal?

He sat up, swung his legs carefully down; they stiffened any time they were out straight for long; returned the stares of the adjutant, the signallers and the two runners by the door and put on his cloth-covered trench helmet.

"I regret the absence of the chocolate, the postal-cards and cigarettes," he said. "I am, however, wearing the uniform."

"The major is coming back at once," the adjutant said. In that army an adjutant is not a commissioned officer.

"The uniform is not very correct," Nick told them. "But it gives you the idea. There will be several millions of Americans here shortly."

"Do you think they will send Americans down here?" asked the adjutant.

"Oh, absolutely. Americans twice as large as myself, healthy, with clean hearts, sleep at night, never been wounded, never been blown up, never had their heads caved in, never been scared, don't drink, faithful to the girls they left behind them, many of them never had crabs, wonderful chaps. You'll see."

"Are you an Italian?" asked the adjutant.

"No, American. Look at the uniform. Spagnolini made it but it's not quite correct."

"A North or South American?"

"North," said Nick. He felt it coming on now. He would quiet down.

"But you speak Italian."

"Why not? Do you mind if I speak Italian? Haven't I a right to speak Italian?"

"You have Italian medals."

"Just the ribbons and the papers. The medals come later. Or you give them to people to keep and the people go away; or they are lost with your baggage. You can purchase others in Milan. It is the papers that are of importance. You must not feel badly about them. You will have some yourself if you stay at the front long enough."

"I am a veteran of the Iritrea campaign," said the adjutant stiffly. "I fought in Tripoli."

"It's quite something to have met you," Nick put out his hand. "Those must have been trying days. I noticed the ribbons. Were you, by any chance, on the Carso?"

"I have just been called up for this war. My class was too old."

"At one time I was under the age limit," Nick said. "But now I am reformed out of the war."

"But why are you here now?"

"I am demonstrating the American uniform," Nick said. "Don't you think it is very significant? It is a little tight in the collar but soon you will see untold millions wearing this uniform swarming like locusts. The grasshopper, you know, what we call the grasshopper in America, is really a locust. The true grasshopper is small and green and comparatively feeble. You must not, however, make a confusion with the seven-year locust or cicada which emits a peculiar sustained sound which at the moment I cannot recall. I try to recall it but I cannot. I can almost hear it and then it is quite gone. You will pardon me if I break off our conversation?"

"See if you can find the major," the adjutant said to one of the two runners. "I can see you have been wounded," he said to Nick.

"In various places," Nick said. "If you are interested in scars I can show you some very interesting ones but I would rather talk about grasshoppers. What we call grasshoppers that is; and what are, really, locusts. These insects at one time played a very important part in my life. It might interest you and you can look at the uniform while I am talking."

The adjutant made a motion with his hand to the second runner who went out.

"Fix your eyes on the uniform. Spagnolini made it, you know. You might as well look, too," Nick said to the signallers. "I really have no rank. We're under the American consul. It's perfectly all right for you to look. You can stare, if you like. I will tell you about the American locust. We always preferred one that we called the medium-brown. They last the best in the water and fish prefer them. The larger ones that fly making a noise somewhat similar to that produced by a rattlesnake rattling his rattlers, a very dry sound, have vivid colored wings, some are bright red, others yellow barred with black, but their wings go to pieces in the water and they make a very blowsy bait, while the medium-brown is a plump, compact, succulent hopper that I can recommend as far as one may well recommend something you gentlemen will probably never encounter. But I must insist that you will never gather a sufficient supply of these insects for a day's fishing by pursuing them with your hands or trying to hit them with a bat. That is sheer nonsense and a useless waste of time. I repeat, gentlemen, that you will get nowhere at it. The correct procedure, and one which should be taught all young officers at every small-arms course if I had anything to say about it, and who knows but what I will have, is the employment of a seine or net made of common mosquito netting. Two officers holding this length of netting at alternate ends, or let us say one at each end, stoop, hold the bottom extremity of the net in one hand and the top extremity in the other and run into the wind. The hoppers, flying with the wind, fly against the length of netting and are imprisoned in its folds. It is no trick at all to catch a very great quantity indeed, and no officer, in my opinion, should be without a length of mosquito netting suitable for the improvisation of one of these grasshopper seines. I hope I have made myself clear, gentlemen. Are there any questions? If there is anything in the course you do not understand please ask questions. Speak up. None? Then I would like to close on this note. In the words of that great soldier and gentleman, Sir Henry Wilson: Gentlemen, either you must govern or you must be governed. Let me repeat it. Gentlemen, there is one thing I would like to have you remember. One thing I would like you to take with you as you leave this room. Gentlemen, either you must govern—or you must be governed. That is all, gentlemen. Good-day."

He removed his cloth-covered helmet, put it on again and, stooping, went out the low entrance of the dugout. Para, accompanied by the two runners, was coming down the line of the sunken road. It was very hot in the sun and Nick removed the helmet.

"There ought to be a system for wetting these things," he said. "I shall wet this one in the river." He started up the bank.

"Nicolo," Paravicini called. "Nicolo. Where are you going?"

"I don't really have to go." Nick came down the slope, holding the helmet in his hands. "They're a damned nuisance wet or dry. Do you wear yours all the time?"

"All the time," said Para. "It's making me bald. Come inside."

Inside Para told him to sit down.

"You know they're absolutely no damned good," Nick said. "I remember when they were a comfort when we first had them, but I've seen them full of brains too many times."

"Nicolo," Para said. "I think you should go back. I think it would be better if you didn't come up to the line until you had those supplies. There's nothing here for you to do. If you move around, even with something worth giving away, the men will group and that invites shelling. I won't have it."

"I know it's silly," Nick said. "It wasn't my idea. I heard the brigade was here so I thought I would see you or some one else I knew. I could have gone to Zenzon or to San Dona. I'd like to go to San Dona to see the bridge again."

"I won't have you circulating around to no purpose," Captain Paravicini said.

"All right," said Nick. He felt it coming on again.

"You understand?"

"Of course," said Nick. He was trying to hold it in.

"Anything of that sort should be done at night."

"Naturally," said Nick. He knew he could not stop it now.

"You see, I am commanding the battalion," Para said.

"And why shouldn't you be?" Nick said. Here it came. "You can read and write, can't you?"

"Yes," said Para gently.

"The trouble is you have a damned small battalion to command. As soon as it gets to strength again they'll give you back your company. Why don't they bury the dead? I've seen them now. I don't care about seeing them again. They can bury them any time as far as I'm concerned and it would be much better for you. You'll all get bloody sick."

"Where did you leave your bicycle?"

"Inside the last house."

"Do you think it will be all right?"

"Don't worry," Nick said. "I'll go in a little while."

"Lie down a little while, Nicolo."

"All right."

He shut his eyes, and in place of the man with the beard who looked at him over the sights of the rifle, quite calmly before squeezing off, the white flash and clublike impact, on his knees, hot-sweet choking, coughing it onto the rock while they went past him, he saw a long, yellow house with a low stable and the river much wider than it was and stiller. "Christ," he said, "I might as well go."

He stood up.

"I'm going, Para," he said. "I'll ride back now in the afternoon. If any supplies have come I'll bring them down tonight. If not I'll come at night when I have something to bring."

"It is still hot to ride," Captain Paravicini said.

"You don't need to worry," Nick said. "I'm all right now for quite a while. I had one then but it was easy. They're getting much better. I can tell when I'm going to have one because I talk so much."

"I'll send a runner with you."

"I'd rather you didn't. I know the way."

"You'll be back soon?"

"Absolutely."

"Let me send——"

"No," said Nick. "As a mark of confidence."

"Well, Ciaou then."

"Ciaou," said Nick. He started back along the sunken road toward where he had left the bicycle. In the afternoon the road would be shady once he had passed the canal. Beyond that there were trees on both sides that had not been shelled at all. It was on that stretch that, marching, they had once passed the Terza Savoia cavalry regiment riding in the snow with their lances. The horses' breath made plumes in the cold air. No, that was somewhere else. Where was that?

"I'd better get to that damned bicycle," Nick said to himself. "I don't want to lose the way to Fornaci."

FIFTY GRAND

"How ARE you going yourself, Jack?" I asked him.

"You seen this, Walcott?" he says.

"Just in the gym."

"Well," Jack says, "I'm going to need a lot of luck with that boy."

"He can't hit you, Jack," Soldier said.

"I wish to hell he couldn't."

"He couldn't hit you with a handful of bird-shot."

"Bird-shot'd be all right," Jack says. "I wouldn't mind bird-shot any."

"He looks easy to hit," I said.

"Sure," Jack says, "he ain't going to last long. He ain't going to last like you and me, Jerry. But right now he's got everything."

"You'll left-hand him to death."

"Maybe," Jack says. "Sure. I got a chance to."

"Handle him like you handled Kid Lewis."

"Kid Lewis," Jack said. "That kike!"

The three of us, Jack Brennan, Soldier Bartlett, and I were in Hanley's. There were a couple of broads sitting at the next table to us. They had been drinking.

"What do you mean, kike?" one of the broads says. "What do you mean, kike, you big Irish bum?"

"Sure," Jack says. "That's it."

"Kikes," this broad goes on. "They're always talking about kikes, these big Irishmen. What do you mean, kikes?"

"Come on. Let's get out of here."

"Kikes," this broad goes on. "Whoever saw you ever buy a drink? Your wife sews your pockets up every morning. These Irishmen and their kikes! Ted Lewis could lick you too."

"Sure," Jack says. "And you give away a lot of things free too, don't you?"

We went out. That was Jack. He could say what he wanted to when he wanted to say it.

Jack started training out at Danny Hogan's health farm over in Jersey. It was nice out there but Jack didn't like it much. He didn't like being away from his wife and the kids, and he was sore and grouchy most of the time. He liked me and we got along fine together; and he liked Hogan, but after a while Soldier Bartlett commenced to get on his nerves. A kidder gets to be an awful thing around a camp if his stuff goes sort of sour. Soldier was always kidding Jack, just sort of kidding him all the time. It wasn't very funny and it wasn't very good, and it began to get to Jack. It was sort of stuff like this. Jack would finish up with the weights and the bag and pull on the gloves.

"You want to work?" he'd say to Soldier.

"Sure. How you want me to work?" Soldier would ask. "Want me to treat you rough like Walcott? Want me to knock you down a few times?"

"That's it," Jack would say. He didn't like it any, though.

One morning we were all out on the road. We'd been out quite a way and now we were coming back. We'd go along fast for three minutes and then walk a minute, and then go fast for three minutes again. Jack wasn't ever what you would call a sprinter. He'd move around fast enough in the ring if he had to, but he wasn't any too fast on the road. All the time we were walking Soldier was kidding him. We came up the hill to the farmhouse.

"Well," says Jack, "you better go back to town, Soldier."

"What do you mean?"

"You better go back to town and stay there."

"What's the matter?"

"I'm sick of hearing you talk."

"Yes?" says Soldier.

"Yes," says Jack.

"You'll be a damn sight sicker when Walcott gets through with you."

"Sure," says Jack, "maybe I will. But I know I'm sick of you."

So Soldier went off on the train to town that same morning. I went down with him to the train. He was good and sore.

"I was just kidding him," he said. We were waiting on the platform. "He can't pull that stuff with me, Jerry."

"He's nervous and crabby," I said. "He's a good fellow, Soldier."

"The hell he is. The hell he's ever been a good fellow."

"Well," I said, "so long, Soldier."

The train had come in. He climbed up with his bag.

"So long, Jerry," he says. "You be in town before the fight?"

"I don't think so."

"See you then."

He went in and the conductor swung up and the train went out. I rode back to the farm in the cart. Jack was on the porch writing a letter to his wife. The mail had come and I got the papers and went over on the other side of the porch and sat down to read. Hogan came out the door and walked over to me.

"Did he have a jam with Soldier?"

"Not a jam," I said. "He just told him to go back to town."

"I could see it coming," Hogan said. "He never liked Soldier much."

"No. He don't like many people."

"He's a pretty cold one," Hogan said.

"Well, he's always been fine to me."

"Me too," Hogan said. "I got no kick on him. He's a cold one, though."

Hogan went in through the screen door and I sat there on the porch and read the papers. It was just starting to get fall weather and it's nice country there in Jersey, up in the hills, and after I read the paper through I sat there and looked out at the country and the road down below against the woods with cars going along it, lifting the dust up. It was fine weather and pretty nice-looking country. Hogan came to the door and I said, "Say, Hogan, haven't you got anything to shoot out here?"

"No," Hogan said. "Only sparrows."

"Seen the paper?" I said to Hogan.

"What's in it?"

"Sande booted three of them in yesterday."

"I got that on the telephone last night."

"You follow them pretty close, Hogan?" I asked.

"Oh, I keep in touch with them," Hogan said.

"How about Jack?" I says. "Does he still play them?"

"Him?" said Hogan. "Can you see him doing it?"

Just then Jack came around the corner with the letter in his hand. He's wearing a sweater and an old pair of pants and boxing shoes.

"Got a stamp, Hogan?" he asks.

"Give me the letter," Hogan said. "I'll mail it for you."

"Say, Jack," I said, "didn't you used to play the ponies?"

"Sure."

"I knew you did. I knew I used to see you out at Sheepshead."

"What did you lay off them for?" Hogan asked.

"Lost money."

Jack sat down on the porch by me. He leaned back against a post. He shut his eyes in the sun.

"Want a chair?" Hogan asked.

"No," said Jack. "This is fine."

"It's a nice day," I said. "It's pretty nice out in the country."

"I'd a damn sight rather be in town with the wife."

"Well, you only got another week."

"Yes," Jack says. "That's so."

We sat there on the porch. Hogan was inside at the office.

"What do you think about the shape I'm in?" Jack asked me.

"Well, you can't tell," I said. "You got a week to get around into form."

"Don't stall me."

"Well," I said, "you're not right."

"I'm not sleeping," Jack said.

"You'll be all right in a couple of days."

"No," says Jack, "I got the insomnia."

"What's on your mind?"

"I miss the wife."

"Have her come out."

"No. I'm too old for that."

"We'll take a long walk before you turn in and get you good and tired."

"Tired!" Jack says. "I'm tired all the time."

He was that way all week. He wouldn't sleep at night and he'd get up in the morning feeling that way, you know, when you can't shut your hands.

"He's stale as poorhouse cake," Hogan said. "He's nothing."

"I never seen Walcott," I said.

"He'll kill him," said Hogan. "He'll tear him in two."

"Well," I said, "everybody's got to get it sometime."

"Not like this, though," Hogan said. "They'll think he never trained. It gives the farm a black eye."

"You hear what the reporters said about him?"

"Didn't I! They said he was awful. They said they oughtn't to let him fight."

"Well," I said, "they're always wrong, ain't they?"

"Yes," said Hogan. "But this time they're right."

"What the hell do they know about whether a man's right or not?"

"Well," said Hogan, "they're not such fools."

"All they did was pick Willard at Toledo. This Lardner, he's so wise now, ask him about when he picked Willard at Toledo."

"Aw, he wasn't out," Hogan said. "He only writes the big fights."

"I don't care who they are," I said. "What the hell do they know? They can write maybe, but what the hell do they know?"

"You don't think Jack's in any shape, do you?" Hogan asked.

"No. He's through. All he needs is to have Corbett pick him to win for it to be all over."

"Well, Corbett'll pick him," Hogan says.

"Sure. He'll pick him."

That night Jack didn't sleep any either. The next morning was the last day before the fight. After breakfast we were out on the porch again.

"What do you think about, Jack, when you can't sleep?" I said.

"Oh, I worry," Jack says. "I worry about property I got up in the Bronx, I worry about property I got in Florida. I worry about the kids. I worry about the wife. Sometimes I think about fights. I think about that kike Ted Lewis and I get sore. I got some stocks and I worry about them. What the hell don't I think about?"

"Well," I said, "tomorrow night it'll all be over."

"Sure," said Jack. "That always helps a lot, don't it? That just fixes everything all up, I suppose. Sure."

He was sore all day. We didn't do any work. Jack just moved around a little to loosen up. He shadow-boxed a few rounds. He didn't even look good doing that. He skipped the rope a little while. He couldn't sweat.

"He'd be better not to do any work at all," Hogan said. We were standing watching him skip rope. "Don't he ever sweat at all any more?"

"He can't sweat."

"Do you suppose he's got the con? He never had any trouble making weight, did he?"

"No, he hasn't got any con. He just hasn't got anything inside any more."

"He ought to sweat," said Hogan.

Jack came over, skipping the rope. He was skipping up and down in front of us, forward and back, crossing his arms every third time.

"Well," he says. "What are you buzzards talking about?"

"I don't think you ought to work any more," Hogan says. "You'll be stale."

"Wouldn't that be awful?" Jack says and skips away down the floor, slapping the rope hard.

That afternoon John Collins showed up out at the farm. Jack was up in his room. John came out in a car from town.

He had a couple of friends with him. The car stopped and they all got out.

"Where's Jack?" John asked me.

"Up in his room, lying down."

"Lying down?"

"Yes," I said.

"How is he?"

I looked at the two fellows that were with John.

"They're friends of his," John said.

"He's pretty bad," I said.

"What's the matter with him?"

"He don't sleep."

"Hell," said John. "That Irishman could never sleep."

"He isn't right," I said.

"Hell," John said. "He's never right. I've had him for ten years and he's never been right yet."

The fellows who were with him laughed.

"I want you to shake hands with Mr. Morgan and Mr. Steinfelt," John said. "This is Mr. Doyle. He's been training Jack."

"Glad to meet you," I said.

"Let's go up and see the boy," the fellow called Morgan said.

"Let's have a look at him," Steinfelt said.

We all went upstairs.

"Where's Hogan?" John asked.

"He's out in the barn with a couple of his customers," I said.

"He got many people out here now?" John asked.

"Just two."

"Pretty quiet, ain't it?" Morgan said.

"Yes," I said. "It's pretty quiet."

We were outside Jack's room. John knocked on the door. There wasn't any answer.

"Maybe he's asleep," I said.

"What the hell's he sleeping in the daytime for?"

John turned the handle and we all went in. Jack was lying asleep on the bed. He was face down and his face was in the pillow. Both his arms were around the pillow.

"Hey, Jack!" John said to him.

Jack's head moved a little on the pillow. "Jack!" John says, leaning over him. Jack just dug a little deeper in the pillow. John touched him on the shoulder. Jack sat up and looked at us. He hadn't shaved and he was wearing an old sweater.

"Christ! Why can't you let me sleep?" he says to John.

"Don't be sore," John says. "I didn't mean to wake you up."

"Oh no," Jack says. "Of course not."

"You know Morgan and Steinfelt," John said.

"Glad to see you," Jack says.

"How do you feel, Jack," Morgan asks him.

"Fine," Jack says. "How the hell would I feel?"

"You look fine," Steinfelt says.

"Yes, don't I," says Jack. "Say," he says to John. "You're my manager. You get a big enough cut. Why the hell don't you come out here when the reporters was out! You want Jerry and me to talk to them?"

"I had Lew fighting in Philadelphia," John said.

"What the hell's that to me?" Jack says. "You're my manager. You get a big enough cut, don't you? You aren't making me any money in Philadelphia, are you? Why the hell aren't you out here when I ought to have you?"

"Hogan was here."

"Hogan," Jack says. "Hogan's as dumb as I am."

"Soldier Bahtlett was out here wukking with you for a while, wasn't he?" Steinfelt said to change the subject.

"Yes, he was out here," Jack says. "He was out here all right."

"Say, Jerry," John said to me. "Would you go and find Hogan and tell him we want to see him in about half an hour?"

"Sure," I said.

"Why the hell can't he stick around?" Jack says. "Stick around, Jerry."

Morgan and Steinfelt looked at each other.

"Quiet down, Jack," John said to him.

"I better go find Hogan," I said.

"All right, if you want to go," Jack says. "None of these guys are going to send you away, though."

"I'll go find Hogan," I said.

Hogan was out in the gym in the barn. He had a couple of his health-farm patients with the gloves on. They neither one wanted to hit the other, for fear the other would come back and hit him.

"That'll do," Hogan said when he saw me come in. "You can stop the slaughter. You gentlemen take a shower and Bruce will rub you down."

They climbed out through the ropes and Hogan came over to me.

"John Collins is out with a couple of friends to see Jack," I said.

"I saw them come up in the car."

"Who are the two fellows with John?"

"They're what you call wise boys," Hogan said. "Don't you know them two?"

"No," I said.

"That's Happy Steinfelt and Lew Morgan. They got a pool-room."

"I been away a long time," I said.

"Sure," said Hogan. "That Happy Steinfelt's a big operator."

"I've heard his name," I said.

"He's a pretty smooth boy," Hogan said. "They're a couple of sharpshooters."

"Well," I said. "They want to see us in half an hour."

"You mean they don't want to see us until a half an hour?"

"That's it."

"Come on in the office," Hogan said. "To hell with those sharpshooters."

After about thirty minutes or so Hogan and I went upstairs. We knocked on Jack's door. They were talking inside the room.

"Wait a minute," somebody said.

"To hell with that stuff," Hogan said. "When you want to see me I'm down in the office."

We heard the door unlock. Steinfelt opened it.

"Come on in, Hogan," he says. "We're all going to have a drink."

"Well," says Hogan. "That's something."

We went in. Jack was sitting on the bed. John and Morgan were sitting on a couple of chairs. Steinfelt was standing up.

"You're a pretty mysterious lot of boys," Hogan said.

"Hello, Danny," John says.

"Hello, Danny," Morgan says and shakes hands.

Jack doesn't say anything. He just sits there on the bed. He ain't with the others. He's all by himself. He was wearing an old blue jersey and pants and had on boxing shoes. He needed a shave. Steinfelt and Morgan were dressers. John was quite a dresser too. Jack sat there looking Irish and tough.

Steinfelt brought out a bottle and Hogan brought in some glasses and everybody had a drink. Jack and I took one and the rest of them went on and had two or three each.

"Better save some for your ride back," Hogan said.

"Don't you worry. We got plenty," Morgan said.

Jack hadn't drunk anything since the one drink. He was standing up and looking at them. Morgan was sitting on the bed where Jack had sat.

"Have a drink, Jack," John said and handed him the glass and the bottle.

"No," Jack said, "I never liked to go to these wakes."

They all laughed. Jack didn't laugh.

They were all feeling pretty good when they left. Jack stood on the porch when they got into the car. They waved to him.

"So long," Jack said.

We had supper. Jack didn't say anything all during the meal except, "Will you pass me this?" or "Will you pass me that?" The two health-farm patients ate at the same table with us. They were pretty nice fellows. After we finished eating we went out on the porch. It was dark early.

"Like to take a walk, Jerry?" Jack asked.

"Sure," I said.

We put on our coats and started out. It was quite a way

down to the main road and then we walked along the main road about a mile and a half. Cars kept going by and we would pull out to the side until they were past. Jack didn't say anything. After we had stepped out into the bushes to let a big car go by Jack said, "To hell with this walking. Come on back to Hogan's."

We went along a side road that cut up over the hill and cut across the fields back to Hogan's. We could see the lights of the house up on the hill. We came around to the front of the house and there standing in the doorway was Hogan.

"Have a good walk?" Hogan asked.

"Oh, fine," Jack said. "Listen, Hogan. Have you got any liquor?"

"Sure," says Hogan. "What's the idea?"

"Send it up to the room," Jack says. "I'm going to sleep to-night."

"You're the doctor," Hogan says.

"Come on up to the room, Jerry," Jack says.

Upstairs Jack sat on the bed with his head in his hands.

"Ain't it a life?" Jack says.

Hogan brought in a quart of liquor and two glasses.

"Want some ginger ale?"

"What do you think I want to do, get sick?"

"I just asked you," said Hogan.

"Have a drink?" said Jack.

"No, thanks," said Hogan. He went out.

"How about you, Jerry?"

"I'll have one with you," I said.

Jack poured out a couple of drinks. "Now," he said, "I want to take it slow and easy."

"Put some water in it," I said.

"Yes," Jack said. "I guess that's better."

We had a couple of drinks without saying anything. Jack started to pour me another.

"No," I said, "that's all I want."

"All right," Jack said. He poured himself out another big shot and put water in it. He was lighting up a little.

"That was a fine bunch out here this afternoon," he said. "They don't take any chances, those two."

Then a little later, "Well," he says, "they're right. What the hell's the good in taking chances?"

"Don't you want another, Jerry?" he said. "Come on, drink along with me."

"I don't need it, Jack," I said. "I feel all right."

"Just have one more," Jack said. It was softening him up.

"All right," I said.

Jack poured one for me and another big one for himself.

"You know," he said, "I like liquor pretty well. If I hadn't been boxing I would have drunk quite a lot."

"Sure," I said.

"You know," he said, "I missed a lot, boxing."

"You made plenty of money."

"Sure, that's what I'm after. You know I miss a lot, Jerry."

"How do you mean?"

"Well," he says, "like about the wife. And being away from home so much. It don't do my girls any good. 'Who's your old man?' some of those society kids 'll say to them. 'My old man's Jack Brennan.' That don't do them any good."

"Hell," I said, "all that makes a difference is if they got dough."

"Well," says Jack, "I got the dough for them all right."

He poured out another drink. The bottle was about empty.

"Put some water in it," I said. Jack poured in some water.

"You know," he says, "you ain't got any idea how I miss the wife."

"Sure."

"You ain't got any idea. You can't have an idea what it's like."

"It ought to be better out in the country than in town."

"With me now," Jack said, "it don't make any difference where I am. You can't have an idea what it's like."

"Have another drink."

"Am I getting soused? Do I talk funny?"

"You're coming on all right."

"You can't have an idea what it's like. They ain't anybody can have an idea what it's like."

"Except the wife," I said.

"She knows," Jack said. "She knows all right. She knows. You bet she knows."

"Put some water in that," I said.

"Jerry," says Jack, "you can't have an idea what it gets to be like."

He was good and drunk. He was looking at me steady. His eyes were sort of too steady.

"You'll sleep all right," I said.

"Listen, Jerry," Jack says. "You want to make some money? Get some money down on Walcott."

"Yes?"

"Listen, Jerry," Jack put down the glass. "I'm not drunk now, see? You know what I'm betting on him? Fifty grand."

"That's a lot of dough."

"Fifty grand," Jack says, "at two to one. I'll get twenty-five thousand bucks. Get some money on him, Jerry."

"It sounds good," I said.

"How can I beat him?" Jack says. "It ain't crooked. How can I beat him? Why not make money on it?"

"Put some water in that," I said.

"I'm through after this fight," Jack says. "I'm through with it. I got to take a beating. Why shouldn't I make money on it?"

"Sure."

"I ain't slept for a week," Jack says. "All night I lay awake and worry my can off. I can't sleep, Jerry. You ain't got an idea what it's like when you can't sleep."

"Sure."

"I can't sleep. That's all. I just can't sleep. What's the use of taking care of yourself all these years when you can't sleep?"

"It's bad."

"You ain't got an idea what it's like, Jerry, when you can't sleep."

"Put some water in that," I said.

Well, about eleven o'clock Jack passes out and I put him to

bed. Finally he's so he can't keep from sleeping. I helped him get his clothes off and got him into bed.

"You'll sleep all right, Jack," I said.

"Sure," Jack says, "I'll sleep now."

"Good night, Jack," I said.

"Good night, Jerry," Jack says. "You're the only friend I got."

"Oh, hell," I said.

"You're the only friend I got," Jack says, "the only friend I got."

"Go to sleep," I said.

"I'll sleep," Jack says.

Downstairs Hogan was sitting at the desk in the office reading the papers. He looked up. "Well, you get your boy friend to sleep?" he asks.

"He's off."

"It's better for him than not sleeping," Hogan said.

"Sure."

"You'd have a hell of a time explaining that to these sport writers though," Hogan said.

"Well, I'm going to bed myself," I said.

"Good night," said Hogan.

In the morning I came downstairs about eight o'clock and got some breakfast. Hogan had his two customers out in the barn doing exercises. I went out and watched them.

"One! Two! Three! Four!" Hogan was counting for them. "Hello, Jerry," he said. "Is Jack up yet?"

"No. He's still sleeping."

I went back to my room and packed up to go in to town. About nine-thirty I heard Jack getting up in the next room. When I heard him go downstairs I went down after him. Jack was sitting at the breakfast table. Hogan had come in and was standing beside the table.

"How do you feel, Jack?" I asked him.

"Not so bad."

"Sleep well?" Hogan asked.

"I slept all right," Jack said. "I got a thick tongue but I ain't got a head."

"Good," said Hogan. "That was good liquor."

"Put it on the bill," Jack says.

"What time you want to go into town?" Hogan asked.

"Before lunch," Jack says. "The eleven o'clock train."

"Sit down, Jerry," Jack said. Hogan went out.

I sat down at the table. Jack was eating a grapefruit. When he'd find a seed he'd spit it out in the spoon and dump it on the plate.

"I guess I was pretty stewed last night," he started.

"You drank some liquor."

"I guess I said a lot of fool things."

"You weren't bad."

"Where's Hogan?" he asked. He was through with the grapefruit.

"He's out in front in the office."

"What did I say about betting on the fight?" Jack asked. He was holding the spoon and sort of poking at the grapefruit with it.

The girl came in with some ham and eggs and took away the grapefruit.

"Bring me another glass of milk," Jack said to her. She went out.

"You said you had fifty grand on Walcott," I said.

"That's right," Jack said.

"That's a lot of money."

"I don't feel too good about it," Jack said.

"Something might happen."

"No," Jack said. "He wants the title bad. They'll be shooting with him all right."

"You can't ever tell."

"No. He wants the title. It's worth a lot of money to him."

"Fifty grand is a lot of money," I said.

"It's business," said Jack. "I can't win. You know I can't win anyway."

"As long as you're in there you got a chance."

"No," Jack says. "I'm all through. It's just business."

"How do you feel?"

"Pretty good," Jack said. "The sleep was what I needed."

"You might go good."

"I'll give them a good show," Jack said.

After breakfast Jack called up his wife on the long-distance. He was inside the booth telephoning.

"That's the first time he's called her up since he's out here," Hogan said.

"He writes her every day."

"Sure," Hogan says, "a letter only costs two cents."

Hogan said good-by to us and Bruce, the nigger rubber, drove us down to the train in the cart.

"Good-by, Mr. Brennan," Bruce said at the train, "I sure hope you knock his can off."

"So long," Jack said. He gave Bruce two dollars. Bruce had worked on him a lot. He looked kind of disappointed. Jack saw me looking at Bruce holding the two dollars.

"It's all in the bill," he said. "Hogan charged me for the rubbing."

On the train going into town Jack didn't talk. He sat in the corner of the seat with his ticket in his hat-band and looked out of the window. Once he turned and spoke to me.

"I told the wife I'd take a room at the Shelby tonight," he said. "It's just around the corner from the Garden. I can go up to the house tomorrow morning."

"That's a good idea," I said. "Your wife ever see you fight, Jack?"

"No," Jack says. "She never seen me fight."

I thought he must be figuring on taking an awful beating if he doesn't want to go home afterward. In town we took a taxi up to the Shelby. A boy came out and took our bags and we went in to the desk.

"How much are the rooms?" Jack asked.

"We only have double rooms," the clerk says. "I can give you a nice double room for ten dollars."

"That's too steep."

"I can give you a double room for seven dollars."

"With a bath?"

"Certainly."

"You might as well bunk with me, Jerry," Jack says.

"Oh," I said, "I'll sleep down at my brother-in-law's."

"I don't mean for you to pay it," Jack says. "I just want to get my money's worth."

"Will you register, please?" the clerk says. He looked at the names. "Number 238, Mister Brennan."

We went up in the elevator. It was a nice big room with two beds and a door opening into a bath-room.

"This is pretty good," Jack says.

The boy who brought us up pulled up the curtains and brought in our bags. Jack didn't make any move, so I gave the boy a quarter. We washed up and Jack said we better go out and get something to eat.

We ate a lunch at Jimmy Hanley's place. Quite a lot of the boys were there. When we were about half through eating, John came in and sat down with us. Jack didn't talk much.

"How are you on the weight, Jack?" John asked him. Jack was putting away a pretty good lunch.

"I could make it with my clothes on," Jack said. He never had to worry about taking off weight. He was a natural welter-weight and he'd never gotten fat. He'd lost weight out at Hogan's.

"Well, that's one thing you never had to worry about," John said.

"That's one thing," Jack says.

We went around to the Garden to weigh in after lunch. The match was made at a hundred forty-seven pounds at three o'clock. Jack stepped on the scales with a towel around him. The bar didn't move. Walcott had just weighed and was standing with a lot of people around him.

"Let's see what you weigh, Jack," Freedman, Walcott's manager said.

"All right, weigh *him* then," Jack jerked his head toward Walcott.

"Drop the towel," Freedman said.

"What do you make it?" Jack asked the fellows who were weighing.

"One hundred and forty-three pounds," the fat man who was weighing said.

"You're down fine, Jack," Freedman says.

"Weigh *him*," Jack says.

Walcott came over. He was a blond with wide shoulders and arms like a heavyweight. He didn't have much legs. Jack stood about half a head taller than he did.

"Hello, Jack," he said. His face was plenty marked up.

"Hello," said Jack. "How you feel?"

"Good," Walcott says. He dropped the towel from around his waist and stood on the scales. He had the widest shoulders and back you ever saw.

"One hundred and forty-six pounds and twelve ounces."

Walcott stepped off and grinned at Jack.

"Well," John says to him, "Jack's spotting you about four pounds."

"More than that when I come in, kid," Walcott says. "I'm going to go and eat now."

We went back and Jack got dressed. "He's a pretty tough-looking boy," Jack says to me.

"He looks as though he'd been hit plenty of times."

"Oh, yes," Jack says. "He ain't hard to hit."

"Where are you going?" John asked when Jack was dressed.

"Back to the hotel," Jack says. "You looked after everything?"

"Yes," John says. "It's all looked after."

"I'm going to lie down a while," Jack says.

"I'll come around for you about a quarter to seven and we'll go and eat."

"All right."

Up at the hotel Jack took off his shoes and his coat and lay down for a while. I wrote a letter. I looked over a couple of times and Jack wasn't sleeping. He was lying perfectly still but every once in a while his eyes would open. Finally he sits up.

"Want to play some cribbage, Jerry?" he says.

"Sure," I said.

He went over to his suitcase and got out the cards and the cribbage board. We played cribbage and he won three dollars off me. John knocked at the door and came in.

"Want to play some cribbage, John?" Jack asked him.

John put his hat down on the table. It was all wet. His coat was wet too.

"Is it raining?" Jack asks.

"It's pouring," John says. "The taxi I had got tied up in the traffic and I got out and walked."

"Come on, play some cribbage," Jack says.

"You ought to go and eat."

"No," says Jack. "I don't want to eat yet."

So they played cribbage for about half an hour and Jack won a dollar and a half off him.

"Well, I suppose we got to go eat," Jack says. He went to the window and looked out.

"Is it still raining?"

"Yes."

"Let's eat in the hotel," John says.

"All right," Jack says, "I'll play you once more to see who pays for the meal."

After a little while Jack gets up and says, "You buy the meal, John," and we went downstairs and ate in the big dining-room.

After we ate we went upstairs and Jack played cribbage with John again and won two dollars and a half off him. Jack was feeling pretty good. John had a bag with him with all his stuff in it. Jack took off his shirt and collar and put on a jersey and a sweater, so he wouldn't catch cold when he came out, and put his ring clothes and his bathrobe in a bag.

"You all ready?" John asks him. "I'll call up and have them get a taxi."

Pretty soon the telephone rang and they said the taxi was waiting.

We rode down in the elevator and went out through the lobby, and got in a taxi and rode around to the Garden. It was

raining hard but there was a lot of people outside on the
streets. The Garden was sold out. As we came in on our way
to the dressing-room I saw how full it was. It looked like half a
mile down to the ring. It was all dark. Just the lights over the
ring.

"It's a good thing, with this rain, they didn't try and pull
this fight in the ball park," John said.

"They got a good crowd," Jack says.

"This is a fight that would draw a lot more than the Garden could hold."

"You can't tell about the weather," Jack says.

John came to the door of the dressing-room and poked his
head in. Jack was sitting there with his bathrobe on, he had
his arms folded and was looking at the floor. John had a couple
of handlers with him. They looked over his shoulder. Jack
looked up.

"Is he in?" he asked.

"He's just gone down," John said.

We started down. Walcott was just getting into the ring.
The crowd gave him a big hand. He climbed through between
the ropes and put his two fists together and smiled, and shook
them at the crowd, first at one side of the ring, then at the
other, and then sat down. Jack got a good hand coming down
through the crowd. Jack is Irish and the Irish always get a
pretty good hand. An Irishman don't draw in New York like
a Jew or an Italian but they always get a good hand. Jack
climbed up and bent down to go through the ropes and Walcott came over from his corner and pushed the rope down for
Jack to go through. The crowd thought that was wonderful.
Walcott put his hand on Jack's shoulder and they stood there
just for a second.

"So you're going to be one of these popular champions,"
Jack says to him. "Take your goddam hand off my shoulder."

"Be yourself," Walcott says.

This is all great for the crowd. How gentlemanly the boys
are before the fight. How they wish each other luck.

Solly Freedman came over to our corner while Jack is band-

aging his hands and John is over in Walcott's corner. Jack puts
his thumb through the slit in the bandage and then wrapped
his hand nice and smooth. I taped it around the wrist and twice
across the knuckles.

"Hey," Freedman says. "Where do you get all that tape?"

"Feel of it," Jack says. "It's soft, ain't it? Don't be a hick."

Freedman stands there all the time while Jack bandages
the other hand, and one of the boys that's going to handle him
brings the gloves and I pull them on and work them around.

"Say, Freedman," Jack asks, "what nationality is this Walcott?"

"I don't know," Solly says. "He's some sort of a Dane."

"He's a Bohemian," the lad who brought the gloves said.

The referee called them out to the center of the ring and
Jack walks out. Walcott comes out smiling. They met and
the referee put his arm on each of their shoulders.

"Hello, popularity," Jack says to Walcott.

"Be yourself."

"What do you call yourself 'Walcott' for?" Jack says. "Didn't
you know he was a nigger?"

"Listen—" says the referee, and he gives them the same old
line. Once Walcott interrupts him. He grabs Jack's arm and
says, "Can I hit when he's got me like this?"

"Keep your hands off me," Jack says. "There ain't no
moving-pictures of this."

They went back to their corners. I lifted the bathrobe off
Jack and he leaned on the ropes and flexed his knees a couple
of times and scuffed his shoes in the rosin. The gong rang and
Jack turned quick and went out. Walcott came toward him
and they touched gloves and as soon as Walcott dropped his
hands Jack jumped his left into his face twice. There wasn't
anybody ever boxed better than Jack. Walcott was after him,
going forward all the time with his chin on his chest. He's a
hooker and he carries his hands pretty low. All he knows is
to get in there and sock. But every time he gets in there close,
Jack has the left hand in his face. It's just as though it's automatic. Jack just raises the left hand up and it's in Walcott's

face. Three or four times Jack brings the right over but Walcott gets it on the shoulder or high up on the head. He's just
like all these hookers. The only thing he's afraid of is another
one of the same kind. He's covered everywhere you can hurt
him. He don't care about a left-hand in his face.

After about four rounds Jack has him bleeding bad and his
face all cut up, but every time Walcott's got in close he's socked
so hard he's got two big red patches on both sides just below
Jack's ribs. Every time he gets in close, Jack ties him up, then
gets one hand loose and uppercuts him, but when Walcott gets
his hands loose he socks Jack in the body so they can hear it
outside in the street. He's a socker.

It goes along like that for three rounds more. They don't talk
any. They're working all the time. We worked over Jack plenty
too, in between the rounds. He don't look good at all but he
never does much work in the ring. He don't move around
much and that left-hand is just automatic. It's just like it was
connected with Walcott's face and Jack just had to wish it in
every time. Jack is always calm in close and he doesn't waste
any juice. He knows everything about working in close too
and he's getting away with a lot of stuff. While they were in
our corner I watched him tie Walcott up, get his right hand
loose, turn it and come up with an uppercut that got Walcott's
nose with the heel of the glove. Walcott was bleeding bad and
leaned his nose on Jack's shoulder so as to give Jack some of
it too, and Jack sort of lifted his shoulder sharp and caught him
against the nose, and then brought down the right hand and
did the same thing again.

Walcott was sore as hell. By the time they'd gone five
rounds he hated Jack's guts. Jack wasn't sore; that is, he wasn't
any sorer than he always was. He certainly did used to make
the fellows he fought hate boxing. That was why he hated
Kid Lewis so. He never got the Kid's goat. Kid Lewis always
had about three new dirty things Jack couldn't do. Jack was as
safe as a church all the time he was in there, as long as he was
strong. He certainly was treating Walcott rough. The funny

thing was it looked as though Jack was an open classic boxer. That was because he had all that stuff too.

After the seventh round Jack says, "My left's getting heavy."

From then he started to take a beating. It didn't show at first. But instead of him running the fight it was Walcott was running it, instead of being safe all the time now he was in trouble. He couldn't keep him out with the left hand now. It looked as though it was the same as ever, only now instead of Walcott's punches just missing him they were just hitting him. He took an awful beating in the body.

"What's the round?" Jack asked.

"The eleventh."

"I can't stay," Jack says. "My legs are going bad."

Walcott had been just hitting him for a long time. It was like a baseball catcher pulls the ball and takes some of the shock off. From now on Walcott commenced to land solid. He certainly was a socking-machine. Jack was just trying to block everything now. It didn't show what an awful beating he was taking. In between the rounds I worked on his legs. The muscles would flutter under my hands all the time I was rubbing them. He was sick as hell.

"How's it go?" he asked John, turning around, his face all swollen.

"It's his fight."

"I think I can last," Jack says. "I don't want this bohunk to stop me."

It was going just the way he thought it would. He knew he couldn't beat Walcott. He wasn't strong any more. He was all right though. His money was all right and now he wanted to finish it off right to please himself. He didn't want to be knocked out.

The gong rang and we pushed him out. He went out slow. Walcott came right out after him. Jack put the left in his face and Walcott took it, came in under it and started working on Jack's body. Jack tried to tie him up and it was just like trying to hold on to a buzz-saw. Jack broke away from it and missed with the right. Walcott clipped him with a left-hook and Jack went down. He went down on his hands and knees and looked at us. The referee started counting. Jack was watching us and shaking his head. At eight John motioned to him. You couldn't hear on account of the crowd. Jack got up. The referee had been holding Walcott back with one arm while he counted.

When Jack was on his feet Walcott started toward him.

"Watch yourself, Jimmy," I heard Solly Freedman yell to him.

Walcott came up to Jack looking at him. Jack stuck the left hand at him. Walcott just shook his head. He backed Jack up against the ropes, measured him and then hooked the left very light to the side of Jack's head and socked the right into the body as hard as he could sock, just as low as he could get it. He must have hit him five inches below the belt. I thought the eyes would come out of Jack's head. They stuck way out. His mouth come open.

The referee grabbed Walcott. Jack stepped forward. If he went down there went fifty thousand bucks. He walked as though all his insides were going to fall out.

"It wasn't low," he said. "It was a accident."

The crowd were yelling so you couldn't hear anything.

"I'm all right," Jack says. They were right in front of us. The referee looks at John and then he shakes his head.

"Come on, you polak son-of-a-bitch," Jack says to Walcott.

John was hanging onto the ropes. He had the towel ready to chuck in. Jack was standing just a little way out from the ropes. He took a step forward. I saw the sweat come out on his face like somebody had squeezed it and a big drop went down his nose.

"Come on and fight," Jack says to Walcott.

The referee looked at John and waved Walcott on.

"Go in there, you slob," he says.

Walcott went in. He didn't know what to do either. He never thought Jack could have stood it. Jack put the left in his face. There was such a hell of a lot of yelling going on. They were right in front of us. Walcott hit him twice. Jack's face was the worst thing I ever saw—the look on it! He was holding himself and all his body together and it all showed on his face. All the time he was thinking and holding his body in where it was busted.

Then he started to sock. His face looked awful all the time. He started to sock with his hands low down by his side, swinging at Walcott. Walcott covered up and Jack was swinging wild at Walcott's head. Then he swung the left and it hit Walcott in the groin and the right hit Walcott right bang where he'd hit Jack. Way low below the belt. Walcott went down and grabbed himself there and rolled and twisted around.

The referee grabbed Jack and pushed him toward his corner. John jumps into the ring. There was all this yelling going on. The referee was talking with the judges and then the announcer got into the ring with the megaphone and says, "Walcott on a foul."

The referee is talking to John and he says, "What could I do? Jack wouldn't take the foul. Then when he's groggy he fouls him."

"He'd lost it anyway," John says.

Jack's sitting on the chair. I've got his gloves off and he's holding himself in down there with both hands. When he's got something supporting it his face doesn't look so bad.

"Go over and say you're sorry," John says into his ear. "It'll look good."

Jack stands up and the sweat comes out all over his face. I put the bathrobe around him and he holds himself in with one hand under the bathrobe and goes across the ring. They've picked Walcott up and they're working on him. There're a lot of people in Walcott's corner. Nobody speaks to Jack. He leans over Walcott.

"I'm sorry," Jack says. "I didn't mean to foul you."

Walcott doesn't say anything. He looks too damned sick.

"Well, you're the champion now," Jack says to him. "I hope you get a hell of a lot of fun out of it."

"Leave the kid alone," Solly Freedman says.

"Hello, Solly," Jack says. "I'm sorry I fouled your boy."

Freedman just looks at him.

Jack went to his corner walking that funny jerky way and we got him down through the ropes and through the reporters' tables and out down the aisle. A lot of people want to slap Jack on the back. He goes out through all that mob in his bathrobe to the dressing-room. It's a popular win for Walcott. That's the way the money was bet in the Garden.

Once we got inside the dressing-room Jack lay down and shut his eyes.

"We want to get to the hotel and get a doctor," John says.

"I'm all busted inside," Jack says.

"I'm sorry as hell, Jack," John says.

"It's all right," Jack says.

He lies there with his eyes shut.

"They certainly tried a nice double-cross," John said.

"Your friends Morgan and Steinfelt," Jack said. "You got nice friends."

He lies there, his eyes are open now. His face has still got that awful drawn look.

"It's funny how fast you can think when it means that much money," Jack says.

"You're some boy, Jack," John says.

"No," Jack says. "It was nothing."

THE SHORT HAPPY LIFE OF
FRANCIS MACOMBER

IT WAS now lunch time and they were all sitting under the double green fly of the dining tent pretending that nothing had happened.

"Will you have lime juice or lemon squash?" Macomber asked.

"I'll have a gimlet," Robert Wilson told him.

"I'll have a gimlet too. I need something," Macomber's wife said.

"I suppose it's the thing to do," Macomber agreed. "Tell him to make three gimlets."

The mess boy had started them already, lifting the bottles out of the canvas cooling bags that sweated wet in the wind that blew through the trees that shaded the tents.

"What had I ought to give them?" Macomber asked.

"A quid would be plenty," Wilson told him. "You don't want to spoil them."

"Will the headman distribute it?"

"Absolutely."

Francis Macomber had, half an hour before, been carried to his tent from the edge of the camp in triumph on the arms and shoulders of the cook, the personal boys, the skinner and the porters. The gun-bearers had taken no part in the demonstration. When the native boys put him down at the door of his tent, he had shaken all their hands, received their congratulations, and then gone into the tent and sat on the bed until his wife came in. She did not speak to him when she came in and he left the tent at once to wash his face and hands in the portable wash basin outside and go over to the dining tent to sit in a comfortable canvas chair in the breeze and the shade.

"You've got your lion," Robert Wilson said to him, "and a damned fine one too."

Mrs. Macomber looked at Wilson quickly. She was an extremely handsome and well-kept woman of the beauty and social position which had, five years before, commanded five thousand dollars as the price of endorsing, with photographs, a beauty product which she had never used. She had been married to Francis Macomber for eleven years.

"He is a good lion, isn't he?" Macomber said. His wife looked at him now. She looked at both these men as though she had never seen them before.

One, Wilson, the white hunter, she knew she had never truly seen before. He was about middle height with sandy hair, a stubby mustache, a very red face and extremely cold blue eyes with faint white wrinkles at the corners that grooved merrily when he smiled. He smiled at her now and she looked away from his face at the way his shoulders sloped in the loose tunic he wore with the four big cartridges held in loops where the left breast pocket should have been, at his big brown hands, his old slacks, his very dirty boots and back to his red face again. She noticed where the baked red of his face stopped in a white line that marked the circle left by his Stetson hat that hung now from one of the pegs of the tent pole.

"Well, here's to the lion," Robert Wilson said. He smiled at her again and, not smiling, she looked curiously at her husband.

Francis Macomber was very tall, very well built if you did not mind that length of bone, dark, his hair cropped like an oarsman, rather thin-lipped, and was considered handsome. He was dressed in the same sort of safari clothes that Wilson wore except that his were new, he was thirty-five years old, kept himself very fit, was good at court games, had a number of big-game fishing records, and had just shown himself, very publicly, to be a coward.

"Here's to the lion," he said. "I can't ever thank you for what you did."

Margaret, his wife, looked away from him and back to Wilson.

"Let's not talk about the lion," she said.

Wilson looked over at her without smiling and now she smiled at him.

"It's been a very strange day," she said. "Hadn't you ought to put your hat on even under the canvas at noon? You told me that, you know."

"Might put it on," said Wilson.

"You know you have a very red face, Mr. Wilson," she told him and smiled again.

"Drink," said Wilson.

"I don't think so," she said. "Francis drinks a great deal, but his face is never red."

"It's red today," Macomber tried a joke.

"No," said Margaret. "It's mine that's red today. But Mr. Wilson's is always red."

"Must be racial," said Wilson. "I say, you wouldn't like to drop my beauty as a topic, would you?"

"I've just started on it."

"Let's chuck it," said Wilson.

"Conversation is going to be so difficult," Margaret said.

"Don't be silly, Margot," her husband said.

"No difficulty," Wilson said. "Got a damn fine lion."

Margot looked at them both and they both saw that she was going to cry. Wilson had seen it coming for a long time and he dreaded it. Macomber was past dreading it.

"I wish it hadn't happened. Oh, I wish it hadn't happened," she said and started for her tent. She made no noise of crying but they could see that her shoulders were shaking under the rose-colored, sun-proofed shirt she wore.

"Women upset," said Wilson to the tall man. "Amounts to nothing. Strain on the nerves and one thing'n another."

"No," said Macomber. "I suppose that I rate that for the rest of my life now."

"Nonsense. Let's have a spot of the giant killer," said Wilson. "Forget the whole thing. Nothing to it anyway."

"We might try," said Macomber. "I won't forget what you did for me though."

"Nothing," said Wilson. "All nonsense."

So they sat there in the shade where the camp was pitched under some wide-topped acacia trees with a boulder-strewn cliff behind them, and a stretch of grass that ran to the bank of a boulder-filled stream in front with forest beyond it, and drank their just-cool lime drinks and avoided one another's eyes while the boys set the table for lunch. Wilson could tell that the boys all knew about it now and when he saw Macomber's personal boy looking curiously at his master while he was putting dishes on the table he snapped at him in Swahili. The boy turned away with his face blank.

"What were you telling him?" Macomber asked.

"Nothing. Told him to look alive or I'd see he got about fifteen of the best."

"What's that? Lashes?"

"It's quite illegal," Wilson said. "You're supposed to fine them."

"Do you still have them whipped?"

"Oh, yes. They could raise a row if they chose to complain. But they don't. They prefer it to the fines."

"How strange!" said Macomber.

"Not strange, really," Wilson said. "Which would you rather do? Take a good birching or lose your pay?"

Then he felt embarrassed at asking it and before Macomber could answer he went on, "We all take a beating every day, you know, one way or another."

This was no better. "Good God," he thought. "I am a diplomat, aren't I?"

"Yes, we take a beating," said Macomber, still not looking at him. "I'm awfully sorry about that lion business. It doesn't have to go any further, does it? I mean no one will hear about it, will they?"

"You mean will I tell it at the Mathaiga Club?" Wilson looked at him now coldly. He had not expected this. So he's a bloody four-letter man as well as a bloody coward, he thought.

I rather liked him too until today. But how is one to know about an American?

"No," said Wilson. "I'm a professional hunter. We never talk about our clients. You can be quite easy on that. It's supposed to be bad form to ask us not to talk though."

He had decided now that to break would be much easier. He would eat, then, by himself and could read a book with his meals. They would eat by themselves. He would see them through the safari on a very formal basis—what was it the French called it? Distinguished consideration—and it would be a damn sight easier than having to go through this emotional trash. He'd insult him and make a good clean break. Then he could read a book with his meals and he'd still be drinking their whisky. That was the phrase for it when a safari went bad. You ran into another white hunter and you asked, "How is everything going?" and he answered, "Oh, I'm still drinking their whisky," and you knew everything had gone to pot.

"I'm sorry," Macomber said and looked at him with his American face that would stay adolescent until it became middle-aged, and Wilson noted his crew-cropped hair, fine eyes only faintly shifty, good nose, thin lips and handsome jaw. "I'm sorry I didn't realize that. There are lots of things I don't know."

So what could he do, Wilson thought. He was all ready to break it off quickly and neatly and here the beggar was apologizing after he had just insulted him. He made one more attempt. "Don't worry about me talking," he said. "I have a living to make. You know in Africa no woman ever misses her lion and no white man ever bolts."

"I bolted like a rabbit," Macomber said.

Now what in hell were you going to do about a man who talked like that, Wilson wondered.

Wilson looked at Macomber with his flat, blue, machine-gunner's eyes and the other smiled back at him. He had a pleasant smile if you did not notice how his eyes showed when he was hurt.

"Maybe I can fix it up on buffalo," he said. "We're after them next, aren't we?"

"In the morning if you like," Wilson told him. Perhaps he had been wrong. This was certainly the way to take it. You most certainly could not tell a damned thing about an American. He was all for Macomber again. If you could forget the morning. But, of course, you couldn't. The morning had been about as bad as they come.

"Here comes the Memsahib," he said. She was walking over from her tent looking refreshed and cheerful and quite lovely. She had a very perfect oval face, so perfect that you expected her to be stupid. But she wasn't stupid, Wilson thought, no, not stupid.

"How is the beautiful red-faced Mr. Wilson? Are you feeling better, Francis, my pearl?"

"Oh, much," said Macomber.

"I've dropped the whole thing," she said, sitting down at the table. "What importance is there to whether Francis is any good at killing lions? That's not his trade. That's Mr. Wilson's trade. Mr. Wilson is really very impressive killing anything. You do kill anything, don't you?"

"Oh, anything," said Wilson. "Simply anything." They are, he thought, the hardest in the world; the hardest, the cruelest, the most predatory and the most attractive and their men have softened or gone to pieces nervously as they have hardened. Or is it that they pick men they can handle? They can't know that much at the age they marry, he thought. He was grateful that he had gone through his education on American women before now because this was a very attractive one.

"We're going after buff in the morning," he told her.

"I'm coming," she said.

"No, you're not."

"Oh, yes, I am. Mayn't I, Francis?"

"Why not stay in camp?"

"Not for anything," she said. "I wouldn't miss something like today for anything."

When she left, Wilson was thinking, when she went off to

cry, she seemed a hell of a fine woman. She seemed to understand, to realize, to be hurt for him and for herself and to know
how things really stood. She is away for twenty minutes and
now she is back, simply enamelled in that American female
cruelty. They are the damnedest women. Really the damnedest.

"We'll put on another show for you tomorrow," Francis
Macomber said.

"You're not coming," Wilson said.

"You're very mistaken," she told him. "And I want *so* to see
you perform again. You were lovely this morning. That is if
blowing things' heads off is lovely."

"Here's the lunch," said Wilson. "You're very merry, aren't
you?"

"Why not? I didn't come out here to be dull."

"Well, it hasn't been dull," Wilson said. He could see the
boulders in the river and the high bank beyond with the trees
and he remembered the morning.

"Oh, no," she said. "It's been charming. And tomorrow. You
don't know how I look forward to tomorrow."

"That's eland he's offering you," Wilson said.

"They're the big cowy things that jump like hares, aren't
they?"

"I suppose that describes them," Wilson said.

"It's very good meat," Macomber said.

"Did you shoot it, Francis?" she asked.

"Yes."

"They're not dangerous, are they?"

"Only if they fall on you," Wilson told her.

"I'm so glad."

"Why not let up on the bitchery just a little, Margot," Macomber said, cutting the eland steak and putting some mashed
potato, gravy and carrot on the down-turned fork that tined
through the piece of meat.

"I suppose I could," she said, "since you put it so prettily."

"Tonight we'll have champagne for the lion," Wilson said.
"It's a bit too hot at noon."

"Oh, the lion," Margot said. "I'd forgotten the lion!"

So, Robert Wilson thought to himself, she *is* giving him a ride, isn't she? Or do you suppose that's her idea of putting up a good show? How should a woman act when she discovers her husband is a bloody coward? She's damn cruel but they're all cruel. They govern, of course, and to govern one has to be cruel sometimes. Still, I've seen enough of their damn terrorism.

"Have some more eland," he said to her politely.

That afternoon, late, Wilson and Macomber went out in the motor car with the native driver and the two gun-bearers. Mrs. Macomber stayed in the camp. It was too hot to go out, she said, and she was going with them in the early morning. As they drove off Wilson saw her standing under the big tree, looking pretty rather than beautiful in her faintly rosy khaki, her dark hair drawn back off her forehead and gathered in a knot low on her neck, her face as fresh, he thought, as though she were in England. She waved to them as the car went off through the swale of high grass and curved around through the trees into the small hills of orchard bush.

In the orchard bush they found a herd of impala, and leaving the car they stalked one old ram with long, wide-spread horns and Macomber killed it with a very creditable shot that knocked the buck down at a good two hundred yards and sent the herd off bounding wildly and leaping over one another's backs in long, leg-drawn-up leaps as unbelievable and as floating as those one makes sometimes in dreams.

"That was a good shot," Wilson said. "They're a small target."

"Is it a worth-while head?" Macomber asked.

"It's excellent," Wilson told him. "You shoot like that and you'll have no trouble."

"Do you think we'll find buffalo tomorrow?"

"There's a good chance of it. They feed out early in the morning and with luck we may catch them in the open."

"I'd like to clear away that lion business," Macomber said.

"It's not very pleasant to have your wife see you do something like that."

I should think it would be even more unpleasant to do it, Wilson thought, wife or no wife, or to talk about it having done it. But he said, "I wouldn't think about that any more. Any one could be upset by his first lion. That's all over."

But that night after dinner and a whisky and soda by the fire before going to bed, as Francis Macomber lay on his cot with the mosquito bar over him and listened to the night noises it was not all over. It was neither all over nor was it beginning. It was there exactly as it happened with some parts of it indelibly emphasized and he was miserably ashamed at it. But more than shame he felt cold, hollow fear in him. The fear was still there like a cold slimy hollow in all the emptiness where once his confidence had been and it made him feel sick. It was still there with him now.

It had started the night before when he had wakened and heard the lion roaring somewhere up along the river. It was a deep sound and at the end there were sort of coughing grunts that made him seem just outside the tent, and when Francis Macomber woke in the night to hear it he was afraid. He could hear his wife breathing quietly, asleep. There was no one to tell he was afraid, nor to be afraid with him, and, lying alone, he did not know the Somali proverb that says a brave man is always frightened three times by a lion; when he first sees his track, when he first hears him roar and when he first confronts him. Then while they were eating breakfast by lantern light out in the dining tent, before the sun was up, the lion roared again and Francis thought he was just at the edge of camp.

"Sounds like an old-timer," Robert Wilson said, looking up from his kippers and coffee. "Listen to him cough."

"Is he very close?"

"A mile or so up the stream."

"Will we see him?"

"We'll have a look."

"Does his roaring carry that far? It sounds as though he were right in camp."

"Carries a hell of a long way," said Robert Wilson. "It's strange the way it carries. Hope he's a shootable cat. The boys said there was a very big one about here."

"If I get a shot, where should I hit him," Macomber asked, "to stop him?"

"In the shoulders," Wilson said. "In the neck if you can make it. Shoot for bone. Break him down."

"I hope I can place it properly," Macomber said.

"You shoot very well," Wilson told him. "Take your time. Make sure of him. The first one in is the one that counts."

"What range will it be?"

"Can't tell. Lion has something to say about that. Won't shoot unless it's close enough so you can make sure."

"At under a hundred yards?" Macomber asked.

Wilson looked at him quickly.

"Hundred's about right. Might have to take him a bit under. Shouldn't chance a shot at much over that. A hundred's a decent range. You can hit him wherever you want at that. Here comes the Memsahib."

"Good morning," she said. "Are we going after that lion?"

"As soon as you deal with your breakfast," Wilson said. "How are you feeling?"

"Marvellous," she said. "I'm very excited."

"I'll just go and see that everything is ready." Wilson went off. As he left the lion roared again.

"Noisy beggar," Wilson said. "We'll put a stop to that."

"What's the matter, Francis?" his wife asked him.

"Nothing," Macomber said.

"Yes, there is," she said. "What are you upset about?"

"Nothing," he said.

"Tell me," she looked at him. "Don't you feel well?"

"It's that damned roaring," he said. "It's been going on all night, you know."

"Why didn't you wake me," she said. "I'd love to have heard it."

"I've got to kill the damned thing," Macomber said, miserably.

"Well, that's what you're out here for, isn't it?"

"Yes. But I'm nervous. Hearing the thing roar gets on my nerves."

"Well then, as Wilson said, kill him and stop his roaring."

"Yes, darling," said Francis Macomber. "It sounds easy, doesn't it?"

"You're not afraid, are you?"

"Of course not. But I'm nervous from hearing him roar all night."

"You'll kill him marvellously," she said. "I know you will. I'm awfully anxious to see it."

"Finish your breakfast and we'll be starting."

"It's not light yet," she said. "This is a ridiculous hour."

Just then the lion roared in a deep-chested moaning, suddenly guttural, ascending vibration that seemed to shake the air and ended in a sigh and a heavy, deep-chested grunt.

"He sounds almost here," Macomber's wife said.

"My God," said Macomber. "I hate that damned noise."

"It's very impressive."

"Impressive. It's frightful."

Robert Wilson came up then carrying his short, ugly, shockingly big-bored .505 Gibbs and grinning.

"Come on," he said. "Your gun-bearer has your Springfield and the big gun. Everything's in the car. Have you solids?"

"Yes."

"I'm ready," Mrs. Macomber said.

"Must make him stop that racket," Wilson said. "You get in front. The Memsahib can sit back here with me."

They climbed into the motor car and, in the gray first daylight, moved off up the river through the trees. Macomber opened the breech of his rifle and saw he had metal-cased bullets, shut the bolt and put the rifle on safety. He saw his hand was trembling. He felt in his pocket for more cartridges and moved his fingers over the cartridges in the loops of his tunic front. He turned back to where Wilson sat in the rear seat of the doorless, box-bodied motor car beside his wife, them both grinning with excitement, and Wilson leaned forward and whispered,

"See the birds dropping. Means the old boy has left his kill."

On the far bank of the stream Macomber could see, above the trees, vultures circling and plummeting down.

"Chances are he'll come to drink along here," Wilson whispered. "Before he goes to lay up. Keep an eye out."

They were driving slowly along the high bank of the stream which here cut deeply to its boulder-filled bed, and they wound in and out through big trees as they drove. Macomber was watching the opposite bank when he felt Wilson take hold of his arm. The car stopped.

"There he is," he heard the whisper. "Ahead and to the right. Get out and take him. He's a marvellous lion."

Macomber saw the lion now. He was standing almost broadside, his great head up and turned toward them. The early morning breeze that blew toward them was just stirring his dark mane, and the lion looked huge, silhouetted on the rise of bank in the gray morning light, his shoulders heavy, his barrel of a body bulking smoothly.

"How far is he?" asked Macomber, raising his rifle.

"About seventy-five. Get out and take him."

"Why not shoot from where I am?"

"You don't shoot them from cars," he heard Wilson saying in his ear. "Get out. He's not going to stay there all day."

Macomber stepped out of the curved opening at the side of the front seat, onto the step and down onto the ground. The lion still stood looking majestically and coolly toward this object that his eyes only showed in silhouette, bulking like some super-rhino. There was no man smell carried toward him and he watched the object, moving his great head a little from side to side. Then watching the object, not afraid, but hesitating before going down the bank to drink with such a thing opposite him, he saw a man figure detach itself from it and he turned his heavy head and swung away toward the cover of the trees as he heard a cracking crash and felt the slam of a .30–06 220-grain solid bullet that bit his flank and

ripped in sudden hot scalding nausea through his stomach.
He trotted, heavy, big-footed, swinging wounded full-bellied,
through the trees toward the tall grass and cover, and the crash
came again to go past him ripping the air apart. Then it
crashed again and he felt the blow as it hit his lower ribs and
ripped on through, blood sudden hot and frothy in his mouth,
and he galloped toward the high grass where he could crouch
and not be seen and make them bring the crashing thing close
enough so he could make a rush and get the man that held it.

Macomber had not thought how the lion felt as he got out
of the car. He only knew his hands were shaking and as he
walked away from the car it was almost impossible for him to
make his legs move. They were stiff in the thighs, but he could
feel the muscles fluttering. He raised the rifle, sighted on the
junction of the lion's head and shoulders and pulled the trigger. Nothing happened though he pulled until he thought his
finger would break. Then he knew he had the safety on and as
he lowered the rifle to move the safety over he moved another
frozen pace forward, and the lion seeing his silhouette now
clear of the silhouette of the car, turned and started off at a
trot, and, as Macomber fired, he heard a whunk that meant
that the bullet was home; but the lion kept on going. Macomber shot again and every one saw the bullet throw a spout
of dirt beyond the trotting lion. He shot again, remembering
to lower his aim, and they all heard the bullet hit, and the lion
went into a gallop and was in the tall grass before he had the
bolt pushed forward.

Macomber stood there feeling sick at his stomach, his hands
that held the Springfield still cocked, shaking, and his wife
and Robert Wilson were standing by him. Beside him too were
the two gun-bearers chattering in Wakamba.

"I hit him," Macomber said. "I hit him twice."

"You gut-shot him and you hit him somewhere forward,"
Wilson said without enthusiasm. The gun-bearers looked very
grave. They were silent now.

"You may have killed him," Wilson went on. "We'll have to
wait a while before we go in to find out."

"What do you mean?"

"Let him get sick before we follow him up."

"Oh," said Macomber.

"He's a hell of a fine lion," Wilson said cheerfully. "He's gotten into a bad place though."

"Why is it bad?"

"Can't see him until you're on him."

"Oh," said Macomber.

"Come on," said Wilson. "The Memsahib can stay here in the car. We'll go to have a look at the blood spoor."

"Stay here, Margot," Macomber said to his wife. His mouth was very dry and it was hard for him to talk.

"Why?" she asked.

"Wilson says to."

"We're going to have a look," Wilson said. "You stay here. You can see even better from here."

"All right."

Wilson spoke in Swahili to the driver. He nodded and said, "Yes, Bwana."

Then they went down the steep bank and across the stream, climbing over and around the boulders and up the other bank, pulling up by some projecting roots, and along it until they found where the lion had been trotting when Macomber first shot. There was dark blood on the short grass that the gunbearers pointed out with grass stems, and that ran away behind the river bank trees.

"What do we do?" asked Macomber.

"Not much choice," said Wilson. "We can't bring the car over. Bank's too steep. We'll let him stiffen up a bit and then you and I'll go in and have a look for him."

"Can't we set the grass on fire?" Macomber asked.

"Too green."

"Can't we send beaters?"

Wilson looked at him appraisingly. "Of course we can," he said. "But it's just a touch murderous. You see we know the lion's wounded. You can drive an unwounded lion—he'll move on ahead of a noise—but a wounded lion's going to charge.

You can't see him until you're right on him. He'll make himself perfectly flat in cover you wouldn't think would hide a hare. You can't very well send boys in there to that sort of a show. Somebody bound to get mauled."

"What about the gun-bearers?"

"Oh, they'll go with us. It's their *shauri*. You see, they signed on for it. They don't look too happy though, do they?"

"I don't want to go in there," said Macomber. It was out before he knew he'd said it.

"Neither do I," said Wilson very cheerily. "Really no choice though." Then, as an afterthought, he glanced at Macomber and saw suddenly how he was trembling and the pitiful look on his face.

"You don't have to go in, of course," he said. "That's what I'm hired for, you know. That's why I'm so expensive."

"You mean you'd go in by yourself? Why not leave him there?"

Robert Wilson, whose entire occupation had been with the lion and the problem he presented, and who had not been thinking about Macomber except to note that he was rather windy, suddenly felt as though he had opened the wrong door in a hotel and seen something shameful.

"What do you mean?"

"Why not just leave him?"

"You mean pretend to ourselves he hasn't been hit?"

"No. Just drop it."

"It isn't done."

"Why not?"

"For one thing, he's certain to be suffering. For another, some one else might run onto him."

"I see."

"But you don't have to have anything to do with it."

"I'd like to," Macomber said. "I'm just scared, you know."

"I'll go ahead when we go in," Wilson said, "with Kongoni tracking. You keep behind me and a little to one side. Chances are we'll hear him growl. If we see him we'll both shoot. Don't worry about anything. I'll keep you backed up. As a matter of fact, you know, perhaps you'd better not go. It might be much better. Why don't you go over and join the Memsahib while I just get it over with?"

"No, I want to go."

"All right," said Wilson. "But don't go in if you don't want to. This is my *shauri* now, you know."

"I want to go," said Macomber.

They sat under a tree and smoked.

"Want to go back and speak to the Memsahib while we're waiting?" Wilson asked.

"No."

"I'll just step back and tell her to be patient."

"Good," said Macomber. He sat there, sweating under his arms, his mouth dry, his stomach hollow feeling, wanting to find courage to tell Wilson to go on and finish off the lion without him. He could not know that Wilson was furious because he had not noticed the state he was in earlier and sent him back to his wife. While he sat there Wilson came up. "I have your big gun," he said. "Take it. We've given him time, I think. Come on."

Macomber took the big gun and Wilson said:

"Keep behind me and about five yards to the right and do exactly as I tell you." Then he spoke in Swahili to the two gun-bearers who looked the picture of gloom.

"Let's go," he said.

"Could I have a drink of water?" Macomber asked. Wilson spoke to the older gun-bearer, who wore a canteen on his belt, and the man unbuckled it, unscrewed the top and handed it to Macomber, who took it noticing how heavy it seemed and how hairy and shoddy the felt covering was in his hand. He raised it to drink and looked ahead at the high grass with the flat-topped trees behind it. A breeze was blowing toward them and the grass rippled gently in the wind. He looked at the gun-bearer and he could see the gun-bearer was suffering too with fear.

Thirty-five yards into the grass the big lion lay flattened

out along the ground. His ears were back and his only movement was a slight twitching up and down of his long, black-
tufted tail. He had turned at bay as soon as he had reached this
cover and he was sick with the wound through his full belly,
and weakening with the wound through his lungs that
brought a thin foamy red to his mouth each time he breathed.
His flanks were wet and hot and flies were on the little open-
ings the solid bullets had made in his tawny hide, and his big
yellow eyes, narrowed with hate, looked straight ahead, only
blinking when the pain came as he breathed, and his claws
dug in the soft baked earth. All of him, pain, sickness, hatred
and all of his remaining strength, was tightening into an absolute concentration for a rush. He could hear the men talking
and he waited, gathering all of himself into this preparation
for a charge as soon as the men would come into the grass. As
he heard their voices his tail stiffened to twitch up and down,
and, as they came into the edge of the grass, he made a coughing grunt and charged.

Kongoni, the old gun-bearer, in the lead watching the blood
spoor, Wilson watching the grass for any movement, his big
gun ready, the second gun-bearer looking ahead and listening,
Macomber close to Wilson, his rifle cocked, they had just
moved into the grass when Macomber heard the blood-choked
coughing grunt, and saw the swishing rush in the grass. The
next thing he knew he was running; running wildly, in panic
in the open, running toward the stream.

He heard the *ca-ra-wong!* of Wilson's big rifle, and again
in a second crashing *carawong!* and turning saw the lion,
horrible-looking now, with half his head seeming to be gone,
crawling toward Wilson in the edge of the tall grass while
the red-faced man worked the bolt on the short ugly rifle and
aimed carefully as another blasting *carawong!* came from
the muzzle, and the crawling, heavy, yellow bulk of the lion
stiffened and the huge, mutilated head slid forward and Macomber, standing by himself in the clearing where he had run,
holding a loaded rifle, while two black men and a white man

looked back at him in contempt, knew the lion was dead. He came toward Wilson, his tallness all seeming a naked reproach, and Wilson looked at him and said:

"Want to take pictures?"

"No," he said.

That was all any one had said until they reached the motor car. Then Wilson had said:

"Hell of a fine lion. Boys will skin him out. We might as well stay here in the shade."

Macomber's wife had not looked at him nor he at her and he had sat by her in the back seat with Wilson sitting in the front seat. Once he had reached over and taken his wife's hand without looking at her and she had removed her hand from his. Looking across the stream to where the gun-bearers were skinning out the lion he could see that she had been able to see the whole thing. While they sat there his wife had reached forward and put her hand on Wilson's shoulder. He turned and she had leaned forward over the low seat and kissed him on the mouth.

"Oh, I say," said Wilson, going redder than his natural baked color.

"Mr. Robert Wilson," she said. "The beautiful red-faced Mr. Robert Wilson."

Then she sat down beside Macomber again and looked away across the stream to where the lion lay, with uplifted, white-muscled, tendon-marked naked forearms, and white bloating belly, as the black men fleshed away the skin. Finally the gun-bearers brought the skin over, wet and heavy, and climbed in behind with it, rolling it up before they got in, and the motor car started. No one had said anything more until they were back in camp.

That was the story of the lion. Macomber did not know how the lion had felt before he started his rush, nor during it when the unbelievable smash of the .505 with a muzzle velocity of two tons had hit him in the mouth, nor what kept him coming after that, when the second ripping crash had smashed his hind quarters and he had come crawling on toward the crashing, blasting thing that had destroyed him. Wilson knew something about it and only expressed it by saying, "Damned fine lion," but Macomber did not know how Wilson felt about things either. He did not know how his wife felt except that she was through with him.

His wife had been through with him before but it never lasted. He was very wealthy, and would be much wealthier, and he knew she would not leave him ever now. That was one of the few things that he really knew. He knew about that, about motor cycles—that was earliest—about motor cars, about duck-shooting, about fishing, trout, salmon and big-sea, about sex in books, many books, too many books, about all court games, about dogs, not much about horses, about hanging on to his money, about most of the other things his world dealt in, and about his wife not leaving him. His wife had been a great beauty and she was still a great beauty in Africa, but she was not a great enough beauty any more at home to be able to leave him and better herself and she knew it and he knew it. She had missed the chance to leave him and he knew it. If he had been better with women she would probably have started to worry about him getting another new, beautiful wife; but she knew too much about him to worry about him either. Also, he had always had a great tolerance which seemed the nicest thing about him if it were not the most sinister.

All in all they were known as a comparatively happily married couple, one of those whose disruption is often rumored but never occurs, and as the society columnist put it, they were adding more than a spice of *adventure* to their much envied and ever-enduring *Romance* by a *Safari* in what was known as *Darkest Africa* until the Martin Johnsons lighted it on so many silver screens where they were pursuing *Old Simba* the lion, the buffalo, *Tembo* the elephant and as well collecting specimens for the Museum of Natural History. This same columnist had reported them *on the verge* as least three times in the past and they had been. But they always made it up.

They had a sound basis of union. Margot was too beautiful for Macomber to divorce her and Macomber had too much money for Margot ever to leave him.

It was now about three o'clock in the morning and Francis Macomber, who had been asleep a little while after he had stopped thinking about the lion, wakened and then slept again, woke suddenly, frightened in a dream of the bloody-headed lion standing over him, and listening while his heart pounded, he realized that his wife was not in the other cot in the tent. He lay awake with that knowledge for two hours.

At the end of that time his wife came into the tent, lifted her mosquito bar and crawled cozily into bed.

"Where have you been?" Macomber asked in the darkness.

"Hello," she said. "Are you awake?"

"Where have you been?"

"I just went out to get a breath of air."

"You did, like hell."

"What do you want me to say, darling?"

"Where have you been?"

"Out to get a breath of air."

"That's a new name for it. You *are* a bitch."

"Well, you're a coward."

"All right," he said. "What of it?"

"Nothing as far as I'm concerned. But please let's not talk, darling, because I'm very sleepy."

"You think that I'll take anything."

"I know you will, sweet."

"Well, I won't."

"Please, darling, let's not talk. I'm so very sleepy."

"There wasn't going to be any of that. You promised there wouldn't be."

"Well, there is now," she said sweetly.

"You said if we made this trip that there would be none of that. You promised."

"Yes, darling. That's the way I meant it to be. But the trip was spoiled yesterday. We don't have to talk about it, do we?"

"You don't wait long when you have an advantage, do you?"

"Please let's not talk. I'm so sleepy, darling."

"I'm going to talk."

"Don't mind me then, because I'm going to sleep." And she did.

At breakfast they were all three at the table before daylight and Francis Macomber found that, of all the many men that he had hated, he hated Robert Wilson the most.

"Sleep well?" Wilson asked in his throaty voice, filling a pipe.

"Did you?"

"Topping," the white hunter told him.

You bastard, thought Macomber, you insolent bastard.

So she woke him when she came in, Wilson thought, looking at them both with his flat, cold eyes. Well, why doesn't he keep his wife where she belongs? What does he think I am, a bloody plaster saint? Let him keep her where she belongs. It's his own fault.

"Do you think we'll find buffalo?" Margot asked, pushing away a dish of apricots.

"Chance of it," Wilson said and smiled at her. "Why don't you stay in camp?"

"Not for anything," she told him.

"Why not order her to stay in camp?" Wilson said to Macomber.

"You order her," said Macomber coldly.

"Let's not have any ordering, nor," turning to Macomber, "any silliness, Francis," Margot said quite pleasantly.

"Are you ready to start?" Macomber asked.

"Any time," Wilson told him. "Do you want the Memsahib to go?"

"Does it make any difference whether I do or not?"

The hell with it, thought Robert Wilson. The utter complete hell with it. So this is what it's going to be like. Well, this is what it's going to be like, then.

"Makes no difference," he said.

"You're sure you wouldn't like to stay in camp with her yourself and let me go out and hunt the buffalo?" Macomber asked.

"Can't do that," said Wilson. "Wouldn't talk rot if I were you."

"I'm not talking rot. I'm disgusted."

"Bad word, disgusted."

"Francis, will you please try to speak sensibly!" his wife said.

"I speak too damned sensibly," Macomber said. "Did you ever eat such filthy food?"

"Something wrong with the food?" asked Wilson quietly.

"No more than with everything else."

"I'd pull yourself together, laddybuck," Wilson said very quietly. "There's a boy waits at table that understands a little English."

"The hell with him."

Wilson stood up and puffing on his pipe strolled away, speaking a few words in Swahili to one of the gun-bearers who was standing waiting for him. Macomber and his wife sat on at the table. He was staring at his coffee cup.

"If you make a scene I'll leave you, darling," Margot said quietly.

"No, you won't."

"You can try it and see."

"You won't leave me."

"No," she said. "I won't leave you and you'll behave yourself."

"Behave myself? That's a way to talk. Behave myself."

"Yes. Behave yourself."

"Why don't *you* try behaving?"

"I've tried it so long. So very long."

"I hate that red-faced swine," Macomber said. "I loathe the sight of him."

"He's really *very* nice."

"Oh, *shut up,*" Macomber almost shouted. Just then the car came up and stopped in front of the dining tent and the driver and the two gun-bearers got out. Wilson walked over and looked at the husband and wife sitting there at the table.

"Going shooting?" he asked.

"Yes," said Macomber, standing up. "Yes."

"Better bring a woolly. It will be cool in the car," Wilson said.

"I'll get my leather jacket," Margot said.

"The boy has it," Wilson told her. He climbed into the front with the driver and Francis Macomber and his wife sat, not speaking, in the back seat.

Hope the silly beggar doesn't take a notion to blow the back of my head off, Wilson thought to himself. Women *are* a nuisance on safari.

The car was grinding down to cross the river at a pebbly ford in the gray daylight and then climbed, angling up the steep bank, where Wilson had ordered a way shovelled out the day before so they could reach the parklike wooded rolling country on the far side.

It was a good morning, Wilson thought. There was a heavy dew and as the wheels went through the grass and low bushes he could smell the odor of the crushed fronds. It was an odor like verbena and he liked this early morning smell of the dew, the crushed bracken and the look of the tree trunks showing black through the early morning mist, as the car made its way through the untracked, parklike country. He had put the two in the back seat out of his mind now and was thinking about buffalo. The buffalo that he was after stayed in the daytime in a thick swamp where it was impossible to get a shot, but in the night they fed out into an open stretch of country and if he could come between them and their swamp with the car, Macomber would have a good chance at them in the open. He did not want to hunt buff with Macomber in thick cover. He did not want to hunt buff or anything else with Macomber at all, but he was a professional hunter and he had hunted with some rare ones in his time. If they got buff today there would only be rhino to come and the poor man would have gone through his dangerous game and things might pick up. He'd have nothing more to do with the woman and Macomber would get over that too. He must have gone through plenty of that before by the look of things. Poor beggar. He must have a way of getting over it. Well, it was the poor sod's own bloody fault.

He, Robert Wilson, carried a double size cot on safari to accommodate any windfalls he might receive. He had hunted for a certain clientele, the international, fast, sporting set, where the women did not feel they were getting their money's worth unless they had shared that cot with the white hunter. He despised them when he was away from them although he liked some of them well enough at the time, but he made his living by them; and their standards were his standards as long as they were hiring him.

They were his standards in all except the shooting. He had his own standards about the killing and they could live up to them or get some one else to hunt them. He knew, too, that they all respected him for this. This Macomber was an odd one though. Damned if he wasn't. Now the wife. Well, the wife. Yes, the wife. Hm, the wife. Well he'd dropped all that. He looked around at them. Macomber sat grim and furious. Margot smiled at him. She looked younger today, more innocent and fresher and not so professionally beautiful. What's in her heart God knows, Wilson thought. She hadn't talked much last night. At that it was a pleasure to see her.

The motor car climbed up a slight rise and went on through the trees and then out into a grassy prairie-like opening and kept in the shelter of the trees along the edge, the driver going slowly and Wilson looking carefully out across the prairie and all along its far side. He stopped the car and studied the opening with his field glasses. Then he motioned to the driver to go on and the car moved slowly along, the driver avoiding wart-hog holes and driving around the mud castles ants had built. Then, looking across the opening, Wilson suddenly turned and said,

"By God, there they are!"

And looking where he pointed, while the car jumped forward and Wilson spoke in rapid Swahili to the driver, Macomber saw three huge, black animals looking almost cylindrical in their long heaviness, like big black tank cars, moving at a gallop across the far edge of the open prairie. They moved at a stiff-necked, stiff bodied gallop and he could see the upswept wide black horns on their heads as they galloped heads out; the heads not moving.

"They're three old bulls," Wilson said. "We'll cut them off before they get to the swamp."

The car was going a wild forty-five miles an hour across the open and as Macomber watched, the buffalo got bigger and bigger until he could see the gray, hairless, scabby look of one huge bull and how his neck was a part of his shoulders and the shiny black of his horns as he galloped a little behind the others that were strung out in that steady plunging gait; and then, the car swaying as though it had just jumped a road, they drew up close and he could see the plunging hugeness of the bull, and the dust in his sparsely haired hide, the wide boss of horn and his outstretched, wide-nostrilled muzzle, and he was raising his rifle when Wilson shouted, "Not from the car, you fool!" and he had no fear, only hatred of Wilson, while the brakes clamped on and the car skidded, plowing sideways to an almost stop and Wilson was out on one side and he on the other, stumbling as his feet hit the still speeding-by of the earth, and then he was shooting at the bull as he moved away, hearing the bullets whunk into him, emptying his rifle at him as he moved steadily away, finally remembering to get his shots forward into the shoulder, and as he fumbled to re-load, he saw the bull was down. Down on his knees, his big head tossing, and seeing the other two still galloping he shot at the leader and hit him. He shot again and missed and he heard the *carawonging* roar as Wilson shot and saw the leading bull slide forward onto his nose.

"Get that other," Wilson said. "Now you're shooting!"

But the other bull was moving steadily at the same gallop and he missed, throwing a spout of dirt, and Wilson missed and the dust rose in a cloud and Wilson shouted, "Come on. He's too far!" and grabbed his arm and they were in the car again, Macomber and Wilson hanging on the sides and rocketing swayingly over the uneven ground, drawing up on the steady, plunging, heavy-necked, straight-moving gallop of the bull.

They were behind him and Macomber was filling his rifle, dropping shells onto the ground, jamming it, clearing the jam, then they were almost up with the bull when Wilson yelled "Stop," and the car skidded so that it almost swung over and Macomber fell forward onto his feet, slammed his bolt forward and fired as far forward as he could aim into the galloping, rounded black back, aimed and shot again, then again, then again, and the bullets, all of them hitting, had no effect on the buffalo that he could see. Then Wilson shot, the roar deafening him, and he could see the bull stagger. Macomber shot again, aiming carefully, and down he came, onto his knees.

"All right," Wilson said. "Nice work. That's the three."

Macomber felt a drunken elation.

"How many times did you shoot?" he asked.

"Just three," Wilson said. "You killed the first bull. The biggest one. I helped you finish the other two. Afraid they might have got into cover. You had them killed. I was just mopping up a little. You shot damn well."

"Let's go to the car," said Macomber. "I want a drink."

"Got to finish off that buff first," Wilson told him. The buffalo was on his knees and he jerked his head furiously and bellowed in pig-eyed, roaring rage as they came toward him.

"Watch he doesn't get up," Wilson said. Then, "Get a little broadside and take him in the neck just behind the ear."

Macomber aimed carefully at the center of the huge, jerking, rage-driven neck and shot. At the shot the head dropped forward.

"That does it," said Wilson. "Got the spine. They're a hell of a looking thing, aren't they?"

"Let's get the drink," said Macomber. In his life he had never felt so good.

In the car Macomber's wife sat very white faced. "You were marvellous, darling," she said to Macomber. "What a ride."

"Was it rough?" Wilson asked.

"It was frightful. I've never been more frightened in my life."

"Let's all have a drink," Macomber said.

"By all means," said Wilson. "Give it to the Memsahib." She drank the neat whisky from the flask and shuddered a little when she swallowed. She handed the flask to Macomber who handed it to Wilson.

"It was frightfully exciting," she said. "It's given me a dreadful headache. I didn't know you were allowed to shoot them from cars though."

"No one shot from cars," said Wilson coldly.

"I mean chase them from cars."

"Wouldn't ordinarily," Wilson said. "Seemed sporting enough to me though while we were doing it. Taking more chance driving that way across the plain full of holes and one thing and another than hunting on foot. Buffalo could have charged us each time we shot if he liked. Gave him every chance. Wouldn't mention it to any one though. It's illegal if that's what you mean."

"It seemed very unfair to me," Margot said, "chasing those big helpless things in a motor car."

"Did it?" said Wilson.

"What would happen if they heard about it in Nairobi?"

"I'd lose my licence for one thing. Other unpleasantnesses," Wilson said, taking a drink from the flask. "I'd be out of business."

"Really?"

"Yes, really."

"Well," said Macomber, and he smiled for the first time all day. "Now she has something on you."

"You have such a pretty way of putting things, Francis," Margot Macomber said. Wilson looked at them both. If a four-letter man marries a five-letter woman, he was thinking, what number of letters would their children be? What he said was, "We lost a gun-bearer. Did you notice it?"

"My God, no," Macomber said.

"Here he comes," Wilson said. "He's all right. He must have fallen off when we left the first bull."

Approaching them was the middle-aged gun-bearer, limping along in his knitted cap, khaki tunic, shorts and rubber sandals, gloomy-faced and disgusted looking. As he came up he called out to Wilson in Swahili and they all saw the change in the white hunter's face.

"What does he say?" asked Margot.

"He says the first bull got up and went into the bush," Wilson said with no expression in his voice.

"Oh," said Macomber blankly.

"Then it's going to be just like the lion," said Margot, full of anticipation.

"It's not going to be a damned bit like the lion," Wilson told her. "Did you want another drink, Macomber?"

"Thanks, yes," Macomber said. He expected the feeling he had had about the lion to come back but it did not. For the first time in his life he really felt wholly without fear. Instead of fear he had a feeling of definite elation.

"We'll go and have a look at the second bull," Wilson said. "I'll tell the driver to put the car in the shade."

"What are you going to do?" asked Margaret Macomber.

"Take a look at the buff," Wilson said.

"I'll come."

"Come along."

The three of them walked over to where the second buffalo bulked blackly in the open, head forward on the grass, the massive horns swung wide.

"He's a very good head," Wilson said. "That's close to a fifty-inch spread."

Macomber was looking at him with delight.

"He's hateful looking," said Margot. "Can't we go into the shade?"

"Of course," Wilson said. "Look," he said to Macomber, and pointed. "See that patch of bush?"

"Yes."

"That's where the first bull went in. The gun-bearer said when he fell off the bull was down. He was watching us helling along and the other two buff galloping. When he looked up there was the bull up and looking at him. Gun-bearer ran like hell and the bull went off slowly into that bush."

"Can we go in after him now?" asked Macomber eagerly.

Wilson looked at him appraisingly. Damned if this isn't a strange one, he thought. Yesterday he's scared sick and today he's a ruddy fire eater.

"No, we'll give him a while."

"Let's please go into the shade," Margot said. Her face was white and she looked ill.

They made their way to the car where it stood under a single, wide-spreading tree and all climbed in.

"Chances are he's dead in there," Wilson remarked. "After a little we'll have a look."

Macomber felt a wild unreasonable happiness that he had never known before.

"By God, that was a chase," he said. "I've never felt any such feeling. Wasn't it marvellous, Margot?"

"I hated it."

"Why?"

"I hated it," she said bitterly. "I loathed it."

"You know I don't think I'd ever be afraid of anything again," Macomber said to Wilson. "Something happened in me after we first saw the buff and started after him. Like a dam bursting. It was pure excitement."

"Cleans out your liver," said Wilson. "Damn funny things happen to people."

Macomber's face was shining. "You know something did happen to me," he said. "I feel absolutely different."

His wife said nothing and eyed him strangely. She was sitting far back in the seat and Macomber was sitting forward talking to Wilson who turned sideways talking over the back of the front seat.

"You know, I'd like to try another lion," Macomber said. "I'm really not afraid of them now. After all, what can they do to you?"

"That's it," said Wilson. "Worst one can do is kill you. How does it go? Shakespeare. Damned good. See if I can remember. Oh, damned good. Used to quote it to myself at one time. Let's see. 'By my troth, I care not; a man can die but once; we owe God a death and let it go which way it will, he that dies this year is quit for the next.' Damned fine, eh?"

He was very embarrassed, having brought out this thing he had lived by, but he had seen men come of age before and it always moved him. It was not a matter of their twenty-first birthday.

It had taken a strange chance of hunting, a sudden precipitation into action without opportunity for worrying beforehand, to bring this about with Macomber, but regardless of how it had happened it had most certainly happened. Look at the beggar now, Wilson thought. It's that some of them stay little boys so long, Wilson thought. Sometimes all their lives. Their figures stay boyish when they're fifty. The great American boy-men. Damned strange people. But he liked this Macomber now. Damned strange fellow. Probably meant the end of cuckoldry too. Well, that would be a damned good thing. Damned good thing. Beggar had probably been afraid all his life. Don't know what started it. But over now. Hadn't had time to be afraid with the buff. That and being angry too. Motor car too. Motor cars made it familiar. Be a damn fire eater now. He'd seen it in the war work the same way. More of a change than any loss of virginity. Fear gone like an operation. Something else grew in its place. Main thing a man had. Made him into a man. Women knew it too. No bloody fear.

From the far corner of the seat Margaret Macomber looked at the two of them. There was no change in Wilson. She saw Wilson as she had seen him the day before when she had first realized what his great talent was. But she saw the change in Francis Macomber now.

"Do you have that feeling of happiness about what's going to happen?" Macomber asked, still exploring his new wealth.

"You're not supposed to mention it," Wilson said, looking in the other's face. "Much more fashionable to say you're scared. Mind you, you'll be scared too, plenty of times."

"But you *have* a feeling of happiness about action to come?"

"Yes," said Wilson. "There's that. Doesn't do to talk too much about all this. Talk the whole thing away. No pleasure in anything if you mouth it up too much."

"You're both talking rot," said Margot. "Just because you've chased some helpless animals in a motor car you talk like heroes."

"Sorry," said Wilson. "I have been gassing too much." She's worried about it already, he thought.

"If you don't know what we're talking about why not keep out of it?" Macomber asked his wife.

"You've gotten awfully brave, awfully suddenly," his wife said contemptuously, but her contempt was not secure. She was very afraid of something.

Macomber laughed, a very natural hearty laugh. "You know I *have,*" he said. "I really have."

"Isn't it sort of late?" Margot said bitterly. Because she had done the best she could for many years back and the way they were together now was no one person's fault.

"Not for me," said Macomber.

Margot said nothing but sat back in the corner of the seat.

"Do you think we've given him time enough?" Macomber asked Wilson cheerfully.

"We might have a look," Wilson said. "Have you any solids left?"

"The gun-bearer has some."

Wilson called in Swahili and the older gun-bearer, who was skinning out one of the heads, straightened up, pulled a box of solids out of his pocket and brought them over to Macomber, who filled his magazine and put the remaining shells in his pocket.

"You might as well shoot the Springfield," Wilson said. "You're used to it. We'll leave the Mannlicher in the car with the Memsahib. Your gun-bearer can carry your heavy gun. I've this damned cannon. Now let me tell you about them." He had saved this until the last because he did not want to worry Macomber. "When a buff comes he comes with his head high and thrust straight out. The boss of the horns covers any sort of a brain shot. The only shot is straight into the nose. The only other shot is into his chest or, if you're to one side, into the neck or the shoulders. After they've been hit once they take a hell of a lot of killing. Don't try anything fancy. Take the easiest shot there is. They've finished skinning out that head now. Should we get started?"

He called to the gun-bearers, who came up wiping their hands, and the older one got into the back.

"I'll only take Kongoni," Wilson said. "The other can watch to keep the birds away."

As the car moved slowly across the open space toward the island of brushy trees that ran in a tongue of foliage along a dry water course that cut the open swale, Macomber felt his heart pounding and his mouth was dry again, but it was excitement, not fear.

"Here's where he went in," Wilson said. Then to the gun-bearer in Swahili, "Take the blood spoor."

The car was parallel to the patch of bush. Macomber, Wilson and the gun-bearer got down. Macomber, looking back, saw his wife, with the rifle by her side, looking at him. He waved to her and she did not wave back.

The brush was very thick ahead and the ground was dry. The middle-aged gun-bearer was sweating heavily and Wilson had his hat down over his eyes and his red neck showed just ahead of Macomber. Suddenly the gun-bearer said something in Swahili to Wilson and ran forward.

"He's dead in there," Wilson said. "Good work," and he turned to grip Macomber's hand and as they shook hands, grinning at each other, the gun-bearer shouted wildly and they saw him coming out of the bush sideways, fast as a crab, and the bull coming, nose out, mouth tight closed, blood dripping, massive head straight out, coming in a charge, his little pig eyes bloodshot as he looked at them. Wilson, who was ahead was kneeling shooting, and Macomber, as he fired, unhearing his shot in the roaring of Wilson's gun, saw fragments like slate burst from the huge boss of the horns, and the head jerked, he shot again at the wide nostrils and saw the horns jolt again and fragments fly, and he did not see Wilson now and, aiming carefully, shot again with the buffalo's huge bulk almost on him and his rifle almost level with the on-coming head, nose out, and he could see the little wicked eyes and the head started to lower and he felt a sudden white-hot, blinding flash explode inside his head and that was all he ever felt.

Wilson had ducked to one side to get in a shoulder shot. Macomber had stood solid and shot for the nose, shooting a touch high each time and hitting the heavy horns, splintering and chipping them like hitting a slate roof, and Mrs. Macomber, in the car, had shot at the buffalo with the 6.5 Mannlicher as it seemed about to gore Macomber and had hit her husband about two inches up and a little to one side of the base of his skull.

Francis Macomber lay now, face down, not two yards from where the buffalo lay on his side and his wife knelt over him with Wilson beside her.

"I wouldn't turn him over," Wilson said.

The woman was crying hysterically.

"I'd get back in the car," Wilson said. "Where's the rifle?"

She shook her head, her face contorted. The gun-bearer picked up the rifle.

"Leave it as it is," said Wilson. Then, "Go get Abdulla so that he may witness the manner of the accident."

He knelt down, took a handkerchief from his pocket, and spread it over Francis Macomber's crew-cropped head where it lay. The blood sank into the dry, loose earth.

Wilson stood up and saw the buffalo on his side, his legs out, his thinly-haired belly crawling with ticks. "Hell of a good bull," his brain registered automatically. "A good fifty inches, or better. Better." He called to the driver and told him to spread a blanket over the body and stay by it. Then he walked over to the motor car where the woman sat crying in the corner.

"That was a pretty thing to do," he said in a toneless voice. "He *would* have left you too."

"Stop it," she said.

"Of course it's an accident," he said. "I know that."

"Stop it," she said.

"Don't worry," he said. "There will be a certain amount of unpleasantness but I will have some photographs taken that will be very useful at the inquest. There's the testimony of the gun-bearers and the driver too. You're perfectly all right."

"Stop it," she said.

"There's a hell of a lot to be done," he said. "And I'll have to send a truck off to the lake to wireless for a plane to take the three of us into Nairobi. Why didn't you poison him? That's what they do in England."

"Stop it. Stop it. Stop it," the woman cried.

Wilson looked at her with his flat blue eyes.

"I'm through now," he said. "I was a little angry. I'd begun to like your husband."

"Oh, please stop it," she said. "Please, please stop it."

"That's better," Wilson said. "Please is much better. Now I'll stop."